The Diary of an IMMORTAL

(1945-1959)

DAVID J. CASTELLO

ISBN (Print) 978-1-48357-862-0 (Ebook) 978-1-48357-863-7

Evil is selfishness to the point of destruction.

Albert Harrison

CHAPTER
❖ 1 ❖

Death. I was so sick and tired of death. By April of 1945, I considered death, not the German Wehrmacht or the SS, to be my real enemy. I was a twenty-one-year old medic assigned to Rifle Company I, Third Battalion, 157th Regiment, 45th Division of the Seventh United States Army, and though it was obvious we were winning the war I did not count myself among its victors. My job was to save lives, not take them, and I failed many more times than I succeeded.

On Saturday, April 28th, we were approximately thirty miles west of the Bavarian capitol of Munich. The Nazi war machine was convulsing in the final grip of its death throes and nearly every German man, woman, and child was fighting with suicidal desperation to defend what little was left of their precious Fatherland. And every day I bore witness to the desecration of one more law, ethic, or code of humanity as we journeyed one muddy step at a time into the depths of the abyss.

That afternoon, the other company medic stumbled upon a wounded German boy. The child couldn't have been more than twelve or thirteen and was huddled tightly on the frozen ground curled in the fetal position while clenching his stomach. This medic was fresh off an LST at Marseilles—six feet of smiling, buck-toothed, corn-fed Omaha farm boy. Full of idealistic fervor, he was quite vocal in his belief that we were all on a sacred crusade to save Europe from fascism.

"There, there," the Nebraskan said tenderly, kneeling beside the boy and softly brushing his dusty hair off his mud caked forehead as if he were calming a newborn calf on his daddy's farm. "You'll see, we're going to get you all fixed up in no time."

I'd just stretched my legs and was walking over to assist him when I saw something that froze me in my tracks. There was a double black thunderbolt crudely sewn onto the boy's upper right shirtsleeve. Up until to that point, I'd never suspected the Nazis would recruit children for combat, but all the Nebraskan medic saw was a wounded child writhing in unbearable agony. His senses were so consumed with seeking the source of the boy's pain that he never noticed that the innocence naturally native to a child's eyes had slowly transformed into a cold, calculating stare. And that stare was now fixed upon him with a boiling ferocity.

He never heard the first word of my scream.

In a flash of sweaty earthen gray wool, the German youth unleashed a pistol out of the waistband of his greasy pants and shot the unsuspecting medic point-blank through his freckled forehead. Blood, bone, and brain matter exploded out of the back of the Nebraskan's skull and splattered the face of a curious corporal who'd been standing behind him. The child's crooked smile of satisfaction was nothing less than demonic. As the corporal furiously wiped the human debris from his eyes, he began stomping the tiny SS warrior with his steel-toed boot, instantly transforming one of Hitler's fearless youth into an ordinary little boy wailing for his mother.

Boys.

That day I tried to save, patch up or repair at least a dozen boys. Not men, boys. Boys with their intestines sliding out through their fingers, their flesh torn out in chunks, their limbs so shattered it was only a question of where to amputate. Do you know what the face of a nineteen-year-old boy looks like when he knows he's about to die? It's one of absolute disbelief. For regardless of the bullets whizzing by his ears, the mortars exploding around his head and the bombs shaking the ground beneath his feet, a nineteen-year-old truly believes he is invincible. He truly believes he is immortal.

For youth is the great deceiver.

And when one of those anonymous German projectiles found its fragile mark, when white-hot shrapnel ripped through tender flesh, the universal truth was finally revealed to him. The truth that just as surely as he was powerless to choose the day he entered this world he was just as powerless to determine the day he would leave it. And if he was an American soldier, and if that day came in the spring of 1945, it was someone like me who rushed pell-mell through the smoking haze of cordite to find him sprawled flat on his back with that twisted look of shock etched across his face. The rousing ideals that had previously sustained him, the siren's song of patriotism, bravado and glory were now all cast aside in a desperate struggle to preserve what little life was pumping through his veins. And it was at that moment he would look up at me with the eyes of a lost and lonely child, and always whisper the same last word:

"Please."

That night I listened to the cries of the dying and fought a losing battle with sleep before we geared up the next morning for our march on Munich and the possibility of liberating our first POW camp. The camp was located in a small town called Dachau about halfway between our position and Munich. Scuttlebutt was that Josef Stalin's son and other political prisoners were being held there. We'd also heard reports from the hordes of refugees streaming westward towards us about medical experiments and medieval style torture; stories almost too fantastical to believe. On the other hand, what kind of civilized nation used children for combat? That night I covered my ears to mute the sound of dying men and tried to shake the feeling that something I'd never experienced before was waiting for me just beyond the smoky Bavarian horizon. At 0730 we broke camp with Companies L and K leading the assault towards Munich. Our Company I was held back as the reserve unit with instructions to mop up any resistance that survived L and K's onslaught. We followed a comfortable distance behind, meeting little resistance, until we reached a town of tightly shuttered cottages called Prittlbach. There we received news that all bridges forward of our position had just been sabotaged by the Germans. We were milling around wondering what to do next when our point man motioned for us to take cover. I dropped to the ground, slamming my stomach against the cobblestone street, and waited for the gunfire to snap. As I held my breath I heard a continuous squeaking sound steadily making its way toward us. I peered up from under my helmet to see a young woman sedately bicycling in our direction.

As she came into view I could see she was a classic Nordic beauty with long blonde hair cascading past her bare shoulders. It fell all the way down her back in the longest pony-tail I'd ever seen bouncing atop a lithe body festively adorned in a brightly patterned yellow and blue sundress. She was busily looking up at the sky, distracted by a squadron of silver P-51 Mustangs flying high overhead, and didn't notice us lying directly in her path until our point man jumped up and grabbed her handlebars, eliciting an adolescent squeal of surprise.

Private Doug "Lucky" Morrison was a red-haired Irish middleweight Golden Gloves boxer from Chicago with a face like a forever smiling English Bulldog and his nickname carved on the butt of his M1 carbine. Lucky and I were the only surviving members who'd come ashore in Sicily during Operation Husky in July of 1943. He held tightly onto her bicycle's handlebar and flagged me forward to translate. The poor girl was shaking, stuttering and probably scared to death we were going to rape her. My mother's grandparents were from Germany and I knew enough of the language to learn she had traveled here from Munich to check on her ailing grandfather in Prittlbach. We couldn't have cared less about her sick grandfather in Prittlbach. What was important to us was that she had made it safely from Munich by crossing a bridge a little further down an unmarked side road. This was the kind of paradox in war that could drive a man over the edge. All day long we'd been crouching low behind our Sherman tank escort looking out for Volksturm snipers taking aim at us from behind any window or tree and this girl comes wheeling along like she's taking a Sunday ride in the park.

Satisfied she presented no danger, I warned her to get to her grandfather's house and off the street as soon as possible. She nodded nervously and pedaled away as fast as she could. With a throaty growl and a belch of oily smoke, our Sherman escort revved its engine and we cautiously proceeded around the sharp turn ahead. We soon discovered the girl had told the truth. Barely visible at the end of a narrow street was a narrow but thick wooden suspension bridge spanning a placid canal about thirty feet wide. But would it hold? We stepped back as our thirty-three ton steel behemoth gingerly began to curl its metal treads over the lip of the entrance.

Boom! There was an incredible flash of light, as if a photographer had popped a flashbulb in my face, accompanied by a deafening explosion as the center of the bridge disintegrated into a roaring orange fireball that mushroomed hundreds of feet into the air. The tank pitched forward, tottered for a moment, but miraculously stopped short of flipping into the murky water. Enraged, every man spun around on his stomach and leaned tightly into his Ml, hell bent on placing a well-aimed .30 caliber bullet between the shoulder blades of a young German girl. Luckily for her, she had bicycled around the bend and was safely out of sight.

While we were checking the bridge to see if the center could be patched, Lucky poked his head underneath and spotted a small cable footbridge strung below. We scampered down the embankment and seconds later I found myself standing on the other side of the canal in Dachau.

At first glance, Dachau had all of the Old World charm of a sleepy Bavarian village on a Sunday morning. But there was a war going on and anything that appeared this quiet was usually sinister. A stained glass window could conceal a sniper, a vegetable garden could be mined, and anything else was probably booby-trapped. We were cautiously making our way down one of Dachau's narrow cobblestone streets when we began detecting a strange, rank odor. An odor even stranger and more disconcerting than that omnipresent combat cocktail of decaying flesh, caked perspiration and cordite. In fact, the last time I'd smelled anything remotely like it was in the monkey house back home at the Miami Zoo. Off to our left we caught sight of a large siding of forty to fifty sealed railroad freight cars positioned on the far side of an open field. As we crept up to the first car, I nearly stumbled over the badly decomposing corpse of a young female hidden in the tall grass her filthy, faded, blue and white striped pajamas barely visible beneath a dense carpet of hungry flies. Lucky grabbed the latch of the first freight car and shoved open the door. I wish I'd closed my eyes because the sight that greeted us will forever haunt me. It was a vertical wall of decomposing corpses that completely filled the freight car from wooden floor to roof. Dozens of dulled eyes stared back at us from the depths of starved eye sockets, each pair set in an ivory face frozen in a grimace of agony. There were men and women of all ages, of all shapes and sizes, many locked in death embraces. And huge piles of human excrement everywhere.

A couple of the guys vomited, some cried, but most just cursed under their breath and looked away. Every soldier knows that in war there are no rules, but this was different. This was wholesale murder. We later estimated that there were at least two thousand bodies packed into those freight cars. We were ordered to proceed and secure the Dachau concentration camp. This was a good thing because, after seeing those corpses inside those freight cars, nothing would have stopped us. We followed a line of winding railroad tracks until we reached a road marked by a lamppost with the words *SS Konzentrations Lager* suspended from its ornate arms. Above these words were two sets of three brightly painted enamel figures, one trio pointing right, the other to the left. The trio pointing right was of two peasants, one playing an accordion and the other holding an umbrella accompanied by a soldier leaning on a cello. These innocuous fellows pointed the way toward the entrance of the camp. We approached an imposing steel gate emblazoned with the words *Arbeit Macht Frei*—Work Makes One Free. Finding it locked, we scaled the adjoining brick wall and ran headlong into some SS troops and their German Shepherds. The early morning chill erupted with the sounds of gunfire and barking dogs. In less than a minute every Nazi man and beast was shot dead and an unsettling silence had descended upon the camp.

The quiet was broken by the sound of boots clanking down one of the guard tower's staircases. We turned to see a spit and polished SS officer stiffly making his way down the steps. He was a veritable blueprint for one of Hitler's Aryan supermen: blond and Nordic, powerfully built, about six foot three and clean-shaven with his uniform perfectly pressed. I could smell the citrusy bergamot scent of his cologne from twenty yards away. Ignoring the fact that every one of our carbines were aimed at him, he proudly held his head high, jutted his chin out and marched directly up to our commander, Lieutenant Colonel Sparks. The German briskly saluted him and said in perfect English, "I hereby surrender to you the prisoner of war camp at Dachau. We have a total population of twenty-nine thousand, seven hundred and thirty with two thousand, nine hundred and forty-one sick cases and five hundred and fifty-one guards and soldiers remaining. Heil Hitler!"

Taken aback, Sparks motioned for the SS officer to join a group of about fifty other surrendering Germans who were being guarded by one of our machine gun squads against the brick wall of the camp. Without warning, the machine gunner opened fire, dropping the SS officer and at least a dozen other German prisoners who'd been standing with their hands in the air. Every one of us hit the ground except for Sparks who angrily rushed the gunner and kicked him clear of his weapon. He lifted the private, who couldn't have been a day over nineteen, up by his collar and brought the boy's terrified face close to his.

"You dumb shit, what in the hell are you doing?!"

"I'm sorry, sir," he stammered. "I thought they were trying to get away."

His answer was so ludicrous that Sparks was at a loss for words. Shaking his head in disgust, he assigned another gunner and was beginning to address us when he was interrupted by the feeblest, most heart-wrenching voice I've ever heard.

"Americans?"

Sparks raised his hand for silence as the pitiful wail reverberated again throughout the camp.

"Americans?"

I've heard hundreds of dying men beg for mercy in a voice that claws at every fiber of your soul, but I'd never heard a human sound like this. This was a voice long devoid of hope. This was the voice of a man echoing from the bottom of an abyss.

"Yes, we are Americans!" Sparks shouted back at the empty camp.

With a terrific bang, every wooden door in the camp simultaneously slammed open and a tidal wave of human corpses hobbled across the ground swarming toward us. We were terrified of being trampled and braced ourselves against each another. The prisoners were horribly emaciated and dressed in the same filthy blue and white striped pajama type garments we'd seen on the corpses in the freight car. They were so physically weak that their hands felt like feathers brushing against our faces. Even their voices sounded avian, their sinus cavities deteriorated so badly they sounded like high-pitched, raspy birds. But for me, the gnawing question of "What are we really fighting for?" had finally been answered. Good had triumphed over Evil. And Evil was about to pay a heavy price. There were some major scores to settle in the camp and a number of prisoners appointed themselves both judge and executioner. Traitorous inmates called *Capos*, whom I later learned had enjoyed the easy life as Nazi collaborators, were tossed screaming in terror above the crowd like human beach balls before being pulled down and torn limb from limb. And considering how physically weak the inmates were, these Capos did not die quickly.

While this mass retribution was taking place, I followed Lucky, Private Robert Torello and Corporal John Hanson over to the SS administrative area. In stark contrast to the inhumane conditions of the prisoners' quarters, it was obvious that the Nazi officers here had lived the good life. Freshly scrubbed cobblestone walkways gave way to meticulously tended gardens of cabbage and leeks surrounding quaint living quarters.

We followed one pathway to the end of a cul-de-sac with a small cottage marked *Kommandant*. Torello kicked in the door and we stepped into a lavish room decorated with French watercolors and carved German furniture. It reminded me somewhat of my parents' living room in Florida, but with two notable exceptions. In the center of the room was a giant aquarium at least ten feet long and five feet deep filled with dozens of colorful tropical fish and other exotic forms of marine life. Next to it was a small lampshade with a flaming dragon emblazoned upon it. On closer inspection, we were revolted to discover that the lampshade was constructed from tattooed human skin. If the former inhabitants of the cottage had been present we would have summarily executed them on the spot.

We explored the bedroom in search of any spoils we could cart away. Lucky rifled through the dresser drawers while Torello and Hanson ransacked the closets. They were coming up empty-handed until Lucky pulled a massive oil painting of Hitler dressed as a Teutonic knight off the wall and discovered a combination safe. Torello immediately volunteered to open it. A wiry, street-smart Italian kid from Brooklyn, Torello often bragged that his uncle was a safecracker for the mob and had taught him a couple tricks of the trade. Torello cracked his knuckles and quickly went to work with all the confidence of a brain surgeon.

I was wolfing down some hard cheese and rye bread in the kitchen when I heard Torello mutter "Got it," followed by a barely audible metallic click. A mad rash ensued as the men scrambled to view the contents of the safe. Stacks of Reichsmarks and assorted jewelry were snapped up in a flash. Christmas for these boys arrived early that year. Exhausted, I fell back into an overstuffed leather chair and watched them go to town. It was the first time I'd seen them smile or laugh in a while and I was just beginning to doze off when one of them said, "Hey, Doc! We've got something for you!"

Torello wheeled around to hand me a heavy, but beautifully polished mahogany case the size of a large tackle box. My first impression was that it had once belonged to a doctor or surgeon of high rank and probably contained precision instruments. I waited until the men returned to pilfering the safe before I flicked open the brass snaps and peered into the case. There were two envelopes stacked atop dozens of bottled pills. The first letter was hand-addressed to SS-Hauptsturmführer Dr. Sigmund Rascher from SS-Reichsführer Heinrich Himmler. My heart raced at the sight of the double-thunderbolt S's embossed in black on the letterhead. I opened the envelope and translated the contents:

Sept. 9, 1943

Hauptsturmführer Rascher,

I am in receipt of your letter dated August 30th. I share neither your enthusiasm, nor your vision. Immortality is nonsense. I don't care how successful your experiments have been, I order you to destroy all of the shark extract and any research pertaining to it immediately.

The Führer has never, I repeat, never, expressed any desire to live beyond what is considered the average human life span. This Dr. Otto Krueger must be disciplined and possibly dismissed. I believe the only reason the Führer appointed him to perform research at Dachau was because of his family's association with Dr. Rosenberg. Therefore, please be discreet in this matter.

I want you to use every means possible and find out who is responsible for ordering Krueger to circumvent me on these experiments and report the findings directly to the Führer. I am glad that our beloved Führer was not bothered with this idiocy. Your demonstration of loyalty to me in intercepting this shipment will be rewarded. I look forward to hearing the results of more practical experimentation, such as the High Altitude tests.

> *Reichsführer-SS*
> *Heinrich Himmler*
> *Berlin SW 11*
> *Prinz-Albrecht-Straße No.8*

The other envelope was dated earlier and I found the content of its letter to be even more incredible.

> *July 1, 1943*

My Beloved Führer,

It is with great pride that I inform you that my experiments have been more successful than I would have dreamed possible. I will not belabor you with the scientific terminology.

I believe that I have discovered a way to stop the aging process in humans. Please tell Dr. Gravitz to relay my personal thanks to our cooperative Japanese counterparts in Kobe. Their research papers were invaluable. The pills enclosed are extracted from the liver of the tiger shark. There are no side effects. Take one a day on an empty stomach immediately before bed-time. I have already produced enough pills for a fifty year supply. However, the anti-aging results will probably not be noticeable for ten to fifteen years.

Theoretically, you should be able to personally enjoy the fruits of your thousand year Reich. My Beloved Führer, may you truly live forever!

Your obedient and grateful servant,
Dr. Otto Krueger

I was lightheaded from sleep deprivation and it took a moment to comprehend what I was reading. Sitting in my lap were fifty large hermetically sealed deep sapphire colored bottles packed in columns of five with ten across. Each bottle contained hundreds of tiny gold speckled pills. The insanity of war had just become a little more insane. My first thought was that it would be the ultimate irony if such an efficient factory of death had discovered a way to actually prolong life. I neatly refolded the letters, placed them on top of the bottles and resealed the case as the others finished cleaning out the safe.

"Hey Doc, we hit the jackpot!" Torello said, flashing a fistful of Reichsmarks in my face. "Find anything in the box?"

"No, not really," I replied. "Just some sedatives. After seeing what they've done here, I'm sure some of these guys had trouble getting to sleep at night. However, this box is solid mahogany and the quality of craftsmanship is quite remarkable. I've never seen anything like it. You guys can keep the rest. I'm going to hang on to this."

Lucky, Torello and Hanson stopped counting the money and looked at me as if I was shell-shocked. They grinned mischievously at one another and shrugged their shoulders. What the hell, now they only had to split the loot three ways.

Weighed down with Reichsmarks, gold, silver and a large wooden box, we scurried out of the administration area and slipped back undetected into the compound. By now, more units of the 45th Division had arrived and the place was humming with activity as Dachau's floodlights casted an eerie glow over the concentration camp. Exhausted from celebrating and meting out justice, the majority of the former inmates milled about, unsure of where to go or what to do with their newly liberated lives.

The next day, April 30th, Munich fell to the Allies. And, except for the fanatical SS and Hitler Youth, the majority of the Germans were quickly losing their will to fight. The populace of Munich signaled their surrender by simply hanging white sheets from their balconies and rooftops, but the memory I will forever attach to that day is much, more personal. That afternoon my closest friend, Private Douglas "Lucky" Morrison, was killed in action two days short of his twenty-first birthday.

We were cautiously rounding one of Munich's identical battle scarred, cobblestone streets when a rifle shot cracked the cloudless sky like a thunderbolt on a sunny day. Everyone instinctively slammed themselves to the street in a desperate attempt to get out of the sniper's sightline. Everyone, except Lucky. I was horrified to peer up and see him still standing tall in the sunshine, oblivious to my whispered pleas to get down. His right hand slowly opened and his M1 clattered the cobblestones. Then, he sank to his knees, crumpling over onto his side. Ignoring the sniper, I dashed over to him praying for the umpteenth time that the red crosses attached to my helmet and jacket would somehow guarantee my safety. When I reached Lucky, his face was so tightly contorted in pain that, despite the hundreds of times I'd seen it on a wounded soldier, it still tied my stomach in knots. I ripped open his shirt to see blood pulsing from a small circular chest wound. As his lungs filled with fluid and he began to struggle for breath, he grabbed my jacket and gasped the last word I wanted to hear. *"Please."*

There was absolutely nothing I could do except whisper the battlefield lie I'd come to master so well. "Hang in there buddy, everything's going to be okay."

As I cradled him in my arms, his eyes rolled into the back of his head and his gritted facial muscles relaxed, slowly transforming his agonized expression into one of a man serenely at peace. I gently laid him on the cobblestones as a bazooka team lined up and dispatched the sniper with surgical precision. It was all over that fast. One minute you're joking with someone who's survived the war long enough to qualify as your best friend and the next minute he's gone.

I was now, at the age of twenty-one, the only surviving member of my original unit. And I had no idea why I was still alive. It was certainly not because I was a medic. The Germans had been sniping medics left and right. And I didn't believe in luck. All of the four leaf clovers in Erin couldn't have saved Lucky Morrison. The bottom line was that I could be killed at any time. I sat in my tent that night contemplating my fate while I studied one of the sapphire colored bottles I'd found in Dachau. The three hundred and sixty-five round white pills packed tightly inside reminded me of tiny pearls, each embedded with tiny gold iridescent flakes that glistened when I turned the bottle against the moonlight. I cracked open the seal and detected an odor that smelled vaguely of the sea, reminiscent of many a seaweed encrusted seashell I'd plucked from the warm sands of Miami Beach. I reached in with my finger and fished out one of the pills. No longer shielded by the deep blue glass it sparkled so brightly that it illuminated the palm of my hand. It certainly looked as if it was imbued with magical properties. What did I have to lose? Perhaps I could cheat the Grim Reaper until I'd made it safely home to Florida. I hesitated when I thought about my strict Southern Baptist upbringing and the soul-searing penalties of eternal damnation for attempting to alter my destiny in such a supernatural way. But I mostly thought about Lucky Morrison and the dozens of other good men who died struggling for breath in my arms after realizing they would never see their loved ones again. And then I thought of the one word I never wanted to hear escape my lips.

Please.

I popped the pill into my mouth and washed it down with a swig from my canteen. I winced at its metallic taste and patiently waited for some sort of reaction. Eventually, I fell asleep after experiencing nothing more earth shattering than if I'd swallowed an aspirin.

The next morning I walked into an intact Munich *café*, a miraculous escapee of the thousands of Allied bombs that had been dropped upon the city. The only thing available was coffee.

I slapped a dime on the black walnut bar and was rewarded with a steaming cup of joe poured into a badly chipped porcelain teacup. Through a cigarette haze I spotted Torello and Hanson with their muddy boots propped up on a sawhorse table as they quietly sipped their coffee behind a plume of smoke rings. Blowing on the brew I made my way over to their table, pulled up a chair and endured a full minute of tense silence before Torello spoke.

"I can't believe this shit. Lucky made it all that way, only to get it at the very end."

"Yeah, I know," I replied, searching for something profound to say. "I wish there was some way I could have saved him."

"Saved him?" Hanson said, resting his coffee cup on the table. "Listen Ronson, you may be a very brave medic. You may be a very good medic, but you're not God. When it's a man's time to die, his time is up. His fate has already been decided by a higher power."

Torello solemnly nodded his approval while I avoided Hanson's gaze and stared down into my steaming cup of joe. "I don't believe any of our destinies are written in stone," I said. "We've all got more control over our lives than we think."

Torello and Hanson frowned skeptically at each other before exploding with laughter. Embarrassed, I got up and walked away to seek refuge against a window frame. Hanson was laughing so hard he was practically choking back tears.

"Hey, Doc, no hard feelings, I just didn't know this war had made you, uh, so philosophical!"

I returned a feeble grin and rested my head against the shattered frame. I didn't know why I bothered to waste my time. Torello and Hanson were tough, cynical men who had long ceased to wonder why a random bullet fired in the heat of battle would choose one man over another. It was more of a comfort for them to believe they were unwitting pawns in a greater plan.

I was deep in thought, watching an endless stream of jeeps, trucks and tanks roll down the muddy snow strewn boulevard, when I became aware of a strange reflection in the shattered glass of someone standing behind me. I spun around to face a beautiful German girl. A young woman with brilliant blue eyes, flawless alabaster skin and blond hair pulled into a ridiculously long pony-tail. It was the same girl we'd encountered on her bicycle in Prittlbach. At first, her beauty and soft smile were so disarming that I could only stare at her in a daze, until I realized what would have happened if I'd been anywhere near that bridge when it exploded. I grabbed her wrists and pulled her against me.

"I should break your arms right here," I hissed.

"Please, you must listen to me," she pleaded in heavily German-accented English, squirming against my grip. "I came here to tell you the truth."

I stared into those Nordic baby blues and paused. If she'd really been trying to kill me, she sure as hell wouldn't have been trying to talk to me about it. I pushed her away.

"Talk fast."

She claimed she didn't know the bridge had been rigged with explosives. She admitted seeing a couple of German soldiers fumbling around on the Dachau side of the canal, but didn't think anything of it as one of them smiled and waved her across. Her story made sense and even though I was attempting to maintain a cold, angry disposition, my resistance was crumbling. She was talking in broken English a mile a minute with her blue eyes flashing in all directions while begging for absolution in a breathless, schoolgirl-like voice. I stopped her just as I was about to crack a smile. "All right, come with me." I said, grabbing one of her delicate hands and spiriting her out of the cafe before Torello or Hanson could react.

"So, you are a doctor?" she shouted above the din of the military vehicles as we walked along the boulevard.

"No, I'm not a doctor. I'm what's called a combat medic. I give first-aid to the wounded in the battlefield until we can get them to a real doctor."

"But I heard your friends in the cafe call you Doc."

"It's just a nickname. When a wounded soldier looks up and sees a guy wearing red crosses on his helmet working as fast as he can to keep him alive, he has a tendency to call him Doc." I craned my neck and looked up and down the boulevard. "You know, I'm not supposed to be fraternizing with you."

She looked at me quizzically and asked, "What does fraternizing mean?"

"It means I shouldn't be standing here in public talking to you and acting as if a war isn't going on. In other words, it's against Army regulations to be strolling along with a German girl in a German city we occupied only a couple of days ago. I could get into serious trouble." "That's ridiculous! How could I hurt you?"

I couldn't believe she was that naive. There were more than enough stories floating around about drugged GIs awakening to find their genitals sliced to ribbons.

"We'd better get back," I said.

She jerked me to a stop. "I have a solution to this fraternizing problem. If anybody asks, you can say that I am injured and you were kind enough to escort me home. I don't understand how you could get into trouble for helping an unarmed civilian." And with that brilliant, humanitarian solution that could only be born of an adolescent mind, she tucked her arm inside mine with determination and pulled me forward. Christ, what could I say to that?

"Okay, you win," I laughed. "But just remember to limp every now and then."

Her name was Erika Orsic. Nineteen years old and, from all outward appearances, amazingly unaffected by the war. She lived with her adopted family on a small dairy farm on the outskirts of Munich. Her biological mother abandoned her soon after birth, but she retained her last name. Ironically, her adoptive parents had been ardent Nazi supporters until one morning when they awakened to discover the SS carting away an old Jewish woman who lived across the street. She had been a surrogate grandmother to the family and their political loyalties switched in a heartbeat. I just hoped the old woman had a better fate than the poor souls I'd seen at Dachau. Dachau! Erika must have bicycled right past the camp.

"What do you know about the concentration camp at Dachau?"

She glared at me as if I'd asked if she was a Nazi.

"Dachau? Why would I know anything about that godforsaken place? My father went to Dachau to retrieve a cousin who was sent there for making a joke about Hitler at a dinner party. When he came home his face was pale and he was trembling. I remember his hand shaking so badly that he couldn't pour himself a glass of Schnapps. He said that his cousin had died of fever and that I was to never go near there under any circumstances."

Erika also told me about a friend of hers who was mistakenly sent to Dachau and lived to tell about it. This man was incarcerated there for almost two years before his misidentification was discovered. After he was released, he was nearly locked up again for telling Erika and her friends what he'd witnessed. My heart began to race when she told me no one believed his fantastic stories about torture and medical experiments. This man might know something about the origin of the pills. I asked Erika if there was any way she could locate him.

"Of course. He's the owner of the *café* where I found you."

Our conversation was interrupted by an angry voice shouting Erika's name from across the street. I looked over her shoulder to see the weathered face of a white-haired man in a green canvas trench coat glaring at me through the endless procession of military traffic.

"It's my father!" she said. "He'll horsewhip me just for speaking to you. I must go."

"Wait a minute," I said, pulling her back to the curb. "I need to talk to your friend who was at Dachau."

Erika yanked free of my grasp and gestured obscenely at me with her upturned middle finger as her father nodded his approval behind her.

"You can." she winked. "Meet me tomorrow afternoon at the *café*."

I arrived at the *café* the next day at 1700 to find Erika seated beside a rotund middle-aged man who looked as if he'd stepped out of a magazine advertisement for a Bavarian beer, complete with a waxed handlebar mustache and round, silver wire-rimmed, glasses. His appearance was highlighted by a ruffled white shirt that barely contained his swollen beer belly straining behind a leather vest. Before Erika could introduce us, he stood up to shake my hand.

"I'm sorry," I said, while his outstretched hand remained empty, "but it's against Army regulations to shake your hand."

"Ridiculous," Erika said, rolling her eyes.

"It's quite all right," the man said, retaking his wooden stool. "My name is Walter Dietrich. Erika tells me you want to talk about Dachau. How did you come to know this place?"

"My army unit liberated the camp."

He eyed the other patrons in the *café* suspiciously. "It would be better if we go someplace quiet where we can speak freely," he whispered. "Please follow me."

Walter led us outside and up a wrought iron spiral staircase. The upper floor of the *café* consisted of a long musty green carpeted corridor with numbered rooms. Unlocking door number three, we entered a sparsely furnished room with nothing more than an oak bookcase and torn leather couch on one side and a small brass bed on the other. However, what was impressive was the view—a stunning panorama of the distant snowcapped Bavarian Alps.

"What was your personal experience with Dachau?" Walter asked as we seated ourselves on the couch.

"I was one of the first Americans to enter the camp. I saw what the Nazis did to the prisoners."

Walter immediately turned to Erika. "My dear, I would appreciate it if you went downstairs and waited until I called on you."

"No!" she protested. "I need to hear this!"

"Erika, you forget your place," Walter said, his voice swelling with anger. "Respect my wishes and leave here at once or I will notify your father!"

With a huff, Erika rose and stormed from the room. Ignoring her reaction, Walter locked the door and pulled the bookcase away from the wall. Reaching around, he withdrew a dusty bottle of wine.

"What is your name and what do you do in the American Army?" he asked, pouring himself a glass as I politely declined.

"My name is Steven Ronson. I'm a medic."

"Ah, a medic," he nodded. "Well, you may come to appreciate some of the duties I performed at the camp. I had the unfortunate privilege of being imprisoned at Dachau from January of 1942 until November of 1943.

The Gestapo picked me up one night as I was leaving my café after celebrating my wife's birthday. They accused me of fostering anti-Nazi sentiment, whatever that meant. Believe me, I may never have supported the views of Adolf Hitler, but I knew enough to keep my mouth shut. And as incredible as it sounds, there was another man named Walter Dietrich who also frequented my *café*. After a couple of drinks, he'd start loudly criticizing Hitler, calling him 'That worthless Bohemian corporal' and other such insults. This other Walter Dietrich was a veteran of the Great War and claimed that Hitler's Iron Cross First Class was unjustified. In Germany, the walls have ears and it wasn't long before someone told the Gestapo that a certain Walter Dietrich at the Sonnenrad *Café* in Munich was labeling Hitler a coward. They picked me up, not believing a word I said about the other Walter Dietrich, and carted me off to Dachau. The other Walter Dietrich heard about my fate and took to the hills. I rotted in Dachau for twenty-two months before an SS officer interrupted me as I was performing my medical duties. He led me to the front gate, pointed me in the direction of Munich and simply said, 'Don't return.'"

"I later learned that the other Walter Dietrich had come out of hiding and, after a few drinks, started laughing aloud about his good fortune. The bastard actually thought it was funny! Unfortunately for him, the Gestapo has no sense of humor. When they got wind of it, they took him away and pumped a bullet into the back of his neck." He paused to clear his throat and sip his wine. As he lifted the glass, I noticed his hand was shaking. I made my move.

"What medical duties did you perform at Dachau?"

"First," he said, putting down his glass, "I want your word that anything I tell you will not be used against me in any way."

Even though I didn't have the authority to do so, my intuition told me anything Walter did at Dachau was not of his free will. "I won't say anything."

Walter took a deep breath and began to speak in a barely audible voice. "I was told the charges against me were quite severe, that I might be sent to a camp much worse than Dachau. Since I was a German, and not a Pole, Russian, or Jew, I was given the choice of assisting in the medical and scientific laboratories at Dachau or being relocated to another camp further east."

"Did you know Sigmund Rascher?"

Walter eyes widened as he gulped his wine. "Of course I knew Sigmund Rascher! He was called *The Captain*. He was my boss."

Walter said that Doctor Rascher was originally a captain in the German Air Force Medical Service and a personal favorite of Heinrich Himmler. He smirked at the memory. "Rascher was a real boot licker. He eventually persuaded Himmler to allow human experimentation at Dachau to benefit the pilots of the Luftwaffe."

Walter described one of the experiments, named the High Altitude test. This was the same experiment that Himmler had referred to in his letter to Rascher. A mobile decompression chamber, referred to in the camp as the *Sky Ride Wagon*, was set up next to Block 5. The chamber could simulate rapid ascent and descent to an atmospheric pressure of 70,000 feet. German fighters couldn't fly that high, but the Nazis were curious to see what would happen if they did and the cabin became depressurized. A prisoner was strapped in and observed through a thick glass portal. Walter said what happened next was practically indescribable. The prisoners would start to rip the hair from their heads and claw the flesh from their faces in an attempt to relieve the pressure expanding inside their skulls.

"I was sent in to clean up the mess," he said. "In the beginning, inmates happily volunteered to enter the Sky Ride Wagon because The Captain promised them better food rations, but when no one returned from the tests, he forcibly selected his next victims."

In addition to the High Altitude tests, Walter recalled the equally horrific Freezing Experiments, Sea Water Experiments and Malaria

Experiments. All of these tests had produced nothing but incalculable human suffering and death. Nevertheless, for his achievements, Dr. Rascher was promoted to the rank of captain in the SS.

I was relieved Walter had mentioned nothing about any immortality experiments. He had been at Dachau during the time when Krueger had written his letters and surely would have known if any human medical experimentation was done in conjunction with them. If there had been any human experimentation, I would stop taking the pills. I couldn't live with that and wanted to be sure.

"Did you know a Dr. Otto Krueger?"

Walter shrugged. "I have never heard of this person."

"Are you sure? Maybe this Dr. Krueger didn't have anything to do with prisoner experimentation."

Walter dismissed the idea. "That would have been impossible. Anyone with the title of Doctor would've been involved to some degree with prisoner experimentation at Dachau."

"Did anyone in the camp experiment with sharks?"

Walter paused in thought for a moment before his eyes brightened. "Sharks? Why, yes! There was someone who worked with sharks." He drained his wine glass and sank back into the leather couch. "We called him *Der Fischer*. The Fisherman. He was a handsome man from Munich in his forties who took great pride in the large aquarium installed in his private laboratory. It was filled with all kinds of beautiful fish, including some baby sharks. He maintained the tank himself and I wasn't allowed to go near it. He was not a Nazi or a member of the SS. In fact, the Nazi doctors disliked and distrusted him because he displayed nothing but contempt for their human experimentation. When Rascher accused him of stealing laboratory supplies, the Fisherman laughed in his face and walked away, and I later learned he'd been transferred. How did you come to know about Rascher or this Otto Krueger person?"

I unfolded the two letters from my jacket pocket and handed them to Walter. He read each and returned them without questioning their authenticity or contents. After living for so many years in Nazi Germany, Walter had learned that curiosity could be a very dangerous thing. All he cared about was that someone had finally listened to his Dachau story and believed him.

Walter smiled warmly. "Would you like to be alone with Erika? I can see she fancies you. Please, finish my bottle of wine. It's a splendid pre-war vintage. Stay here and drink, while I fetch her for you."

I pulled out my lighter and examined the bottle. It was a 1934 Chateau La Mission Haut-Brion and there wasn't a drop left. After a light tapping on the door, Erika reappeared and, noticing the empty wine bottle, reached behind the bookcase and pulled out another. "Would you like a glass?" she asked, straining to uncork it. "This is an excellent Liebfraumilch. It's my family's favorite."

"Sure." I replied. "I'll definitely need a drink after what I just heard."

She poured us both a glass and sat close enough to me on the couch so that her partially bare slender, long legs rubbed up against my drab olive winter combat trousers.

"And what exactly did you hear?"

Walter had just bared his soul to me and I didn't feel I had the right to share it. Even though I believed that young Germans like Erika needed to know the truth, I wasn't about to assume that responsibility. Besides, after two years of war I was now alone with a beautiful girl and a bottle of wine. I could think of a million other things I'd rather do than to talk about torture and human experimentation.

"Erika, I don't feel comfortable discussing this right now. Walter told me things in confidence. You should ask him yourself."

"Ridiculous," she said.

"There's nothing ridiculous about it. A good number of your fellow Germans committed unspeakable crimes."

"So what?" she replied. "War is always terrible." As mature as she was attempting to act, it was painfully obvious that Erika didn't grasp the magnitude of how terrible war could be. And if I hadn't heard Walter's story or seen firsthand the condition of the prisoners at Dachau, I would've had trouble believing it myself. The problem was that Dachau wasn't the work of a solitary deranged man. It was the result of a nation allowing itself to be seduced by a deranged man. Everyone in Germany shared the blame, including Erika, her friends and her family.

And she wasn't about to take no for an answer. She slid off the couch, rested her chin on my knee and looked up at me with her beguiling blue eyes.

"Enough of these ridiculous reasons." she said. "Please, tell me what you saw at Dachau."

Fine. I could see this going on all night. I finished my glass of wine and launched into a vivid account of everything I'd witnessed including the bodies of the men and women entwined in death in the railroad cars, the diseased and near-death condition of the inmates and the vengeful murders of the SS guards. I didn't tell Erika about the pills. That was my business.

Erika curled up against the couch and began to cry. "I'm so ashamed," she sobbed. "At this moment I'm ashamed to call myself a German. Now I know why my father told me never to go near there. He was trying to protect me."

I felt terrible. In less than twenty minutes, I'd managed to destroy whatever shred of innocence Erika had retained throughout the war. And I wondered if her reaction was a prelude to what millions of her countrymen would experience when the reality was revealed to them about Hitler and his Third Reich. Nevertheless, I felt more than pity for Erika. As I watched her cover her face and sob, something inside me began to stir. Something

I hadn't felt in nearly two years. Something I'd begun to believe I would never feel again.

I slid off the couch, wrapped my arms around her and held her until she stopped crying. Lifting her chin, I tenderly kissed her tear stained face, her forehead, her temples, her lips. She pulled away and stared at me with desirous eyes. Then she rose to her feet, grabbed my hand, and silently led me to the brass bed. That night, I made passionate love to Erika Orsic while the guns of war thundered off in the distance. I released every emotion I'd kept bottled up for the past two years in a flood of desire. For the rest of my life I want to remember how badly I wanted her. I want to remember how her skin felt, how her hair smelled and how her lips tasted. I could feel my senses returning to me. I was becoming human again.

After closing my eyes for what seemed like an instant, I woke to find Erika asleep snuggled against me. I didn't want to move a muscle. I didn't want to ruin the moment. I could have laid there in that small brass bed with her forever. Then, reality set in.

It was late.

Very late.

A.W.O.L. late.

I bolted out of bed and looked out the window. The dark streets of Munich were completely deserted with not a soul in sight. The German spring moon was full, gorgeously opaque and positioned so low in the sky that it appeared to be sitting just above the snowy Bavarian mountain peaks. As I watched in awe, a thick layer of clouds seemed to bounce off the mountain tops and swirled majestically upward toward the moon like five gigantic cosmic fingers extending to embrace it. For a brief moment, I felt as if I could have reached out and touched eternity. I looked back at Erika. Her bare ivory skin glistened softly in the glow of the moonlight. God, she was beautiful. I reached across the bed and gently stroked her blonde hair. She opened her eyes, stretched contentedly and smiled up at me.

And again, reality set in.

"Oh my God!" she cried. "What time is it? My father will kill me!"

"It's very late," I replied, quickly pulling on my boots. "Where is Mr. Dietrich?"

"He lives down the hall in room number six." We dressed quickly and hurried down the hallway.

"Mr. Dietrich, it's Erika," she said, tapping on his door. "Please help us."

The door slowly unbolted to reveal a half-naked Walter, his naked beer belly hanging grotesquely over the lip of a bath towel slung low around his waist. He grinned lasciviously as he rubbed the sleep from his blood-shot eyes. "Ah, you kids," he croaked. "Erika, don't worry. I'll talk to your father. But Steven, I'm sorry. I have no desire to tangle with the U.S. Army."

"You won't have to. Just make sure Erika gets home safely."

I kissed Erika on the lips and scurried down the staircase. This time I had my hands full. There was a curfew on. A shoot-to-kill curfew. I'd confided to Torello that I was going to meet Erika and my only hope was that he'd covered for me. The streets were deathly serene and, no matter how softly I lifted my feet, the sound of my combat boots slapping against the cobblestones made my presence known. My unit had been bivouacked in the wine cellar of an abandoned warehouse. Torello told me there was a makeshift tunnel that led out of the cellar and surfaced about a hundred yards south at a market square. I had only a couple of blocks to cover, but under the conditions that night it might as well have been a mile. U.S. Army patrols were everywhere and it took me a good thirty minutes of furtively darting in and out of shadows to bridge the distance. Finally, I spotted the tunnel entrance across the deserted square. It was nothing more than a jagged hole of broken cobblestones. A large upside-down red arrow was crudely painted on the wall above it. The Germans must have been using it as a bomb shelter entrance.

I inhaled deeply and made a mad dash, the sound of my footsteps ricocheting off of every building in the market square. Breathless, I reached the tunnel entrance and began to feel my way down into the darkness when I was startled by the roar of an army patrol jeep racing in my direction from across the square. Convinced that a pair of MPs would soon be storming in to arrest me, I groped my way wildly, raking my fingertips bloody along the rocky walls until I entered a dimly lit tunnel that led to a wine cellar filled with snoring men. The last thing I heard before I closed my eyes was Torello leaning over to whisper, "You fucking owe me."

Germany surrendered on May 7th, 1945. I should have been elated, but I was in no mood to celebrate. Erika was gone. Not from this world, but from mine. Dietrich told me that he personally escorted her home the morning after our night of passion, telling her father that she had accidentally locked herself in the basement of the *café*. Her father would have swallowed the story, but Erika made the mistake of telling one of her girl-friends that she wanted to follow me home to America and word reached her family. When confronted by her father, Erika broke down and told him everything.

I cringed. "Everything?"

"Well, not quite everything." Walter smiled, deviously. "But enough to send her father into a rage. He has her locked up in her room like Rapunzel. He's also threatened to speak to your commanding officer."

My stomach tightened.

"Don't worry. When he said that, Erika practically became suicidal and the old man backed down. He won't come forward against you, but I can promise you that her father will make sure you never see her again."

I was devastated. "I don't understand. Erika told me her parents hated Hitler and the Nazis."

"They do. But that doesn't mean they like you Americans."

My journey home began unexpectedly that evening when Torello informed me that he'd finagled us onto a troopship departing France in a few days. I have no idea how he pulled it off, but he mumbled something about his family's black market connections and assured me that if we didn't leave immediately we'd be stuck in Europe for a very long time.

The next morning we huddled under a tarp in the back of an empty supply truck and sped west to the French port of Le Havre. The scenes that flashed before us were of total devastation. Twisted German and Allied aircraft littered the countryside like crumpled metal birds, resting alongside huge bomb craters. Most of the towns and cities had been annihilated, reduced to nothing more than a field of brick and cobblestones resting silently under a heavy gray sky that hung down from the heavens like the final curtain on this *Götterdämmerung*.

By now, I'd been taking the pills daily for almost a week. Before we boarded the truck in Munich, Torello pulled me aside and, in his inimitable Brooklyn style, asked, "So what was the deal between you and that hot German broad?" Word spread fast and practically everyone in my unit had heard the rumors about Erika and noticed my deepening depression. As insensitive as he sounded, Torello was simply voicing his concern in the only way he knew how.

As I told him the story, I began to envision Erika. We'd only known each other for less than a day, but if there is such a thing as "love at first sight" this was it times ten. I simply could not stop thinking about her. A flood of anguish welled up inside of me and tears rolled down my face. Torello was shocked. He'd seen a dozen men die in my arms and I'd never once allowed my emotions to get the best of me.

"Hey buddy, get a hold of yourself," he said, resting his hand on my shoulder. "She's just a German broad for Christ's sake."

I could barely hear him because I felt as if my heart was being crushed in a vise. In just one night, Erika had managed to pierce a protective shell I'd carefully constructed around myself during the past two years. To preserve my sanity, I'd steadily disconnected myself from my emotions and allowed myself to become more machine than man. I would smile, but there was no happiness or joy behind it. Now I was paying a price for embracing my humanity again. Torello's lips moved and he said something, but I couldn't hear him. I was in too much pain. At the moment, I felt as if my heart would burst. Suddenly, I was jolted by a blinding flash of light as if a firecracker exploded deep inside my brain. I began to lose consciousness as my knees buckled and the ground rose to embrace me. Torello caught me just in time and prevented my face from crashing into the street. The next thing I knew I was lying flat on my back, blinking my eyes up at the sullen gray sky as a fog slowly lifted from my brain.

Regaining my senses, I realized that something was missing. The heart-wrenching pain had disappeared and was replaced by the most comforting feeling of calm I'd ever experienced. It was as if I'd been empowered with the paradoxical belief that everything and nothing in the world mattered at the same time. That everything and nothing in the universe lasted forever. I also saw something—a vision that flashed quickly and evaporated. When I closed my eyes, I could still see its image imprinted across my closed lids like a photo negative. I strained to distinguish the outline of what appeared to be some type of ancient fortress. My initial impression was that the pills were governing my mind and body, and possibly feeding me information. Regardless, I wasn't afraid simply because I'd never felt better in my life.

I believe my reaction was the result of my mortal side conflicting with the immortal part of my transformation. If my body had truly stopped aging, then every part of me from the smallest cell to my subconscious mind would be aware that there were no longer any time constraints. The biological and instinctive deadlines had vanished. The attraction between Erika and me was extremely powerful. If our relationship had been allowed to progress I would have probably chosen her as a mate. In a normal life span, there are only so many people a person meets who can be considered truly compatible. Some people never find that person. There's only so much time.

With immortality, time is on your side and the omnipresent tick of the biological clock is silenced. When I lost Erika, my mortal side plunged into a conventional state of despair. I have no doubt I was quickly falling in love with Erika as she slipped away. Every mortal instinct and emotion was thrown into an evolutionary induced turmoil. It was at that point that the immortal part of my being attacked my mortal reaction as if it were some sort of virus. Finding no justification for the severity of such a response, and seeing it as a threat to my well-being, my immortal side simply shut it down. Afterwards, I still thought about Erika but the devastating and debilitating heartbreak was gone. It was as if the whole experience had been placed in its proper perspective—that of a microscopic piece of an infinitely larger picture.

The experience was so fantastic that it convinced me to abandon my original plan and continue taking the pills after I returned home to Florida. As our troopship, *John Ericsson*, glided out into the open Atlantic, I leaned against the rail and watched the war ravaged French shoreline slowly slip into the horizon. For the other soldiers aboard, their journey had finally ended. They were on their way home to embrace their loved ones and tell them all about the horrors they'd survived. From that day forward, they would lead relatively normal lives. Many would marry, have children and someday sit around the fireplace to tell their grandchildren what it was like during that terrible time in the 1940s when the world descended into war. But no such safe harbor awaited me. I knew that destiny had other plans for my restless soul.

My journey had just begun.

CHAPTER

After stopping in Southampton to pick up wounded soldiers and ex-POWs, I endured an uneventful week crossing the Atlantic before disembarking on a west side pier in Manhattan. I taxied to Central Park where I stretched out on a cedar bench and nourished my war ravaged senses, filling my lungs with the sweet, lemony fragrance of saucer magnolias and feeling rejuvenated with every breath. The atmosphere was one of laughter and celebration as the troop ships began returning home from Europe. War still raged on in the Pacific, but Japan stood alone against the world and her defeat would happen in only a matter of time.

Time.

On the cruise home, I realized that the psychological portion of my transformation might take a while. My body was the product of thousands, perhaps millions, of years of evolution. I had altered this evolutionary process and I was still in a state of shock. My dreams on the voyage were strange and distorted. Every night I was bombarded by fleeting images of people and places alien to me and none of those images appeared to be

American or European. On the contrary, what little I could discern seemed to be Asian. While my subconscious mind grappled with those images, I confronted a philosophical dilemma. The cycle of life and death is natural for all living organisms. Immortality is not. By consuming that formula, I had challenged the universal powers and I knew it. And now I believed they knew it, too.

Regardless, I was ecstatic about the possibility of recapturing the youth the war had stolen from me. But with whom could I share it? My future appeared to be limited to one of two destinies: that of the luckiest man in the world or that of the loneliest.

Home.

It was a strange word to me in the late spring of 1945. Something inside me told me that I could never really go home again, but there I was, back in Miami with my head buried deep in my pillow on the same pine bed where I'd slept my entire life. Black and white glossy pictures of Humphrey Bogart, Gary Cooper and other matinee idols stared down at me with mute intimidation from every corner of the room. Those movie stars were my childhood heroes and I now cringed at the thought of ever placing a Hollywood actor in such a lofty position again. During the war I'd had the honor of becoming acquainted with real heroes. The battlefields in Europe were strewn with them.

Mom, Dad and the entire Ronson clan were out in force waiting for me at the Florida East Coast Railway station in Miami. As the train entered the station I was awakened by the soldier seated next to me grumbling, "Who in the hell is Steven?" I popped my head out the window into a breeze of humid sunshine to see my cousins, aunts and uncles briskly waving miniature stars and stripes underneath a giant "Welcome Home Steven!" banner stretched above the crowd.

I stepped into a sea of hugs, carelessly planted kisses and hearty pats on the back. Then the crowd parted and I saw my father smiling proudly with his arm around my mother, tears glistening on his weathered cheeks.

He was a World War I veteran from the coal mines of West Virginia, whose powerful physique and gruff demeanor disguised the generous heart and enlightened soul beneath. He hugged me so hard he cracked my back.

On the train ride to Florida I'd made the decision to tell my father about the pills. The secret was burning inside me and he was the only person I knew who would accept my discovery and decision without condemnation. But, I had no illusions as to my mother's reaction. A former local beauty queen and photographer's model from Jacksonville, she had left her "flapper with a cigarette" image far behind when she embraced religion with a fervor that would have given Aimee Semple MacPherson pause. And the last place I wanted to be was held hostage while my mother circled the kitchen table, unleashing an impromptu diatribe on the evils of defying God's will. But I so wanted to ask her, where was God when the SS was throwing Jewish babies alive into the ovens at Auschwitz?

The truth that I no longer belonged in Miami was dawning on me. Everything around me was a reflection of my former life. It was time to move on and let the memories stay sweet. I just didn't know where or when to go, and that was another reason I wanted to talk to my father. At the age of twenty five he traded coal mining for a life of palm trees and orange groves with a born-again beauty queen. And he escaped, too. Away from a dead-end life that had sent both his father and grandfather to an early grave, their bodies riddled with black lung disease.

The next morning I accompanied my father in his blue 1939 Packard sedan on his way to work at his Miami Beach print shop. He knew something was weighing heavily on my mind as I stared mutely out the window. We both loved the New York Yankees and during the baseball season it used to be a morning ritual to review every team member's batting statistics as printed in the sports section of the Miami Daily News.

"Looks like the war's ending soon," he ventured.

"Yep."

"That means the Yankees can start putting a real team together again."

"Guess so."

That was the entire extent of our conversation until he pulled into his parking space, turned off the ignition and faced me.

"I may not be the smartest guy in the world, but it wouldn't take a genius to know you've got something on your mind. Want to talk about it?"

"Got an hour?"

"As a matter of fact, I do."

I followed him through the back door of the shop, pausing briefly to acknowledge a smattering of applause from his four employees and walked into his office.

"Dad, it's important that you listen with an open mind," I said as he slid into a brass buttoned leather chair behind his desk. "I've seen some pretty strange things that have nothing to do with war."

"Strange things that have nothing to do with war," he slowly repeated to himself.

"Son, you've got to be kidding me. 'Strange' pretty much sums up what war is all about. What do you think I saw in France in 1918? War is humanity operating at its lowest level. Believe me, there's nothing you saw that will surprise me."

"Well, it's not exactly what I saw. It's what I discovered."

"Discovered?"

I proceeded to tell my father how I'd discovered the pills in Dachau and Walter's confession. My father leaned back in his chair, folded his hands behind his head and waited patiently until I finished. "So, let me get this straight," he said. "You're taking these pills?"

"Yes."

"And you think they work?"

"I believe they do."

"And why do you believe that?"

"Because I can feel it."

"That's your proof?" He chuckled. "Because you can feel it?"

I told him about my reaction to losing Erika and the bizarre visions on the voyage home. After a couple of minutes he began to fidget in his chair. I could see this wasn't sitting well with him. He turned away to stare at the yachts skimming across the azure waters of Biscayne Bay. "Steven, you left us two years ago as a boy and now you've come home a man. You've seen terrible things that most people won't and shouldn't experience in their lifetime. Don't you think the only reason you're taking these pills is because you're trying to counter all the horrors you've experienced?"

"Yes, that's one reason why I'm taking them. I also wanted to make it home alive. But that's not the reason I believe they work. At any rate, we'll both know for sure in about ten to fifteen years. If I've truly stopped aging it will be obvious by then."

Something in those words caused my father to close his eyes.

"Ten to fifteen years," he muttered under his breath. "What I wouldn't give for ten to fifteen more years."

I felt a chill tighten the base of my spine. "What is that supposed to mean?" When he opened his eyes I saw something I'd seen too many times during the war.

Fear.

Dad came from a long line of decorated war heroes, dating back to the formation of West Virginia during the Civil War. Despite my rejection of a professional career in the armed services, we'd managed to forge a closeness he'd never enjoyed with his father. Now, for the first time in my life, I felt as though he was hiding something from me.

"You're the only person who knows I'm taking these pills. I told you about them because I trust you with my life. I'd like to think you feel the same way about me."

He pursed his lips and nodded in agreement. "Okay. Steven, I'm very sick. I was going to wait a couple of days before I broke the news because I didn't want to ruin your homecoming, but…I have leukemia. It's in a very advanced stage and my time is limited at best. That's it." He shrugged. "There's nothing that can be done about it."

It took an effort to breathe. He looked so solid. So himself. He was a sergeant under Pershing with the Allied Expeditionary Force in World War I, a real bad ass according to all of his military buddies. At the age of sixty, he could still bench press three hundred pounds and here he was calmly reciting his death sentence.

"Relax kid. It's not the end of the world. Let's have a drink and change the subject." I was astounded at his resignation, but somehow managed a weak smile.

"Sure, I'll have a drink with you."

He opened his file cabinet and withdrew a bottle of his favorite scotch, a 1928 Macallan.

"Does Mom know?"

"Oh, yeah." He grinned. "She's got God working overtime on me."

I tried to laugh, but I couldn't get past the lump in my throat. "Dad, I am so sick and tired of dealing with this. For the last two years I've lived with nothing but the sight, sound and smell of death. And every time I began to feel close to someone I'd wake up to find them gone. The only way I could keep my sanity was to disconnect myself from everyone around me. Then I met this German girl. In one night she made me feel human again. And then she was gone, too. Not dead, but she may as well be. And now you. It feels like this nightmare has followed me home."

My father reached over and tenderly rested his hand upon mine. "Nothing has followed you home. All of this is beyond our control. Things just happen and we don't know the reason. But trust me, in time we will."

Time.

He poured a shot of scotch and slid it over it to me.

"Now, let's suppose, just for the sake of argument, these pills are the real thing. First of all, everything I've ever heard about these Nazi folks indicates they are nothing less than evil incarnate. And these pills are a product of that evil. You don't really know much about this Otto Krueger character besides the fact he was producing these pills for Adolf Hitler, which is a pretty frightening thought. And besides, what kind of a life are you planning to have? Do you know that Kathy's been calling the house practically every hour since you arrived? You can't expect to get involved with someone like her knowing she wants a normal life."

As far as Otto Krueger was concerned, Walter had made it perfectly clear that Otto was vehemently opposed to human experimentation. And the fact that those pills had been developed for Hitler didn't make them any more evil than if I'd bought a Mercedes-Benz that had been manufactured for him, but Kathy Livingston was an entirely different matter. She'd been my high school sweetheart in Miami for almost three years. We broke up right before I went overseas, agreeing to see other people. Gee, I wonder who got the better half of that deal? I guess I'd seen too many Errol Flynn movies. Before I met Erika in Munich, I'd never had the opportunity to even have a conversation with another woman during the entire two years I was in Europe.

Dad lit his cream colored, meerschaum pipe and the soothing aroma of vanilla Cavendish wafted across the room.

"One more thing," he said, blowing out his match. "You're taking one hell of a gamble. You're only twenty-one years old. According to this Otto Krueger's letter, the results shouldn't be obvious for ten to fifteen years and you're probably planning on structuring your life around the premise that these pills work. And if you're wrong that means you will have squandered ten to fifteen of the best years of your life chasing a hoax."

I could only think of one response.

"In 1918, you fought in combat. I'm sure it affected you when someone you knew died, but you had the benefit of a warrior mentality and were able to accept it as a part of battle. But, my role was that of a healer. My job was to save men, not kill them. Every time one of my men died, a part of me went with him. I felt I'd failed. I can tell you that I failed exactly eighty-six times. I may not remember their names, but I can certainly remember their faces because they haunt me in nightmares that seem to go on forever. I believe these pills are my only salvation and I want those memories to become so old that the nightmares fade away. And because I believe these pills are real, I've already found a degree of hope."

My father took a long drag on his pipe. "In that case, I won't bother trying to dissuade you, but as far as your assessment of me is concerned, your dispassionate warrior theory is only partially correct. You see, Steven, I still have nightmares."

I telephoned Kathy and within minutes she screeched her car to a stop in our driveway and was knocking on the door. Kathy had been an adorable sixteen-year-old brunette cheerleader when we first met at a Miami Senior High School dance. I opened the door and was surprised to see a beautiful woman who bore an uncanny resemblance to Vivian Leigh.

She embraced me tightly and whispered into my ear, "Am I still your baby?"

That was our ritual question while we were dating. I held her quietly for a moment before I gave her only answer she wanted to hear, "Yes, and you always will be."

We held hands as we walked into the kitchen where my mother was busy whipping up some scrambled eggs and bacon, and juicing fresh grapefruits picked from the trees in our backyard.

Mom was in rare comedic form that morning, mercilessly grilling Kathy with questions such as "How is that Ferguson boy? You know, the one Charles and I saw you with at the movies last month?"

Flustered, Kathy could only sputter monosyllabic responses and I was laughing so hard my ribs ached.

My mother was relentless, going in for the kill with comments like, "You went out with him? Good Lord, I guess the war really did take all of the good boys away!"

None of it mattered to me. Whatever Kathy did while we were apart was none of my business. On the other hand, both Kathy and my mother were curious to know if I'd met anyone during the war. I really didn't want to talk about Erika, but they kept pressing me until I admitted to having a brief friendship with a German girl.

"A German girl?' my mother snapped, in a tone intimating I'd been consorting with the daughter of Satan. "I can't believe that my God-fearing son would associate with an enemy of our country!"

"She wasn't the enemy," I replied, testily. "She was someone very special I met under extremely difficult circumstances. Now, can we please change the subject? I didn't come home to face an interrogation."

My mother slowly raised her coffee cup to her lips in stony silence. I'd never addressed her that way before and she could be notoriously thin-skinned.

Sensing the tension, Kathy reached under the table and clasped my hand. "Steven, some friends are getting together tonight at Casey's to play pool. Will you come with me?"

"Yeah, that sounds swell. It'll be nice to see the old gang again."

Kathy finished her breakfast and left. After I watched her pull out of the driveway, I walked back into the kitchen to find my mother bent over a sink full of dirty dishes, scrubbing away with an unnatural fervor. This wasn't going to be easy.

"Mom, I'm sorry. I didn't mean to snap at you like that."

She carefully wiped the last dish, turning off the faucets and methodically drying her hands. "No need to apologize," she said, forcing a smile. "I can see you're still dealing with the effects of the war, but don't you worry about me. I know that sooner or later my old Steven will return!"

I looked into my mother's eyes, and realized how different our worlds had become. Her life from birth had been comprised of a carefully structured cocoon of relatives, religious holidays and a predictability that gave her a sense of security. Though I'd been raised in the same environment, the war had presented me with a reality I could never forget and an uncertain future I couldn't resist. I gently kissed her forehead and whispered, "I'm sorry, Mom, but he's never coming back."

I jumped in the shower, lathered my face and was beginning to shave when I was startled by the crash of broken glass as my mother burst into tears in the kitchen. I jerked my head towards the sound and slashed myself across my left nostril. I watched in the shower mirror as bright red blood dribbled down my chin before grabbing a towel and holding it firmly against the wound as my nose began to itch ferociously, as if it had been bitten by a hundred mosquitoes. After a few seconds the itching stopped and I gingerly lifted the towel to see the side of my nose smeared with blood.

The wound had completely disappeared.

I don't know how long I stood there staring at my reflection. A minute earlier I'd practically sliced my nostril open and now it was completely healed. The pills had far more power than I'd imagined. And I was still standing there dripping wet and naked when Kathy rang the doorbell.

Originally intended as a fishermen's private club, Casey's was built along the waterfront of Biscayne Bay during the 1920's Miami real estate boom. By 1945, those days were long gone. It was now frequented by New England retirees who had no idea how ridiculous they looked in their captain's hats and black Guernsey sweaters in the sweltering Miami heat.

There were four other couples waiting for us at the bar with one notable exception– my best friend and high school football teammate Rick Lavoy and his girlfriend, Gloria.

"Where is that cracker?" I joked. No one laughed as they looked down at their drinks. My Miami High football teammate, Arnie Simmons, discreetly pulled me aside to inform me that Rick had been killed in the Pacific a month earlier during the invasion of Okinawa. I couldn't believe it. When was it all going to end?

Rick's death wasn't the only one I learned of that night and I was shocked to learn that quite a few of my former classmates had been killed in the war. The men and women who gathered at Casey's were indeed the survivors of their generation. And that night was the first time I began to feel it was their generation but not mine.

I'd already begun to distance myself.

All of the guys spent the remainder of the evening excitedly discussing their plans to get married and raise a family. Every guy, except me. Kathy didn't say a word to me and moved away whenever I tried to stand next to her. I got an earful as soon as I closed my car door.

"I can't believe you embarrassed me like that!" she shouted.

"I did nothing to embarrass you," I calmly replied. "I didn't know that accompanying you here tonight placed me under an obligation to make some kind of an announcement."

Kathy broke down, sobbing on the dashboard. God, it was amazing. For two years I'd learned to live with the heart-wrenching sound of men fighting for their last breath and I still couldn't bear to hear Kathy cry.

"Kathy, please listen to me. I'm not the same person you knew two years ago. I may look and sound the same, but believe me, I'm not. The truth is, I do love you and I always will, but I'm not interested in getting married and raising a family. I know how important that is to you and I love you too much to string you along. We were friends before we were lovers and it's very important to me that we always have our friendship."

Kathy pulled a tissue out of her purse and began to wipe away the mascara streaking her face.

"Everything will be okay." She sniffed. "Most of the guys who came back from overseas were in some kind of emotional distress for a while. Whatever it is we'll work it out, but, please, don't leave me alone. Promise me that no matter what happens, I won't end up being alone."

Some things never change. For a beautiful and intelligent girl, Kathy had always been incredibly insecure. I tilted her chin up and looked into her swollen eyes.

"Stop it!" I said. "You've got more going for you than any ten girls put together. You're stronger than this."

When Kathy was nine years old, her father said that he was going out to buy the Sunday paper. He never came back. Fearing that he'd fallen in harm's way, Kathy and her mother notified the police and prayed every morning, noon and night for his safe return. A week later they received a package with a Seattle postmark and no return address. Inside was three thousand dollars in cash and a letter explaining that he'd started a new life with a twenty-five-year-old cocktail waitress he'd met at the Hialeah Park Race Track. The remainder of Kathy's childhood was spent with empty holidays and listening to her mother cry herself to sleep.

Kathy dried her tears, sat up in her seat and focused coldly on the road ahead.

"Fine," she snapped, reaching up to pull a pin out to loosen her hair.

"In that case I'd rather not be alone tonight. Or is that too much to ask of an old friend?"

I wasn't the only one who'd changed in two years.

"Kathy, are you sure that's what you want?"

"Just shut-up and drive," she replied, never taking her eyes off the road. We parked down the street from her mother's white washed, wooden two story house, slipping through the mango and sarsaparilla trees in the backyard and tiptoed up the stairs.

Kathy lost her virginity to me on her seventeenth birthday. Sex with her was always fantastic. Her desperate need for emotional security was always simmering just beneath the skin deep veil of her cool demeanor. The moment I entered her she unleashed a passion that still surprised me as much as it had the first time we were together. Kathy wrapped her legs tightly around my waist and passionately clawed my back as she surrendered herself to me. A wash of moonlight cascaded across her athletic body as she writhed and moaned in ecstasy. She closed her eyes and smiled to herself with content as she slipped away to a world where there was no painful past, only the pleasure of the present. And I slipped away, too. Far away to a place where the Florida coconut trees gently swaying in the balmy breeze were replaced by the chill of crisp winds rolling down the face of Bavarian snowcapped mountains. Kathy shuddered with orgasmic release as she arched her back and her face became illuminated by a beam of moonlight.

Suddenly, I had to close my eyes.

Her hair was blonde.

After Kathy fell asleep, I quietly slipped out her screen back door and returned home to find my father sitting in the den silently sipping scotch from a brandy snifter as he thumbed through a cracked black vinyl photo album. He turned the pages with careful reverence, studying the faces and pausing to smile at the sight of a familiar figure.

"If it wasn't for you and your mother, I would've rather taken a bullet in the Argonne than die a slow death like this," he said, not taking his eyes off the old black and white photos.

"C'mon Dad, you don't mean that."

"Like hell, I don't. I've always believed it's better to go out in a flash than fade away. This is worse than death."

I'd never heard him talk this way before and I didn't like it. The thought of any type of surrender had always been foreign to my father. I tried to change the subject by telling him I wasn't interested in taking over the print shop and that we should start advertising for a manager. He ignored me. Nothing mattered anymore.

"Do you really believe those pills are real?" he asked, turning a page of the photo album.

"I do."

He exhaled deeply. "Life is so short. I hope to God you know what you're doing."

"Dad, something truly extraordinary happened today. I now have proof these pills work."

"Proof?" He smirked, closing the photo album. "This I have to see."

"Could I see your hunting knife?"

He reached into his desk drawer and unsheathed a Bowie Texas Special with a six-inch blade. "What do you plan on doing with this?"

"Not me. You. I want you to cut my hand."

He recoiled in horror. "What are you, some kind of a nut?"

"You said you wanted proof."

"Look, I took you at your word the first time you told me. You're my son and I've never given you any reason to lie to me. What is this, some kind of macho crap you learned overseas?"

"Just think of it as an experiment. Come on, Dad, you're not getting soft on me in your old age, are you?"

That pushed his button. With a determined grimace he grabbed my wrist and sliced the razor-sharp knife across the palm of my hand. Instantly, the blood welled and drizzled down my fingers. He tossed the knife onto his desk and turned away in disgust.

"Satisfied now, tough guy?"

"Dad, you need to see this."

He glanced back to see the wound in my hand begin to vibrate with small lightning quick pulses. The sliced skin resealed itself as if an invisible zipper had been pulled across my palm. He thrust my hand under his desk lamp to prove with his eyes what his mind couldn't understand.

"Well I'll be goddamned."

I felt completely vindicated.

"This is incredible. Absolutely incredible." he muttered, pressing his thumb deep into the unblemished palm of my hand. "Do you intend to keep this discovery to yourself? Have you considered talking to the press? I have a friend at the Miami Daily News who would kill for a story like this. People need to know."

I'd thought about it, but I was all too familiar with the military mentality. I told my father I knew I'd never see the pills again. The powers that be would find some obscure law or regulation that would make them the property of the U.S. Government and I had no intention of becoming anyone's guinea pig. Then I suggested that he take the pills to see if they had the power to cure his leukemia.

"That's most kind of you, but these pills are your destiny, not mine." He pushed back in his chair and gazed up at an oil painting of him and my mother. It was painted over twenty-five years ago, right after they were married and had always hung above our fireplace. I've always loved that painting, but something about it appeared different to me that night. It was no longer my mother and father. It was simply a portrait of an attractive young couple looking forward to spending the rest of their lives together. They had that look of supreme confidence and joy that comes when one is young and beautiful and in love.

And immortal.

"It's obvious these pills have some kind of incredible powers," he said, sipping his scotch. "Whatever you choose to do with your life, I believe your mother and I have taught you to be a God fearing man and I know you'll never use these powers for anything selfish or destructive. Perhaps fate brought these pills to you. In that case, no one has the right to take them away. My only advice is that you leave Miami as soon as possible and find your destiny. There's really nothing left for you here." He drained his snifter and sank back into his chair. "It's true, you don't regret the things you did in life as much as the things you didn't do." My father's eyes grew misty and I got an uneasy feeling he was looking far beyond the walls of his study. "Who knows?" he said softly. "Maybe through you I can really live forever."

If I live for a million years I will never forget those words.

At first, I thought I was dreaming that an explosion woke me from my sleep, like I was having a flashback from the war. Then I heard my mother scream and I realized it had been a gunshot. I knew it was my Dad. I ran downstairs to find my mother sobbing hysterically.

She sat on our living room couch, cradling my father's bleeding head in her bloodstained lap, feverishly rocking him back and forth to no avail. His stainless steel Colt 45 handgun was lying in the middle of a dark crimson puddle rapidly seeping across the carpet. Spread out on his desk was a collection of faded photos arranged in chronological order beginning with Dad as a boy on his mother's lap, then his military years, his wedding and honeymoon with Mom, my baby pictures and ending with a group shot of the three of us taken on the day I graduated high school. Next to the photos were two envelopes labeled Steven and June.

I felt as if I'd accidentally stumbled onto the set of a horror film. Every birthday, Easter, Thanksgiving, Christmas and New Year's Eve we'd ever celebrated as a family in this room flashed before my eyes. I began to cry and then I felt a strange calm settle over my emotions, as if an old friend had rested a comforting hand over my heart. I mouthed the words "Thank you" and dialed the police. Then I sat down on the floor and held my mother.

Within minutes, sirens were splitting the early morning air and without a knock the police charged in. The officers kept our curious neighbors at a distance and cleared the way for my father to be taken away in an ambulance. Mom accompanied him, desperately praying for a miracle that would never come. One of the officers read the contents of both envelopes, stuffed the pages back inside and handed them to me without a word as he left.

The envelope addressed to my mother felt as if it held four or five pages, but mine was quite thin. I sat down at the kitchen table and opened it. There was only one page:

My Beloved Steven. Don't ever look back. I will always love you. Dad.

I was riveted as I sat there reading my father's words–words that slowly became distorted, as my eyes filled with tears. Then I reached for the phone and called Kathy.

There's a timelessness I love about the ocean. Waves are born as a wind induced ripple before building into a towering crescendo crashing onto the beach in all of their explosive glory and humbly receding back in a continuous motion of life, death and rebirth. I sat on the beach that afternoon after my father's funeral and watched the waves crash and crawl back out to the sea, over and over again. Somewhere in those waves were the ashes of my father. The universe had reclaimed him.

Kathy arrived and sat beside me in silent contemplation. The final chapter of my mortal life was coming to an end. Kathy had enrolled at the University of Miami to study Political Science. My mother was selling the house and moving in with her sister Ruth in West Palm Beach. I'd decided to relocate to New York City where I believed I'd have the best chance of realizing my most immediate goal.

Anonymity.

After fifteen minutes of watching the waves break onto the beach, I said to Kathy, "Let's go for a walk."

We strolled north along the water's edge. I knew what I wanted to say, but I couldn't think of where to begin. As if she knew, Kathy stopped and said, "Please don't feel guilty if you've decided to move on without me.

I'll be all right. That night at Casey's, I'd been drinking and my emotions got the best of me. No matter what, I'll be fine."

Her selflessness moved me and I pulled her down to the sand beside me.

"Kathy, I'm going to tell you something that will either sound insane or incredible, probably both. I'm going to tell you this because not only do I love you, but I trust you. I trust that you really believe in me."

"Of course. You know I would never betray you."

I proceeded to tell her everything about the pills. At first she cracked an uneasy smile as if she thought I was playing a macabre joke, but the more I talked about what I'd seen at Dachau, the more she realized this was no joke. Her smile disappeared as she scooped a handful of sand and began trickling the crystal granules from her fist into the palm of her other hand in a motion that reminded me of an hourglass. She kept doing it over and over until I mentioned the shaving incident. Then she dusted off her hands and stood up.

"Steven," she said flatly. "You need professional help."

I couldn't believe it. My first thought was to grab a piece of jagged coral out of the foaming surf and slice my arm open, but I quickly discarded the idea. Deep down I was hoping there'd be some measure of blind faith between us. After I moved to New York, I planned to cut all my ties to Florida except for my mother and Kathy. Obviously, this wasn't meant to be. Kathy had just made it very easy for me to say good-bye.

Foolishly, she tried to make light of the situation. "Immortality?" She laughed. "Tiger shark liver extract? Come on Steven, think! Think how idiotic you sound! I hope to God you haven't told this story to anyone else!"

My heart sank at her betrayal. And what she said next only made it worse.

"I know this doctor. His name is Samuels. He has an office on Collins Avenue. A lot of the guys who came back from the war with problems like yours swear by him. He also happens to be a good friend of my mother. I'll make sure she calls him tonight and schedules an emergency appointment for you first thing Monday morning."

"Why are you doing this to me?" I moaned, burying my face in my hands.

"Because I love you and you need help! Now promise me you'll see him tomorrow! Promise me!"

She was shaking me as if I was a candidate for a Section 8. I wanted to push her away and run as fast and far away as possible. Instead, I numbly nodded in agreement just to stop her from saying another word. Inside, my heart was breaking. She hugged me tightly and whispered, "Don't worry darling. Everything will be fine."

Kathy was a stranger to me now–a compassionate, caring, loving stranger, but a stranger, nonetheless. Of course my story was fantastic. And that was exactly the reason why I'd told her. My father was a skeptic, but at least he'd always given me the benefit of the doubt. He could look me straight in the eye and know right away if I was telling the truth because he knew me. Now I knew Kathy never did.

We were interrupted by a loud cheer erupting just north of us at the Miami Beach pier. We walked up just as a group of fisherman hoisted the winning catch of the 1945 Kiwanis Club fishing tournament.

"My God," Kathy exclaimed. "Look at the size of that fish!"

I studied the massive dorsal fin, the razor sharp teeth and the barely perceptible stripes lining the sides of its powerful body. I had never seen one before, but I knew exactly what it was.

"Kathy, that's not a fish. That's a shark. A tiger shark."

Her jaw dropped. "Well, what do you know?" She smirked, regaining her composure. "Isn't that one hell of a coincidence?"

I ran my hand along the sandpapery skin of the fifteen-foot-long beast as thick blood oozed from its gaping jaws and a pungent fishy odor brewed under the hot tropical sun. The animal was magnificent and I was spellbound by the thought that I was facing the creature that was the source of my destiny.

"I'm sorry Kathy, but I don't believe in coincidences."

Seeing that tiger shark was no coincidence. It was an omen. And it told me that the time had come to leave Florida. That weekend I found myself in a sentimental slump. I curled up by our family's Philco radio and listened to Amos and Andy. I knew I was living in the past and I wanted to recapture and savor every nostalgic moment just a minute longer.

I packed two suitcases. One had my personal effects: my prized silver 1940 Conn 6M VIII Alto Saxophone, assorted clothes, some toiletries and a soft red leather bound diary to record my experiences as I journeyed into the unknown. The other suitcase contained the fifty bottles of immortality pills, each now carefully wrapped in a protective strip of white linen, and five thousand dollars in cash my mother advanced me from my father's estate. I purchased a one-way bus ticket on a Greyhound for twenty-nine dollars that departed that Sunday night at eight o'clock for Manhattan. Kathy thought she was picking me up the next morning to drive me to my appointment with Dr. Samuels. When she arrived, I had instructed my mother to hand her an envelope with the following letter enclosed:

My Dearest Kathy,

I've decided this is the best way to say good-bye. Believe it or not, what happened to me in Germany was real. I realize now what I told you was too incredible for anyone to believe unless they'd experienced it themselves. The only person who believed me was my father, and it tortures me to think that the knowledge of my secret may have hastened his death. Your reaction to my story only reinforces my belief that I have to be alone. You must accept the truth that my change is permanent. The Steven you knew doesn't exist anymore and will never return. The only thing I have in common with the person I once was is that I love you— very deeply. And that is why I must let you go. I can't tell you how elated I am that you've enrolled in college and are finally on your way to realizing your dream of becoming an attorney. There is nothing more important in life than having your dreams come true

May they all.
Steven

Through the corner of my eye, I could see tears streaming down my mother's cheeks as we drove in awkward silence to the bus station. I stared out the window and watched a blur of houses, faces, automobiles and neon storefronts of my hometown flash by. At the station, I hugged my mother and mumbled something about promising to write. Words at this point were nothing more than a painful obstacle to a foregone conclusion. When the bus driver finally shut the door, I knew I would never see home again.

After three days of traveling up US 1, the bus reached its destination in New York City near Penn Station. The trip was uneventful save for the insistent reminders of racism, still so glaringly prevalent in the South. Two of the most blatant examples were the bathrooms in Jacksonville labeled Men, Women and Colored, and a giant billboard on the Georgia/South Carolina state line proclaiming "Welcome to Klan Country!" complete with a white hooded rider carrying a shield and joust on horseback. After dealing firsthand with the horrific results of Hitler's hatred, I thought it was high time we started working on our own backyard.

The moment I stepped off the bus in Manhattan at Greyhound's Pennsylvania terminal on 34th Street my senses were assaulted by the acrid smell of stale urine. Shuffling my way through the teeming masses of humanity, I picked up a copy of the New York Sun and zeroed in on a one-bedroom, third-floor apartment in Greenwich Village for eighty-five dollars a month. I hailed a taxicab and drove to a brownstone at 137 Waverly Place, only to be told by the landlord that he'd promised the space an hour earlier. Not to be deterred, I flashed six months' worth of rent money in his face and was promptly handed the keys.

As I sat cross-legged on the hardwood floor and read the newspaper, I came across a page filled with advertisements for Manhattan's jazz clubs located on 52nd Street between 5th and 6th Avenue. Before the war, I'd stand in front of my bedroom mirror practicing my sax for hours playing along to Johnny Hodges of the Duke Ellington Band on my father's Victrola. I became proficient enough to seriously entertain the idea of becoming a professional saxophonist. But, the sixty hour work week necessary to keep the family print shop alive in post-depression Miami made that an impossibility. Now, time would never be an obstacle for me again. I wanted nothing more than to pursue the one thing in life that brought me happiness and music had always been my secret passion. "You can make all the money in the world and you'll still be mortal," my mother had once told me, "but the arts will make you immortal." Little did she know how prophetic those words would become. I decided to brush up on my technique and make the rounds on Swing Street when I felt confident.

That first night in New York, I lay awake wondering what Kathy's reaction was to my letter had been. My conscience had been prodding me and I wondered if I could have let her go in a more sensitive manner, but there was no other way. She was firmly convinced that I'd suffered some sort of mental trauma. By the time I arrived in New York I'm sure she'd probably resigned herself to the idea that I was on my way to becoming just another strung-out alcoholic, endlessly wandering the streets of the Bowery's skid row.

For the next couple of days, I traipsed around the Village familiarizing myself with my new surroundings. I found the area to be mostly populated with coffeehouses, bookstores and New York University students delightfully willing to debate liberal politics or social causes at the drop of a hat. Strolling north up 8th Avenue, I noticed a large, silver Navy dirigible churning majestically through the sky as it headed up the Hudson River.

A blast from the ship's powerful foghorn split through the air, the sound ricocheting off the buildings and resonating through my bones. Whatever ship making that sound had to be gigantic.

In response, everyone walking beside me picked up their pace and began to hurry towards the docks. I flagged down a taxi who informed me that it was the Queen Mary arriving from Europe and packed with soldiers. I rode the cab up to 48th Street before the traffic became so thick that I decided to get out and walk. I turned westward on 50th Street and followed the crowd streaming towards the docks. As I approached Pier 90, I caught a glimpse of the leviathan's massive smokestacks trailing plumes from her steam turbines. Despite her wartime coat of gray, the Queen Mary was still a breathtaking sight and I couldn't believe how many troops were jammed onto her decks. The cabbie told me he'd heard there were at least fifteen thousand men aboard. As the ship neared the dock, the roar of the crowd became as loud as if Joe DiMaggio had just hit a homer in the Bronx, but, most of the soldiers aboard were booing something below them. I stood on my toes and spotted the objects of their derision– the dock was lined with hundreds of grim faced military policemen.

It felt strange to be standing there as both civilian and spectator. Less than a month earlier I'd landed not far from here on a much smaller ship with almost zero reception. And at that moment, I thought of Kathy. Flower-toting girls around me all had the same look of wide-eyed anticipation as she had when she ran to embrace me in my parents' driveway. Forcing the image from my mind, I focused on the faces of the men striding down the gangplanks. A generation of thousands of young faces eagerly anticipating the celebration of life, love, children and the promise of a steady job. And save for one fateful night in Dachau, my expectations would have been exactly the same. Standing in the midst of all that joyous humanity, I became aware of just how far in a short time I'd distanced myself from my fellow man.

I was learning to embrace solitude.

CHAPTER
❖ 3 ❖

On the evening of Sunday, July 1st, 1945, I carted my saxophone up to the Onyx Club at 57 West 52nd Street to check out their jam session. I'd practiced every night and was shocked at my progression. My technique had advanced more in weeks than I would have expected in a year and I had a sneaking suspicion the pills were playing their hand there as well.

I arrived at the club just before the house band took the stage, seated myself directly in front of them and ordered a Gibson. A couple of dry martinis and I was feeling no pain, swaying along with the audience to the four musicians improvising just a few feet from me. They were playing a new style of jazz called Bebop that was nothing like the big-band swing I'd learned. I found it exhilarating. My inhibitions were quickly lowering and I was dying to get up there. It was obvious from the familiar banter between the band and the audience that much of the local scene was in attendance. An outsider like me would never get a second chance to make a first impression, but the more I listened and the more I drank, the more confident I became that I could hold my own. The music stopped and the front man stepped up the stage to lean into the microphone.

"Do we have a sax man in the house tonight with some hair on his balls?" he cracked in a thick Caribbean accent.

My sax was lying in its case across an empty chair next to me. There was no way he could miss it. And he didn't. My adrenaline surged as he flashed a toothy grin directly at me and began to bounce his eyes back and forth between my sax case and me like a Warner Brothers' cartoon character. He finally settled his gaze on me.

"C'mon, my man," he said, warmly waving me up. "Don't be shy. We're always looking for new blood. Give it a shot."

Encouraged by the three martinis coursing through my veins, I snatched my case and bounded up onto the stage. After I unpacked my sax and put the reed to my lips, the bandleader leaned over and said, "Let's see how long you can ride this train before you fall off."

I took a deep breath, waited until the rhythm section had played a couple of bars, and chimed in. Within seconds I felt as if I'd glided off a mountaintop. My playing felt completely effortless. Very easy: in fact, much too easy. I began to hear myself as if from a distance and my brain began to feel detached from my fingers. More than once I had to glance down at the instrument to confirm it was really my fingers dancing across the sax pads. I heard myself improvising melodies that seemed influenced by some sort of exotic tonality. They were sounds that shouldn't have been compatible with the free form jazz style the band was playing, but somehow they dovetailed. I looked around to see the rhythm section nodding at each other with intense affirmation. The drummer and bassist never smiled or returned my gaze; they just kept on nodding while the trumpet player, pianist and I took turns trading licks. I was having the time of my life. The odd thing was I had to keep resisting an overwhelming temptation to close my eyes.

I began to have the distinct feeling that a strange force would completely overwhelm me if my eyelashes touched for more than a split-second and it got so bad that I was afraid to blink. I barely managed to remain wide-eyed and in control until the very last measure of the jam. After the drummer signaled the finale with an explosive cymbal crash, the audience applauded enthusiastically as the bandleader patted me on the back and asked me to stick around.

At the end of the set, he joined me at the bar. He was a Cuban émigré who went by the name Hines Winston. Hines was in his early thirties with black hair slicked straight with pomade and neatly dressed in a navy blue pin-striped suit. I must have made one hell of an impression on him because he wouldn't stop showering me with compliments that seemed a bit excessive. He then told me that the only person he'd heard come close to my style of playing was someone called *The Bird*.

"The Bird? Who's that?"

"C'mon man," he laughed. "You've never heard of the great Charlie Parker, Jr?"

I shook my head.

"Seriously? Where in the hell have you been?"

"That's exactly where I've been. Hell. I've just returned from Germany."

Hines invited me to return to the next Sunday jam session and said he was going to "pull some heavy strings" and invite some important friends to hear me play. As he walked back to the stage he wagged a tanned, bony finger at me and cautioned, "Whatever you do, don't be late."

I was ecstatic and yet, I had no one to share it with. Solitude certainly has its limitations. By this time I was pretty drunk, so I called it a night and taxied back to the Village. I was so intoxicated that I forgot whether I'd already taken my daily pill, so to be on the safe side I took another. Within seconds I instantly fell into the deepest sleep I'd ever known.

In what only seemed like a minute, I awoke to the sound of cars incessantly honking their horns. I tried to open my eyes, but found that I could do little more than arch my eyebrows. My arms tingled from lack of circulation and felt as if they were cast in lead. Mustering my strength, I reached up and felt greasy hairs matting my face. My throat felt like sandpaper and it was impossible to swallow. I gently pried my mouth open and massaged my tongue to generate some saliva. My eyes were sealed shut with a sheet of entrusted mucus. I delicately picked my eyelashes clean and opened them. By the angle of the sunlight flooding across my floor, I guessed it to be late afternoon. I tried to sit up, but fell back nauseous and disoriented. Sliding up against the headboard, I pulled myself into a sitting position. The windows were shut and the air in the apartment was stifling from lack of ventilation. After sitting there for about twenty minutes and enduring the cacophony of noise outside, I draped my legs over the side of the bed and painstakingly pulled myself up by the bedpost. Using baby steps, I made my way to the bathroom.

My jaw dropped in revulsion when I looked in the mirror and saw a bearded, puffy-eyed, stranger staring back at me. I gargled with a handful of cool tap water and felt it slowly work its way down my esophagus to my empty stomach. Judging by the length of my beard, my first thought was that the pills had somehow sped up my metabolism overnight, but that didn't make sense. There was only one logical answer.

I'd been asleep for a long time.

Fortunately, I'd paid the landlord six months' rent in advance. I didn't have a phone and no one knew where I lived, so I remained undisturbed. But for how long? And why did I awake now? It couldn't have been the noise outside. I'd slept through many a barrage of 155mm guns during the war.

I pulled on some clothes and stumbled outside. It was as if the whole world had gone mad. As if Mardi Gras had been transplanted from New Orleans and descended on Greenwich Village. Strangers were running up and hugging each other, dancing in the streets and jumping on top of lamp posts. I hadn't taken more than a couple of steps before a very attractive and intoxicated Italian girl grabbed me and kissed me full on the mouth. I was starting to think maybe I was imagining all of this, but then I realized that I must have accidentally taken two pills that day. In other words, an overdose. I turned a corner and came upon the news stand on 6th Avenue. I focused my eyes on the New York Sun's headline:

TRUMAN PROCLAIMS V-J DAY!

And then the date: Wednesday, August 14th, 1945.

I had been unconscious for six weeks! The war was over! The last thing I'd heard was that we were fighting in Okinawa, but that the Japs were stonewalling with such ferocity that we'd probably have to invade the Japanese mainland early next year. Right below the headline I found the reason for Japan's sudden change of heart. An incredible bomb had destroyed the cities of Hiroshima and Nagasaki on August 6th and 9th. Faced with such a doomsday machine, the Japanese had no other choice but to capitulate. How could one bomb destroy an entire city?

August 14th, 1945 was an important day in history and I believe its significance awakened me. While I was unconscious I'd felt as if I was floating on a raft down a river of twisting and turning glass. If the current of time is analogous to a river, then I believe that dates of historical importance may cause a kind of ripple or wave. I distinctly recall being bumped by something right before I drifted back into consciousness.

My light-headedness soon got the better of me and I departed the sights and sounds of celebration for the quiet relief of my apartment. I drifted in and out of consciousness for two more days before my strength returned enough to shave, shower and clean myself up. I taxied up to the Onyx Club to find Hines hunched over the bar, leering drunkenly into an empty martini glass. He didn't move a muscle when I called out his name. As far as he knew, I'd broken an agreement to return that Sunday last month and had never bothered to call with an explanation. I took a deep breath, walked up and tapped him on the shoulder.

"Hines, may I speak to you for a second?"

He blinked his bleary eyes and peered up at me. "You know," he slurred, "you never told me your name, so that if I ever saw you again, I could properly tell you to go fuck yourself. So, what is your name?"

"It's Steven Ronson."

"Good to meet you, Steven Ronson. Now please go fuck yourself."

He turned away from me and I pulled on his suit covered bicep.

"Hines, it was a situation that was beyond my control."

He spun around with a speed I would've thought impossible in his condition and clenched my hand in a crushing, steely grip.

"You must be one stupid motherfucker to ever touch me like that."

I could smell the alcohol on his breath and I was expecting a punch, but he hesitated. Even in his drunken state, Hines was probably torn between knocking the daylights out of me and giving me another chance.

"Do you have any idea how bad you made me look when you didn't show up?" He was eyeball to eyeball with me now, but I didn't dare utter a word. As long as he kept talking I knew I was safe. "The day after you played I called everyone in the business and shot my mouth off about this new boy wonder in town. I invited the cream of the crop to hear you that Sunday. Sitting out there were some of the best saxophonists on the scene including Ben Webster and Don Byas. He was wheezing hard and stopped to catch his breath. I sensed I was out of the woods so I apologized.

"Hines, I can't tell you how sorry I am. The reason I–"

He cupped my mouth with a brown, calloused hand. "Shut the fuck up. Don't waste your breath because I'm not going to believe you. I don't care if it's drugs, women or whatever. I'm going to let this slide, one time, but if you ever do that to me again," he whipped a switchblade out of his coat pocket and pressed the razor sharp blade underneath my Adam's apple, "I'll carve your fucking throat out. Do we understand each other?"

"Perfectly."

"Good, now get your sorry white ass home and practice. I'll see you here Sunday night at nine o'clock sharp."

That week I did nothing but eat, sleep and drink alto saxophone. On Sunday I taxied up to the Onyx Club, ready to take on the world. From my first step inside the smoky club it was obvious that Hines had done an extraordinary amount of damage control. The place was packed with curious club luminaries such as Art Tatum, Red Allen, Cozy Cole, Roy Eldridge, Ben Webster, Billie Holiday, Dizzy Gillespie and Sarah Vaughan. He introduced me to at least a dozen of them, and that was just on my way to the stage.

Any nervousness I felt performing before such an intimidating audience dissipated the moment I exhaled into my first note. On the other hand, I found myself expending a considerable amount of energy to keep my eyes open. I found it somewhat distracting and I began to wonder what would happen if I stopped resisting. I decided against it because I didn't want to chance anything negatively affecting my performance and enraging Hines.

As my fingers furiously glided across the saxophone's pads, I looked out into the cigarette haze of bopping heads and caught sight of someone in the darkest recess of the room. She had the most beautiful eyes I'd ever seen. I couldn't make out the face to whom they belonged, but through the smoky darkness I became aware of these magnificent, sparkling eyes framed by reddish hair capped with a black beret. She firmly held my gaze as I wailed away and from then on I found it much easier to keep my eyes open. It felt as if I'd performed only a couple of minutes when Hines raised his trumpet and signaled the end of the improvisation. He politely acknowledged the audience's enthusiastic applause with a suave, toothy smile and said, "Thank you all so very much and welcome to the Onyx Club."

And then he invited another saxophonist to the stage to take my place.

"You did good." Hines said, patting me on the back. "I just wanted to give them a taste. Now go wait at the bar and have a drink until I call on you again."

I made my way to the bar, pausing briefly along the way to shake some hands, and ordered a Gibson. As the bartender dropped two pearl onions into my martini glass, a tall, elderly gentleman standing next to me with thinly combed over white hair dressed in a black leather trench coat leaned stiffly across the bar and said in a refined British accent, "Bartender, would you kindly put this musician's drink on my tab."

I nodded and lifted my drink appreciatively. He leaned over and whispered, "I simply wanted to tell you that I found your playing most intriguing. The last time I heard melodies like that was when I was doing missionary work in the Far East, deep inside of mainland China."

I told him I'd never studied Chinese music.

"I didn't say it sounded Chinese." He sniffed. "I simply said the last time I heard anything like that was in the Far East, in a Buddhist monastery, performed by monks on ancient religious instruments."

"I'm glad you liked it." I smiled.

"Well, I'm not sure if I liked it. I may have to digest it for a while. Actually, it brought back some memories I'd rather forget." I had absolutely no idea what this guy was driving at, but I decided to be polite and let him ramble on. Besides, the Gibson tasted great and it was on his dime.

"You see, I discovered those wonderfully musical monks were far from harmless. One evening, I accidentally walked in on them while they were performing some sort of bestial ceremony. When my missionary zeal got the best of me I attempted to intervene and the bastards nearly murdered me."

His story was starting to give me the creeps, but I also found him to be somewhat pitiful. He labored for every breath and had these sad, beagle-type eyes that looked as if they hadn't seen better days for quite a while.

I extended my hand. "It's a pleasure to meet you, sir. My name is Steven Ronson."

When he didn't react I looked down and was mortified to see he didn't have a right hand. Sensing my embarrassment, he smiled, turned his shoulder and reached out from under his leather coat with a deformed left hand.

"Like I said, the bastards nearly killed me. My name is Albert Harrison."

"So, you're a missionary?"

"Not anymore. Let's just say I've had my fall from grace. From where do you hail?"

"Miami."

"Is that where you developed your unique musical style?"

"Not what you heard tonight. I've just returned from Europe where I spent the last two years in the army as a medic. Before the war, I was influenced by a lot of big band saxophonists, but the stuff you heard tonight seemed to come out of nowhere."

The ex-missionary eyed me suspiciously. That's okay, I thought to myself. I wouldn't have bought it either.

"As I was saying," he continued. "I don't understand where you could have learned to play like that. Legend has it that no one but those Buddhist monks can create those types of melodies. They use them in their secret ceremonies and I've heard bizarre stories about their behavior behind closed doors—sexual orgies, animal sacrifice and possibly human sacrifice."

"They don't sound like Buddhist monks to me. Why weren't they simply arrested?"

"Because the locals were terrified. One must understand that these beliefs, no matter how preposterous they may seem to us, have been held by these people for hundreds, perhaps, thousands of years. After that long, even the most absurd rumors tend to gain some sort of credibility. Furthermore, many of the locals believe these monks can't be killed."

"Why not?" I asked, sipping the last of my martini.

He bent over until his chapped lips almost touched my ear and whispered n a ragged voice, "Because legend has it they are immortal."

I coughed up a mouthful of gin and a pearl onion.

"Are you okay, old boy?" he asked, patting me on the back with his withered hand. "I didn't mean to startle you."

"What do you mean legend has it that they are immortal?"

"What do you think I mean? The locals believe these monks can actually live forever. My housemaid was an old Chinese woman who was quite intelligent and not susceptible to superstition. One night, I pulled her aside and asked her if she believed there was anything strange or supernatural about the monks. She carefully checked every room in the house to make sure we were alone before she reached into her dresser and handed me a portrait of a Buddhist monk named Chow Li. I knew Chow Li quite well and assumed him to be twenty-five to thirty years old. She told me the photo was taken in the mid-1880s."

"Are you sure it was him?"

"Absolutely. I saw Chow Li at least once a week."

Though I found his story fascinating, I couldn't see the connection between a remote Chinese monastery and the Nazis.

"Mr. Harrison, I've always been fascinated by the idea of immortality. Do you think it's possible?"

"Call me Albert. I haven't discussed this chapter of my life with many people and I'd feel a lot more comfortable if I thought I was entrusting this information to someone who was more than a stranger. Before all of this,

I would've thought the idea of physical immortality was utterly preposterous. Now, I don't know what to think. I was curious enough at the time to do a little research on the subject. Legend had it that these monks ingested some daily concoction and that once a year they made a pilgrimage to the South China Sea to replenish its main ingredient. I'd been trading dry goods with them during their weekend visits to the city to acquire this wonderfully luxurious silk only they know how to create. One weekend they didn't appear and I decided to hike out to their mountain monastery to see them. By this time I was convinced we'd become friends or had become as friendly as any outsider could become with them. Foolishly, I slid through the partially opened massive iron door to their monastery and stepped into total darkness echoing with this fascinating music emanating from deep inside. I followed this seductive sound and the aromatic scent of sandalwood incense until I reached a wooden door. Never in my life had I heard anything so hauntingly beautiful and politely knocked while cradling a bag of goods. No one answered and, after a respectable pause, I opened the door to see their head monk, or whatever you'd call him, draped in a cape and performing bestial sex on a young Chinese woman chained to a stone altar. After I'd recovered from my initial shock, I screamed at them to stop what they were doing in the name of our Lord Jesus Christ. Monks who'd been silently prostrated in prayer viciously attacked me with knives and clubs. As I ran backward, I shielded myself with my hands. Though that action undoubtedly saved my life, it also cost me the loss of one hand and injured the other so badly that it's no longer good for anything except holding a good cigar. I nearly bled to death as I fled through the darkness and made my way back to the mission.

"Legend has it that these monks have been preying on wayward travelers for centuries without retribution. This time was different. I had become quite popular with the locals and word of my attack spread quickly. The next night the Japanese army pulled up in a truck convoy and raided the place while the monks escaped into the mountains."

I was confused. "What was the Japanese army doing there?"

"This was in 1938, one year after the Japanese invaded the area. I was with the China Inland Mission. We were housed in the ancient walled city of Sian and the monks' monastery was in the mountains about fifteen miles away. Even though Sian is located approximately nine hundred miles west of Shanghai, Japanese reconnaissance troops had been steadily patrolling the area because Sian was less than seventy-five miles southwest of the Japanese Army's front line that had swept down from Manchuria. By this time, the Japanese had their hands full controlling both the Chinese Nationalist and Communist factions.

"I doubt if they cared about the troubles of one English missionary. What caught their attention was that the news of my attack included information describing the monastery as resembling some kind of military fortress. Its appearance had nothing in common with any of the traditional Buddhist or Taoist structures in Sian. My guess is that when the Japanese came upon this fortified building, they saw it as a potential threat and neutralized it."

"Did they find anything to substantiate the local folklore?"

"I have no idea. They picked the place clean and carted everything back to Japan."

I'd become so engrossed in Albert's story that I didn't realize someone was eavesdropping.

"You'll have to excuse my Uncle Albert," said a suggestive female voice behind me. "He's quite fond of boring his victims to death with one of his crazy missionary tales."

I turned to face a gorgeous woman in her early twenties. She was dressed in a shoulder-padded black dress and heels. Her matching black beret capped long, Veronica Lake-styled auburn hair that framed eyes so intimidatingly emerald green that I found it difficult to maintain eye contact with her.

"Good evening," she said, extending a black suede glove. "I'm Jennifer Harrison."

"It's a pleasure to meet you," I replied, firmly squeezing her hand. "My name is Steven Ronson, and I must admit you have the most stunning green eyes I've ever seen."

"Gee, that's original," she deadpanned. "Anyway, I didn't want to interrupt and just stopped by to say I enjoyed your performance even though you really need to brush up on your stage presence."

Albert slammed his deformed hand upon the bar so hard my drink jumped.

"Damn it, Jennifer, your rudeness is inexcusable! This is a fine young man who's just returned from war, and if he's not too insulted by your behavior, I'd like to invite him to join us for a cup of coffee."

Jennifer smirked devilishly, as if she enjoyed eliciting such an emotional reaction from the old man. "Whatever," she replied, sailing off into the darkness.

Albert stared tight-lipped down at the bar, shaking his head in anger. I got the feeling he'd played this part many times before.

"Please excuse my niece. When she was a child both of her parents were killed in an automobile accident and I've cared for her ever since. After her parents' death, she became very shy and withdrawn and in an effort to correct her introverted personality, I encouraged her to vocalize whatever was on her mind. As you can see, I've more than succeeded."

"Please, don't worry about it." I laughed. "You have an extremely beautiful niece and I have to admit that I was impressed with her honesty."

"Honesty?" He chuckled. "Is that what you Yanks call it?"

Hines waved me up to rejoin him. "I'd like to invite someone back to the stage who jammed with us earlier tonight. Steven, c'mon up here, my man."

The band kicked into gear as I put my lips against the saxophone reed and exhaled into the instrument. I was soon alone in my own private universe, except for the one thing I found impossible to block out of my mind. I locked onto Jennifer's beautiful green eyes through the haze.

I could sense her desperation.

I could sense her hunger.

Spurred on by her presence, I played with a freedom I'd never experienced as the band did their best to follow me into uncharted musical waters. And again, I felt the powerful tug of seduction, the inescapable desire to close my eyes and surrender to whatever force was attempting to take control of my senses. So, I did the only sensible thing.

I closed my eyes.

Instantly, my brain exploded into a kaleidoscope of brilliantly illuminated rectangular images that rocketed through my subconscious mind like a thousand tracer bullets on either side of me. I watched spellbound as an endless stream of people and places materialized out of the blackest void I'd ever seen. The images would first appear as a glowing pinpoint on the horizon before quickly magnifying in size as they rushed toward either side of me. There were so many of them moving so quickly that it was difficult to focus on a particular image for more than a fraction of a second. By the time I could distinguish one that contained the frozen image of a woman with ringlet chestnut hair in a powder blue nineteenth century antebellum hoop dress, it had already streaked past me and disappeared. As I peered into the inky void, I noticed a dot that seemed to behave differently than the rest. It was pulsating erratically like a cosmic Morse code, as if it demanded my attention. I ignored the fusillade of colorful images streaking by and concentrated on it. As if on command, it flickered brightly, and began to shoot towards me. Quickly enlarging in size, the image began to reveal itself. It contained a woman lying in a hospital bed, twisting her head from side to side as she writhed in agony. Streaks of long black sweaty hair clung to her face and brow. She was quite attractive in a tanned bathing beauty way, perhaps in her early twenties, but something about her was uncomfortably familiar. Just as the image zoomed past, I saw a masked doctor guiding a baby out from between her legs. And then I knew.

She was my mother.

The shock instantly bolted me from the subconscious to the conscious world. I yanked the saxophone from my mouth and gasped for breath as I opened my eyes to see every face in the Onyx audience staring at me in amazement.

"Okay people," Hines said softly to a smattering of confused applause. "We're gonna take five." Disoriented, I sat down on the stage and rested my head in my hands.

"Hines, I'm sorry."

Hines knelt down beside me. "Don't apologize. You were fantastic, but your damn eyes were closed the whole time and I couldn't get your attention!"

I squinted through the stage lights and scanned the club. Albert and Jennifer were gone. Hines draped his arm around me and helped me over to the bar.

"Steven, I think we should talk some serious business," he said, sliding a barstool underneath me. "I know a very powerful *Artists and Repertoire* man over at RCA-Victor. I could get him down here next Sunday."

"Don't you think that's a little premature? This is only my second night here and you want to bring an A and R guy down?"

Hines was adamant. "I know it sounds crazy, but to tell you the truth, what you're playing is crazy. I've never heard anything like it in my life. And that covers a lot of territory. The guys and I could barely keep up with you, but the important thing is that we did keep up with you. Do you know that you were so outrageous that none of the cats I brought down tonight have any desire to jam with you?"

I didn't know what to think about that. It was definitely the most backhanded compliment I'd ever received. Regardless, I already knew one thing for sure. Hines wasn't going to put his reputation on the line again unless he thought he'd hit the jackpot.

"Sure, bring him down," I shrugged. "You know this business better than I do."

"That's the spirit, brother!" he said, slapping me on the back. "I'll see you next Sunday!"

He shook my hand furiously, but before I let go, I pulled him closer.

"Hines, do you know anything about that old man I was talking to earlier or that young woman with him?

"Yeah, I noticed you were talking to them." He frowned. "They're here all the time. Rumor has it that he was a missionary who got his ass thrown out because he lost his faith or something. He's always getting drunk and pissing people off with his religious arguments and crazy views about Jesus. One time I thought I'd impress him with the ancient religion in Cuba called Santería. Turns out he knows more about it than I do. The girl is his niece. A real piece of ass and she knows it. Forget about her. She loves to lead guys on and screw with their heads. The saying around here is that she's shot down more guys than Zeros at Midway. The regulars keep their distance from her. I suggest you do the same."

I thanked him for the advice, grabbed my sax case and bounded out into the damp Manhattan night. The rain-slicked streets were empty and there wasn't a cab in sight and I began walking down 5th Avenue. Suddenly, a taxi's headlights barreled toward me and before I could raise my arm, it pulled over and the rear door opened.

"Care to join us for that cup of coffee?" Albert shouted.

"Sure," I answered, stepping into the cab.

I squeezed into the back seat next to Jennifer as we roared off into the neon illuminated night. She coldly stared ahead and ignored my presence while Albert directed the driver to a diner on the corner of 50th and 9th Avenue, deep in the heart of Hell's Kitchen. The street was lined with high-heeled hookers dressed in slit-thigh skirts, preening and seductively positioning themselves while their zoot-suited pimps patiently chain smoked in their prewar sedans guarding their inventory. A couple of girls began strutting in our direction when our cab pulled up, but they spun on their heels the second they saw Jennifer. I opened the door and offered my hand. Extending his forearm, Albert politely thanked me as I helped him out of the cab while Jennifer pushed past us.

We entered the diner and seated ourselves at an isolated booth in the back. Jennifer was obviously bored with the company and made sure everyone knew it by propping her head against her hand and staring blankly out the window. When our eyes met briefly in the reflection, she blinked and looked away.

"When you performed tonight, could you hear what you were playing?" Albert asked.

"Not after I closed my eyes. After that I couldn't hear a thing, but I could see things that were incredible. Thousands of square shaped images of people and places, brilliantly illuminated against the blackest void I could ever imagine. They were mostly images of people—men and women of all ages and races, from the past, present and maybe even the future.

"Did you recognize anyone?"

"There were too many of them moving too quickly. The one image I was able to recognize was the image of my birth. Needless to say, the shock of witnessing my mother in labor snapped me out of my trance and ended my performance."

Albert nodded assuredly. "It sounds like your mind entered a portal exposing you to the Akashic Records. They contain all of the knowledge of the universe. You didn't recognize anyone at first because they were unfamiliar to you, perhaps from another lifetime. Billions of people have existed since the beginning of time. When you finally locked onto someone familiar, it was most likely going to be the first person you saw when you entered this world in this lifetime—your mother."

He was right. Unless I'd been lucky enough to see someone I'd known personally or who someone was famous, I'd have no idea who or what I was viewing.

I took a sip of my coffee and noticed that Jennifer had taken more than an interest in our conversation.

Albert excused himself to use the restroom. I now found myself in the precarious position of being alone with Jennifer. She stared down into her coffee, slowly swirling her cream and sugar with a spoon. And in the bright lights of the diner, I got a really good look at her. She was even more beautiful than I thought with flawless ivory skin, straight shiny auburn hair, full ruby lips and those fantastic sparkling emerald green eyes. She would've made for one hell of a pin-up during the war. All that was missing was a personality. And as much as I wanted to know what made her tick, I'd rather have crawled on my belly across a field of broken glass than have initiated a conversation with her.

And then I saw those sensuous red lips move.

"I wish I could see my mother again," she murmured in a voice so soft it sounded as if it had come from another person.

I felt an overwhelming desire to reach across the table and comfort her, but I didn't dare act on it. She knew I'd heard her and raised her head until our eyes met. I was stunned by her sudden transformation. The callousness had disappeared and was replaced by a demure loveliness that was absolutely breathtaking. There was another person trapped inside of that beautiful face and body. We stared at each other in silence and then she caught herself. In one blink those alluring green eyes flashed angry as if a steel curtain had been ripped across her soul. With a vicious flick of her delicate wrist, she whipped the spoon out of her coffee cup and flung it at me, striking me square between the eyes with such velocity it felt as if it had cracked my forehead.

I calmly picked up my napkin and wiped the coffee off my face. Without saying a word, she turned her head and dispassionately stared out the window as if nothing had happened as Albert reappeared.

"Sorry, I left so abruptly. At my age, when nature calls, she can't be ignored. Did I miss anything?" Jennifer ignored him and continued staring out of the window.

"Nothing, Albert," I replied. "Nothing at all."

"Very well, then. I believe we should–"

Suddenly, Jennifer shoved past her uncle, nearly knocking the old man to the floor as she charged out of our booth.

"Jennifer!" Albert shouted after her. "Where on earth are you're going?"

"Nowhere," she replied, her voice breaking, as she stormed off to the ladies room. Albert watched her retreat in disbelief.

"My Lord, was Jennifer crying?"

"Yes, I believe she was."

"That's incredible! I can't remember the last time she cried. What on earth did you say to her?"

"That's the funny thing. I didn't say a word to her the entire time you were gone."

Jennifer reappeared at our table with puffy eyes and trembling lips.

"I want to go!" she said folding her arms and angrily tapping her foot. "I want to leave right now!"

I pulled out a five spot and tossed it on the table as Jennifer stomped out of the diner.

We should call it a night," I said to Albert.

"You're probably right." he answered. "But would you mind accompanying me down to 42nd Street? It'll be easier to catch a cab there this time of night and I'd rather not walk alone."

By the time Albert and I made it out the front door, Jennifer was already a block ahead of us walking down 9th Avenue.

"Will she be all right?" I asked. "Hell's Kitchen isn't the safest place for a woman to be walking alone at three-thirty in the morning."

"Oh, let her go," Albert replied, waving her off in exasperation. "She'll wait up for us on 42nd Street."

Nevertheless, I kept an eye on her as the street lights illuminated her quickly disappearing silhouette.

"Steven, I'm going to be honest with you and say what's on my mind. I believe you're holding something back from me. You'll never convince me it's simply a coincidence that in addition to the music you create, you now have another supernatural trait in common with those Buddhist monks I knew in China."

I stopped to face him. "What do you think I'm holding back? And what do you mean by saying that I have another supernatural trait in common with the monks?"

"Visions. Your description of your experience on stage tonight mirrors exactly what I'd heard in China. There's only one difference between you and those monks. They must ingest some kind of substance to achieve these powers. Are you asking me to believe you were born with these gifts?"

I was racking my brain for an acceptable answer when I glanced down 9th Avenue. Jennifer had vanished. I strained my eyes across the empty streets until I recognized the neon lights flashing seven blocks away on busy 42nd Street. Jennifer was nowhere in sight.

"Albert, look!" I yelled, pointing down the faintly lit avenue. "Jennifer's gone! She couldn't have possibly walked that fast!" I shoved my saxophone case against his chest. "Hold this," I commanded as he fought to juggle the bulky case with his forearms. My heart raced with anxiety as I sprinted down 9th Avenue. Somehow I knew Jennifer was in extreme danger. I didn't think. I knew. The shuttered buildings whizzed past and my legs ran faster than I would've thought possible. Within seconds I reached the corner of 48th Street and jumped off the curb, clearing the road in one hurdle and stumbling on the sidewalk when I landed from the shock of being airborne so long. The harder I ran the more I could feel my senses opening up. I began to smell Jennifer's jasmine floral perfume hanging in the damp asphalt night air. I bulleted across 47th Street, 46th Street, 45th Street, and then I stopped.

I could no longer smell her perfume.

I backtracked toward 46th Street. Halfway up the block, I once again detected her scent. I stopped and listened. I was picking up something. It was the barely audible, barely perceptible thump-thump-thump of a terrified heartbeat. It was coming from somewhere beneath the sidewalk. I pushed open an unlocked door and crept down a flight of concrete steps to enter a faintly lit maze of whitewashed corridors and boiler rooms. I heard the heartbeat racing faster now and I knew I was running out of time. Jennifer did not have long to live.

I frantically turned a corner, then another, and there she was. She was pinned against a sweaty basement wall, her dress hiked up to her waist, held captive by a leather jacketed man that had one hand covering her mouth as he fumbled to undo his belt buckle with the other. And then I saw those eyes. Those amazing, brilliant green eyes that had already begun to captivate my soul. Eyes that were now as wide-eyed in terror as an animal being led to slaughter. Eyes that were about to be devoured by an evil harbored in the hearts of sick and selfish men. And in my agitated supernatural condition I could only think of one logical solution.

Destroy the receptacle.

Jennifer could see me now. Her pupils dilated in fear as she watched me stealthily approach her attacker from behind, like a leopard bearing down on its prey. I paused a few feet behind him before I exploded forward with lightning fury. Gripping the back of his head with my right hand, I slammed him face first into the concrete wall. He was probably knocked unconscious from the blow because no sound or word ever uttered from his lips. I slammed him repeatedly with the force of a jack hammer until his facial features pancaked into an unrecognizable bloody pulp. Jennifer raised her hands to shield her eyes from the particles of flesh, bone and brain tissue that spattered heavily in the misty light. As my primal rage dissipated, I slowly released him from my grasp and his nearly decapitated body crumpled to the basement floor.

A voice boomed from around the comer. "Hey, Jake, are you done with that bitch, yet? Leave something on the bone for me."

I put a finger to my lips and signaled Jennifer to be quiet, but it wasn't necessary. She was much too terrified to speak. I crouched down hidden in the shadows.

The hunter had now become the hunted.

Another hulking figure turned the corner.

"I said, are you–"

Before he could say another word I punched him in the throat, bursting through the soft tissue of his trachea and esophagus. Clawing maniacally, I tore out fist-sized chunks of flesh until my fingertips reached down and touched the spongy warmth of his lungs. He grabbed his mutilated neck in terror, vomiting convulsively and drowning in his own liquids as he collapsed to the floor. Neither of them ever knew what hit them.

And I didn't know there were three of them.

A high-pitched bang shattered my eardrums as the walls around me illuminated in a burst of white light and searing hot lead punched through my back. I grabbed my side and dropped to the floor. Jennifer screamed as a dark figure fled down the hallway. The faint echo of his retreating footsteps was soon replaced by the clanking sound of someone coming down the stairs.

"Oh my God!" Albert exclaimed when he saw my motionless body wallowing in a puddle of blood. "Help! Someone call the police!" he yelled, running back up the stairs.

So this is what it felt like, I thought to myself. How ironic that I would make it through two years of combat without a scratch, only to get shot back home in the States in a basement in Hell's Kitchen. I was fading fast and starting to lose consciousness. I'd been shot right beneath my left shoulder blade into my heart and I was starting to choke as blood filled my lungs.

Jennifer knelt down beside me and tenderly cradled my head in her arms. "Steven, please don't die," she begged, rocking me back and forth, reminding me of how my mother held my father after he'd shot himself. I could hear a siren wailing in the distance as a rapid tingling sensation began shooting up and down my spine with urgent intensity. This wound was far more serious than a mere shaving cut and my back muscles contracted violently as the power of an unknown force surged through them. Within seconds the pain began to disappear, my breathing cleared, and then—I felt fine.

I tried to stand, but Jennifer protectively pushed me back down. "Don't move," she said, tenderly. "The ambulance will be here soon."

"Jennifer, please. I want to get up." I said, standing and wiping myself off. Jennifer looked up at me agape. Without saying a word, I led her up and out of the basement. At the top of the stairs, we nearly collided with Albert and two New York City policemen, their guns drawn. They took one look at me and stepped back in disgust. My shirt was soaked in blood and my hair was riddled with flecks of flesh and brain matter. The first policeman, a tall, chiseled Italian, holstered his gun and reached out to help us out as the other cop, a freckled Irishman, who reminded me somewhat of Lucky Morrison, walked downstairs, flashlight in hand, to check out the crime scene.

"Don't worry about me, I'm fine," I told the Italian officer. "Take care of her. She's the one who was attacked."

"Do you need to go to a hospital?" he asked.

"No, I'm fine," Jennifer softly responded.

A minute later, the Irish policeman poked his head above street level and beckoned his partner with a jerk of his head. "Tony, I think you'd better take a look at this."

There was no mistaking the nervousness in his voice.

"Stay put," the Italian cop commanded. "I need all of you to come down with me to the station."

As the policemen descended the stairs, Albert approached me.

"Well, I'm glad to see you're okay," he said with a hint of sarcasm in his voice. "You really had me worried, but then again, I should've known better. Wouldn't you agree?"

Albert was on to me, but I was in no mood to reply. I had precious little time to concoct my story before we arrived at the police station. It was very dark in that basement and I was pretty sure Jennifer couldn't have seen what had actually happened. The policemen reappeared at the top of the stairs. The Italian officer approached me with his hand resting firmly on his holstered gun.

"What's your name, pal?"

"Steven Ronson."

"Mr. Ronson, do you want to tell me exactly what happened down there?"

"Yes, I was walking down 9th Avenue with Albert Harrison and his niece, Jennifer, on our way to 42nd Street to catch a cab. Jennifer decided to walk ahead of us. A short time later I realized she'd disappeared. I ran after her and discovered her down in that basement in the midst of being attacked."

"Were you raped, lady?" asked the Irish cop, with all the subtlety of a man who had worked the Hell's Kitchen beat for too long.

"No," Jennifer replied. "Steven stopped them in time."

"I'll say he stopped them!" the Italian bellowed. "He tore those guys to pieces! It looks like a Chicago slaughterhouse down there. One of them is nearly missing his head and the other one's got his throat ripped out so badly I can see his spinal cord. Where the hell did you learn to fight like that?"

"I was in the army for the past couple of years. My company saw some pretty nasty action in Germany."

"Jesus." He laughed, shaking his head. "No wonder we won the war."

The Irish cop eyeballed me as he rubbed his chin. "Mr. Ronson, how did you know they were going to rape her?"

"One of them had her pinned against the wall. He was holding one of his hands over her mouth and loosening his belt with the other. By the look on her face, I didn't get the impression he was asking for her phone number."

He turned to Jennifer. "Miss Harrison, is that true?"

"Yes. My attacker and the other two were standing in the alley between the buildings as I walked down 9th Avenue. They grabbed me, covered my mouth and forced me down into the basement."

"It seems to all make for a pretty good case of justifiable homicide, but there's one thing that doesn't add up." The Irish cop cocked his head suspiciously. "If this guy had her mouth covered with his hand the entire time, how did you know where to find her?"

Good question. What could I say to that? And unless I wanted to spend the night in Bellevue, telling the truth was out of the question. I threw up my hands in mock resignation. "Honestly guys, I don't know. I saw the partially open door and the stairs leading down into the basement and it's the first place I checked. I guess it was just a lucky break."

The cops looked at each other, shrugged their shoulders and led us back to their squad car.

Albert trotted over and fell in line next to me. "My boy, I don't buy your ridiculous explanation for a second," he whispered. "Not one second. I know what I saw down in that basement!'

"And what did you see, Albert?" I asked wearily.

"I saw you drowning in a pool of your own blood!" he replied, stepping in front of me to block my path.

"Don't be ridiculous!" I replied. "First of all, it wasn't my blood I was lying in. And if I was really dying, then what am I doing here?"

"Precisely!" he exclaimed, sticking his deformed left hand in my face. "I'm on to you, my boy! Just remember, I'm on to you!"

Without saying a word I reached under his arms and lifted him completely out of my way. Albert stood there aghast as I climbed into the back of the squad car next to Jennifer. She leaned over and gently kissed my cheek.

"That was a very brave thing you did. If there's anything I can do to repay you, just ask."

"Dinner," I answered without hesitation. "Just the two of us, without your pain-in-the-ass uncle."

"Yes, that would be fine." she smiled. "I think I'd like that very much."

Albert insisted on sitting up front, wedging himself between the two police officers as we sped to the Midtown Precinct station on 54th Street. I checked my sax at the front desk where I was relieved of my bloody shirt, handed a faded blue short-sleeve replacement and instructed to clean up in the restroom. I washed the blood from my face and ran my fingers through my hair to comb out the sticky pieces of human tissue glued to my scalp. I was taken into a windowless room, reeking of stale tobacco and coffee, and seated across a gaunt, balding man in his forties who looked like he wanted to be anyplace but there. He introduced himself as Detective Sullivan, cleared his throat and began to reel off a string of questions in a bored monotone. He noted my answers on a pad as he chain-smoked.

"Full legal name?"

"Steven Woodrow Ronson."

"Residence?"

"One thirty-seven Waverly Place."

"How long?"

"A couple of months."

"Previous address?"

"Nine-oh-nine Biscayne Boulevard, Miami, Florida."

"Telephone number?"

"I don't have a phone."

"Age?"

"Twenty-one."

"Occupation?"

I paused to think about that one. "Musician."

"Place of occupation?"

"Various clubs throughout the city."

"Previous occupation?"

"I was drafted into the army in 1943 and honorably discharged in May. I served as a combat medic."

Detective Sullivan leaned back and took a long drag from his cigarette. "Did you see any action?"

"Plenty. I was with the 45th Thunderbird Division from the time we landed in Sicily until we occupied Munich."

He nodded respectfully. "That was one hell of a run."

After interviewing the police officers, he seemed satisfied that my killing of the two suspects was justified, but he was curious about the attack on me. I explained that after I dealt with the second assailant, someone jumped me from behind and knocked me unconscious. That would pretty much have covered what Albert saw. However, it was what Jennifer might say that concerned me.

The detective quickly scribbled down a couple more notes, stood up and told me to stay put. About ten minutes later he re-entered the room accompanied by a Detective Spinelli. Talk about hard-boiled. This guy looked like he'd just stepped out of an Edward G. Robinson movie complete with cauliflower ears, a thick furrowed brow, blood-shot eyes and a nose that'd been broken too many times to piece back together.

"Mr. Ronson," he began in a tired, gravelly voice, "we have a small problem."

I didn't react.

"We have no doubt this girl was attacked. We've identified the bodies and both of them have a rap sheet a mile long. They belonged to a Hell's Kitchen Irish gang called the Westies. They were small time hoods who made their money pick pocketing, the occasional car theft and anything else they could get their hands on. My guess is they thought Miss Harrison was a hooker and decided they could get for free what everybody else has to pay for. It was insane for her to be walking alone at that hour in that neighborhood. Regardless, the problem we have is that Albert Harrison told us he heard a gunshot. You haven't said a word about it. Would you care to explain?"

Damn. It hadn't occurred to me that Albert wouldn't have known where to find us unless he'd heard that gunshot. My intuition told me these guys had heard every fabrication in the book and any attempt to get too creative would backfire. So, I just played dumb.

"I don't know." I shrugged. "Maybe a gun did go off."

"What?" Spinelli laughed, sticking his finger into his ear and making an exaggerated digging motion. "Did I hear you correctly? Are you asking me to believe you wouldn't know if a gunshot went off next to you?" He leaned across the table until his flattened nose almost touched mine. "Do I look that stupid to you?"

"No, sir," I answered calmly, "but you have to understand that I've just returned from two years of combat. I was at the front for most of the time and guns of every shape and size were going off at all hours of the day and night. After a while you learn to live with it or go crazy. On the other hand, I've never seen an attempted rape. That was a first for me. Both of those guys were huge and I was fighting for my life. I was so preoccupied with staying alive that a bomb could've gone off next to my head and I wouldn't have noticed."

Spinelli and Sullivan sat there poker-faced, studying me. Their years of outwitting every conceivable type of human deviant and con-man were coming into play. They scrutinized me for anything–a nervous twitch, a spastic flinch, darting eye contact, an unwarranted smile, anything they could pounce on. I may have been hiding something, but I knew I'd done nothing wrong. Finally they relaxed and leaned back in their seats.

"Okay," Spinelli said, drumming his fingers on the desk. "That may explain part of it, but how do you explain this?"

He opened an evidence bag, pulled out my bloodied shirt and pointed to the bullet hole in the back. I was caught off guard and both smiled when they saw my look of surprise. The powder burn encircling the hole was plainly obvious. There was no doubt I'd been shot–and at very close range.

"I–I can't explain it," I stammered, looking down at the cigarette burnt desk.

"Didn't think so," he smirked. "Would you mind taking off your shirt?"

The detectives closely examined my naked back holding their table lamp.

"Yeah, right here. Take a look at this pink spot," Sullivan said, poking his finger into the skin below my left shoulder blade. "It appears to be about the size of a thirty-eight, but the skin's not even broken. What do you make of it? Did it deflect off him or something?"

"I haven't the faintest idea." Sullivan replied. "I've never seen anything like that before."

"Okay, Ronson." Spinelli said. "You can get dressed and go, but I'll tell you one thing. You are one lucky son-of-a-bitch. If that bullet had gone through, I can guarantee you'd be tagged and slabbed by now."

I nodded appreciatively and shook their hands as Spinelli opened the door.

"Oh, and one other thing. I'd stay out of that neck of the woods for a while. You've just killed two guys from the Westies. On the street that's like signing your death warrant. I'm going to record this as a justifiable homicide, but in their minds you've killed two of their brothers over nothing more than a piece of ass. Take it from someone who knows, these guys are as vicious as they come and revenge is a part of their heritage. They don't forgive and they don't forget."

He accompanied me to the front desk where Jennifer rushed forward and threw her arms around me. Brooding in the background, Albert kept his distance.

"Is everything okay?" she asked.

"Yeah, everything's fine," I replied as I retrieved my sax and we walked out into the early morning Manhattan light.

"I was wondering," Jennifer said. "Do you like Italian food?"

"Love it. I first managed to get a taste of the real thing in Sicily."

"There's a place in the Village on MacDougal Street called the San Remo Café where they serve great Italian food. If you like, I can meet you there this Friday night at eight."

"Alone?"

"Yes, alone."

Albert expelled an irritated sigh and staggered across the street.

"Where's Mister Personality going?"

"To catch us a cab."

"I'll find my way back to the Village." I yawned. "You'd better hurry or you'll lose your uncle."

"I should be so lucky!" She laughed, rushing after him.

CHAPTER

The following week I practiced my sax every night until I fell asleep with the instrument in my hands. By the time Friday rolled around, I was a bit stir crazy and all I could think about was having a quiet, romantic Italian dinner with Jennifer.

I strolled over to 93 MacDougal Street and found the San Remo Café to be more of a boisterous artist and writer's rendezvous with pressed-tin ceilings and black-and-white tile floors. Seating myself, I was handed a menu by a waiter who seemed irked that I was the sole recipient of his last available table. But when I informed him I was waiting for a young lady named Jennifer Harrison, the pained smile on his face made it apparent that he was a veteran of her charming personality. I ordered a carafe of the house Chianti and tried my best to tune out the table next to me who were slapping their hands on the table every time one of them felt like he'd made a winning point debating the literary merits of *The Lost Weekend*.

Minutes later, Jennifer waltzed in overdressed to the nines in an elegant black evening ensemble accessorized with long black velvet gloves, heels and a pearl necklace. Every guy in the place froze in mid-bite as she walked past their tables and every guy in the place caught a stiff jab in the ribs from the woman seated beside him. When she stooped to give our waiter a kiss, leaving a lipstick tattoo on the top of his bald head, I thought the guy was going to keel over in shock.

"I missed you," she breathed into my ear as we embraced. "I wanted to talk to you so badly this week. Why don't you get a phone?"

"I didn't think it was a necessity, but I guess I've got a good reason to get one now."

"Steven, I'd like you to meet Mario," Jennifer said as our waiter poured her wine. "He's such a sweet man, always taking good care of me and my uncle whenever we dine here. I just adore him."

Mario was so taken aback by Jennifer's gracious behavior that he could barely force a smile. She ordered the house special of spinach ravioli and I opted for the linguine with white clam sauce. When I raised my glass to toast I was surprised to see that she had already finished hers off in one gulp.

"I want to thank you again," she said, refilling her wine glass to the brim. "I really believed I was going to die down in that basement."

She paused to take a deep breath as her eyes began to well.

"Don't think for a second I don't know the kind of person I've become. I've always resented the world because of the way I lost my parents. After they died, the only family I had was my uncle and all of his missionary friends who constantly reminded me that losing my parents was God's will. And when a child is taught that God is the reason you've lost your mother and father, you begin to blame God. And since the world and all its inhabitants are the creation of God, you begin to hate them as well. When I was in that basement, I prayed. I prayed for the first time in my life. I prayed that if God would just let me live, I would really try to make myself a better person." She buried her face in my shoulder as her body convulsed with sobs. "And then I saw your face coming through the darkness."

I don't think I've ever seen anyone cry so hard. I took my napkin and dabbed the tears from her eyes before I gently kissed her lips. The moment was interrupted by the sound of Mario intentionally clearing his throat.

"Spinach ravioli for the beautiful young lady and linguine with white clams for the gentleman," he announced, placing our respective dishes in front us with a dramatic flourish.

"Thank you, Mario. It all looks quite delicious," I said in a hushed voice, cocking my head toward Jennifer who was snuggled tightly against me. Mario flushed with embarrassment and quickly stepped away from the table.

"I am so sorry. Excuse me!" he said as he beat a hasty retreat back to the kitchen.

"I don't think we'll be seeing him anytime soon."

"No." Jennifer laughed, wiping her eyes. "I don't think so either."

"Your uncle. How is he?"

"Oh, he's fine." she said, examining her face in her compact mirror. "He's still a little upset with you. I don't know what you said to him, but you did a pretty good job of bruising his ego. You may find this hard to believe, but my uncle can be quite sensitive."

"I think all of our nerves were stretched to the limit that night. When you see your uncle, please give him my apologies."

Jennifer smiled slyly as she sipped her wine. "I wouldn't let him off the hook that easily."

"Why not?"

"Because it'll probably do him some good to get a dose of his own medicine. I heard him trying to badger you into a corner all night. He prides himself on being a master chess player and when he feels he's scored a point in an argument, he has this nasty habit of hounding his opponent into submission. Sometimes he'll even say, 'Checkmate!'"

"It must have made him an effective missionary."

"Actually, he was one of the best. He was the first missionary to successfully convert the cannibalistic headhunters of the mountain highlands of Papua, New Guinea."

"Were you with him up in the mountains?"

"Heavens, no!" Jennifer said. "I waited down in Port Moresby for three months until he returned. It was much too dangerous and he was responsible for my safety. My parents died when I was six, while we were visiting my uncle in London. Uncle Albert was my father's older brother and he adopted me. I traveled with him all over the world."

"It must have been very exciting to see so much of the world at such an early age."

Jennifer shook her head as she swallowed her wine. "Exciting? You have no idea how miserable I was."

"Why were you so miserable?"

"Where do I start? For one, I was tutored by missionaries. They were all male and cut from the same Victorian cloth. The first time I menstruated I was eleven and thought I was bleeding to death. Not one of them had the nerve to tell me the truth. Thank God it happened while my uncle was stationed in the Philippines because our Spanish housemaid saved my sanity. Her name was Maya and she became the closest thing I've ever had to another mother. We cooked and shopped together. She would even sing me to sleep. This was in 1937. One morning in December, my uncle barged into my bedroom and excitedly announced that we were being assigned to a remote city deep in China. I didn't want to leave Maya and barricaded myself in my room. The other missionaries had to break the door down with an ax and they carried me out kicking and screaming. I felt as if I'd lost my mother all over again. Anyway, it's all ancient history. Except for the nightmares, I don't think about that time anymore."

"Nightmares?"

"For as long as I can remember. They're usually about my parents. I was born in England. Northampton to be exact. My mother was visiting her English relatives there when she met my father, fell in love, and became pregnant with me. After I was born, my father decided to wait until I was old enough to attend elementary school before relocating the family to America. When I was six, we drove to London to visit Uncle Albert for the Christmas holidays. My father took me shopping for presents while my uncle drove my mother to his missionary school for a tour. After Uncle Albert finished showing my mother around, he decided he was too tired to join us for dinner and gave my mother the keys to his car. He didn't realize that Mother had never driven in England and wasn't accustomed to driving on the left side of the road. The first roundabout disoriented her and she smashed head-on into a garbage truck."

"My God, I'm sorry."

"I bet my uncle told you that both of my parents were killed in an automobile accident."

"Yes, he did."

"That accident also killed my father, but not directly. When no one came to pick us up, my father called the missionary school. Uncle Albert told him that my mother had left an hour earlier in his car to pick us up. I can still hear my father screaming at him while we stood crammed in that tiny red telephone booth. When he hung up, he was trembling with anger. A short time later, two police cars showed up, one containing Uncle Albert. My father got into one and I got into the other with my uncle and all of my Christmas presents. I couldn't understand why we drove off in different directions.

"That night, my father came into my bedroom and told me that he'd always love me. Then he went out into the garden and blew his head off with his hunting rifle."

I put down my fork.

"My uncle didn't tell me the truth about my father for years. He told me that my father died of a broken heart. That may be true, but I'll tell you one thing–you'll never hear me say I miss him. My mother didn't have a choice when she left me, but my father did."

She took a sip of wine and noticed I'd stopped eating. "Oh Steven!" she said, throwing her gloved arms around my neck. "How incredibly selfish of me! I've never revealed this much about myself to anyone."

"Well, we have at least one thing in common," I said, forcing a forkful of linguine into my mouth.

"And what's that?"

"My father also shot himself. He was terminally ill. It happened three months ago at my parents' home in Florida."

"I'm so sorry. What about your mother, is she still alive?"

"Yeah, she's fine. I mean, she's about as fine as anyone could be under the circumstances. They'd been married for over twenty-five years. I haven't written to her since I moved to New York. After tonight, I think I will."

"I wonder why both of our lives have been surrounded by so much death."

"You don't know the half of it. I saw enough death during the war to last a hundred lifetimes. Anyway, enough about that. I'm curious to hear your version of what happened to your uncle in China."

"Not now," she replied. "Let's enjoy our dinner first."

Jennifer and I spent the next hour chatting about New York City nightlife, particularly the jazz clubs on 52nd Street. She told me that Hines had hit on her the first night she visited the Black Onyx. Obviously, he'd received the royal treatment. When Jennifer revealed that she'd relocated to New York because her uncle had been booted out of the China Inland Mission, I saw my opening.

"Why was your uncle asked to leave the China Inland Mission?"

"Because he doesn't know when to keep his big mouth shut. Shortly after he was attacked we left China and sailed back to England to recover. War broke out in Europe the following year and we found ourselves stuck there, doing office work in the China Inland Mission's London headquarters. We stayed in London until the Blitz scared the hell out of everyone and we relocated to my uncle's family estate outside of Cambridge. One evening after dinner, my uncle was entertaining two Anglican missionaries interested in joining the China Inland Mission. He opened a bottle of port, had too much to drink and launched into this fantastic tale from his travels in China. The missionaries found his story unbelievable and promptly told him so in the most condescending manner. Uncle Albert has never been much of a diplomat and when challenged he can be downright nasty. He shouted insults until they left the room and addressed them afterwards as Brother Idiot and Brother Moron. Word filtered back to London about his behavior and my uncle was asked to leave the China Inland Mission in July of 1944. We packed our bags and moved to New York."

"Do you know the story your uncle told the missionaries?"

Jennifer opened her mouth to speak, but caught herself as if two opposing thoughts had collided in her brain. She gazed at me in confusion, as if she suddenly realized that certain people, places and events which had long seemed unimportant had now become extremely relevant.

She chose her words slowly. "My uncle claimed to have met someone in China who had met Jesus Christ."

"Did you know this person?"

"He was a Buddhist monk who told my uncle he was over two thousand years old, even though he appeared to be no older than his early thirties. I can't remember his name, but I will never forget his face. I'm afraid that I've repressed a lot of memories from that period. It was a difficult time for me."

"How did your uncle meet this man?"

"My uncle loves to hear stories about local folklore and superstition, and then disprove them using a combination of philosophy, science and the word of God. He's what you would call a Theosophist. One night he challenged our Chinese housemaid in Sian to tell him the most incredible story she knew. She produced what appeared to be a recent photo of a monk with a little boy sitting on his lap. The monk was a man whom my uncle knew quite well. Then the maid swore on her life that the picture was almost seventy years old, taken in the late eighteen hundreds. When my uncle laughed, she left the room and returned with an old man who claimed he was the little boy sitting on the monk's lap."

"Your uncle related that same story to me, minus the anecdote about the little boy. The monk's name was Chow Li."

"Yes, that's him! Chow Li! I haven't heard that name in quite a while. Supposedly, Chow Li is the oldest of a group of immortal Buddhist monks who live on the outskirts of Sian. The only difference is that Chow Li lives a solitary life and wants nothing to do with the other monks."

"Why is that?"

"Because the other monks have become corrupted. Like Chow Li, they possess an ancient immortality formula that prevents them from aging and seems to have other miraculous properties, but they have long abused those powers for their own selfish and immoral purposes. Chow Li told my uncle that he originally concocted this immortality formula so that monks and other holy men who had strayed from the path of righteousness would be forced to continue their penance on earth without the glory and rewards of death."

"Wait a minute. Are you trying to tell me these pills were originally created as a form of punishment?"

Jennifer furrowed her brow and cocked her head. "Who said anything about pills?"

"I—I just assumed—they swallowed a pill or something like that," I stammered, silently cursing my carelessness.

"Well, the answer to your question about punishment is yes. However, the monks of this monastery abused its original intent. They had succumbed to every pleasure of the flesh and the most evil is their leader, Chang Sou. Legend has it that he was a criminal. Chang Sou's family was very wealthy and said to be related to one of the three original Chang families that founded the Chinese Taoist church. When Chang Sou's mother accused him of murdering one of their male servants, his father had him exiled to the monastery under Chow Li's supervision for life. Then, the most incredible thing happened. After only two years, Chow Li publicly announced that Chang Sou had renounced his earthly desires and accepted spiritual enlightenment. Unfortunately, the truth was something completely different.

"Chow Li had become infatuated with Chang Sou. He'd fallen platonically in love with him! Chang Sou came to know the immortality formula because Chow Li wanted Chang Sou to live with him forever. By the time Chow Li discovered that Chang Sou had manipulated him it was too late. And to this day, Chow Li controls their movements and keeps them contained in their mountain fortress monastery. Chang Sou and his monks can't travel very far unless he permits them."

"What happened the night your uncle was attacked?"

"My uncle had become obsessed with a beautiful silk fabric that only Chang Sou's monks knew how to create. Every weekend they would trudge into town shepherded by Chow Li to pick up supplies for their monastery. Uncle Albert decided to trade surplus canned goods from the mission for their silk. I remembered thinking that he must have been an idiot for believing he could do business with those people. Except for Chow Li, every one of them, especially that giant, Chang Sou, gave me the creeps. They had dead man's eyes, that glazed-over look like something you'd see packed in ice at the fish market—utterly devoid of emotion. One weekend they didn't come into town and Uncle Albert decided to hike out into the mountains to visit their monastery to barter for their silk. Our Chinese housemaid became hysterical and begged him not to leave. Of course, he didn't listen and trekked out into the snow alone.

"That night I was awakened by a horrible high-pitched scream steadily growing louder in the distance. At first it sounded like a wounded animal with a leg crushed in a trap, but as it came closer you could tell it was human. I got dressed and ran outside to see a handful of Chinese men with torches carrying my uncle into the mission. The other missionaries wrapped his hands in gauze and cauterized his wounds. Fortunately, a renowned Canadian physician was in the area and saved his life."

"How did the locals react?"

"They were furious at the monks. My uncle and the other missionaries were very popular and generous with the citizens of Sian. Word of the incident spread quickly and the Japanese Army got wind of it. A week later they showed up at the mountain monastery with truckloads of soldiers and a couple of tanks. The monks were terrified and scattered into the mountains. The Japanese ransacked the monastery, stuffed everything into wooden boxes and carted it off to Japan."

"Even the secret formula?"

"Yes, but it didn't matter. The monks would just make another trek with Chow Li overland to the South China Sea and come back with whatever ingredients they needed to concoct another batch."

"Did your uncle ever learn what those ingredients were?"

"No, but I'll tell you one thing. They all smelled terrible when they returned."

"How so?"

Jennifer wrinkled her nose at the memory. "They smelled like rotting fish! It was disgusting. Regardless, the villagers would start celebrating the moment they saw the long caravan of monks snaking across the horizon."

"And why was that?"

"Because it meant they'd soon be feasting on one of the most popular Chinese delicacies, Shark Fin Soup. Upon their return, the monks would present the city with burlap sacks stuffed to the brim with dozens of smelly shark fins." Jennifer noticed that my hand was trembling as I filled my glass with wine. "Steven, what's wrong? Did I say something to upset you? Do you want to talk about it?"

I drained my glass and closed my eyes. "No, not now. Maybe never."

Jennifer tenderly rested her head on my shoulder. "That's perfectly all right. There's one thing I want you to know about me. I'll always respect your privacy and I'll never force you to talk about something. My uncle did that to me for years. I know what it feels like, and I would never do that to someone else."

I gently kissed her forehead. "Thank you, Jennifer," I said, as Mario slipped the check onto the table.

That Sunday night at the Black Onyx, Hines introduced me to an A and R man from RCA-Victor named Jack Scoville. After Scoville ribbed me about the flowery praises Hines had used in describing my talent, he got down to business. He was curious about my musical background. Since I didn't have one, I answered him as vaguely as possible, spicing my responses with colorful theories of how the trauma of combat somehow impacted creativity. Under normal circumstances, I'd have been extremely nervous at the thought of auditioning for such a prestigious label as RCA-Victor, but, I'd had the whole weekend to mull over an interesting offer Jennifer made to me after dinner as we strolled through the streets of Little Italy. Out of the blue, she suggested that I accompany Albert and her on a trip back to Sian. She'd already discussed the idea with him and I was surprised to hear that he'd not only gone along with the idea, but had agreed to foot the bill. Despite the tempting offer, the first thing I needed to do was sit down with Albert and find out exactly what I was getting myself into.

All of this weighed heavily on my mind as I discussed the business of music with Jack Scoville. Deep in conversation, I was startled by the warm sensation of a pair of lips softly planting themselves at the nape of my neck. And, judging by the wry smile on Scoville's face and the arched eyebrow on Hines, I knew it had to be Jennifer.

"I'll be waiting for you at the end of the bar," she purred.

"That is certainly one fine looking woman," said Scoville.

Hines was impressed. "My man, I've got to hand it to you. You certainly have walked where angels fear to tread."

Scoville clapped his hands together. "Okay guys. Let's go. I'd love to hear some music."

Hines leaned into me as we made our way to the stage. "All you've got to do is the same thing you did last week. Just jump in and play whenever you feel like it. Don't think. Just play."

I readied myself as Hines welcomed the crowd with his trademark toothy grin to "an extra special Sunday night at the Black Onyx." Scoville got up from his table and positioned himself directly in front of me. Hines counted off and the rhythm section jumped to life. He raised his trumpet dramatically and chimed in. I paused a moment, took a deep breath and let go.

Once again, I watched in awe as my fingers telegraphed complex melodies completely alien to me. My eyelids became heavy and I gave into their weight as the syncopated sounds of improvised bebop trailed off into the distance and I soon found myself standing alone in the silence of infinity. In the distance, thousands, perhaps millions, of brilliant pin-points clustered together in a narrow jeweled band stretching across the horizon as if all the stars in the universe had gathered on the rim of an inky bowl. They pulsated in unison before one by one they slowly began to launch in my direction, much like phantom skiers spilling down an invisible slope, a thin luminescent golden tail trailing behind each. They were soon upon me, a torrent of multi-colored images streaking past on either side.

It was like standing on the IRT platform in Times Square as two subway trains sped by on either side and trying to make out the features of those passengers seated inside. Albert was right, these were the portals of the Akashic Records and I was now extremely curious to examine their contents.

Narrowing my eyes, I locked onto an exceptionally bright sapphire pin spot speeding in from my left. Closer and closer it came, growing in size and sparkling with intensity. I concentrated my will upon it, as if to say, "I want you to stop" and a split-second before it would have raced past, the image popped out of the speeding torrent and stabilized in front of me, bobbing weightlessly in the black void.

It was the crystal clear image of an Asian man's face with his black hair completely shaved off in the style of a Buddhist monk. He smiled serenely and glowed with peace and harmony. Though his smooth skin looked no more than thirty years old, his eyes conveyed the wisdom of the ages and I had no doubt I was looking into the tranquil image of Chow Li. Then his image slid back and continued past me.

My attention was then diverted by an equally intense purple pin-point zooming in on my right. I focused on it and, sure enough, it popped out of the kaleidoscopic torrent and situated itself directly in front of me, glowing brightly as it wavered back and forth in the darkness. This portal also contained the image of a young man with ageless eyes, but this man's cold blue eyes were terrifying with huge, black pupils that were vacant windows to a lifeless soul rotting for centuries in a body that would not die. I was staring straight into the face of Chang Sou and I had an unsettling feeling that he was actually looking back at me. I caught my breath as his frozen image shifted and came to life. He raised an upturned, long-nailed index finger and, ever so slowly, curled it back. Chang Sou was beckoning me to China.

And he knew I would come.

His image began to magnify in size and rise above me. I was gripped with the worst feeling of desolation I'd ever experienced, trapped somewhere alone in the darkest recesses of my mind as a tidal wave of ancient evil towered above and threatened to engulf me. My heartbeat raced and my lungs would not respond to my drowning desire for breath. I was literally suffocating with terror. Just as his glowering face seemed poised to devour me, I managed to force open my eyes and escape the subconscious world.

Chang Sou's horrific image was instantly quickly replaced by what appeared to be a cloudy sky filled with a multitude of suns. I blinked my eyes and realized I was lying on the floor of the stage, gazing up at the white lights. As my vision cleared, the concerned faces of Scoville and Hines came into focus as they hovered above me.

"He's okay, people." Hines calmly announced to the audience.

"Hey man, you're lucky you didn't crack your skull open," Scoville said. "Hines reached out and caught the back of your head just in time."

"Thanks, Hines," I said groggily as he and Scoville lifted me off the stage. "Guys, I'm really sorry about this."

Hines broke out into a sly, toothy grin. "Sorry about what?"

"That was incredible," said Scoville. "My only regret is that I wasn't able to record it."

"Excuse me, but I'm a little confused," I said as they helped me on to a barstool.

"I've never heard anything like it," Scoville marveled. "Your melodies have the power to evoke very emotional responses in the listener. I don't even want to tell you the memories you dredged up inside of me."

"But how did I end up on the floor like that?"

"You were holding this incredibly high note—I think it was a double altissimo A," Scoville replied. "You were hyperventilating, turning red and leaning so far back that your sax was practically inverted while you held that note for at least a solid minute. The next thing I knew, your mouthpiece popped out, you dropped your sax and collapsed to the stage. And frankly, I'm not sure if your performance tonight was more style or substance. Regardless, I'm very curious to see how it all translates in the recording studio."

"My man!" Hines whooped, slapping me on the back. "This calls for a little celebration! Bartender, crack open a bottle of your finest gin. The good stuff from England. Not that rack shit. Pour everybody a round on me!"

I wanted to celebrate, but I was emotionally and physically drained. "Hines, if you don't mind, I'd like to call it a night."

"No problem, man Go home and relax. Tonight you did what you needed to do."

I picked up my case and dragged it down to the other end of the bar where Jennifer was waiting anxiously.

"What were you trying to do up there? Kill yourself?"

"Well, that would be impossible," I muttered under my breath.

"What did you say?"

"I said that I think I've done the impossible. I've just landed my first recording session."

"Are you serious?"

"Serious as a heart attack. Just don't ask if I'm excited about it."

"Why on earth wouldn't you be?"

"Three years ago, I would've done anything for a break like this. It's every musician's dream. There's just one small problem. That wasn't me playing up there. I don't deserve credit for something I didn't do."

Jennifer looked at me incredulously. "What do you mean it wasn't you playing up there?"

"It wasn't. I mean, yeah, it was my fingers running up and down my sax and my lips blowing into the reed. It's just that none of it was being directed by my brain, at least not consciously. I can't remember anything I played."

"Are you saying you were actually unconscious?'

"That's exactly what I'm saying. I completely lost all sense of time. How long was I up there?"

"About thirty minutes."

"It felt like two. Like I told your uncle in the coffee shop, when I'm in that state I can't hear anything. I only see visions. It's as if I'm some kind of human radio receiver. When I play certain notes, they seem to act as frequencies that attract transmissions from another time and place. It's like dialing across a radio until you pick up a station. That's why I don't feel so good about the recording session. If Benny Goodman has a hit song playing on the radio, you give credit to Benny Goodman, not the radio."

"Who or what did you see this time?"

"Let me put it this way, when I finally meet Chow Li and Chang Sou, it won't be the first time."

"What? You saw them?"

"I believe I did. Chow Li has a boyish, cherubic face with shaved black hair like a monk. In my vision, he exuded warmth and kindness. Chang Sou is huge with long dirty-blonde hair, faded blue almond-shaped eyes and high, sunken cheekbones. He looked at me with absolute contempt. And another thing—he doesn't appear to be Asian. If anything I'd say his ancestry is more Germanic or Scandinavian. He kind of reminded me of a Viking."

Jennifer rested her gin and tonic on the bar. "You've just described both of them perfectly. You must tell my uncle about this. He wanted me to invite you over to our apartment after the show tonight."

Scoville told me that he was going to book a recording session for ten o'clock that Friday morning at RCA-Victor's Studio A on East 24th Street. He couldn't understand why I wasn't more excited and probably thought my reservation was due to exhaustion. He repeatedly assured me that everything was going to be fine. Jennifer and I caught a cab uptown to her uncle's luxury apartment at 942 Park Avenue. The elevator operator took us up to the fifteenth floor where I found Albert comfortably nestled in his study, puffing on an enormous cigar.

"Steven, my boy," he said cheerfully. "Would you like a cigar and something to drink? I have a wonderful box of Cuban *Partagás* and I've just cracked open a bottle of Remy."

"Both sound good to me," I replied as Albert reached over and took one of the Cuban cigars out of its box. I snipped the end of the cigar as Jennifer poured a generous snifter of cognac.

"Steven is going to be recording for RCA-Victor," Jennifer proudly announced. "He auditioned tonight at the Black Onyx for an important A and R guy that Hines brought down. He wants to record him this Friday."

"Congratulations!" Albert exclaimed. "Most musicians wait years to get a break like that."

"To be honest, I came very close to telling them I wasn't interested."

"Why on earth would you do something like that?"

"Come on Albert, you know why. The only reason I'll bother to show up Friday is because I'm curious to hear what everybody else is raving about."

"I see." He nodded, puffing on his cigar. "Did you have another vision tonight?" "Actually, I had two."

"What made you stop this time?"

"Let's just say that I didn't appreciate Chang Sou's invitation."

"Chang Sou! Dear God, you saw Chang Sou? How do you know it was him?"

"He described him perfectly," Jennifer interjected.

Albert walked over to the window and stared out across the flickering Manhattan skyline.

"He's using you to get to me."

"That may not be his only consideration. I got the distinct feeling that Chang Sou considers me to be an adversary."

"Oh, he doesn't consider you an adversary," he said, with a dismissive wave of his cigar. "You mean nothing to him. The only way he'd feel threatened would be if he thought that–" Albert stopped as he realized the only logical answer and turned to face me. "The only reason Chang Sou would want to lure you to China would be if he believed you shared his powers. That would be completely unacceptable to him. And the only way you could share his powers would be if you had somehow obtained the immortality formula."

I kept the best poker face I could muster as I looked him straight in the eyes and calmly took another sip of cognac.

"My God, you discovered it in Germany, didn't you? Please Steven, do show some honor and don't insult an old man's intelligence!"

I had to hand it to him. Albert had me cornered in one of his famous mental chess games Jennifer warned me about. Whatever. It didn't matter. He and I were now in the same boat. The truth was that we needed each other.

"Checkmate," I answered.

Jennifer covered her mouth.

"I knew it!" Albert exclaimed. "For a while there you had me believing that I'd lost my mind. Damn you, Steven. Damn you for bringing this nightmare back into my life. But, God bless you for having the decency to admit it. You must tell me. How did you get your hands on the immortality formula?'

I savored another sip of the aromatic Remy and exhaled a plume of Cuban smoke.

"I was in the army unit that liberated the concentration camp at Dachau. We looted the officer's quarters. Since I was a medic, the other men handed me what they thought was a box of medical supplies. It turned out to be a fifty year supply of the immortality formula processed into pill form. There were also two envelopes. One was from the doctor who manufactured the pills. He had designed them for Hitler so he could survive his thousand year Reich. The other letter was from the commander of the camp. He'd intercepted the shipment and reported it to Himmler. I guess Himmler had his own ideas about who should succeed Hitler."

"Incredible," said Albert. "I wonder how the Nazis got their hands on the formula?"

"Thanks to you and your niece, I believe I've got that figured out. The Japanese stole it from Chang Sou's monastery and passed it onto the Germans. The German doctor's letter specifically thanked his counterparts in Kobe."

"What made you decide to take the pills?" Jennifer asked.

"Death. Not the fear of my own death, but the round the clock agony of continuously losing those around me. For two years I was inundated with death. Until you've been in a war zone, you have no idea how death can completely rob you of your spirit and drain you of your will to live. Death is so final, so complete, with absolutely no second chance. I lost a lot of friends who were just beginning their life. Many of them died in my arms while they begged me to do anything I could to save them. They had done nothing wrong except for being in the wrong place at the wrong time. A lot of them were really good people–"

I could feel the lump building in my throat as I paused to clear it with another sip of cognac.

"Call it my irrational way of dealing with the pain. Call it my personal vendetta against the laws of nature. Call it what you will. But, one day at a time, I'm slowly getting back what was stolen from me."

"Believe it or not, I do see your point," Albert said with the effective warmth of a man of faith. "How long have you been taking these pills?"

"Since April 30th. I probably won't notice most of the results for quite some time. However, if you count the visions, my body's phenomenal ability to heal itself and my supernatural musical abilities, I'd say that we're pretty much dealing with the real thing."

"Why do you want to live forever?" Jennifer asked.

"I didn't say I want to live forever. I just want to laugh again. I want to smile again. I want to live for so long that I can forget everything I experienced during the war and it's going to take a while to clean the slate. When that finally happens, and I believe it will, I'd like to enjoy it in a body that hasn't been genetically programmed to fall apart."

"Where do you keep these pills?" Albert asked.

"In my apartment." I shrugged. "Where else?"

"You're keeping them in your apartment? Good heavens. I'd think you'd want to keep something that valuable in a much safer place."

"Yeah, you're probably right. I think I'll stick 'em in a safe deposit box somewhere."

Jennifer sat down beside me and held my hand. "Will you come with us to Sian?"

"Well, I have less than a fifty-year supply of these pills and it may be a good idea to visit the source. But before I decide anything, I want to know a little more about this Chow Li character. Is he really over two thousand years old? Is he more powerful than Chang Sou?"

"Yes, to both," Albert replied. "Chow Li was born in the year 156BC during the Western Han Dynasty. His birthplace was Sian in the Shensi Province, which at that time was named Chang'an and was the ancient capital of China. He was appointed as an assistant to the great Taoist magician, or *fang-shih*, Li Shao-Chun in the court of Emperor Wu Ti in 127 B.C. Li Shao-Chun was the first to teach Chow Li that it was indeed possible for man to become an immortal, or *hsien,* through a process of transformation by ingesting a magical concoction. He would never divulge the exact formula he used to prolong life except to say the main ingredient was extracted from an animal caught near the legendary Isles of the Blessed. It had to be derived from some kind of sea-life because Li Shao-Chun never ate the flesh of any land based animal. When this maritime substance was mixed with cinnabar, the cinnabar flakes would convert into gold. Only then would the immortality formula be ready for human consumption. The process of attaining immortality was quite different back then. It was achieved only after death. The immortality formula would create an identical embryo inside the person. After death, this embryo would gorge on the decaying flesh before breaking free of the old body shell, much like a butterfly bursting out of its chrysalis, but to maintain immortality, the process would have to be repeated over and over again through countless lifetimes. When Li Shao-Chun decided his work was finished on this plane of existence and prepared to die, he entrusted his recipe for the immortality formula to Chow Li. Soon after, Chow Li rose to the position of Chief Magician for Emperor Wu-Ti where he was commanded to create a formula that would indefinitely prolong life for wayward Taoist monks without the need to physically die repeatedly to become immortal. This new formula forced these corrupt men to serve out their sentences on earth indefinitely until the emperor set them free, allowing them to die and go on to their heavenly reward."

"That's the part Jennifer told me that I found most interesting," I said. "This immortality formula was originally created to keep people here on earth as a form of punishment?"

"That is correct," Albert replied. "The ancients did not fear death the way we do today. Death was their pathway to receive their reward in the afterlife. But, Chang Sou and his monks are infatuated with the material world and have no desire to leave it. Their dream is to control the world and they will consume the immortality formula forever to achieve that goal. Chow Li is a pacifist and the polar opposite of Chang Sou and his monks.

He blames himself for Chang Sou and will serve his penance indefinitely on this planet to keep him and his monks contained. Twice a year he makes a pilgrimage to Tibet to visit the Buddhist monasteries around Lhasa and teach at the Mentsikhang, the ancient medical school atop Chakpori Hill. The present building was constructed in the late seventeenth century, but Chow Li has been traveling there to teach since the second century. I've heard amazing stories about that medical school such as people levitating and self-warming themselves in sub-freezing temperatures. When I was stationed in the Bahamas, I befriended a missionary who was probably the only person on earth who didn't think my immortality stories were the rants of an insane man. Over the years, he'd written a Tibetan monk in Lhasa. One afternoon I found him laughing as he read a letter from his Tibetan friend that was so fantastic it left no doubt in his mind that Germany was losing the war. The monk had learned that the Nazis were making a number of secret expeditions to Tibet. His responsibility was to restrict public access to the Chakpori Hill medical school to stop those without the proper religious intent or credentials. He'd become suspicious of a German he'd seen milling about the base of the hill. The monk befriended him under the false pretense of helping him gain entrance to the school and discovered the man was a Nazi researcher from the German Ancestral Heritage Organization. The organization was ordered by Himmler to journey to Tibet to substantiate Nazi ideology. The German Ancestral Heritage Organization eventually became so powerful that in 1940 it was incorporated as an official organization of the S.S."

Himmler! He must have already known the truth about the immortality formula when he wrote that letter to Sigmund Rascher and ridiculed Otto Krueger's research.

"Have you ever heard of the Thule Society in Germany?" Albert asked.

"No."

"Have you ever wondered how Hitler came to power? Have you ever wondered how a World War One corporal with a ridiculous Charlie

Chaplin mustache could rise so quickly to reign over the most techno-
logically advanced country on the planet? Have you ever wondered
where he learned the power to so easily control millions of people?"

"I have to admit that it all never made much sense," I replied.

"Precisely. Did you ever read a popular nineteenth century book titled *The
Coming Race*?"

"I read it when I was teenager. It was a science fiction novel about
an underground ancient super-race called the Vril-ya who were stranded
here from another solar system and founded the Sumerian culture. What
about it?"

"What if I were to tell you that book was fact disguised as fiction?"

"I would say you've been drinking too much cognac."

Albert smiled. "Allow me to share some historical facts with you. The
Thule Society was founded in 1918 in Munich on beliefs espoused in *The
Coming Race*. In addition, there was a sub-group of the Thule Society comprised of beautiful Germanic women who happened to be powerful mediums. This group was called the Vril Society. It is important to note that one
of the Thule Society's founders, Dietrich Eckhart, was Adolf Hitler's best
friend. He coached him on how to communicate with the masses. One
of the Vril-ya's powers was psycho-kinetic energy and Hitler mastered it
well. He could literally convince an audience that only he knew the truth
and by the end of his speech they would believe him without question.
Essentially, he seduced the German nation using the powers of the Vril-ya.
Dietrich Eckhart died in 1923 and Hitler dedicated the second volume
of *Mein Kampf* to him. Pardon the pun, but that alone speaks volumes.
Other prominent members of the Thule Society read like a Who's Who
in the Nazi Party hierarchy. Rudolf Hess, Alfred Rosenberg, Hans Frank,
Hermann Göring, Julius Streicher, Wilhelm Frick and Heinrich Himmler
were all members. The Thule Society founded the Nazi Party and even gave
them their symbol, the Tibetan Buddhist Swastika, which they inverted to

turn clockwise, renaming it the *Hakenkreuz*. Once Hitler attained power he banned the Thule Society and other occult organizations from the Reich."

"Why would he do that?" I asked.

"Oh, let's just say that Hitler didn't want to risk the chance of any future competition. Fortunately for mankind, Hitler used the ancient powers of the Vril-ya only to attain power, not maintain it. Once he became dictator, his ego became so intoxicated with power that he forever disassociated himself from the Thule Society and attempted to shut it down. Hitler truly believed he'd assumed God-like abilities and from thereafter became law only unto himself. The reality was that his power became limited to his own military experience and the production capabilities of the German war machine. Then it all boiled down to a numbers game. There was no way Nazi Germany could survive long against the combined men and machinery of America and the Soviet Union. Until the very end Hitler thought he could win the war, but his generals knew better as early as 1943."

"How do Chow Li and Chang Sou play into all of this?"

"I believe the immortality formula was originally created by the Vril-ya and that Chow Li is the last keeper of the gate. Only the Vril-ya would possess that type of knowledge. Li controls Chang Sou and his monks by giving them a less potent immortality formula that limits their ability to travel far beyond their monastery. You either possess Chow Li's formula or the Germans discovered a way to modify Chang Sou's. Regardless, Chow Li lives in a small structure just outside Chang Sou's monastery and he's closely monitored them for thousands of years. But make no mistake, Chang Sou is an extremely power hungry creature from an ancient super-race who must never be set free upon the world. If he escapes, Chang Sou would make Hitler's destruction look like child's play. Only Chow Li can control him and has steadfastly done so for thousands of years, but their world is rapidly changing and my greatest fear is that technological advances may accidentally liberate him. I now believe it is my life's mission to assist Chow Li in insuring that never happens. It was by sheer chance that the Japanese stumbled upon Chang Sou's monastery and the formula found its way to Germany. Luckily, it ended up in your hands, but that may be a harbinger of darker things to come. Furthermore, it is not what's inside of Chang Sou's monastery that frightens me. My fear is what may lie beneath it."

"And what might that be?"

Albert paused to sip his cognac.

"The entrance to the underworld of the Vril-ya."

CHAPTER 5

RCA-Victor's studio A was located in an old seven-story stable building on the ground floor of 155 East 24th Street between 3rd and Lexington Avenue. I followed the alluring syncopated beat of improvised jazz down the hallway until I found Hines, Carter the pianist, Simon the bassist, and Jackson the drummer, studiously rehearsing their instruments in the center of a large rectangular room illuminated by two pipes of fluorescent light. Ignoring their musical banter, Scoville was perched high atop a ladder above them attaching a large microphone to the end of a towering boom stand. Hines laid down his trumpet when he spotted me.

"Steven–my–man!" he shouted, punching each word like a fist in the air. "Are you ready to make some music?"

"I'm as ready as I'll ever be."

"That's the spirit!" Hines exclaimed, sounding like he'd downed his fourth cup of coffee. The excitement in his voice only added to my anxiety and I could tell it was going to be a long morning. Scoville finished fastening the microphone and slid down the ladder.

"I need you guys to assemble in a semi-circle in front of the drums while I check the levels," he said, shuffling the five of us into position.

Unfortunately, he stuck me right next to Hines who seized every opportunity to playfully pinch my arms and poke my ribs. I could understand that this session was his big break and he was all excited, but I really needed to relax and focus on the task ahead. Seated behind us on his white pearl Slingerland drum kit, Jackson could see what was going on.

"Hines, why don't you knock it off and leave the kid alone?"

Hines wheeled around and glared back at him. "Hey boy, don't forget who's your boss and meal ticket. Mind your own business and shut the fuck up or you'll be hitchhiking back home to Meridian, Mississippi."

Scoville returned from the control booth and clapped his hands. "Okay, are we ready to make some music?"

"Yeah, we're ready," Hines fumed, narrowing his eyes at Jackson.

"First, I need to set some levels. I'd like you all to play at once."

We launched into a chaotic chorus of musical scales and drum fills until he waved his hands for us to stop. "Good, we're set. Which song do you want to record first?"

"We're gonna do 'The Black Diamond of 52nd Street,'" Hines answered.

I'd never heard of it. "What is 'The Black Diamond of 52nd Street'?" I whispered, just loud enough for Scoville to hear as Hines blushed with embarrassment.

"Hey man, don't worry about it," he snapped. "All you've gotta do is exactly what you did at the club. Just listen to what we're playing and jump in whenever you want. Trust me, everything's gonna be fine."

The method to Hines' madness became clear to me. He and his sidemen had been performing together for years, rehearsing the same songs to back up various musicians every Sunday at the Black Onyx. Hines figured that it didn't matter what I played as long as the rest of the band kept it together. Scoville went behind the window of the control booth and signaled a thumbs-up. Hines silently mouthed a four-count and the band launched into the song. I waited for the first twelve bars to pass, pressed my lips against the saxophone's reed and exhaled.

I'd barely heard my sax breathe the first note before I slipped away into the infinite void of my subconscious world. The jewels of the Akashic Records flickered brightly in the distance, awaiting my command. They returned my gaze with frenzied pulsation and began streaming toward me.

I searched the multitude of images rushing past for anything unusual. I didn't have long to wait. On the left, an exceptionally brilliant emerald portal streaked toward me. I focused my will upon it until it stopped to pop out, wavering in front of me.

I was mesmerized by the softly illuminated image of a man and woman passionately making love while framed against the blackness of infinity. The man's muscular buttocks thrust into her as she feverishly raked his back with long, scarlet fingernails, clawing deep welts that quickly filled with blood. I watched in fascination as she responded with raw, primal urgency to his movements, her legs tightly intertwined with his. I couldn't see their faces because he was kissing her mouth and the portal's view was from directly above them, but it was the first time I'd seen two people make love and I watched with a voyeur's curiosity. My heart began to race with anxiety. There was something strangely familiar about the quilted powder-blue comforter and the antique brass bed frame. The man shifted his head and kissed her neck, exposing her face as she looked straight up into my eyes.

It was Kathy.

I jerked back into consciousness as an angry voice echoed inside my skull.

"Wake the fuck up!" Hines shouted.

I blinked to see him kneeling over me. "What in the hell is wrong with you?' he yelled as Scoville quietly offered me a glass of water. I gulped down a mouthful and nodded that I was fine.

"Steven, can I asked you a personal question?" Scoville asked softly.

"Yeah, sure," I said.

"Are you an epileptic or something like that?"

"Not as far as I know. I suffered a mild concussion during the war, but I made a full recovery."

"It sure as fuck don't look that way to me!"

"Hines, please give us a moment," Scoville said, waving him off. "Steven, here's the situation. Your melodies, your technique, and your phrasing– they're all absolutely brilliant beyond anything I've ever heard. But, short of physically restraining you, there appears to be no way of directing you once you start playing. Come with me, I want to show you something." Dazed, I followed him into the control booth. "Now tell me the truth. Have you ever recorded before?"

"No," I replied sheepishly.

"Relax." he smiled. "I had a feeling you hadn't. Recording is actually a very simple process. Out there, suspended over your heads, is a condenser microphone. It's connected to this vacuum tube amplifier, which in turn is connected to this electromagnetically controlled curing stylus," he explained, patting each piece of equipment with his hand. "The dilemma I'm facing is that at seventy-eight RPMs there's only enough room for a little more than three minutes of music on a ten inch disc. That's it. If we go over then we have to re-record the whole performance. Do you know how long you were playing out there?"

"I have no idea."

"After I signaled the band to stop, you were still in your own world and kept racing along like a runaway train. The interesting thing was that while the band played you followed their changes perfectly and never strayed too far. However, once they stopped you roared off into some very bizarre musical territory. And believe me, I'd love to record it. The problem is that if you can't control the length of your performance, there's no way I can produce it properly."

"Do you have any suggestions?"

"I'll have to mull it over for a while. There's some experimentation going on now with magnetic tape. My research engineers believe it could give us the freedom to record uninterrupted for a very long time. Unfortunately, we're at least two to three years away from it becoming a reality. But, as far as today is concerned, this recording session is over."

We were startled by the crash of metal as Hines angrily threw his trumpet down. He'd been eavesdropping as he stood outside the control booth.

"Damn it, Hines!" Scoville yelled, storming after him. "I've just about had it with your Cuban temper tantrums. This boy's got a gift. All we've got to do is find a way to capture it properly. If you can't be professional about it, I'll work with him. Alone."

Hines stared down at his cream and coffee wingtips as if he was a schoolboy being admonished by his teacher. "I'm sorry man, I'm just a little frustrated and confused by the whole situation."

"I understand. Here's what I want to do. I'm not going to record it, but I'm curious to hear what Steven sounds like when he doesn't close his eyes."

In that case, we had to play a song I was familiar with. Hines suggested "Body and Soul." As we played, Scoville sat inside the control both and nodded approvingly. After the last note, he smiled and motioned us to join him.

"That was good guys. It was very good. Unfortunately, it wasn't great. I'm just going to have to find a way to record the magic that happens when Steven goes into that trance of his."

"Would you play what you recorded?" I asked.

"Sure," Scoville replied, reaching down to pull the master off the curing stylus. He placed the disc on a turntable and clicked on the machine. As the needle circulated through the grooves the up-tempo syncopated sounds of Hines, Simon, Carter and Jackson filled the room. Everyone began tapping their feet in unison. Then I heard the wail of my sax swell in intensity as it crescendoed into the mix. I couldn't believe what I was hearing and glanced around the control room nervously to check everyone's reaction. No one was tapping their feet now. It was very difficult to describe what I was hearing because there was nothing of a contemporary nature that compared to it. The closest thing would be a mélange of Middle-Eastern, Indian and Asian tonalities. My phrasing was scattered, yet I somehow managed to weave in and out of the other musicians' parts without conflicting with them. I listened in amazement until I realized that the band was pushing the tempo as they repeated the same phrase over and over again in a frantic attempt to end the song before the cutting stylus ran out of room. Finally, the band stopped, but I continued playing. I found my solo performance to be extremely disturbing. My saxophone cried alone in the dimly lit control room, screeching in agony like a wounded animal. Then it hit me. I was unconsciously responding to the painful vision of Kathy making love to another man. The memory of their bodies intertwined flashed before me and I swept my hand across the turntable, loudly scratching the needle off the record.

"Easy!" Scoville yelled. "That's a diamond needle for Christ's sake!"

"Sorry, I guess it was all a little too much for me."

"You might as well take it," he said, slipping the record into a wax paper jacket. "But I wouldn't play it too many times because it's only meant to be used as a mold for a master and will start to deteriorate after four or five plays," he said, handing me the disc. "Now, if you gentlemen wouldn't mind, I'd appreciate it if you'd permit Hines and me to speak alone."

This was the band's big chance and I'd blown it. Regardless, they each made a point of approaching me as I packed my saxophone to offer words of encouragement.

A few minutes later, Hines stepped out of the booth. The sight of his flashy Caribbean grin spoke volumes. Whatever Scoville said had calmed him.

"Listen up everybody," Hines announced. "Let's get this gear packed and meet downstairs for coffee at Dimitri's. We've got some business to discuss."

"There ain't nothin' to discuss," Jackson muttered under his breath. "Hines is going to do all the talking and we're going to do all the listening."

We grabbed our instruments and walked single file into the coffee shop next door. The black-haired, mustached Greek owner barely looked up from behind his cash register to acknowledge us as we stacked our equipment cases into a towering pile beside the front door and seated ourselves in a window booth.

"Coffee! Coffee! Coffee!" Hines shouted obnoxiously as he pounded his palm on the table.

A thinner, younger version of the proprietor, presumably his son, emerged from the steam of the kitchen, wiped his hands on his dishwater-stained apron, marched over to our booth and stared down coldly at the band.

"We don't serve black people," he said in a deadpan Greek accent.

I nearly died.

"That's good," Hines replied, jumping up to face him. "Because we don't eat 'em."

Both men hugged each other and broke into raucous laughter as I sank back into my seat. "It's damn fine to see you, Dimitri Junior!"

"And you too, my brother!" the young Greek replied.

"We're all gonna have a round of your Turkish coffee and that sweet stuff you made us last time. What's that stuff called?"

"Baklava."

"Yeah," said Hines, smacking his lips. "Get everybody a piece of that."

"Okay, here's the deal," Hines said, leaning across the table. "Scoville has agreed to take us under his wing. He's got some really good ideas. The fact that Steven uses an alto sax works in our favor because combos with altos are really hot right now. Even Charlie Parker plays an alto. Scoville suggested we call the band The Hines Winston Quintet featuring Steven Ronson. I think it's a fantastic idea because everyone knows me from hosting the jam night at the Black Onyx and I believe it will give us some instant name recognition."

At the sound of that Simon turned his head and coughed loudly into his napkin as the other guys bit their tongues and resisted the urge to laugh.

"We'll become a featured band and then we'll start making some real money. We've all paid our dues and I want everyone here to get a piece of the action. The kicker is that Scoville promises we'll be back in the studio as soon as he figures a way around our little problem with Steven."

Now I faced a terrible dilemma. I knew there was no way Hines and the band were going to be signed to RCA-Victor without me. And Hines was talking about a long-term commitment. The bottom line was that as soon as Albert and Jennifer were ready to depart for China I was going with them because my destiny was ten thousand miles west of 52nd Street.

Dimitri returned with a tray filled with our coffee and pastries. One sip of the thick Turkish brew sent my head spinning. I couldn't take a bite of the honey, nutty pastry fast enough.

Hines gulped down his coffee. "Since I'm the leader of this band, I'll get the standard forty percent of whatever we earn and the rest of you will divide the remaining sixty percent."

I glanced around the table and nobody flinched. I couldn't believe they were going along with such a ridiculous offer.

"You must be joking," I said.

Hines glared at me as if I'd spit in his face. "That's the way it works in this business," he said, emphasizing his point with a sharp slap of his hand on the table. "That's the way it is and that's the way it's gonna be!"

"Well, let me tell you something," I said, setting down my coffee. "If we're a real band, then I want everyone to get an even split. That means twenty percent for everyone or you can count me out"

Hines' lips quivered as he fought to contain his Cuban temper. He was livid, but I had him cornered. I was his meal ticket and he knew it.

He threw up his hands in mock resignation. "Man, why are you busting my balls?" he pleaded in a whiny voice.

"I'm not. I believe everyone seated at this table is exceptionally talented and I couldn't care less whether you use my name, your name or Dimitri Junior's name on the recording. I'm proud to be a part of this group and I haven't felt this close to a bunch of guys since I was in the war. I only know one way to work and that's as a part of an equal team. Everybody pulls their own weight and nobody is made to feel like they're second fiddle to anyone else."

Hines straightened and rubbed the stubble on his chin. What could he say? There was no way he could allow me to leave the group. It was now a matter of how much face he could save in front of his band.

"You know, now that I think about it, I could probably learn a lot from you," Hines said, wagging a finger at me. "What can I say? I'm from Cuba. We have a dictatorship down there. That's the type of leadership I understand, but you're absolutely right. This is America and your idea is very democratic. So, let's put it to a vote. Would you gentlemen feel better if we split everything evenly?"

The guys fidgeted in their seats, avoiding eye contact with Hines as they each slowly raised their hands.

"Got my vote," Carter said cautiously.

Jackson smiled. "I can live with that."

"Sounds fine to me," Simon said.

"Well, God bless America!" Hines said, sliding out of the booth. "Now if you gentlemen will excuse me, I've got to take a piss."

"He's probably going to cry his fucking eyes out," Jackson laughed as Hines kicked the door open to the men's room.

"That was beautiful!" Carter said as each man reached over and slapped me on the back.

"Guys, I've got to level with you," I said. "I don't know how much longer I can stay with the band. It could be a month or a year. I just don't know."

"Are you ill or something?" Jackson asked.

"No, it's nothing like that. It's something personal and I'm not at liberty to discuss it. I just want to enjoy my time with you while I'm still here. There's a bond I feel with all of you every minute we're on stage. You guys are the closest thing I've got to family."

"Hey man, at least you're being honest," Carter said. "Besides, you have no idea how much what you just said means to us. I thought it would be a cold day in hell before I ever heard a white boy from the South call a bunch of black men his family."

Over the next few months, The Hines Winston Quintet featuring Steven Ronson began building a steady following around the Manhattan jazz clubs on 52nd Street. And even though my income had increased to an impressive three hundred dollars a week, the band's rise was not as meteoric as we'd hoped. This was due to the fact that I would not allow myself to succumb to the unknown since our failed recording session.

After that session, I began to have severe headaches, nosebleeds and ear-bleeds, and I'd decided it was time to give my brain and body a chance to heal. We all attended the 1946 New Year's Eve party at the Black Onyx and everyone who was anyone in the New York music scene stopped by to jam or make an appearance. Albert, Jennifer and I watched in awe as an endless parade of stellar musicians were invited up to the stage by a very intoxicated Hines, who was plainly relishing in his position as Master of Ceremonies. It was getting close to 11:30 when I felt a tap on my shoulder.

"Hey man, Hines wants you on stage," Carter said.

As I was making my way through the crowd I could see that Hines had assembled an intimidating collection of all-star players including Thelonious Monk on piano and Dizzy Gillespie on coronet. I was stepping onto the stage when I accidentally bumped into another saxophone player.

"Oh, I'm sorry," I said. "I'll sit this one out."

"No, we'll take turns soloing," the saxophonist replied. "Besides, this is New Year's Eve and this ain't supposed to be no competition."

I was thinking to myself, "What a classy guy" when Hines stumbled over and fell into me, three sheets to the wind.

"Steven, my man," he slurred, his breath reeking of undiluted gin, "I'm glad to see that you've finally met the King of Kings, the one and only, Mr. Charlie Parker."

I could have killed him. Only Hines would be enough of an asshole to stick me next to the greatest sax man on the planet. Through the corner of my eye, I studied the man and couldn't believe that Parker was only twenty-five years old. The rumors on the street about his dalliance with heroin were legendary and his appearance left little doubt. Judging by his sunken cheeks and deeply shadowed eyes, I would've guessed him to be closer to sixty. I respectfully shook his hand and readied my instrument. Unfortunately, the audience wasn't the usual local familiar faces, but consisted mostly of a "bridge and tunnel" crowd who were using New Year's Eve in Manhattan as an excuse to get intoxicated and rowdy. Even worse, Charlie Parker was famous. They had zero idea who I was. It was like being the unknown support act to a popular headliner. You're the only thing standing between them and their idol. I stared out into a sea of happy drunks, most wearing that look of jolly expectation that the ancient Romans must have reserved at the Coliseum whenever a Christian was introduced to a lion.

"You ladies all look so beautiful tonight," Hines slurred into the Black Onyx's chrome microphone. "We've got about twenty more minutes until 1946, so why don't we spend it together with a little 'Body and Soul'?"

Parker leaned over and whispered, "You take it first."

I smiled apprehensively and launched into a solo I'd carefully crafted over the past four months. This was a tune I could play with my eyes open or closed and after twelve bars I stepped back from the center of the stage. Surprisingly, I received a polite smattering of applause. Then Parker raised his instrument high in the air until it nearly eclipsed the floodlights, expanded his cheeks and exhaled. The first word I can think of to describe what I heard would be genius, and within seconds the crowd was wildly cheering him on. For me, the evening was quickly turning into a musician's worst nightmare and I wished for nothing more than to find the largest hole in the stage and drop through it. And I was still searching for that magic hole when Parker ended his solo and nodded at me.

I composed myself, took a deep breath and plowed onward. If I was going to get my musical ass kicked, at least I was going to take the beating with a little dignity. I finished to very little applause with the exception of two patrons cheering enthusiastically from the back of the club. I was encouraged for a moment until I looked out and realized it was Jennifer and Albert.

Parker was embarrassed by the crowd's behavior and frantically motioned behind me for everyone to applaud. Then he stepped to the front of the stage and ripped into a whirlwind of melodies that left me breathless as the audience went ballistic. I was desperately hoping he'd keep right on playing until the song ended and put me out of my misery, but Parker remained the perfect gentleman and paused respectfully when his twelve bars were up to pass the musical baton back to me.

By now the crowd had become downright hostile. Ignoring a growing crescendo of boos, I was ready to jump back in when—whack—an ice cube smacked me in the face. Parker's head was turned and didn't notice, but someone else did. I peered through the haze and watched Jennifer wipe away a tear. Without hesitation, I raised the saxophone to my lips, exhaled and closed my eyes.

It had been almost four months since I'd last journeyed to the center of my mind. The heckling quickly faded into the distance and was replaced by the soothing silence of eternity. The sparkling portals of the Akashic Records were waiting and they launched forward to greet me. As I studied the luminous images streaking past, I could only guess what was happening on the outside. Perhaps Hines had planned it this way all along, or maybe it was Scoville's idea. Regardless, there was one thing I knew for sure—no one in that audience was laughing now.

A pulsating pin-point, glowing as if sheathed in mother-of-pearl, rushed toward me. I concentrated my gaze on it as the bullet of light stopped and hovered silently in front of me. I was startled to see the imposing silhouette of a massive cross with the outline of a man hanging from it as the sun burned brilliantly behind him, nearly blinding me and making it impossible to identify his facial features. A small crowd of men reared back their heads in laughter as they stood around the base of the cross, taunting him. And for the first time I could hear voices that were undeniably Chinese. None of it made any sense. At first I thought I was watching an ancient crucifixion in China, but quickly discarded the idea when I noticed the men were holding rifles.

A rumbling sound akin to rolling thunder reverberated across the portal as two strange aircraft rocketed across the cloudless sky at a very low altitude. I'd never seen anything fly so fast. Even more surprising was the fact that neither had propellers. As I watched the aircraft streak upward at a phenomenal rate, the incredible truth dawned on me.

I was viewing the future.

A soothing, feminine voice began to echo throughout my brain, gently calling my name over and over. The brutal vision of the crucifixion began to fade as I regained consciousness and squinted from the bright lights above me. But this time they weren't stage lights. I'd been transported to the Black Onyx's back office and deposited onto a sofa. My head was resting in Jennifer's lap as she held an ice pack against my forehead and softly spoke my name. Charlie Parker pulled a chair up beside us as the crowd outside shouted down the final ten seconds of 1945.

Parker laughed. "Happy New Year, you crazy motherfucker!"

"Thanks," I replied, weakly shaking his hand. "Happy New Year to you, too."

"Happy New Year, sweetheart," Jennifer whispered, bending over to kiss my lips.

"Happy New Year, baby." I cocked my head and spotted Albert curled up in the corner on the carpet, morosely sipping a martini. "What's wrong with him?"

"You'll have to forgive my uncle. He always gets like this at the singing of 'Auld Lang Syne.' It reminds him of all the friends he lost over the years. It's best to just let him be."

"That was some serious shit you played out there," Parker said.

"Thank you. What did it sound like?"

"Are you telling me you don't know what you played?"

"No, I passed out."

"I thought your first couple of solos were pretty decent, even though the audience was giving you a hard time. The next thing I knew you started jerking and jumping around as if your brain was on fire. I thought you were having a seizure or something until you started playing the most amazing music I've ever heard. You sure shut that crowd up in a hurry."

"How long did I play?"

"Are you kidding me? You were still playing when I carried your ass back here! You were going crazy and spinning around in circles. I thought you were going to knock me down! The audience really ate it up, but the weird thing is that once we got you back here you started playing real sad stuff like you were at a funeral. Are you working with any labels?"

"We did a session with Jack Scoville from RCA-Victor. It didn't work out because I haven't figured out a way to control myself when I get crazy like that."

"Are you telling me that this has happened to you before?"

"Yes. I can turn it on anytime I want. All I have to do is close my eyes. But I don't know how to turn it off. I wouldn't call the situation exactly conducive to recording."

"I can see that," Parker mused. "Damn, that's too bad. Don't get me wrong, your regular playing is pretty good, but that stuff you're ripping when you go crazy is out of this world. I've gotta admit that I'm downright envious you can travel so easily on a road the rest of us have to hitchhike." Parker furrowed his brow as he studied my face. "You should really get that checked out," he said, pointing to my forehead. "Did the ice cube do that?"

Jennifer opened her compact mirror to show me a bleeding, bulging vein that protruded grotesquely from the center of my forehead. This time I'd gone too far. She fumbled through her purse and handed me a couple of aspirin. I took a swig of Parker's beer and swallowed just as the office door crashed open and Hines stumbled into the room holding a half empty bottle of champagne.

"Steven, my man!" he slurred, "Tonight, you definitely slayed the fuckin' dragon!"

Parker rolled his eyes and stood up. "Gotta go, man." He sighed. "I'll see you around."

Parker tried to circumvent the intoxicated Cuban bandleader and leave the office, but Hines wrapped his arms around him and sloppily kissed him on his cheek. "I love you, my brother."

Parker pushed him away in disgust. "Man, get the hell away from me! You're spilling champagne all over my fucking suit!"

Hines apologized and staggered out into the hallway after Parker, who repeatedly warned him to keep his distance. Hines' intoxicated pleadings were cut short by the cracking sound of knuckles impacting with flesh, followed by a sickening thud. The ruckus caused Albert to emerge from his semi-comatose state and crane his neck out the door.

"I do say, Parker knocked that son-of-a-bitch out with one shot!" Albert chuckled as Parker appeared in the doorway dragging an unconscious Hines behind him.

"Where should I dump this sorry sack of shit?" he gasped.

"Just prop him up in a corner," I replied. "Nobody will miss him until Monday."

In January of 1946, the Hines Winston Quintet was awarded a Tuesday residency at the Black Onyx after word spread around town about my New Year's Eve performance. Unfortunately, that night I burst a blood vessel on my forehead and spent a full week cross-eyed, nauseous and bed-ridden. This was one injury even the formula couldn't heal and no record deal, fame or fortune could convince me to view the Akashic Records again. However, I made sure that Hines remained unaware of my decision. The other band members had confided in me about his criminal exploits in Havana including attempted murder and sexual assaults. They convinced me that I was dealing with nothing more than a smiling psychopath in a pinstriped suit.

Regardless, we were packing them in week after week, even though some patrons had voiced their disappointment that they'd yet to see a repeat of my legendary New Year's Eve performance. To alleviate those expectations, Hines spread the rumor that my New Year's Eve performance was simply fueled by too much alcohol. His strategy backfired and every Friday night I faced at least a dozen beautiful females lining up to buy me a drink—much to Jennifer's dismay. On a more positive note, the band had evolved into a tightly knit unit and Scoville was starting to hint that he was seriously considering us for a recording contract, featuring a very conscious Steven Ronson.

On March 12th I looked out into the audience and for the first time in memory didn't see Jennifer or Albert. Since the New Year's Eve incident, Jennifer and I had become inseparable. We'd spent every available moment together and I'd begun to tell her I loved her, but she would never say it back. Jennifer would just smile demurely and say, "I know you do."

Yes, we were inseparable, but not intimate. Emotionally, she was carrying more baggage than a bellhop at the Waldorf and our passion had been limited to marathon kissing and petting sessions in my Greenwich Village apartment. As frustrating as it was, I needed only to remind myself that I went nearly two years during the war without sleeping with a woman. And then as soon as she left my apartment, I would turn my shower's cold water knob all the way counter-clockwise and think about the Yankees.

The band finished its set and I bounded off the stage to use the telephone to call Jennifer. I'd no sooner picked up the receiver when Albert rushed up behind me.

"Steven, my boy! You are hereby advised to get your affairs in order. We're leaving next month for China!"

I turned to face a jubilant Albert and Jennifer fully expecting me to jump for joy. Their smiles quickly turned to consternation when I didn't react. Before I could think of brushing up on my Mandarin, I had to think of a way of explaining all of this to Hines.

"When do we leave?" I asked.

"Wednesday, April 10th," Albert replied. "I don't like to fly so I've arranged for us to travel cross-country by rail to California and across the Pacific by ship."

"In that case, there's a little problem I need to take care of right away."

"'What's wrong?" Jennifer asked.

"I have to tell the guys. Last year, I told them I couldn't make a long-term commitment, but they've probably forgotten about it by now."

"Well, at least Hines can't say he wasn't warned," Albert said.

"Oh, yes he can. He wasn't present when I told the band."

Albert was appalled. "You can't be serious. I've heard that Hines is actually wanted for murder in Cuba. It takes very little to make him snap. Until the time comes, I believe it's best we keep our mouths shut."

"No, that's not my style. I'm not running away from anyone, especially Hines. I don't care how crazy you think he is, I don't want to burn any bridges with the guys in the band."

I walked back to the dressing room and bumped into Scoville in the hallway.

"Congratulations," he said, extending his hand.

"For what?"

"Let them tell you," he replied, jerking his head toward the dressing room.

I opened the door to find the guys dancing around on the chairs and furniture like a bunch of high-school kids who'd just won the state basketball championship.

"We've all paid our dues, we've all had the blues, and now I'm here to bring you the news!" Hines said, waltzing across the room to me with a glass of champagne in his hand. "Scoville has agreed to sign us to a recording contract with RCA-Victor! And it doesn't matter if you play with your eyes open." He winked, "Or closed!"

I couldn't believe it. It was bad enough I'd walked in here to announce I was leaving the group, but now I was about to spoil the greatest moment of their lives and I didn't have the heart to do it. When no one was watching, I slipped out to the bar and poured myself a double shot of vodka that I hoped would numb my aching conscience. As I gulped it down, Jackson walked up to the bar and slapped his hand on my shoulder.

"So brother, when are you leaving us?"

"What?" I asked incredulously.

"Let me tell you a little story," he said, pulling up a bar stool beside me. "About five years ago I was at a big family reunion back home in Mississippi. Sometime before, my sister-in-law had stopped having her time of the month and my mother took her to the hospital. This was big news because my brother and his wife had been trying to have a child for years.

"That evening, right in the middle of this huge family dinner party, the telephone rings. It's the doctor at the hospital and he's got something to tell my mother that just can't wait. We all held our breaths. My mother screamed, slammed down the phone, praised the Lord and joyfully announced that a genuine miracle had occurred. My sister-in-law was pregnant. Everybody in that house went crazy congratulating my brother. He was hugged, kissed, cried on and congratulated by at least thirty people. He seemed the happiest that anybody had ever seen him, except to me. Something about his reaction seemed unnatural. When I cornered him later that evening, he broke down and admitted the truth. He was impotent.

"It turns out that my sister-in-law had been having an affair with her best friend's husband. When I looked at you a minute ago in that dressing room, you reminded me of my brother. So, I'm gonna ask you again. When are you leaving us?"

"April 10th."

Jackson bit his lip and closed his eyes.

"Well, whatever you do, don't tell Hines. He'll cut your heart out. I've never told you this, but he threatens you a lot behind your back. He always tells the guys that the only way you're going to leave the group is in a body bag. Now that you're leaving, can you finally tell me why?"

"Not really. You could say it has a little to do with religion. The one thing I can tell you is that I'm going overseas for a while."

"That's probably a good idea." Jackson said, pouring himself a shot. I guarantee the first thing Hines will do is have some of his street friends come looking for you."

"What friends are those? Why wouldn't he come after me himself?"

"He's crazy, but he's not stupid. He's not going to ruin his career and end up in jail for killing somebody. He's got a lot of friends in a Hell's Kitchen Irish gang called the Westies. "

"The Westies?"

"Yes. Hines claims he's got something on you and all he's got to do is give them the green light to kill you."

I didn't react as I poured myself another vodka. "What does Hines claim he has on me?"

"The Westies have a mole down at the local police station who swears you're the guy who killed two of their members. And not just killed. Rumor has it that these guys were literally ripped to shreds. Apparently, some Westies had mistaken that Jennifer girl of yours for a hooker. When they tried to fuck her, you killed two of them. The one who survived says he shot you in the back."

"That's crazy," I said. "I think it's pretty obvious that I've never been shot."

"This gang member was so shaken by what he saw that nobody believed his story. The Westies figured he got scared, ran for his life and made up the story to save face. The problem is that their mole claims he overheard a detective talking about you surviving a one-in-a-million chance and walking away from a gunshot wound with nothing more than a bruise. Did you know that on the night Scoville first heard you, there were a couple of Westies waiting for you in the audience? Hines had already heard the rumors on the street and got to them just before they got to you. He swore on his mother's grave that you were at his place talking business that night. The Westies bought his alibi and left. Hines couldn't care less if you lived or died. The only reason he stuck his neck out was because Scoville wouldn't record us without you. Man, you have no idea how close you came to getting a knife jammed in your heart that night."

"Wouldn't the Westies be angry if they found out Hines deceived them?"

"Probably." Jackson shrugged. "But you'd be amazed at how easily Hines can weasel his way out of any situation. He's been doing it his whole life. The point is, if Hines gets wind of this you're dead. But don't worry about the other guys. Trust me, they'll understand."

"Thanks, Jackson. You've just taken a huge weight off my mind."

"I knew this day was coming," he said. "Now that Scoville has decided to record some of our originals, it doesn't matter who plays the sax in the band as long as that guy can play the parts. Hines will eventually figure that out when he cools down. The problem is that you'll be long dead before he does."

"What if I just disappear for the next four weeks?"

"No good. The Westies know every nook and cranny in Manhattan. Besides, there's other ways they can get to you."

"Such as?"

"Hines told me that back in Cuba they believed that if you wanted to really hurt someone all you had to do was hurt the person they loved. Then, life would be worse than death. In your case, Hines told me he'd send the Westies after Jennifer."

That son-of-a-bitch. Just knowing he'd even consider harming Jennifer made me want to storm into the dressing room and squeeze the life out of his scrawny Cuban neck.

"Cool down, man." Jackson said. "A blind man could see the hate burning in your eyes. We have an old saying back in Mississippi. Don't get down in the mud with a pig."

"It's more than hate. My God, I'd almost forgotten what it felt like."

"What's that?"

"Fear."

"I'd recommend that you go ahead and record with us. You know all the parts and it'll be a cinch. If one of the songs becomes a hit, we'll have a dozen saxophonists beating down our door to take your place."

On Saturday April 6th, 1946 I recorded with the Hines Winston Quintet inside RCA-Victor's East 24th Street Studio A. In contrast to last year's session, this one was a breeze. In less than an hour we blazed through four of our originals including "The Black Diamond Of 52nd Street." The band was so incredibly tight that three of the songs were keepers on the first take. Unfortunately, every time Scoville gave us the thumbs up and signaled for us to move on to the next number, Hines would insist we re-record the song to see if we could make it better. The third time he pulled that stunt, Scoville charged out of the control booth.

"Damn it, Hines! I'm the producer! I've been recording bands since you were stealing hubcaps in Havana. Stop trying to second guess me. I, not you, will decide which take is best and which is not. And until I say this recording session is over, the only thing I want to hear out of your mouth is music."

Hines could barely mumble an apology as Jackson, Carter and Simon broke into wide grins behind his back.

When the session ended, we retired to the control booth to hear the results. The band sounded fantastic. It was amazing how far we'd progressed in only six months. We'd developed an incredible musical chemistry, and for the first time, I was experiencing pangs of regret over my decision to leave the group. As if he could read my mind, Jackson glanced over at me, but no matter how selfish my actions may have appeared to him, I couldn't remain in the band. I now felt in my heart that some preordained destiny, not random chance, had led me to the immortality formula in Germany and that road was now leading me to China. And for whatever reason that turned out to be, I felt it was more important than my personal ambitions in Manhattan.

"Listen up people," Hines said when the music ended. "I'm canceling Tuesday's show. Scoville and I have some important business to discuss concerning the future of this band and that's the only night he's free to meet with me."

That little announcement meant that today's recording session marked the last time I'd perform with the Hines Winston Quintet.

"One more thing," he added. "There's going to be a band meeting at the club on Wednesday at four o'clock."

That spelled trouble. I was supposed to rendezvous with Albert and Jennifer on Wednesday at 4:30 p.m. at Grand Central Station to board the 20th Century Limited to Chicago. The train didn't depart until 6:00 p.m. If I didn't show up for the 4:00 p.m. meeting Hines would know something was up and his Westies would have a good two hours to find me.

As I turned to walk out of the control room, Hines grabbed my arm.

"Scoville and I need to speak with Steven for a second," he told the band. "The rest of you guys go on down and wait for us at Dimitri's. We'll catch up with you in a little bit."

"It's part of my job to make my company's business interests perfectly clear to the artists," Scoville said, closing the control room door. "The truth of the matter is the only people RCA-Victor are interested in signing are you and Hines. The rest of the group will be your economic concern. My guess is you'll want to employ them as sidemen, same as it's done with the Big Bands. Duke Ellington is signed to Capitol–the rest of the band is paid directly by Ellington."

That may have been the standard in the industry, but it certainly didn't seem fair to me.

"Those guys work just as hard as I do," I said.

"I know, I know," Scoville replied. "But RCA-Victor looks at it quite differently. They're only concerned with essential personnel. The harsh reality is that even though they may be very talented musicians, sidemen like Jackson, Carter and Simon are a dime a dozen in this town. Hines is essential because he's the bandleader, manger and songwriter. You're an exception to the rule. You're essential because you're our insurance."

"Insurance?"

"Yes, you're what I'd call the record company's insurance. I'm still gambling that in a couple of years we'll have the technology that will give us the time to record one of those fantastic solos you create during your seizures. I'm drawing up a one-year contract with four one-year options. I'll have it ready for you to sign by Wednesday's meeting. If the songs we recorded today don't pan out, my company wants you locked into a long-term contract so that they can recoup their investment."

"What if I don't want to sign for that long?"

"In that case, we would not be interested in releasing what we recorded today."

That may have been standard in the music business, but it sure sounded like blackmail to me. Hines could sense my apprehension and glared at me with an unnerving ferocity. He was truly a product of the streets. "I'm sure everything will be fine," I said.

"Excellent!" Scoville exclaimed. "I'll have our attorneys draw up the papers."

"Your problem is you worry too much about the other guy," Hines said as we walked the studio's hallway to the street. "Just worry about yourself." That last comment would have made a perfect epitaph for Hines.

I thought the whole deal reeked of deception and when he opened the door of the coffee shop, I took a step back. "Hines, I'm not feeling well. Tell the guys I'll see them on Wednesday."

"Don't be a minute late for that meeting or else," Hines warned, pulling his finger ominously across his throat.

As I walked past the large window in front of the cafe, I saw the band sitting snugly in their booth. Simon and Carter waved cheerfully at me. Obviously, they hadn't heard the news. On the other hand, Jackson smiled so sadly it made me pause. I stepped closer and flattened my hand against the glass. Jackson reached up and pressed his hand against mine. Simon and Carter looked bewildered until it dawned on them what was happening. I was saying good-bye. Hines was so busy talking to Dimitri Junior that he never noticed the poignant scene unfolding behind him. I stood outside in the gray, Manhattan cold and stared silently at three talented men who'd so wonderfully enriched my life in such a short period of time. Then I turned my leather jacket collar up against the blustery spring wind and headed down 24th Street.

Wednesday morning my spirits soared as I showered, shaved and dressed for the long journey to Asia. The dream of traveling to such an exotic destination was finally becoming a reality and I was practically giddy with excitement. I packed my pills and clothes, and extra toiletry items which Albert warned me would be in short supply in China. In addition to my open bottle of immortality pills, I took along two unopened bottles just in case one of them became lost or contaminated. Albert suspected that we could be gone for as long as a year and I wanted insurance. For safe keeping, I stored my saxophone and remaining forty-seven bottles of pills inside Albert and Jennifer's Park Avenue apartment. While I packed, I constantly checked my watch to make sure I left no later than 3:30 p.m. Any time after that was too close to the 4:00 p.m. band meeting I was supposed to attend at the Black Onyx and could be dangerous. At precisely 3:20 p.m., I picked up my suitcase, walked out of the apartment and taped an envelope to the door addressed to the landlord with my key. As I stepped away, I bumped into someone standing behind me in the shadows.

"Going somewhere, motherfucker?" Hines hissed.

He spun me around, slammed me up against the door and pressed the razor-sharp steel of his pearl handled switchblade against my throat. Standing behind him were two of the most vicious looking human beings I'd ever encountered. Beefy giants in black leather trench coats with greased hair framing faces scarred and pulverized from a lifetime of violence. It didn't take a genius to figure out I was staring at a couple of Westies. I quickly decided that the best defense was an angry offense.

"Are you out of your fucking mind?" I shouted. "Get that knife out of my face before I jam it up your ass!"

Hines was trembling with animalistic fever as he stared me down. It was like being eyeball to eyeball with a rabid Doberman. All he needed to see was a flicker of fear and he'd go for my throat.

"Where were you going with the suitcase?" he demanded.

"After our meeting, I planned on catching a train at Penn Station. Jennifer and I are going to visit her family in Baltimore. What's the big fucking deal? I'll make it back in time for next Tuesday's show."

"So, you're going to Baltimore? Then how come I've heard you're leaving the band?"

Damn. Somebody talked. And the presence of two Westies meant that Hines believed what he'd heard. Or did he? If Hines was really convinced I was leaving the group, he would've simply unleashed the Westies right then and there. He must've had some lingering doubt and wanted to be completely sure before he gave the order. After all, killing me was the same as killing his record deal.

"Why in the hell would I leave the band? Does that make any sense to you? After all that hard work we're finally getting a record deal, and I'm going to bail? Did you forget that RCA-Victor wants me to sign the contract? I think you'd better think twice about trusting the person who told you this shit. Sounds to me like somebody's trying to screw with your head."

Bingo. Paranoia is the Achilles' heel of all criminals and my words found their mark. Hines slowly relaxed his grip. His stare became less fixed as his mind became riddled with doubt. Hines contemplated the situation for a moment, then stepped back to whisper something to the Westies. Without saying a word, they turned on their heels and walked downstairs. I could sense their disappointment.

"Hey man, no hard feelings," Hines said, folding the switchblade and slipping it back into his coat pocket. "I heard some shit and got a little crazy. I've been waiting my whole life for this break and I'll carve a man's heart out and serve it on a silver platter to him before I let anyone take it away from me."

Hines trotted downstairs to flag a cab while I lagged behind with my suitcase and calculated an escape plan. Minutes later we screeched to a halt in front of the Black Onyx. Jackson and Carter broke into smiles when I walked through the door. They probably thought I'd changed my mind, but Simon looked confused and afraid. I'd found my man. It made perfect sense. Simon was timid, the least educated, and by far the most easily manipulated. Hines confirmed my hunch when he made a beeline for Simon and dragged him by his jacket back to the men's room.

"What the hell are you doing here?" Jackson whispered.

"Simon leaked the news to Hines. He showed up at my apartment with a couple of Westies and put a blade to my throat. I barely talked my way out of it."

"I can't believe Simon would do something like that," Carter said.

"Well, believe it. Anyway, I'd love to sit and chat, but I've got a train to catch." I was about to bolt for the entrance when I caught sight of two leather jacketed giants lurking in the lobby. I carefully lowered my suitcase down to the floor and slid back into my seat.

"Are those the same guys Hines had with him at your apartment?" Carter whispered.

"Yeah. Who are they?"

"Mickey Flannigan and Rich O'Malley. They're Westies' hitmen, famous throughout Hell's Kitchen for the dozen different ways they love to torture their victims with blowtorches. Word is they hate to spoil their fun by killing 'em." Taking a deep breath, Carter stood up and walked over to the stone-faced Westies with his hand outstretched. "My man Mickey! My man Rich! Long time no see!"

"Is he out of his mind?" I said to Jackson.

"Just slowly slide over your suitcase," he whispered.

I pushed it across the wooden floor with the tip of my shoe, while Carter continued to chat with the Westies, obstructing their view of our table. Jackson snatched up the suitcase and slipped away, returning a minute later.

"Your bag is in the first stall of the ladies room. There's a window I've unlatched that will drop you into the alley behind the club. As soon as Hines returns, excuse yourself and get your ass out of here."

"I owe you big time, Jackson."

Jackson stared mutely down at the table as if he didn't hear me. I glanced behind to see Hines approaching with Simon in tow. Simon's nose was bloodied and his right eye was swollen shut.

"I'll be right back," I said to Hines. "I've got to take a piss."

"Make it fast," Hines replied. "Scoville will be here any second and he's got a fat contract with your name on it."

As I rose from my seat, one of the Westies took a step in my direction, but Hines motioned him back. I entered the men's room, locked the door behind me, popped the window open, crawled out into the alley and climbed into the adjacent ladies' room window to retrieve my suitcase. Seconds later, I was kicking up a cloud of dust as I sprinted down the alley toward 6th Avenue.

I'll never know how long it took before Hines realized I wasn't coming back. I could only pray that Scoville's threat not to release the four songs if I didn't sign the recording contract was a bluff. Regardless, Hines and the Westies never showed up to intercept me at Grand Central Station. I'd made sure of that when I planted the bug in their heads about Jennifer and me catching a train at Penn Station.

CHAPTER

6

After a brief stop in Cleveland, we arrived at Chicago's Dearborn Station the following morning. The three of us passed the time reading newspapers and working crossword puzzles until we could board the 8:00 p.m. Santa Fe Super Chief to Los Angeles. I read the Chicago Times from cover to cover, scoured the sports pages and even browsed through the classifieds. Then, more out of boredom than hunger, I followed the tantalizing aroma of freshly cooked hot dogs and boiled sauerkraut. While I was counting my change the vendor cordially asked about my destination.

"I'm on my way Los Angeles to catch a slow boat to China," I cracked.

He brightened. "China? My brother was one of the original Flying Tigers who served under Colonel Chennault. He lived the good life on a salary of six hundred dollars a month plus five hundred dollars for each enemy plane he bagged."

The Flying Tigers were volunteer American airmen who fought the Japanese for China before the U.S. entered the war. They were a brave group who achieved an almost legendary reputation and it was well deserved. It took a lot of guts to fly a Curtis P-40 against a lightning fast Japanese Zero.

"What did he think of China?"

"No idea. He never talks about the place. I know more about the country than he does. The only thing he ever says is how much he hates Chiang Kai-shek."

"Chiang Kai-shek? I've read in the paper that the U.S. may support him if the civil war in China heats up again."

"What do you mean *if* it heats up again?" He laughed. "China's civil war never ended! They called a truce so they could unite to fight the Japs. Now that the Japanese are history, Chiang Kai-shek and his Nationalists will return to trying to annihilate the Communists. The worst part of it all is that we're backing the wrong horse. Chiang Kai-shek doesn't have a clue as to what the common Chinese man wants. He and his glitzy wife act westernized and that's what we're comfortable with. We should be helping the Communists, but this country will never stand for that. Where in China are you headed?"

"Sian."

"Sian? That's the ancient capital of China. You'll be almost a thousand miles inland and you'd best be extremely careful."

"Actually, I'm going there with a former British missionary who knows the people and terrain fairly well."

"That may help. Look, I'm not trying to scare you. My brother told me that once you get to know the Communists you'll find that most of what you read about them here is simply propaganda. They're really nice people. Nearly all of them are peasants and they'll give you the shirts off of their backs. What year was your friend over there?"

"1938."

"You should ask him what happened in Sian two years earlier."

"How come you know so much about China?"

"When my brother joined the Flying Tigers nobody in my family knew anything about the country. I did some research and found their culture to be fascinating. It never ceases to amaze me how ignorant most Americans are about China. The first time I walked into a bar and suggested that we support the Communists, I barely got out of there in one piece. But mark my words, the Communists will win and we'll look like idiots for backing Chiang Kai-shek."

I returned with my hands full of steaming hot dogs and sauerkraut, and my head full of questions. As the three of us began to devour our lunch, I asked Albert about Sian.

"What happened in Sian in 1936?"

"How do you know about that?" he asked.

"It just so happens that the hot-dog vendor back there is a walking encyclopedia on China. His brother was one of the original Flying Tigers. What's the real story over there about Chiang Kai-shek and the Communists?"

"For one thing, you might as well forget everything you've read in the American newspapers. Chiang Kai-shek has been trying to eradicate the Communists since the twenties. The Communists are headed by a fellow named Mao Tse-tung. Whereas Chiang Kai-shek is very elitist and quite proficient at playing up to the West—especially to the Americans—Mao Tse-tung truly understands what his countrymen desire. Poor Chiang Kai-shek doesn't have a clue."

"That's exactly what the hot dog vendor said."

"That hot dog vendor spoke the truth. Sadly, I've met very few Americans who really know what's going on over there. The only thing most Americans agree upon is that Communism is evil. What they don't know is that the Soviets, who happen to be very Communist, are also backing Chiang Kai-shek. In 1936, the Chinese Communists captured Chiang Kai-shek in Sian. They could have executed him on the spot. Instead, they told him that Chinese should not be fighting Chinese and suggested they all unite against the Japanese. I consider that pretty reasonable behavior coming from people that Chiang Kai-shek and his Nationalists have labeled bandits."

"How well did you get along with the Communists?"

"I got along with them very well because I believe they represent the heart and soul of the Chinese people. I've never met Mao Tse-tung, but I've had the honor of befriending his second-in-command, Chou En-lai. Even though it's a capital offense to aid the Communist party I smuggled medical supplies to their capital, Yenan, which is about three hundred miles north of Sian."

"So you support the Communists?"

"Absolutely. Chiang Kai-shek simply exists as a symbol of the old corrupt China. He cannot endure."

The Santa Fe Super Chief pulled into sunny Los Angeles exactly forty hours after we departed Chicago. Our western route took us through Kansas City; Santa Fe, New Mexico and Flagstaff, Arizona. This was my first coast-to-coast trip and it was hard to believe it had been only three days since I was living the carefree life of a musician in New York City. The Hines Winston Quintet, the Westies, the Black Onyx and my apartment in Greenwich Village were now almost three thousand miles and another world away. At Union Station we were greeted by an elderly gentleman whose exacting manners and English accent were almost identical to Albert's. He introduced himself as Horace Bentley. Albert informed me that Horace was the sympathetic missionary he befriended in the Bahamas–the same man who told him about the German Ancestral Heritage Organization and secret Nazi expeditions to Tibet.

We piled into his white 1938 Ford Deluxe Convertible Sedan and drove to his modest Tudor home on Wilshire Boulevard in Santa Monica. Horace's living room was plastered with photographs documenting his travels with the China Inland Mission. My eyes quickly found one of Albert and Jennifer, gleefully posing on a beach surrounded by a group of somber-faced missionaries. Horace explained that it was taken in the West End, Bahamas in the summer of 1942. The only thing I noticed was how great Jennifer looked in a bathing suit. We sat down for tea while Horace rambled on about the pleasantries of living in Southern California. My eyelids were becoming heavy when Jennifer excused herself to shower. The moment she locked the bathroom door and turned on the water Horace's jolly demeanor turned somber.

"Let's get down to business," he said.

"What's the current political situation over there?" Albert asked. "Not good. The cease-fire George Marshall brokered in January between Chiang Kai-shek and the Communists is disintegrating. It's the same old song and dance. Chiang still dismisses the Communists as nothing more than stupid peasants and that is precisely the reason he will lose this war. They may be peasants, but they're certainly not stupid. To make matters worse, my sources have informed me that the U.S. is preparing to send millions of dollars in military aid to Chiang Kai-shek. When that happens Americans will lose their neutrality. Fortunately, your situation is an exception. The Nationalists won't touch you because you're an American, and the Communists haven't forgotten your generosity and the medical supplies you smuggled to them in the thirties. I've also learned that the railroad between Shanghai and Sian is still open. Other than that, I've had to pull teeth to get you on a ship."

"Which ship is that?" I asked.

"The S.S. *Marine Lynx*. It's one of the few passenger vessels crossing the Pacific and it's scheduled to depart Hunter's Point in San Francisco tomorrow afternoon at five o'clock."

Albert smiled warmly. "Thank you my dear and trusted friend."

"You're most welcome," Horace replied. "Unfortunately, I have three disturbing messages from my sources in Germany. I will share them in order of severity. First, my British friends with the International Military Tribunal have informed me that no evidence of the occult or the Thule

Society will be presented at the ongoing Nuremberg trials. The umbrella charge will simply be *Crimes Against Humanity*."

"Fools!" Albert thundered. "If they disregard this information the whole damn thing can happen all over again!"

"Precisely," Horace said. "The second message comes courtesy of my Soviet contacts. During the fall of Berlin, the Soviets discovered a thousand dead Tibetans near the Reichstag all dressed as German soldiers. I have no idea what it means, but whatever it is can't be good. It may somehow be connected to the third and most important message of all."

Enraptured by what I'd just heard about the Nuremberg trials and the thousand dead Tibetans in Berlin, I leaned forward to listen, and from the corner of my eye noticed Albert raising a finger to his lips to silence Horace.

"Oh Albert, relax old boy." Horace chuckled. "Steven is now in this adventure up to his neck and we need him completely in the loop from this moment forward."

"Fine. What's the last message?"

"An ex-member of the Thule Society has informed me that Maria Orsic has completely vanished from the face of the earth. She disappeared no later than March 11th of last year and her last message was, 'Nobody is staying here.' It appears she may have traveled to Aldebaran."

"Excuse me," I interjected. "Did you say her last name is Orsic?"

"Yes," Horace said. "Her last name is Orsic. Does it sound familiar to you?"

"I met an Erika Orsic in Munich, but I only knew her for a night."

Albert was puzzled. "What do you mean you only *knew* her for a night?"

I couldn't contain my smile. "I knew her in the Biblical sense. We were intimate." "You were intimate?" Albert asked.

"Yes. Intimate, as in having sex. As in, excuse me gentleman for being human, but I'd been in a war for over two years and I'd just met a German girl who was drop dead gorgeous."

Horace reached into a folder and handed me an eight by ten black and white headshot of what appeared to be a light haired woman with even lighter eyes. "Did she look anything like this?"

I was stunned. She was beyond beautiful, and looked like an older version of Erika. "When was this taken?' I asked.

"In Munich about twenty years ago," Horace said.

"What is so significant about Maria Orsic?"

"She was the leader of a very powerful group of female mediums embedded inside the Thule Society. They were called the Vril Society. Maria had this amazing telepathic ability to communicate with advanced beings sixty-five light years away in the Aldebaran solar system. In 1919, she began receiving information that not only helped bring Hitler to power, but detailed blueprints on how to develop a flying machine to travel there. Various German companies started manufacturing parts for this craft in 1922, each made unaware of the other to keep its development top secret. The first of seven prototypes was tested beginning in 1934, each more successful than its *predecessor,* and in December of 1943 Maria met with Nazi officials in Kolberg to discuss helping Hitler and Himmler escape to Aldebaran via interstellar dimension channels. By then, even the most hardcore Nazis knew the war was lost, but it appears that only Maria Orsic safely departed for the Aldebaran system in March of 1945."

"I don't believe that Erika knew anything about this," I said. "She was adopted soon after birth and, besides retaining her surname, she never knew her biological mother."

"You may be right," Albert mused. "I'm just wondering if this all might be connected."

Horace slipped the photo of Maria Orsic back into his folder. "Well, if they are, there's a good chance you'll find the answer in Asia."

We left Los Angeles early the next morning and drove north hugging the California coastline for most of the nine hour journey. I convinced Horace to put the top down on his convertible and we raced up and down the winding roads with the sun warming our faces as the cool ocean breezes whipped our hair and Albert struggled to keep his hat on. After witnessing some of the most breathtaking scenery imaginable, particularly the mountainous ocean cliffs south of Monterey, we arrived at Hunter's Point in San Francisco Bay by late afternoon. The Marine Lynx was a single-funnel steamer that reminded me of a smaller version of the troopship I'd taken back from Germany. Jennifer fostered no such sentimentality.

"I can't believe we're going to cross the Pacific Ocean in that rust bucket," she moaned as Horace steered onto the pier.

We were the only civilian passengers except for some frightened American businessmen who'd had the misfortune of being selected by their companies to oversee the evacuation of their offices in Shanghai. Horace confirmed with the captain that our papers were in order and hastily bid us farewell. As the Marine Lynx began to pull away from the dock, we leaned over the railing and waved good-bye.

"Give me some bad luck, old boy!" Albert shouted down to Horace.

"Why on earth would you want him to do something like that?" I asked.

"It's an old tradition we started early in the war when German U-boats were sinking every other ship sailing out of England. It's kind of like saying 'break a leg' in the theater, except that you must then come up with a catastrophe that occurred on the same date of your departure. It's based on the theory that lightning doesn't strike twice in the same place. You'll see, he'll think of something."

Deep in concentration, Horace folded his arms and stared down at the water's edge. Suddenly, he looked up with a triumphant grin and cupped his hands around his mouth.

"Do you know that today is April 14th?" he hollered, loud enough for most of the crew and passengers to hear.

"So what if it is?' Albert replied, greatly enjoying his role as the straight man.

"Thirty-four years ago tonight, the Titanic slammed into the bloody iceberg!"

Honolulu was our first port of call, and the first thing I did was visit the place directly responsible for my presence at Dachau.

Pearl Harbor.

Nearly five years after the Japanese attack, the magnitude of the devastation was still visible. I could plainly see the submerged hulls of the battleships Arizona and Utah still lying where they came to rest in the shallow harbor. Even more disconcerting was the fact that the remains of over a thousand American servicemen were still entombed in the twisted hull of the Arizona. As I gazed across the tranquility of those waters, gently lapping against the empty docks of Ford Island, I shuddered to think what those men and women must have felt fast asleep that Sunday morning when they were awakened by the roar of hundreds of Japanese attack planes screaming out of that peaceful Sunday sky to rain fire and destruction down on them.

After crossing thousands of miles of empty Pacific, on May 8th we steamed into Yokohama, Japan. Our ship was greeted at the dock by a truckload of stern-faced American military police. For security reasons, only Japanese nationalists and military personnel who'd boarded in Honolulu were allowed to disembark. Yokohama escaped nuclear annihilation but suffered terribly from conventional bombing. Even from my distant perspective, the devastation wrought by the hordes of B-29s was horrifying. In the eight months since the war's end, the rubble had been carted away and the streets had been swept clean, but the city's skyline remained riddled with the ghostly spires of bombed-out buildings rising out of the morning mist as far as the eye could see. A crowd of about a hundred Japanese gathered outside the dock enthusiastically waving American flags and posters of General MacArthur. When Jennifer appeared on deck and shouted a greeting to them in their native tongue, they went absolutely wild and the MPs had their hands full trying to stop them from rushing her. With her beauty, they probably thought she was a Hollywood starlet.

Three days later, Albert knocked on my cabin door to inform me that we had docked in Kobe. My teeth chattered from the early morning chill as I stood on deck and sleepily surveyed the city where the immortality formula first arrived after the Japanese seized it from Chang Sou's monastery. Kobe suffered much of the same destruction from the B-29s as Yokohama and once again we were under strict orders to remain on board. After taking it all in, I raced back to the warmth of my cabin and dove under the covers.

On May 17th I was awakened by an unnatural silence. The ship's engines had stopped. I glanced at my alarm clock to see it was a little before six in the morning. Dressing quickly, I walked out on deck where I spotted Albert peacefully smoking a cigar as he leaned across the railing, studying the rugged coastline of China, barely visible in the early morning light.

"There was always something so beautiful and mysterious about this country," he said, his eyes fixed on the distant shoreline.

"Why have the engines stopped?" I asked.

"Nothing to fear, it's simply too shallow for us to continue right now. We're stuck here until the tide rolls in at the mouth of the Yangtze. It has an estuary that turns into the Whangpoo River and we'll follow it all of the way into Shanghai."

I retreated to my cabin and buried my head in the pillow. I was fast asleep when I was awakened by a gentle tapping on the door.

"Wake up sleepy head," Jennifer said. "It's almost noon and you're going to miss everything."

I got up and joined Albert and Jennifer as they strolled along the deck. The Marine Lynx was steadily churning through the muddy water as it navigated a series of twists and turns on its way up the Whangpoo. We were nearing the outskirts of Shanghai and I was horrified by the degree of poverty in which its citizens existed. Most of their homes were nothing more than hovels on the shore and the perpetual odor of human and animal excrement hung heavily in the dusty air.

"I thought Shanghai was one of China's most modern cities."

"It is," Albert said. "But the difference between the countryside and the center of the city is absolute. Here in the country is where peasants live and Communist sympathies thrive. Downtown belongs to the warlords and Chiang Kai-shek."

Shanghai's skyline slowly materialized on the horizon and the hovels gradually gave way to warehouses and other industrial structures. The Marine Lynx wheeled sharply around a final bend and we were greeted with a panoramic view of Whangpoo Harbor filled to the brim with thousands of rickety brown sampans dwarfed by dozens of imposing gray American warships. Adjacent to the harbor was the cosmopolitan center of Shanghai, the Bund—an impressive array of tall buildings sculpted in Western architecture and bathed in a spectrum of neon. The warships had already laid claim to all of the larger docks, so we were forced to berth at the Shanghai jetty. We disembarked and were taken by launch to the customs jetty. The customs system in China was virtually nonexistent and we discovered that our passports and visas were good for nothing but identification. Shanghai was a hustler's paradise. After we were cleared, Albert led us onto the concrete shore of the Bund and flagged down a muscular, pony-tailed rickshaw driver as casually as if he were hailing a cab in Manhattan.

"Trust absolutely no one!" Albert shouted above the swirling mass of sweating human bodies as the rickshaw driver trotted us up Nanking Road toward the North Railroad Station. "This city has more prostitutes per capita than any other city in the world. Even the pickpockets and beggars are united in guilds. Always remember to keep your wallet in your front pocket, and whatever you do, don't speak to anyone!"

Not a problem. I couldn't understand a word of Chinese.

When we arrived at the North Railroad Station, it became apparent that Albert had made the classic mistake of not negotiating a price with the rickshaw driver before we left Whangpoo Harbor. A nasty shouting match ensued and we soon found ourselves surrounded by a very irate rickshaw driver who repeatedly counted off some outrageous figure on his fingers while Albert haggled with him to no avail. Attracted by the commotion, a young policeman wandered over to Jennifer who told him that the rickshaw driver was demanding 21,000 Chinese yuan. That sounded excessive until the policeman politely informed her that, under China's skyrocketing inflation, 21,000 yuan roughly equaled three U.S. dollars. Jennifer settled the matter by opening her purse and handing the angry man nearly double his fee—five dollars.

And now we faced a more serious dilemma.

When Jennifer opened her purse, every beggar and thief within sight noticed the huge wad of American currency stuffed inside. Within seconds they were upon us, a swarm of filthy, tattered locusts desperately trying to grab her purse while the policeman, Albert and I struggled to fend them off. It smelled as if we were drowning in a cesspool of flailing limbs and unwashed bodies. Amidst the melee, I managed to snatch the money and bury it under my arm as Jennifer threw the purse into the air, distracting the mob. While the crowd fought for the empty purse, we scooped up our luggage and ran until we reached the ticket booth. Behind a steel encased window, a shrill elderly voice informed Albert that the evening train to Sian was completely booked and another one wouldn't be available until tomorrow.

"There's no way we're going to survive the night in this hell hole," I said.

"We won't have to," Albert replied. "The train to Sian isn't sold-out. That's nonsense. Keep your eyes open."

"For what?"

"A member of the Yellow Ox gang. They control most of the theater and railroad tickets in all of the port cities."

Sure enough, I spotted four cigarette-smoking Chinese teenagers who, with their limp, dank hair, ill-fitting suits, and exaggerated gangster swaggers, looked as if they were auditioning for a Chinese version of *Little Caesar*. After some haggling, Albert slipped one of the boys a ten dollar bill and was promptly handed three railroad passes.

"We didn't fare too badly," Albert said. "I was prepared to give him another ten. That was the going rate eight years ago."

We stepped onto the wooden platform and carefully guarded our possessions for two hours before a pre-war steam locomotive laboriously huffed and puffed its way steaming into the station.

"Does China seem the same to you as it did in 1938?" I asked as we boarded.

"No. The sense of fear and desperation among the lower classes in Shanghai is completely different. In 1938, their struggle to survive was based on overcoming the cruelties imposed upon them by the Japanese Army. Now, I sense that their traditional acceptance of a dead-end life mired in poverty has been replaced by a seething rage and frustration aimed directly at the ruling class. I could see it on their faces when the crowd attacked us. They acted as if that policeman didn't exist. Such blatant disregard for authority was unheard of in 1938. If this rebellious fearlessness is indicative of the state of mind of even the lowliest beggar, Chiang Kai-shek and his cronies won't last much longer."

We covered the nine hundred miles to Sian in roughly thirty-six hours. Our journey took us in a northwesterly direction through the cities of Nanking, Pengpu and Hsu Chou, before turning west towards Kaifeng, Cheng Chou, Loyang and Sian.

I was exceedingly curious to see the city of Nanking. In 1937, the *Rape of Nanking* was one of the most horrific crimes ever perpetrated by an army against a civilian population. The Japanese Army raged out of control for a full month and nearly fifty thousand men, woman and children were tortured and killed in a mass orgy of rape, murder and mutilation that even the Japanese commanders were powerless to stop. It took us seven hours to reach Nanking and by the time we reached the city, the massive iron platform clock read a quarter to midnight. Making sure that Jennifer was asleep, Albert relayed to me eyewitness accounts of the carnage that occurred there only a year before he arrived in China. He described columns of victorious Japanese soldiers marching in formation with a Chinese baby impaled on each of their bayonets. Chinese POWs were buried alive dozens at a time while other unfortunates were selected to have their heads dipped in kerosene and ignited. Public violation of the Chinese women was commonplace, usually after the woman's children were beheaded in front of her. In one instance, a Japanese soldier smothered a crying Chinese baby with one hand while he held down the mother with the other and raped her. After hearing that, I asked Albert to spare me the rest.

As we journeyed deeper into China's interior, American made cars, common throughout Shanghai and Nanking, became replaced by horses and oxen. It was as if we were traveling back in time one year for every mile of rail. The only mechanized vehicles we encountered belonged to Chiang Kai-shek's military and Albert informed me that the Communist's transportation options were strictly limited to foot and horseback. I slept deeply to the sound of the train's metallic heartbeat until I opened my eyes to a breathtaking countryside of yellow and green rolling hills, ancient virgin forests and majestic mountain vistas. Sian, the ancient capital and former terminus of the legendary Silk Road, was completely surrounded by an imposing thirty foot stone wall. Very few dwellings were outside the wall except for the twin classical pagodas known as the Little Goose and the

Big Goose. Both pagodas were constructed in the seventh century and, as impressed as I was at the age of these sacred structures, I only had to remind myself that Chow Li was almost a thousand years older.

After disembarking at Sian's train station, we entered the city via the massive wooden doors of the North Gate and followed Albert to the white-washed stone facade of the China Inland Mission. He asked Jennifer and me to wait outside. We pressed our ears against the mission door and heard Albert's cordial greeting quickly deteriorate into a shouts of accusation. Moments later he emerged, fuming.

"Spineless, hypocritical bastards! Let's go down the street to see the Wu's."

Albert marched off, leaving Jennifer and I behind struggling to keep the pace while carrying the luggage. We traversed a couple of twisting narrow back streets until we reached the adobe brick dwelling of Wu Tso-lin. The wooden door cracked open to reveal a nervous eyeball looking us up and down.

"Tso-lin, please let us in," Albert said, exasperated. "We've traveled such a long way."

"Albert!" a high-pitched voice exclaimed as the door swung open. Out stepped a thin, bespectacled man who practically cried with happiness upon recognizing Albert and Jennifer.

Forty-five-year-old Wu Tso-lin was the owner of Sian's largest wheat noodle shop and one of Albert's first Chinese Christian converts. The warm reception he and his wife Ching-ling showered upon us was a welcome relief after the rigors of our practically non-stop ten thousand mile journey from New York. The Wu's were childless and insisted we stay with them as "one big happy family" for as long as our hearts desired. Albert agreed to accept their hospitable offer on the condition that we were allowed to reciprocate their kindness by helping them with their noodle shop. Tso-lin assented and seated us around a large wooden table as Ching-ling spooned heaping portions of mutton and vegetable soup into clay bowls filled to the brim with steaming noodles.

As I watched Jennifer grab her chopsticks and dig in, it was apparent she'd long adapted to their culture. After dinner, Albert lit up a cigar and inquired about the status of Chow Li and Chang Sou. Tso-lin cast a wary eye in my direction and hesitated.

"It's quite all right. Steven's been taking the immortality formula."

Tso-lin and his wife gaped at me in horror.

"How can this be?" Ching-ling asked. "Neither Chow Li nor Chang Sou would ever permit this."

I explained to the Wu's how I'd acquired the formula through the Sian-Kobe-Dachau connection and told them my reasons for taking it. Satisfied with my logic, Tso-lin gave us an update on Chow-Li and Chang Sou.

"Chow Li is in Tibet, teaching at the medical school atop Chakpori Hill. He usually returns during the summer, but strangely, he did not return last year. I have not seen Chang Sou or his disciples for the last eight years and the monastery is sealed like a tomb. But, I believe that Chang Sou and his monks are still inside."

"Inside?" I asked. "Doing what?"

"I would assume they are hibernating," Tso-lin replied.

"Hibernating? They have the ability to hibernate?"

"I'm sorry, but for some reason I thought you already knew about that," Albert said, scratching his head. "If you overdose on the formula, your metabolic rate will fall drastically, resulting in a state of comatose hibernation."

"That happened to me in New York! I doubled my daily dosage by mistake and slept for weeks, but that was an accident. Why would anyone purposely go into hibernation?"

"Chang Sou and his followers probably went into hibernation soon after the Japanese raided the monastery," Tso-lin answered. "The monastery is built into the side of a mountain. Chang Sou probably assumed the Japanese would eventually overrun this area and attempt to occupy it. Ironically, the battle line north of Sian was one of the few that stabilized for the duration of the war. The Japanese never returned."

"When can we see the monastery?"

"You should wait until Chow Li returns," Tso-lin replied. "Even with your immortality formula, it is not a safe place to visit. I'm sure Albert has told you about his terrible experience there."

"He did, but that was because Albert went inside the monastery and disturbed them. I have no intention of doing that. I'm just curious to see what the place looks like. Besides, we have no idea when or if Chow Li will return."

"I don't believe there is any harm in visiting the monastic grounds," Albert mused. "Let me have a couple of days to catch my breath and think it over."

The next day, Jennifer and I began assisting the Wu's at their noodle shop. Jennifer's handy knowledge of Chinese enabled her to record the customers' orders. I was assigned to the kitchen, mixing the wheat flour and hanging the rubbery sheets of noodles outside to dry. It was easy work, but it took Tso-lin a little while to warm up to me. He kept his distance until I told him I'd been hearing music that reminded me of a church organ every time I walked outside the noodle shop. Tso-lin had no idea what an organ sounded like and asked me to show him. We stepped outside just as a sound similar to a high octave chord played on a pipe organ filled the air and a flock of pigeons scattered overhead. "See, I'm not imagining things. The sound even startled the pigeons!"

Tso-lin exploded with laughter. "That sound *is* the pigeons. We tie bamboo whistles to their tails!"

A week after we arrived in Sian I sat at the breakfast table and waited patiently as Albert swallowed his last mouthful of cabbage soup.

"Caught your breath yet?" I asked as he wiped his mouth.

"What's that supposed to mean?"

"You told me when we arrived here that you needed a couple of days to catch your breath before we headed up to the monastery. It's been a week."

"I needed some time to consider your request to visit the monastery."

"And?"

Albert paused to take a sip of tea. "I've mulled it over and I don't think it's a wise idea."

"Why not?"

"Legend has it that the sacred forest surrounding the monastery is fraught with supernatural powers that may be extremely dangerous."

"And what powers are those?"

"I'm not sure. All I know is that the forest is unlike any forest I've ever seen. Not only does the forest have the power to keep Chang Sou and his disciples imprisoned inside of the monastery, it also has the power to keep intruders out."

"But you made it through."

"True, but I was scared out of my wits. The treetops are so dense that little light can filter through, making it almost as black as night during high noon. I thought I saw things, heard things, as if some creature was stalking me. By the time I reached the monastery I was delirious with fright."

"Is that why you went inside?"

"Yes. And I ran from the clutches of one nightmare straight into the arms of another."

"I agree it would be dangerous to enter the monastery, but the fact that you made it through the forest and back unscathed is enough to convince me that we'd be safe. Besides, I didn't journey ten thousand miles to learn how to make wheat noodles."

Albert cradled his teacup and carefully set it down on the table. "All right, I'll take you up there under one condition."

"What?"

"You agree to leave the moment I say so."

"Not a problem. What about Jennifer?"

"Are you kidding?" Albert snorted. "Wild horses couldn't stop her from going."

Ching-ling packed a Chinese-styled picnic basket of delicious meat-filled dumplings called Dim-sum and we departed through the North Gate. The weather was magnificent, about seventy degrees with low humidity and not a cloud in the sky. The opium poppies were bursting and the pomegranate trees were in full bloom, their beautiful red and white flowers dotting the hillsides around us. It was as if we were headed out on a Sunday afternoon stroll in the country and nothing about it seemed unusual except that we were on the other side of the world.

We hiked northeast along the main road out of Sian for eleven miles until Albert directed us to follow a dirt path that wound up into the mountains. Our legs began to ache as we steadily increased in elevation, but we were soon rewarded with a panoramic view of the walled city of Sian shining in the distance surrounded by miles of cultivated farmland, stretching out below us like a yellow and green checkered carpet.

We continued for another hour until Albert was forced to rest. Between gasps for air, he admitted that he couldn't locate a familiar landmark—a naturally shaped rock formation resembling a primitive Buddha. As he was talking I looked ahead and spotted the Buddha about fifty yards up the path, partially obscured by a bush. It seemed more like a brownish stone snowman than an important totem and sat beside a rocky trail that disappeared up a steep embankment. We climbed and stepped into the shadow of a lush canopied forest. It was impossible to see more than a hundred feet ahead as Albert informed us that we were now standing on sacred ground rarely seen by the outside world.

"See that giant cypress?" he asked, pointing at the massive trunk looming in front of us. "It's over two thousand years old and marks the outer boundary of the sacred forest."

"Does Chow Li remember when it was planted?" I asked.

"No," he replied, "but his father did."

The area teemed with wildlife. Hares, field mice, and pheasants rustled through the fallen leaves and darted across our path. As we trudged ahead, the density of the forest increased and the sunlight began to fade with every step. The upper branches of the pines and cypresses begin to intertwine in an unnatural alliance that soon plunged us into total darkness.

"Keep your eyes on that distant flicker of light," Albert said, pointing directly ahead. "That's our destination."

I peered through the gloom and spotted something sparkling in the distance like a candle flickering on a boat far out at sea. I kept an eye on it as I did my best to ignore the sudden squeals and grunts of unseen animals scurrying around us. The light steadily grew larger until it revealed itself to be sunlight reflecting off the stone wall of a towering mountainside. As the forest receded and sunshine began bleeding through the meshed treetops, I could see that the base of the mountain was barren except for a dozen small pine trees, growing perfectly flat against the center of the stone face. They were positioned precisely in a straight row and all were of uniform height. They also looked as if they had no business being there.

Albert paused to catch what little breath he had left. "This is it," he gasped, mopping the sweat off his brow.

We stepped out of the darkness onto a sun-dappled field of wild grass swaying in the breeze like a swirling emerald carpet. It led to the base of the mountain. Off to our right rested a squat round structure about thirty feet in diameter constructed of what appeared to be highly polished mahogany shaped in the shell of a giant tortoise.

Albert leaned back and stretched. "That is Chow Li's temple."

We walked ahead and soon stood before a vertical wall of glittering stone that shot skyward for thousands of feet. Upon closer inspection I noticed that the pine trees were camouflaging two massive iron doors.

I couldn't understand why Chang Sou and his followers had allowed Chow Li's tortoise temple to remain in such close proximity to their monastery. His temple was the only thing in the area that would attract attention and it wouldn't take much for a passing army patrol or band of thieves to happen upon the monastery.

When I turned to Albert in curiosity, he quickly raised a withered index finger to his lips. He motioned for us to follow him back away from the monastery to a sandy patch in the grass. Then he stiffly traced a message in the dirt with the tip of his shoe:

They can hear you.

I mouthed the question, "They?"

Do not speak again until we're back in the woods

We returned to the wall and silently inspected the outside of the monastery. The stone surface surrounding the iron doors was painfully cold to the touch. The closer I slid my hand along the wall toward the round metal handles in the center, the colder the surface became until it threatened to freeze my skin. I pulled my hand away and warmed it with my breath. It was then that I noticed Jennifer had slid her hand between the pine trees and was pressing her palm flat against the hammered metal door. Suddenly, she was thrown backwards as if she'd been jolted by an electric shock. Albert quickly put his fingers to his lips and reminded us to be silent. I helped Jennifer over to the sandy patch and wrote a question in the dirt:

What did you feel?

Trembling, Jennifer scratched out ten jagged letters: *A heartbeat.* That was it for me, and the three of us bolted for the forest. We'd made it almost to the tree line when it began to feel as if we had stumbled into a knee-deep pool of quickly hardening cement. Jennifer and Albert appeared to be running in slow motion as we struggled against the grasp of an unseen force. Reaching out on either side of me, I wrapped my arms around their waists, thrust my head down and barreled ahead. The moment I pulled us off the grass, the force released its grip and we catapulted forward, rolling and tumbling onto the soft cushion of leaves blanketing the ancient forest floor.

"Is everyone all right?' Albert gasped, lying on his back.

"What in the hell was that?" I asked, brushing off leaves. "A warning. I guess the legend is true that while in hibernation, the monks have the ability to sense movement and vibrations outside the monastery. Thank God for the protection of this forest."

"If Chang Sou and his men are trapped in the monastery, then why doesn't Chow Li just leave them there forever?"

"Steven, my boy," he said, clawing leaves and twigs from his hair, "you've just arrived at the crossroads that separates Eastern and Western philosophy. You must remember that Chow Li blames himself for Chang Sou's existence and believes it is his sole responsibility to redeem his soul. As a Buddhist, Chow Li also believes in mercy. To entomb Chang Sou and his followers forever would be unmerciful, regardless of the many atrocities they've committed. To be frank, every time I look at my wounds I have a problem with Chow Li's beliefs. But, this is his culture in which we've intruded and it is not right to evaluate them according to our Western standards."

"How does Chow Li ensure they return to the monastery after he accompanies them on their trips for provisions into Sian? Why doesn't Chang Sou and the other monks simply flee once they're free of this forest?"

"Chow Li and Chang Sou ingest different recipes of the immortality formula. When Chow Li realized his mistake in trusting Chang Sou, he devised a new immortality formula for himself and planted this forest around the monastery. Its trees emit an invisible pollen-like substance that enters the bloodstream through the lungs. This substance has the power to reverse the immortality process of Chang Sou's formula. Untreated, Chang Sou and his men would die a horrible death within days. Chang Sou is over nineteen hundred years old and his youngest disciple is almost four hundred years old. If they reverted to their mortal ages they would instantly crumble into a pile of dust. Chow Li's formula is immune to the powers of this forest and is the only known antidote. Chow Li gives Chang Sou and his men just enough of his formula so they can make their journey to Sian. If they don't return in time, they will die."

"In that case, wouldn't Chow Li be responsible for their deaths?"

"Not according to his way of thinking. In that situation, Chang Sou and his men would be responsible for their own deaths because they refused to return to the monastery. For almost two thousand years, they've returned in time. They're much too selfish to die."

"This is insane. You're telling me that Chow Li will wait forever until Chang Sou renounces his ways? So, in other words, he's waiting for a miracle."

"Basically, yes."

"Tell me, Albert, As a man of God, do you believe in miracles?"

"Let me put it this way, in all my years of missionary work I've never seen anything I would even remotely classify as a miracle. But if someone as fanatically evil as Chang Sou were to renounce his ways, I'd have to say that such an event would qualify as a miracle. Other than that, I don't believe in miracles. In fact, I don't believe in–" Albert froze mid-sentence and stared up into the treetops to the far right of us.

"What's wrong?" I asked.

"There's something up there," he whispered, squinting up into the darkness.

If there was something up there, I had no idea how he could see it. I followed his line of sight and saw nothing but blackness.

THE DIARY OF AN IMMORTAL (1945-1959) | 163

"Steven, I'm not sure what it is. There it is again! No! I beg of you! Please don't!"

"Don't do what? " I asked.

"Uncle Albert, stop it!" Jennifer pleaded. "You're scaring me!"

"My dear, it's perfectly natural to be afraid," he said, his voice trembling. "I can assure you that I certainly am."

While they were talking, I stealthily reached down and picked up a broken branch about the size of a baseball bat.

"Put that damn thing down!" Albert whispered. "Under no circumstances are you to demonstrate such aggressive behavior. Remember, we pose no threat to whatever it is as long as we remain unarmed."

Despite what I believed to be utter nonsense I dropped the branch and huddled in the darkness with Jennifer, watching intently up at the black canopy. I still saw nothing, but I began to hear something. The ominous sound of crunching underbrush as something of considerable size and weight steadily made its way through the forest.

I closed my eyes to zero in on its position as I'd been taught to do by a Sioux Indian in my battalion. I quickly estimated it was fifty to sixty yards away, approaching from our left, pausing every couple of yards as it steadily made its way toward us. It was so dark that it was almost impossible to see more than a few yards ahead of us. I could only hope that whatever was out there was limited by the same conditions we were. My optimism quickly faded as the crunching footsteps grew progressively louder. I anxiously eyed the large stick at my feet.

And then the forest became deathly still.

I was about to dive for the stick when the bushes in front of us parted and out stepped four grim-faced Chinese with the barrels of their rifles aimed at us. Albert began babbling frantically in Chinese. Other than his own name, the only words I understood were the names Chou En-lai and Mao Tse-tung. Fortunately, it worked. The grim expressions of the soldiers transformed into broad welcoming smiles. After shaking hands with Jennifer and me, they stepped back into the bushes and disappeared.

"My God, we were lucky." Albert sighed. "At first I thought they were bandits, in which case, they would have robbed and murdered us on the spot. Instead, they're veterans of the Great March and due to my previous assistance to their cause, they were quite familiar with my name. They're passing through here on a reconnaissance mission out of Yenan. I don't understand what they're doing this far south. Trouble must be brewing. We must hurry." He said all of this in an extremely soothing English voice, backed by a warm, comforting smile. And then it hit me.

He's lying.

Albert raced ahead through the darkness and we followed closely behind not stopping until we bathed in sunshine again and rested ourselves against the base of the ancient cypress tree that marked the entrance to the forest. After he caught his breath, Albert turned and grinned at me.

"I believe we've forgotten something. Steven, care to go back for that picnic basket?"

When he straightened up to make his way down the embankment, I blocked his path.

"What on earth are you doing?" he asked.

"Albert, what really happened back there in the forest?"

"What are you saying?" he asked, attempting to brush past me. "I told you what happened. What do you want me to say?"

"The truth would be refreshing."

"Steven, why are you acting like this?" Jennifer asked.

"Because your uncle is not being honest with us."

Albert was indignant. "I have absolutely no idea what you're talking about."

"Oh, I think you do. The first time you turned around, I noticed your eyes were fixed on a position about thirty to forty yards to the right of us, up in the treetops."

Albert rolled his eyes. "How militarily accurate of you."

"And the second time you claimed you saw something, it was located at about the same position."

"And what is so peculiar about that?"

"Nothing, except for the fact that those soldiers approached us from the left."

Albert slumped against the cypress tree trunk in perspired resignation. "And what does all of that tell you, Steven?"

"Only one thing. There was something else in that forest besides those soldiers."

Albert eyed me with contempt, but didn't reply. This was one chess game he wasn't going to win.

Jennifer was shocked by her uncle's deceptive behavior. "Uncle Albert, please say something!"

"Oh, shut up you petulant child."

I shoved Albert aside and charged down the embankment. I was absolutely furious with him. I had followed the man halfway around the world on a quest any other rational person would've deemed ridiculous. I had sympathized with his physical, emotional and spiritual plight. Now I felt utterly deceived and had no intention of remaining another day with him. When I reached Sian, I would pack my bags and give Jennifer the option of returning to New York alone with me.

"Steven!" Albert shouted.

I kept walking.

"Steven. Please, I beg of you!" I paused, but didn't turn around.

"What is it, Albert?"

"You forgot to say, 'Checkmate.'"

On our hike back to Sian, Albert apologized repeatedly to me and Jennifer, but he steadfastly refused to divulge what he saw or heard in the forest, except to say that the experience deeply troubled his soul and he would pray about it. I decided to let the matter rest, but the incident dampened our relationship, and our usual fiery after-dinner debates about Chow Li and Chang Sou were replaced by the mundane exchange of newspaper snippets concerning the disintegrating situation between Mao Tse-tung and Chiang Kai-shek. And it wasn't difficult to put Chang Sou on the back burner as I had no intention of returning to the monastery until Chow Li returned to Sian. The mysterious events of our visit proved only one thing–we were way out of our league.

On a positive note, in a very short time I'd fallen irrevocably in love with Sian and its people. Jennifer and I were now working six days a week at the Wu's wheat noodle shop. The place was continuously packed and provided a great way to meet the locals. There was much to learn from their culture and I found myself developing a powerful bond of friendship with those around me.

But there were storm clouds gathering on the horizon.

The fragile six-month-old truce brokered by General Marshall between the Nationalists and the Communists, who now called themselves the People's Liberation Army or the P.L.A., had expired. It seemed only a matter of weeks before the country would explode into full scale civil war. In Sian, we were under the control of General Hu Tsung-Nan and his Nationalist soldiers. But, the capital of the P.L.A., Yenan, was a scant three hundred miles to the north. It was only logical to assume that the Nationalists would eventually make a play for it. Albert confided to me that Tso-lin had been resupplying him with medical supplies and he had resumed funneling them to Yenan utilizing local teenage boys willing to undertake the hazardous journey for a couple of American dollars. He also confessed he blamed himself for the death of a certain Canadian heart specialist named Norman Bethune. Dr. Bethune came here directly from the battlefields of the Spanish Civil War and directed front-line medical services for the Communist's Eight Route Army saving thousands of lives under abysmal sanitary conditions. He happened to be visiting a friend in Sian the night Albert was attacked and was able to save his life with massive blood transfusions donated by mission volunteers.

When Dr. Bethune told Albert that thousands of Communist soldiers were dying in the field from lack of first-aid medication, he arranged for medical supplies pilfered from the mission storeroom to be smuggled to Yenan. Informed he was going to be transferred to the Bahamas, Albert revealed the truth about his clandestine activities to his fellow missionaries. Despite fear of reprisal from the Nationalists, they promised to continue the shipments. In 1940, Chiang Kai-shek imposed a tight blockade around the portion of Shensi province that included Yenan. The remaining missionaries in Sian backed down and terminated the medical supply shipments. Soon after, Dr. Bethune cut his finger during an operation on the battlefield, developed septicemia and died. All he would have needed was a little penicillin. The argument Jennifer and I heard outside of the China Inland Mission on the day we arrived in Sian was Albert venting years of pent-up rage over the needless death of his friend.

After hearing this story I began to consider how desperately the P.L.A. could use an experienced medic such as me. Even though I didn't possess the medical skill of someone like Norman Bethune, I knew enough to save and preserve lives under battlefield conditions and because of my immortality pills, the tragic fate that befell Bethune could never happen to me. There was one potential reality I feared, though: that the U.S. would get pulled into China's civil war and begin sending troops to bail out Chiang Kai-shek. That situation would create a crisis of allegiance for me that would be unthinkable.

CHAPTER

*I pressed my broken pencil firmly against a scrap of paper I could barely
see. The tiny, flickering light illuminating my words emanated from a
slow burning cotton wick immersed in a brass saucer of bean oil. The
shadows dancing on the stone walls around me revealed my bed to be little
more than a wooden door supported by two saw horses. My only protection
against the freezing winds gusting from the Gobi Desert was my cotton padded suit and a tiny brazier by my bed that had to be kept constantly fueled
with charcoal sticks. And all of it was housed in a small cave carved into the
side of Green Ridge Mountain.*

Such were the wretched conditions we shared with Mao Tse-tung and
his People's Liberation Army during the fall of 1946. Jennifer, Albert, and
I made the three hundred mile journey in the Communist Eighth Route
Army's black 1939 Chevrolet. The Communists housed the car in Sian
during the war with Japan so that any disagreements with the Nationalists
could be remedied by making an emergency run up to Yenan. When the
truce expired, the Nationalists confiscated it. The day before we left for

Yenan, Albert brazenly approached General Hu and asked if we could borrow the car for a Christian missionary expedition to deliver the word of God and a trunk full of Bibles to the atheistic rebel capital. Incredibly, General Hu gave his permission. The knot in my stomach didn't abate until we cleared the military checkpoint five miles north of Sian.

Our trunk was stuffed with medical supplies.

Albert decided to risk the trip after he received word that General Hu was preparing to mount a full-scale assault on Yenan sometime after January 1st. The Nationalists were now equipped with American military firepower and had tired of the cat-and-mouse civil war with the Communists that had dragged on since 1927. Propped up by millions of dollars in American aid, Chiang Kai-shek was launching offensives all over the country and by November of 1946 his army outnumbered the P.L.A. three-to-one in manpower and five-to-one in supplies. I didn't see how the Communists could hold out much longer.

All of this convinced Albert that a mad dash up to Yenan would probably be his last chance to see his old Communist friends. Furthermore, the summer had come and gone, and there was still no sign of Chow Li. We dodged bomb craters for most of the journey, trailing a large plume of yellow dust behind us, and arrived in Yenan at dusk. I was surprised how easily we made the trip and asked Albert why Chiang Kai-shek hadn't simply marched on Yenan and taken the rebel city.

"The American tanks haven't arrived in Sian," he said. "When they do, he will."

I was appalled by the devastation the Japanese bombers had wrought upon Yenan. Tokyo must have wanted Mao and his men quite badly, as hardly a structure remained intact. The city's population was left with no choice but to abandon the area and, hide in the surrounding hills, digging caves into them. The streets were deserted except for the distant echo of music, sounding as if it was coming from a muffled phonograph. We followed the unmistakable melody of "She'll Be Coming Round the

Mountain" and discovered the source deep inside the basement of a partially destroyed brick church. The music was too loud for anyone to hear us knock, so we entered uninvited.

It was as if we'd crashed a New Year's Eve party. The room exploded in song as over a dozen Chinese couples danced gracefully around a bare stone floor while six musicians dressed in rebel uniforms played their hearts out of key. Across the room I recognized Mao Tse-tung, easily identifiable with his wide forehead and feminine lips, as he whirled his svelte dance partner around him. He and his men were so caught up in their festive mood that it was a solid minute before any of them noticed three Westerners, including a beautiful red-haired woman, standing in their midst.

Mao saw us first and stopped dancing; instantly everyone froze. It was an intimidating display of how much control Mao commanded over his people. No matter how indifferently anyone acted as they danced around the room, no one had dared take their eyes off him. The tension was broken when Chou En-lai went over to Mao and whispered in his ear. As he spoke, Mao broke out into a wide grin.

"My dear and generous friend!" Mao exclaimed, reaching out to shake Albert's hand. He noticed his deformity and, without missing a beat, patted Albert on the back and welcomed him warmly.

I found Mao to have one of the most powerful, albeit odd, handshakes I'd ever encountered. Strangely, he didn't pump my hand up and down in the standard Western fashion, but held it firmly in an iron grip as he stared into my eyes in an inquisitive manner I found somewhat intrusive. When I mentioned it to Albert, he told me that Mao was renowned throughout China for his ability to see the truth in a person's eyes.

"Don't ever lie to him," Albert cautioned. "He'll see right through you."

I soon discovered we weren't the only Americans in town. There was also a U.S. Army Mission in Yenan actively serving as the liaison between Washington and the Communists. Since the United States had now thrown its weight behind the Nationalists, I was puzzled as to why the Communists tolerated their presence until I learned that Hollywood films were shown in the U.S. Army Mission every Friday night, making that evening a close second in popularity to their Saturday night dances.

After Chou introduced us around the room, Mao clapped his hands and everyone grabbed a partner to dance a Chinese revolutionary tune called "March of the New Democratic Youth." Jennifer and I had never danced to a political song before and I could only hope that everyone interpreted our hysterical laughter as a sign we were simply having a good time. Meanwhile, Albert sat contentedly in a corner sipping a cup of cold bean milk while he caught up on old times with Chou En-lai. At midnight, the bandleader counted off the last song. I didn't recognize the tune, but its slow tempo and sentimental melody seemed oddly familiar. Then I realized they were trying to play my mother's favorite song, "Stardust." I politely excused Jennifer away from her P.L.A. dancing partner and pulled her close against me. As I reveled in the intoxicating warmth of her swaying body, my mind reeled from the surrealism of the moment. Here I was over ten thousand miles from home in the midst of an exploding civil war slowly dancing in the arms of a beautiful woman as a band of Communist soldiers did their best to play my mother's favorite song.

As if she could read my mind, Jennifer raised her lips to my ear and whispered, "Steven, I will love you for as long as I live."

It was the first time Jennifer had ever told me she loved me and I believed she always would.

For as long as she lived.

Since the Communists were atheists, I would've never known a particularly chilly Wednesday morning that December in Yenan was Christmas if Jennifer hadn't awakened me in my room with a Merry Christmas kiss and a small box wrapped in brown paper. I carefully unraveled the twine to find a pine box containing a beautifully polished heart. It was carved from ancient cypress with an inscription etched across it that read:

My love for you will last forever.

To anyone else, that inscription may have read like a sentimental cliché. But since my discovery at Dachau words like *forever* had taken on a much deeper and complex meaning in my life. Over the past year Jennifer had become an irreplaceable part of my world, and yet, until that moment I'd never stopped to consider the stark reality. She would age normally and I would not. While I slowly ran my fingers across the polished wood and pondered this, she looked at me with wide-eyed expectation.

"Do you like it?" she asked, apprehensively.

"Very much so." I reached over the side of my bed to retrieve a bottle of immortality pills. I unscrewed the cap and rolled one of the gold-speckled pills into the palm of her hand.

"Merry Christmas, my love."

"Steven, what on earth are you doing?"

"Giving you the gift of life."

Jennifer dropped the pill onto my bed and started to cry. "I'm sorry. I've often wondered what I'd say if this day ever arrived. The truth is I can't do this."

"Why not?"

"Because I'm afraid. You don't know what long-term effects these pills will have on you. All I can remember is what happened to you down in that basement in Manhattan."

"That's precisely my point. We're smack in the middle of a civil war. That means human flesh versus bullets, bombs and shrapnel. And I can assure you, human flesh will lose every time. If you took the pills I'd know you were protected."

"Steven, I'm not talking about the gunshot you survived. I'm talking about the way you killed those two men. You tore them to pieces. You became something else. You turned into some kind of animal."

"I was only trying to save your life."

"I know you were and I'll always love you for it, but, there's something unholy about this whole idea of immortality. If we were meant to live in our physical bodies forever, God would've made us that way. I'm sorry. I really do love you, but I can't be a part of this."

She kissed me on the cheek and ran sobbing out of the cave. I sat there in stunned silence holding the polished heart in my hand. Suddenly the curtain at the entrance of my cave swept aside and a Chinese man with an unmistakably wide forehead poked his head inside. It was Mao.

"May I enter?" he inquired politely.

"Please, come in," I said, rubbing the last of the sleep from my eyes.

Mao lumbered in, pulled up a chair and sat beside my bed. "Merry Christmas!" he said heartily.

I thought I was dreaming. Since my arrival, I'd been hard at work helping the other revolutionaries dig caves out of Yenan's loess hills. And even though Mao had stood beside me many times, the man had never said more than two words to me.

"You'll have to excuse my English. It is not very good."

"That's all right. It's a lot better than my Chinese."

Mao threw his head back and roared with laughter. This was also unexpected as I had no idea the man possessed anything remotely resembling a sense of humor. He always conducted himself quite formally except when an idea crossed his fertile mind. Then he'd stop whatever he was doing to quote an inspirational line or recite a few verses of poetry. I found this habit of his to be quite strange and bordering on pretentious, but among his followers it was highly revered.

"I saw Albert's niece run out of here. She appeared quite upset. Is everything all right? "

"We had a little disagreement about religion."

"Ah, religion." He frowned. "I have no time for that. Man must learn to rise off his knees and stand. He must take responsibility for his own destiny. All blind faith does is make one blind. Except for Albert, the Western missionaries here have always favored the Nationalists because Chiang Kai-shek pretends to be a Christian. Tell me, which side do you favor?"

"There's really no comparison. From what I've seen, the Communists would treat everyone more fairly."

"Then why does General Marshall and President Truman support Chiang Kai-shek?" he shouted, pounding his fist into my bed. It was the first time I'd seen Mao lose his temper and I got the feeling he didn't have much time.

"Communism has a bad name in America," I said. "For one, you oppose religion and America was founded on it. Also, Chiang Kai-shek and his wife act and dress extremely westernized. He's definitely got you beat in the public relations department."

Mao shook his head in disgust. "The only man who can rule China is one who sees, hears and feels what the people of China sees, hears and feels. Chiang Kai-shek knows none of this."

"What will you do when the Nationalists attack Yenan?"

"Celebrate! Yenan is worthless except as a publicity tool which Chiang Kai-shek will use to extort more financial aid from the Americans. His army is already overextended and to hold onto Yenan will only worsen his situation. More importantly, our soldiers are volunteers while his are conscripts. You'll see, it may take us a few more years, but soon we'll wear Chiang Kai-shek down until he is left with nothing. The truth is that our soldiers are fighting for their freedom and his are fighting for their warlord masters."

"I believe in your cause and I can do much more than digging caves."

Mao was touched. "What can you do? Do you have a special talent?"

"Actually, I have a couple. I was a medic for two years with the American Army in Europe. I'm no Dr. Bethune, but I could save a lot of your soldiers' lives in the field."

"That would be most welcome. What is your other talent?"

"Well, unlike Dr. Bethune, I can't be killed."

Mao's feminine lips broke into an uneasy smile. I could see he was silently translating my words in his head to make sure he'd heard me correctly. As if embarrassed to ask the question aloud, he leaned forward and whispered, "Are you telling me you cannot die?"

"Yes."

Mao reeled back in his seat, slapped his hands on his meaty thighs and exploded with laughter. "That is so good to hear!" he said, wagging a finger at me as if I was telling a bad joke. "You know, with a thousand soldiers like yourself I could defeat Chiang Kai-shek in one day! Tell me, is this something you were born with or are you just lucky?"

"That all depends on your definition of luck."

Mao's smiled faded. "I know you are not crazy."

"No," I replied, exhaling deeply, "I can assure you I am not crazy."

"Then why would you make such a ridiculous statement?"

"Because legend has it that you would know if I was lying,"

Taken aback by my challenge, Mao stared deeply into my eyes seeking an answer that would explain why this American's behavior seemed to deviate between the charitable and the insane. Whatever he saw in my eyes bothered him. He looked away and stood up.

"I truly hope you can help us with your medical knowledge and whatever other talents you feel may be beneficial to our cause," he said somberly. "I also hope you tell your friends back in America the truth about the civil war in this country."

"I'll do whatever I can."

On February 22, 1947 1 re-entered the world of war.

The day before Mao sent a messenger into my cave to inform me that my medical services would be needed. His intuition told him that General Hu was going to attack Yenan sometime after March 15th. Plans were made to evacuate everyone to another rebel base about sixty miles north called the Tile Kiln Fortress. Radio Yenan was broadcasting Communist ideology to the outside world in twenty minute intervals and he didn't want to disconnect the transmitter until the last minute. That meant that a reconnaissance team had to be sent to Sian.

I created a portable first-aid kit by stuffing a backpack with a can of sulfanilamide powder, two pints of plasma, gauze, linen and morphine. Later that day, a P.L.A. soldier came by and presented me with a Japanese Arisaka 38 rifle, complete with a bayonet and five clips of bullets. I respectfully handed it back to him. My mission was to save Chinese lives, not take them.

I was attached to a group of nine P.L.A. soldiers who ranged in age from a sixteen-year-old boy to a white bearded father of three. They were all wearing the standard P.L.A. uniform of home-spun blue-gray padded suits, cloth caps and shoes made of tree bark fibers. We marched vigorously through the hills and woods, keeping away from, but never quite losing sight of, the main road. These guys were in phenomenal physical condition and I could barely keep up with them. I was shocked to discover we were covering nearly sixty miles a day. A typical day on the move consisted of twenty hours traveling and four sleeping while subsisting on precooked rice rolled in cloth accompanied by a vegetable reminiscent of a raw potato.

On the afternoon of the fifth day, we were marching single file through a hilly, wooded area as we approached the outskirts of Sian. I was last in line and had spent most of the journey focusing on the backpack of the man in front of me. Suddenly, our point man raised his arm and we dropped to the ground. As I lay there catching my breath, I heard the familiar growl of tanks revving their diesel engines somewhere on the valley floor below us.

I crawled over on my belly and squirmed in between two of the rebels busy taking notes as they crouched behind a short outcropping of rocks. I looked down to see at least fifty Sherman tanks neatly aligned on the grassy plain. Mao and his men had nothing remotely resembling that kind of firepower. In fact, the P.L.A had neither a single tank nor plane in their possession. My guess was that Chiang Kai-shek was trying to convince the world that the conquest of Yenan was going to be a tough battle.

I turned around and leaned against a rock to catch my breath. Mao was right. Chiang Kai-shek was going to milk the fall of Yenan for every American penny he could get. The world's newspapers would soon trumpet the Nationalist's stunning victory over the fall of the Communist capital and it would all be as staged as perfectly as a Hollywood production.

I was pondering the absurdity of it all when the soldiers on either side of me began to bear down against me with all of their weight. For the past five days I'd been constantly teased about bringing up the rear of the line and their jokes had begun to border on harassment. Not in the mood for that, I pushed them away. To my horror, they tumbled backwards, spurting blood across the sandy ground as machine-gun fire echoed in the distance. I looked around to see that every one of the P.L.A. soldiers, except for the sixteen-year-old, had been hit.

"Help me!" I screamed at the terrified teenager, stripping off my backpack. I paused when I realized the severity of the P.L.A, soldiers' wounds. From the looks of it, the men had been ripped apart by a fifty-caliber Browning and none of them were moving. There was nothing I could do.

"Let's grab their notes and get out of here!"

The boy leaped into action, scurrying from man to man and ripping every scrap of paper out of their tightly clenched fists. I turned to adjust my backpack and BAM! I was hit directly on my lower spine and hurled forward. My legs collapsed underneath me as I lifted my hands to brace my fall onto the sandy ground.

"Go, go!" I shouted, waving the boy off. He hit the ground like a terrified jackrabbit and sprinted into the hills with the observation notes gripped tightly in his hand. As I lay sprawled face down in the dirt, I felt my spinal cord vibrate wildly as it began to rejuvenate itself. I soon heard footsteps and looked up to see five fully armed Nationalists emerge from the woods. One of them shoved the still smoking barrel of an M-1 Garand into my face.

"Do you speak English?" a voice behind him demanded.

I rolled over and saw that the voice belonged to their commanding officer.

"Yes, I'm an American." I said.

"Then why are you with these men?"

"Because I'm a doctor."

He ripped my backpack off and dumped the contents onto the ground, breaking both of the plasma bottles in the process. "Way to go, pal," I said.

"You are a doctor helping the Communists?" he asked. "Do you fancy yourself to be another Dr. Bethune?"

One of the wounded P.L.A. soldiers moaned. I tried to crawl toward him, but I was still paralyzed from the waist down.

"If you will help me," I said to the officer, "I will treat this man's wound."

"Do not help him. Allow me to demonstrate the official method of rendering first-aid to Communist bandits." The officer knelt down and offered his canteen to the dying soldier who feebly parted his lips in anticipation of a soothing drink. Then he jerked the canteen away and replaced it with the barrel of his chrome plated Colt 45.

"Drink this," he said, pulling the trigger.

"You fucking animal," I said, turning away.

"What did you say to me?" he said, wheeling around to press the hot gun barrel into my cheek. I held my breath as I watched his finger tighten on the trigger. Suddenly, his body twitched, his eyes rolling back into his head as he slumped to the ground. His confused subordinates hovered around him and anxiously tried to lift their fallen leader. Those guys must have been as green as their tea because I knew immediately he'd been shot.

A second later, another soldier jerked and silently collapsed back onto the sandy earth. I strained my ears to hear the faint echo of a distant gunshot. It had to be the P.L.A. teenager who'd escaped. He'd probably seen his comrade executed and was taking his revenge from the hillside somewhere above us.

By now, the surviving Nationalists realized what was happening and crashed into one another in a wild Keystone Cops' panic as they attempted to flee the unseen sniper. Almost as an afterthought, one of them spun around and stuck the muzzle of his rifle against my forehead.

Then he pulled the trigger.

I never heard the gunshot and only saw a brief flash of light. That was it. No pain. No sound. Nothing, but instant darkness. The next thing I felt was a splitting headache that reminded me of the last time I'd viewed the Akashic Records.

I woke to find my face solidly coated with a mask of dried blood and dirt. I swept my hands blindly around the sandy ground until I touched my canteen and a roll of gauze. I drenched my face and wiped it clean to find the sun had set and the bodies of the two dead Nationalists were gone. I refilled my canteen from the others and stuffed my backpack with food from the dead rebels' backpacks. Then I pulled myself up and set off for Yenan.

My instincts were good and using dead reckoning I arrived before sunrise five days later. The first person I saw was Chou En-lai standing outside of his cave. When I waved, he dropped his cup of bean milk and ran back inside. Within seconds, the honeycomb of caves along the face of Green Ridge Mountain was buzzing with excitement. The noisy racket roused Mao from his cave wiping his eyes.

Jennifer, clad only in her nightgown, bolted out of her cave with Albert trotting behind as she ran barefoot down the hill in the sub-freezing temperature.

"The boy who returned yesterday said they shot you in the head," she cried, throwing her arms around my neck.

Yesterday? Damn, that kid must've been flying on adrenaline to get back here that fast. I couldn't have been unconscious for more than three or four hours and thought I'd made the trip to Yenan in record time.

Mao trudged down the hill to greet me.

"Congratulations. You are a very brave man and the party is in your debt for the precious information your mission has provided. I have declared today to be an official day of mourning for the eight comrades who died and I would like to speak with you in my quarters."

I escorted Jennifer back to her cave and then followed Mao into his dwelling, the entrance marked by a beautiful apple tree. His living quarters were like the others, albeit a bit more spacious. I sat down on a small wooden chair for the first time in ten days and marveled at the luxurious feeling of such a commonality.

Mao handed me a fresh cup of bean milk. I had never been a fan of the chalky brew, but after having nothing to drink but water for the past ten days, I found it delicious. He reached behind himself and dug into a burlap sack.

"Would you like some onions?" he said, dropping a couple of dirt encrusted bulbs into my lap. "I grow them myself. It's an American variety, and I thought you might like to have some. They make a wonderfully fragrant soup."

"Sure. Thanks," I said, dusting them off.

"You have a strange mark on your face," he said, pointing to a spot on his forehead.

I didn't answer. Right away I knew Mao didn't invite me into his cave to discuss my reconnaissance mission. It seemed he'd never forgotten something I'd said to him on Christmas Day.

"Forgive my curiosity," he persisted. "But what exactly is that mark on your forehead?"

"The same as this," I said, taking off my jacket to show him an identical circular pink bruise on my lower spine. Mao came around and studied the indentation on my back.

"My mother used to tell me stories about religious men who had powers such as this. I used to dismiss them as nothing more than peasant folklore. Tell me, how is this possible?"

Knowing Mao's negative position on religion, the last thing I wanted to do was tell him that my powers were the creation of a Buddhist monk.

"It's a gift I was born with. For some reason, my body has this ability to heal itself."

Mao shook his head as he pulled his chair up to me. "No, you are being untruthful, and you are insulting both of us with your shameful behavior." It seemed that Mao's uncanny ability to tell if someone was lying wasn't folklore after all. "There is no reason to be afraid, and if you insist, I will respect your silence. But, you must understand what an unfair advantage Chiang Kai-shek has over my people. We are becoming desperate and my army would benefit greatly if we were allowed to possess your fantastic powers."

"Mao, your army doesn't need my powers."

"And why is that?"

"Because you have something more powerful on your side. Destiny.

"Mao stared at me stone-faced for what seemed like an eternity before his eyes twinkled and he broke into his trademark smile.

"You have spoken the truth."

On March 19, 1947 Yenan fell to Chiang Kai-shek and his Nationalists. I heard the news the following morning on the radio outside of the China Inland Mission back in Sian. Even though Mao had explained to me that surrendering the city was part of his overall strategy, I couldn't help feel a sense of loss. It was painful to envision the Nationalist troops vandalizing and looting the caves where so few had sacrificed so much.

The first warning sign came on the morning of March 8th when the U.S. Army unexpectedly shuttled all of their liaison officers out of Yenan. They couldn't have cut it any closer because by mid-afternoon the bombers had arrived. I'd never seen a B-29 during the war and they dwarfed the B-17 Flying Fortresses I remembered in Europe. At the sound of a clanging bell, we frantically burrowed deep inside the tunnels as the B-29's bombs exploded above us, causing the roof to rain yellow dust upon our heads. It was as if a legion of giants were stomping across the hilltop. The sounds of the bomb blasts were interrupted by the staccato bursts of machine gun fire as P.L.A. troops stationed on the summit valiantly battled against their four-engine tormentors.

When the bombers left we climbed outside to check on their status and found nothing but empty craters.

The next day we bid an emotional farewell to Mao, Chou and the others as they departed north for the Tile Kiln Fortress. We had decided to wait in Yenan until the Nationalist forces arrived and return to Sian with them. Mao left the 1939 Chevrolet in our possession along with a promise that someday he'd return to retrieve it.

We watched them file out of the city on horseback, all of their worldly possessions slowly dragging behind them. As we waved and cheered, I could think of only one thing—that only true destiny would ever allow such a pitiful collection of men, women and horses to defeat an army as power-ful as Chiang Kai-shek's Sherman tanks and B-29 bombers.

By March 16th there was still no sign of the Nationalists and we had exhausted our food supply. We had no choice but to drive the Chevrolet back to Sian.

I ripped up a white sheet and attached it to the car's antenna as a surrender flag. For added insurance, Jennifer tied a small American flag to the front bumper. We encountered neither man nor machine until we reached the Nationalist checkpoint just outside of Sian. An army patrol stopped us and led us back through the city walls to be interrogated. On the drive down we rehearsed our story—the Communists were not interested in a Christian God or any other God. None of it mattered. All the Nationalists wanted was confirmation that Mao had left Yenan.

We were awakened the next morning by a parade of men and machines rumbling north to Yenan. Chiang Kai-shek soon made headlines around the world for his daring "capture" of the Communist capital. He may have had Mao on the run, but there was one thing even a rank amateur could see—Chiang Kai-shek and his Nationalist Army were now dangerously overextended.

As Mao had predicted, over much of China, the tide quickly turned in favor of the Communists. By September of 1947, Manchuria was practically controlled by the P.L.A. and riots were breaking out in Shanghai. In a desperate attempt to keep a stranglehold on world opinion, the Nationalists created a propaganda campaign about P.L.A. atrocities.

Unfortunately, I knew first-hand one of them to be true. The continued B-29 bombing of the Communists produced dreadful casualties that included thousands of women and children. The P.L.A. had almost no anti-aircraft guns and chose to fight back with messages they hoped would demoralize the Nationalist pilots. One of these messages arrived in Sian that summer strapped across the backs of two mules – the bodies of two mutilated Nationalist airmen who had the misfortune of bailing out over Communist-held territory. Their hands were cut off and their eyes gouged out. Unbelievably, they were still alive and never uttered a sound as I generously injected them with morphine. How foolish I was to believe that even those as good-natured as the Communists would not sink to the lowest level of human behavior when confronted with the brutality of war. Those horrors weighed heavily on my mind as Jennifer and I labored in the noodle shop one typically busy Sunday morning. Inflation in China was wildly out of control and people were walking in carrying bales of near worthless paper currency. Incredibly, no one complained and Wu's customers remained patient as they looked up at the chalkboard behind the counter and studied the daily shop in their monetary worth.

Tso-lin had proved to be an excellent teacher and my mastery of the Chinese language had become so proficient that Jennifer and I could now alternate our duties. I jumped at the chance to get out of the steamy kitchen, but by mid-morning I was cursing my luck. We had a line out the door before 8:00 a.m. and I found myself jotting down the orders of an endless stream of hungry Chinese without even once having the opportunity to look up and see who I was feeding.

Around noon, I handed my two hundredth order to Tso-lin and braced my pencil against the pad for the next customer's request. Instead of the usual rapid-fire request in Chinese, I was addressed in English by a youthful male voice.

"Wu Tso-lin makes some of the most delicious wheat noodles in all of Shensi Province, don't you think?"

I put my pencil down and looked up. Standing before me and grinning from ear to ear was none other than Chow Li. Except for the fact that he was barely five feet tall, he looked exactly as I'd envisioned him.

"Hello, Steven," he said, radiating happiness. "I am glad to see our paths through life have finally crossed."

"How do you know who I am?"

"I have seen your face and heard your voice many times in my visions."

By now, Chow Li had held up the burgeoning line of customers behind him for a moment too long and they were bickering. I shouted back to Jennifer that I was taking a break. She charged out of the kitchen to protest until she saw Chow Li standing beside me.

"Chow Li!" she exclaimed.

"Hello, my dear child," he said, embracing her. "You have blossomed into a beautiful woman. Your uncle must be very proud. Is he in Sian?"

"Yes, he's resting at the Wu's residence."

"Please tell him I am anxious to speak with him, but first I must talk to Steven."

We slipped past the line of hungry customers and exited the city through the South Gate. Chow Li was barefoot and dressed in a simple red Buddhist robe with the hood pulled back from his shaved head. While we walked in silence, I periodically glanced over to study the exposed skin of his hands, feet and face. It was youthful and unwrinkled, and there was nothing about his appearance to suggest he was more than thirty years old. We stopped to sit at the base of an ancient gingko tree.

"For over two thousand years I have sat under this majestic tree to seek wisdom and reflect upon the world around me, but today I did not come here to review my life, I have come to learn about yours."

Chow Li closed his eyes and nodded solemnly, listening as I described my life before and after I discovered the immortality formula. The only time he exhibited any reaction was when I mentioned Chang Sou's name. Then he'd pause briefly before resuming his rhythmic nodding. When I finished, he remained quiet for a while before he reopened his eyes.

"Destiny arrives in many forms. For you, it has come in the form of tiny gold-speckled pills. I am sorry that your hatred of death possesses you to want to live forever. Death is a release, not a condemnation. Someday you will know that, but for now you must do what your destiny desires."

"My destiny has brought me here," I said.

"That is correct. Approximately one thousand years ago, Chang Sou nearly escaped from his monastery. My visions tell me that Chang Sou may attempt another escape soon. If he succeeds, he will shed the blood of many innocents."

"He won't escape. Not if I can help it."

"Your optimism is inspiring," Chow Li said. "Unfortunately, even with your immortal powers, stopping him will be extremely dangerous."

"Can he be killed?"

"Yes, but my personal beliefs forbid me from considering that method."

"Mine don't."

Chow Li winced. "I know this about you. Perhaps that is the reason you are here. You have immortal powers, thus making you invulnerable to Chang Sou and you are not opposed to using them. In two thousand years he has not faced an opponent such as you, and for two thousand years I have successfully contained Chang Sou without resorting to violence or murder. It is my deepest desire to maintain those principles."

"Even if it means that Chang Sou could escape and shed the blood of many innocents?"

"I cannot take another human life. Even if it is to prevent the shedding of more blood."

"I'll never understand that," I said, shaking my head.

"One should never say never."

"Never," I insisted. "I've seen firsthand what happens when evil goes unchecked. I believe it is wrong for any man to stand by and allow innocent people to be slaughtered. When will Chang Sou awaken from his hibernation?"

"This I do not know. Some of my visions have been difficult to interpret, but your presence signifies that this day is fast approaching. It may be next month, or perhaps it could be ten or twenty years from now."

"Ten or twenty years?"

"Ten or twenty years is a short winter in the life of an immortal. You must stop thinking of time in relation to a mortal life span. The first hundred years will seem the longest. After that, the passage of time will become easier to accept. The one weakness you must resist is the temptation to fall in love with a mortal. The ending will never be in doubt and it would be an extremely selfish and painful act on your part."

His warning was a little late. I'd fallen deeply in love with Jennifer and sooner or later I was going to have to deal with it. There was a more pressing problem, though. I had only nine months' worth of the pills remaining in the last bottle of the immortality formula I'd taken with me to China.

"The rest of my formula is in America. Will you keep me supplied until Chang Sou awakens?"

"In return for assisting me with Chang Sou, I will gladly supply you. But I must warn you that, unlike the formula you consume, mine has a smell and taste that will be quite unappealing to your Western palate."

"It can't be any worse than a K-ration," I said, jokingly.

Chow Li stared at me blankly. "What is that?"

"Never mind, I've already told you much about my life. Can I ask you some questions about yours?"

"What would you like to know?"

"Did you really meet Jesus Christ?"

"Yes, and not far from this very spot. He told me he began his journey in Tyre and traveled by way of the Silk Road spreading his belief that love was the greatest of all universal powers. People followed him from village to village and, as word spread of his message of redemption, flocked to hear him speak. I was amazed that, regardless of their native tongue, everyone understood his words. What I found most remarkable was that even though he possessed these incredible powers, I have never met a man so humble. Unfortunately, he never stayed more than a few days in the same village because the local men in power would start to feel very threatened by his powers and popularity."

Chow Li smiled wistfully as he reflected on the ancient memory. "I was deeply saddened when I received word that the Romans had executed him. He was a great holy man who suffered terribly for his beliefs."

I found his story about Christ incredible and I must've been staring at him like he was the star attraction in a freak show because when his eyes met mine something unnerved him.

"No more questions," Chow Li said, abruptly rising to his feet. "I understand your curiosity, but you must control these and other desires you inherited from your mortal past. From now on there will be no communication between us until Chang Sou awakens. You must get on with your life and learn that patience will soon become your most treasured virtue."

True to his word, Chow Li did his best to avoid me. The only time I saw him was when I'd run into him during his weekly sojourns to buy provisions in Sian's busy marketplace. He would acknowledge these awkward meetings with a respectful bob of his shaved head and then disappear into the crowd. Strangely, he never visited Albert. After our meeting he headed straight for his temple in the mountains. When I mentioned this to Albert, he dismissed the snub as nothing out of the ordinary.

"For Chow Li, a day goes by in minutes, a month is measured in hours, and a year passes in less than a week. Even though Chow Li's been back for nine months, in his immortal mind that's the equivalent of a couple of days."

I told Albert that Chow Li agreed to supply me with his immortality formula, saving me a trip back to the states, provided I help him control Chang Sou.

Albert was skeptical. "What sort of help does he have in mind?"

"I'm not sure. Chow Li has had visions about Chang Sou escaping from the monastery. Apparently, he once came very close to succeeding."

"By about thirty feet," Albert said. "Almost a thousand years ago, a fungus nearly destroyed the forest that imprisons him. The world would be a very different place today had Chang Sou and his followers escaped."

"Chow Li said that if Chang Sou escapes he would shed the blood of many innocents."

"I have no doubt that he would. Chang Sou is an incredibly selfish creature with no regard for human life. He looks upon raping and killing human beings as sport and desires the riches of the world by whatever means possible. I've seen enough evil in this world to realize that evil is selfishness to the point of destruction. And believe me, you will never meet anyone as selfishly destructive as Chang Sou."

By April of 1948, 1 was down to my last handful of pills and I hadn't seen Chow Li in over two months. If he didn't show his face soon I'd have no choice but to risk another trip through the sacred forest to see him.

Jennifer hurried back from her lunch break to tell me she'd seen Chow Li wandering through the market square. I raced out of the noodle shop and found him haggling over a bushel of cabbage. When I told him about my dire predicament, he invited me to return with him to his temple and suggested I bring Albert.

After procuring a burlap sack of vegetables, Chow Li accompanied me to the Wu's house where he was reunited with Albert for the first time since 1938. Chow Li was ecstatic to see his old friend, but Albert acted very odd. He appeared distracted and his reaction to Chow Li's invitation was blasé at best.

Albert's only reply was, "That's fine, but I believe it best if we don't take Jennifer."

As we filled our canteens, I asked Albert if anything was wrong, but he acted as if he hadn't heard me.

Along the way Chow Li regaled me with interesting anecdotes about Chinese history. He had witnessed most of China's great historical moments, from the glory days of the Han Dynasty to the fall of the Manchus, and I was spellbound by his vivid eyewitness accounts. I couldn't get him to say another word about Christ, but he did reveal that he'd met Mohammed in 612 on a spice caravan out of Yathrib.

Meanwhile, Albert remained tight-lipped and sullen. He answered most of Chow Li's questions with nothing more than a half-hearted shrug. Chow Li simply ignored his behavior and addressed his questions to me. I found Albert's attitude increasingly irksome and more than a little rude. After he ignored Chow Li for the umpteenth time, I confronted him on the shoulder of the dirt road leading out of Sian.

"If you knew you were going to act like this, why did you bother to come along?"

"Believe me, I don't want to be here. I came along because I felt it was my duty to do so."

"Your duty to do so? What's that supposed to mean?"

"Steven, I think you'd better sit down."

My throat tightened. The last time I heard those words they came from my father's mouth.

"Whatever it is, just say it."

Albert took a long ragged breath. "This morning the mission received a letter from the International Red Cross. I deeply regret to inform you that your mother has passed away. She died in her sleep."

The next thing I knew I was lying on the ground curled in grief, my tears melting into the yellow, sandy earth as I mourned the loss of my beautiful, vivacious mother, dead at the age of only forty-five. Albert told me she'd died of a heart attack in her sleep, but I knew better. When my father put that bullet in his brain, he killed two people. To make matters worse, there was no service or funeral for me to attend. No way to say good-bye. It had taken the news over a month to reach Sian. After an agonizing minute the formula warmed my emotions and I was able to pull myself together and continue the journey. Chow Li and Albert respected my unspoken desire to walk behind them alone and they limited the scope of their conversation to each another.

We reached the stone Buddha and scaled the embankment into the sacred forest. Just as we passed the ancient cypress tree, the ground rumbled beneath our feet. It felt like the beginning of an earthquake.

Albert glanced around in fear. "What in God's name was that?"

"Chang Sou is voicing his displeasure." Chow Li said. "His subconscious mind can see us. But he will be able to neither see nor hear us once we are within the protective confines of my temple."

"Can he harm us?" I asked.

"No, but he will do his best to frighten you. I would compare his powers at this moment to those of a vicious tiger trapped in a cage."

Once again, the ground rumbled. Chow Li cupped his mouth and shouted something in a language that sounded Chinese.

"What did you say?" I asked. "Were you speaking Chinese?"

"I told Chang Sou to leave us alone and go back to sleep. The Chinese dialect I spoke hasn't been used in centuries, but it is one he respects."

The forest became silent around us and we were soon encircled by massive tree trunks, rising out of the ground like giant shadows in the fading fight.

"Which of these trees is shedding the material that neutralizes Chang Sou's immortality formula?" I asked.

"They all are. They're a hybrid of pine and cypress I developed through a process called botanical alchemy."

I turned to say something to Albert and realized he was no longer beside me. He was standing about twenty feet back, staring transfixed up at the black canopy of treetops. Following his line of vision, I was stunned to catch a split second flash of the face of Chang Sou just below the tree canopy before it disappeared. Chang Sou appeared exactly as I had seen him in my vision, right down to his ice-water blue eyes and thick blond hair draping his prominent cheek-bones.

"Do not be alarmed," Chow Li said. "It is an illusion. He cannot harm you."

Chow Li's words of reassurance snapped Albert out of his trance.

"Is that what you saw in the forest that day with me and Jennifer?" I asked.

"Yes."

"So, why didn't you simply tell us?"

"It wasn't his image that frightened me. It was his words I heard resonate in my head."

"What words?" I asked.

"I'd rather not say."

"Albert, there's no time for this. What did Chang Sou say to you?"

"Chang Sou said that because you had desecrated his monastic grounds he would visit your mother in her dreams and frighten her until she died. I prayed for your mother every night." Just the thought of Chang Sou torturing my mother to death in her sleep filled me with a rage I'd never experienced. I wanted to run as fast as I could through the forest, smash down the gate to his monastery, pull him from his hibernation and tear him to pieces with my bare hands. Chow Li sensed my thoughts and placed himself in my path.

"I can feel your thoughts. Please do not act upon your emotions. Never allow your heart to rule your mind. Chang Sou is hungry and feeds off hate. Do not play into his hands. It will only empower him."

I reluctantly agreed to do so and we continued our journey until the forest receded and we stepped onto a sun-splashed carpet of green grass. Chow Li drew an iron key from the folds of his robe and unlocked the door to his tiny temple. We stooped down and entered a cramped, dimly lit room beautifully engraved with intricate ancient Chinese designs of fish, horses, flowers and other wildlife. In one corner sat a small wooden altar adorned with six beeswax candles. Hanging next to the altar was a bronze bell with a mallet and an incense burner. The sweet pungent odor of stale incense swirled around us, but did little to mask the nauseating stench of decomposing fish. The oval-shaped roof was pierced with hundreds of tiny holes configured into various constellations. Even though the afternoon sun blazed outside, the ceiling of the temple twinkled like a starry evening sky in the dome of a planetarium.

Chow Li retrieved a small rectangular box intricately crafted out of jade. As he lifted the cover, an overpowering sniff of something resembling fermenting fish juices nearly made me retch. I quickly covered my nose as Albert buried his face in his shirtsleeve.

"You weren't kidding about the smell," I gasped. "That's worse than a corpse."

Chow Li closed the box and slid open a couple of small air vents along the floor.

"Sorry," he said, as a breeze of fresh mountain air filled the room. "Over the years, I've become quite accustomed to the odor and it no longer affects me. I'll burn some sandalwood which should sufficiently disguise it."

Chow Li lit an incense stick and waved it around the room. I gingerly pulled my hand away from my nose to find the incense was extremely effective. I could only smell a trace of the sea. Chow Li reopened the jade box and extracted a doughy gold-flecked gray ball about the size of a small marble, which he gently placed in the palm of my hand.

"Drink this," he said, handing me a small wooden bowl filled with crimson liquid.

"What is this or do I really want to know?"

"Pomegranate juice."

I took a sip and was pleasantly surprised by its sweet, tangy taste. I then popped the doughy metallic ball into my mouth. It instantly melted and trickled down my esophagus leaving a disgusting aftertaste I could best describe as the putrid entrails of a fish that had been decomposing on a beach.

"That is, without exception, the most disgusting thing I've ever tasted." I groaned, chasing it down with the rest of the pomegranate juice as I fought an urge to retch.

"I can promise it would've been far less palatable without the pomegranate juice. Fortunately, the fruit is native to this region and always in plentiful supply."

Chow Li placed a rack of thirty of the balls in front of me. "I would like you to join me in an oath that will confirm your intentions with this formula. I must ask Albert to wait outside until the ceremony is complete." Albert wordlessly complied and exited into the sunlight as Chow Li struck the bell on his altar three times.

"I am going to ask you five questions. All I request is that you answer them honestly. Will you do this?"

"Yes," I said.

"Good. Let us begin. Is your word your sacred and eternal bond?"

"Yes."

"Do you swear to the powers of the universe that you will use this substance to enlighten mankind?"

"Yes."

"Do you swear to the powers of the universe that you will never use this substance for material gain?"

"Yes."

"Do you swear to the powers of the universe that you will never use this substance to intentionally cause pain or suffering to another human being?"

"Yes."

"Do you swear to the powers of the universe that you will never take a human life, even in self-defense?"

I hesitated and Chow Li repeated the question. Again, I hesitated.

"No. I cannot promise this."

Chow Li opened his eyes. There was no mistaking his disappointment.

"The oath was contained in the first four questions. I added the last one to see how far you had evolved in your own enlightenment."

"I'm sorry if I didn't pass your test, but I have no desire to be a saint or a monk," I said, looking up at the pin-points of light dotting the ceiling of his temple and recognizing the constellation of Taurus the bull. The right eye of the bull appeared to be filled with a red precious stone illuminated by the sunlight behind it. "Is that a ruby?" I asked, pointing to the glowing stone.

"Yes, that is a ruby," Chow Li answered. "It represents the star Aldebaran."

"What's so significant about Aldebaran?"

"For us on Earth there is no star more special in the entire universe than Aldebaran. All human life on Earth originated there."

I stared at Chow Li, lost for words. I knew he wasn't lying simply because there wasn't any reason for him to lie. And I wasn't about to argue with a two thousand year old man. "Are you telling me all mankind on this planet originally came from Aldebaran?"

"Hundreds of thousands of years ago our ancestors arrived here from Aldebaran to colonize this planet. They knew it would be hospitable for life because they encountered primates when they landed. Unfortunately, these colonists were susceptible to many of the same human foibles we have today including greed, lust and pride. They were much more evolved than we are now, but far from perfect. They eventually abused their powers and destroyed not only their colonies, but the land masses they inhabited. The legends of Atlantis and Lemuria are based upon the original colonies of the Aldebaranians. The survivors of those catastrophes were mostly children who retained little knowledge. They bred like locusts. Very ignorant locusts compared to their ancestors, but they built the great civilizations we know today that started after the great flood including Sumer and Egypt."

"Do these Aldebaranians ever return?"

"They monitor us, but consider us too primitive to physically interact. They are an extremely loving and highly evolved species of human beings and will establish contact with us only when they deem it appropriate. Sadly, the last time they sent a messenger here to spread the universal truths it ended terribly."

"Who was this messenger?"

"He is commonly known today as Jesus Christ," Chow Li said.

"Are you saying Christ was some kind of missionary from a more advanced civilization in another solar system?"

"That may be one way of interpreting him."

"I know more than a few people who will have a problem with that information."

"I agree, but it has never made any sense to me," said Chow Li. "The truth about Christ's origin takes nothing away from the truth about his message of love and salvation."

"Does Albert know this?"

"Yes."

Now I understood why Albert had been kicked out of the China Inland Mission.

"Is anyone in contact with Aldebaran today?" I asked.

Chow Li hesitated. "There was an organization in Germany fifty years ago that established contact through telepathy during séances. They gained the trust of some Aldebaranians, but they misused the information that was given to them to better this world and a terrible catastrophe ensued. I believe you know about this."

"You are referring to the Thule Society in Munich, Germany that brought Adolph Hitler to power."

Chow Li smiled. "I can see that Albert has educated you about many things."

"Yes, he has. Albert said he fears that the entrance to the underground world of the Vril-ya lies beneath Chang Sou's monastery."

It was the wrong thing to say. Chow Li's smile quickly faded. "The Vril-ya are no more. Not for many thousands of years. Today, they are us and we are them. Please never ask me about the Vril-ya again. You may now invite Albert back inside."

I pushed open the door while I shielded my face from the sudden blast of sunlight.

"Albert!" I shouted.

I didn't get a reply so I shouted his name even louder. Again, there was no response. Chow Li and I climbed out of the temple and surveyed the area. Albert was nowhere to be seen.

"Well, this isn't good," I said, squinting through the brightness.

Chow Li closed his eyes and pointed towards the monastery's pine tree camouflaged gates. "You will find him over there," he said.

We discovered Albert lying face up and unconscious in the tall grass a few feet in front of the monastery's gates with a dark shadow of urine staining his pants. Chow Li plucked a blade of grass and chewed it while he cupped his hands around Albert's mouth. Then he exhaled powerfully, fully inflating the old man's chest until I thought it would burst.

Chow Li pulled away and Albert sputtered back to life, hacking up a fist-sized wad of bloody yellow phlegm.

"He should be fine now."

"Where did you learn to do that?"

"In Lhasa, at the medical school atop Chakpori Hill."

We helped Albert to his feet and walked him back to the temple. Chow Li gave him one of his Buddhist robes to replace his soiled clothing.

"What happened?" I asked, helping him slip on the robe.

"When I stepped out of the temple, I saw a life-sized image of Chang Sou standing in front of the monastery gates, Albert replied in a croaking voice. "He was dressed in some sort of ancient military uniform. His long blond hair was pulled tightly into a knot and his torso was covered in rows of small metallic plates. Chang Sou began taunting me with vile, sacrilegious obscenities and challenged me to a fight. After what Chow Li told me in the forest, I felt no fear and walked over to confront him. I told Chang Sou that I wasn't one of his local superstitious peasants and that I wouldn't be frightened by an illusion, especially one that looked like it belonged in the London Museum. Well, this illusion viciously backhanded me across the face, knocking me out cold."

"Has something like this ever happened before?" I asked Chow Li.

"Not in a very long time." he said. "Chang Sou is getting stronger and utilizing magic that has not been practiced in thousands of years."

"Is there anything you can do to weaken him?"

"Yes. There is something I can do and it must be done now," he answered, pulling his bronze incense burner off the wall and handing it to me along with some incense sticks and a Zippo lighter with a black crackle finish.

"A Zippo lighter?" I mused. "For some reason, I never imagined this to be one of the meager possessions of a traditional Buddhist monk."

"I consider it to be a religious tool for my altar. It was given to me by a very brave American pilot."

I flipped the lighter over and read the inscription etched on the other side. *For my dear*

friend, Chow Li. A man who taught me how to live and die. A. E. C. 11/18/43.

"Who was A.E.C.?"

"He was an American fighter pilot and a very good man. One of countless soldiers I have met through the ages who realized the folly of war before it claimed his life."

Chow Li handed Albert and me two long polished cylinders of wood about a foot long.

"These are made from the trees in the forest and burn brightly without releasing any smoke. We will light them when we are inside the monastery."

Albert was mortified. "We're going inside the monastery?"

CHAPTER

We climbed out of Chow Li's temple and followed him to the row of pine trees camouflaging the black hammered metal doors of Chang Sou's mountain monastery. He knelt down to the base of the center tree, carefully loosened the dirt around it and pulled the tree forward just enough so we could slip behind it.

"Why don't we just break the roots?" I asked.

"Because these trees are not as they appear. They are Chang Sou's creation and if one of their fragile roots were to break, a wonderful aroma akin to over-ripe bananas would fill the air. When their scent reached your lungs, they would freeze with paralysis and you would die horribly, gasping for breath like a fish pulled from the sea. Because of the immortality formula, you and I would survive, but Albert would not."

Chow Li inserted his temple key into a small slot in the right monastery door. He turned the key counter-clockwise and two giant bolts slowly retracted into the top and bottom of the door. Slipping his nimble fingers into the center crevice, Chow Li slid the right door partially into the mountain wall just enough to for a body to fit through.

"Get in now!" he commanded, quivering from the strain of holding the door open.

Albert and I ducked under his arm and squeezed inside. Once he saw we were safe, Chow Li jackknifed his body through the opening just as the heavy metal door slammed behind him and the bolts shot back into the stone with an echoing bang.

We now found ourselves standing in absolute darkness and the first thing I noticed was the smell. It was an unnerving odor that reeked of the ancients, much like the musty catacombs I'd explored in Italy. Before my imagination could get the better of me, I flipped open the Zippo and touched the flame to the ends of the two wooden cylinders. They didn't burn, but glowed brightly emitting very little heat with no smoke. Their intense illumination revealed the walls around us. They were carved with numerous sado-masochistic vignettes depicting scenes of Chang Sou and his monks engaging in a variety of sexual acts involving every combination of man, woman and child.

Chow Li trembled with anger as he examined the grotesque carvings. "How dare he desecrate this sacred ground!" he shouted, charging ahead of us into the darkness of a narrow corridor. Albert and I rushed after Chow Li and found him standing before a wooden door riddled with more carvings of sacrificial scenes.

"This is the room where I interrupted Chang Sou's ceremony," Albert whispered to me.

Chow Li turned a stone handle and opened the door. The room was barren with the exception of a stone altar in the center shaped like a giant cross, metal chains dangling from the arms and bottom. Chow Li lifted the chains and inspected the ankle and wrist clasps welded to the ends.

"Chang Sou has been wallowing in the very excrement of human behavior. Please bring the light closer to me. There is something on the floor."

I moved my torch to where Chow Li was delicately probing something with his sandaled foot. It was a polished human skull. Chow Li pulled the bronze incense burner from around his neck and lit one of the aromatic sticks inside.

"Gently swing this back and forth and stay close behind me," he said, handing over the chain attached to the burner.

I followed Chow Li around the room swinging the billowing burner side to side as he wandered in a slow figure-eight pattern, chanting in a low monotone. The ceremony lasted a few minutes before he was satisfied that the room had been cleansed. Finally, he knelt down and chanted.

"Do you understand anything he's saying?" I asked Albert.

"Yes. Something about hoping that the poor souls who suffered in this horrible place will find everlasting peace."

When he finished, Chow Li could barely rise to his feet. His normally cherubic face was gaunt with exhaustion and he appeared to have aged.

"Where is Chang Sou?" I asked.

"That is the answer I am seeking," he whispered, gliding his hands across the walls. After probing every crack and carving with his tiny fingers, he sank to the ground. "I'm sorry, but I don't know where to go from here."

"Albert, does this room appear the way you remember it?" I asked.

"I don't recall the altar being in the center."

We leaned our collective weight against the massive block of stone and pushed until it gradually gave way, revealing a staircase spiraling down into the darkness. Chow Li led the way and we descended; our torches scraped against the low stone ceiling showering us with bursts of smokeless sparks. Approximately fifty feet down we came upon an inverted swastika chiseled into the wall surrounded by a fanged winged dragon on either side. Next to it was a narrow passageway that led into a small chamber.

The moment we entered the room it felt as if we'd fallen through the ice of a frozen lake.

Our breaths transformed into white puffs of condensation. In the center of the room was some sort of torture device that resembled a medieval rack. On the rock above it were the symbols for *Level 1* chiseled in Chinese.

"Level 1 of what?" I asked, my teeth chattering.

Chow Li ignored my question and performed the same ceremony we had upstairs. When he finished, Chow Li stormed out of the room and dashed back toward the staircase as we rushed to keep up with him.

"Do you know what this is all about?" I asked Albert.

"I believe I do, and I pray that I'm wrong."

Another fifty feet down, we came upon another inverted swastika surrounded by dragons marking the entrance to another narrow passageway. Again, we followed Chow Li into another freezing room equipped with an instrument of execution that I instantly recognized as the medieval device called the Iron Maiden. I noticed the spikes inside this one had been shortened to a length that would cause a wound of only about a half-inch deep—more than enough to disfigure a victim, but not enough to cause instant death. Chiseled in the wall above it were the Chinese symbols for *Level 2.*

Chow Li feverishly performed another ritual before we hurried down the stairs where we found another torture device and he performed another ceremony on Level 3.

"How many of these are we going to find?" I asked Albert as we descended to Level 4.

"If my hunch is correct, we should find a grand total of eighteen."

Albert was correct in his prediction. We discovered a total of eighteen levels as we descended approximately nine hundred feet into the bowels of the mountain. We encountered eighteen chiseled inverted swastikas encircled with dragons and eighteen rooms each equipped with an exotic array of torture devices. Among them we found a Chinese water machine, a bed of nails with stone weights on each side, giant clay tubs of oil with charred firewood beneath, a collection of razor sharp hooks and pulleys, a selection of branding irons and a bed of sand which looked innocuous until Albert touched it with the butt of the torch and a multitude of tiny scorpions simultaneously arched their poisonous tails in the air. The temperature in the first eight rooms was freezing until we reached Level 9. Then the temperature began rising quickly and by the time we reached Levels 15 and 16 it felt like we had stepped inside an oven. Oddly enough, the temperature in Levels 17 and 18 were quite moderate. Level 17 contained a large bladed ax that swung from the ceiling like a pendulum, dropping a notch closer every time it passed over the victim. Level 18 had dozens of swords imbedded in the floor, walls and ceiling. Together they created a small maze of tight passageways that Chow Li said was called the *Forest of Razors.*

Chow Li performed a cleansing ceremony in each of the eighteen chambers as I dutifully trailed behind him swinging the incense and trailing smoke with every step. Upon reaching the eighteenth level, the staircase ended. On the far side of the torture room containing the Forest of Razors we discovered the opening to a large tunnel.

"We have descended into hell," Chow Li announced. "Chang Sou has created a working replica of the eighteen levels of Buddhist hell: eight of ice, eight of fire, and two of steel. This monastery was once my home and a beautiful, sacred place. Chang Sou has turned it into a dungeon of evil."

Chow Li charged into the tunnel with all the fire and brimstone intensity of a Southern Baptist tent revivalist while Albert and I did our best to keep up with his robed silhouette, barely visible up ahead in the chilly darkness. About a hundred feet into the tunnel, he stopped.

"Steven, please hand me your torch."

I passed the light over to him and we stepped into a magnificent cavern of fossilized white crystal. The room was huge, about the length, width and height of a gymnasium. Chow Li reached up and touched the end of his torch to the unlit portion of another mounted on the cavern wall. The stick silently exploded with light the instant his glowing cylinder rubbed against it. He continued walking the length of the room stopping to ignite a series of torches until the room was ablaze with a wall of cold light. It revealed a small stream bubbling across the center of the cavern. Chow Li instructed us to wait there while he crossed a wooden bridge over the stream and continued lighting torches on the other side.

Ivory white stalactites and stalagmites rose out of the ground and hung from the ceiling on all sides, transforming the chamber into a prehistoric winter wonderland. On our side of the cavern there were five large bamboo bins and a massive rectangular wooden table surrounded by thirteen chairs. Albert's curiosity got the better of him and he lifted the top on one of the bins.

"Oh, my God!" he choked, dropping the top with a resounding thud.

"What's in there?" I asked, running over to him.

"Don't look." He shuddered, bending over to retch.

I lifted the heavy wooden flap and recoiled from the stench, horrified by the sight of dozens of severed human heads bobbing in brine, all neatly shaven and well preserved in the salty bath. "My God," I said in disgust, forcing the lid down with all my weight. "What kind of people are these?"

"The most abysmal," Albert gasped. "Cannibals."

"Steven, hurry with the incense!" Chow Li shouted from the other side of the cavern.

As we trotted across the wooden bridge, I looked down. The clear running stream was teeming with blind albino carp. Some of these eyeless creatures were huge–probably fifty to sixty pounds each. Chow Li stood transfixed before a honeycomb-type structure that contained thirteen separate hexagonal chambers and rose nearly twenty feet above the stone cavern floor. It was three layers high of four chambers across with a very large chamber mounted in the center of the top. Each chamber was sealed with an orange, waxy plug pierced with tiny air holes. I peered into one and saw the unmistakable outline of an unconscious human being.

We had found Chang Sou and his monks.

The numerical coincidence of Chang and his twelve monks, and Christ and his twelve disciples did not escape me. We were startled by a shuffling noise as an attractive, middle-aged woman with auburn hair and green eyes stepped out from behind the honeycomb.

"My dear Albert, have you missed me?"

Albert gripped the side of the giant honeycomb to steady himself. "Anne, it can't be you! You've been dead for over fifteen years!"

It was Albert's sister-in-law– which also meant she was Jennifer's mother.

"Anne, please forgive me!" Albert cried, rushing forward.

"Stay back!" Chow Li shouted. "She is nothing more than an illusion conjured by Chang Sou to torture your soul!"

Illusion or not, I had to admit that Jennifer's mother looked awfully real and bore an uncanny resemblance to her beautiful daughter. Albert was sobbing so hard he looked as if he was about to collapse. Chow Li calmly lit another incense stick and dropped it into the burner. I was softly blowing into the container when I heard the voice of another woman coming from behind the massive honeycomb.

"Steven, I am so cold. Why would you abandon me?"

I glanced up to see my mother. She looked so real that I instinctively rose to comfort her. Fortunately, the sound of Chow Li's shrill voice slapped me back to reality.

"Steven, get away from it!"

It.

I swung the smoking burner wildly around me, releasing a thick plume of white that temporarily obscured the apparition. Chow Li began chanting furiously as Albert tearfully embraced the image of his sister-in-law and begged forgiveness. Through the haze I could see my mother slowly shuffling toward me with her arms outstretched.

"Chow Li!" I shouted, forcing myself to look away. "I can't take much more of this!"

Chow Li began chanting even faster and gradually the illusion of Albert's sister slowly faded and his deformed arms clutched nothing but air. He collapsed to the ground wailing in grief as my mother's tear streaked face receded into oblivion.

"I should climb up there and rip his heart out!" I screamed.

Chow Li blocked my path. "That would not be wise. Chang Sou is an immortal who possesses the strength of ten men. The best thing we can do now is to depart from this garden of evil. In time, we will confront him."

A deep rumble began to boil beneath our feet and the ground convulsed violently, shaking the stalactites and stalagmites loose from their foundations and crashing them to the ground. Razor sharp shards of crystal shot in every direction with shrapnel-like velocity. As Albert and I hunkered down, Chow Li stood his ground, ignoring the exploding maelstrom around him and continued chanting until everything suddenly became still.

"Run as fast as you can!" Chow Li commanded.

Albert and I bolted across the bridge and into the tunnel. Unfortunately, Albert slipped in the darkness and wrenched his back and

I was forced to help him up the nine hundred foot staircase while Chow Li pushed against us and nervously reminded us to hurry.

We threw ourselves on the floor of his temple just as the ground began to rumble again.

"Neither one of you can ever return here," Chow Li gasped, pouring us a round of pomegranate juice. "No matter how long it takes, you must wait in Sian until I can bring Chang Sou to you. He is much too powerful here."

"Have you calculated a more specific time when that might happen?" I asked, dreading the thought of being condemned for an eternity as a noodle shop clerk.

"Chang Sou tends to hibernate during periods of extended warfare. He formulates the length of his hibernation based upon his prophetic visions, but his ignorance of the outside world has increased over the years and he has a tendency to misinterpret his visions. I believe he has combined the last World War into one extended conflict with the present Chinese civil war. Therefore, I believe he will reappear soon after the current civil war has ended. After he awakens he will most likely appear in Sian during a day of religious significance. Historically it has been Buddhist dates, but during the last hundred years he has displayed a peculiar penchant for appearing during Christian holidays."

"Why?"

"Chang Sou has prophesied that when he comes to power all religious dates of all faiths will be renamed in his honor."

On October 1st 1949, the Chinese civil war ended and the People's Republic of China was proclaimed. While everyone was busy celebrating the birth of the new country, a select few of us were keeping an eye on her ancient past. That December 24th the only way I knew that it was Christmas Eve was by the date circled on my calendar. The Communists had made it clear that they wanted nothing to do with this or any other religious holiday and now that they'd won the war their wish was the law of the land. But, in the Wu household Christmas Eve was sacred and we all exchanged gifts. I gave Jennifer a jade necklace dating from the Han Dynasty and she handed me a multicolored wool sweater Ching-ling had taught her to knit.

I presented Albert with a sterling silver ashtray and he gave me a box of imported *Partagás* Cuban cigars, which I had little doubt he'd completely smoke in no time. The Wu's obliged all of us with homemade cookies and Jennifer's favorite—moon cakes. Even though it was heartwarming to see everyone in such a festive mood, I was overwhelmed with sadness every time I gazed out at the dark outline of the distant mountains.

Jennifer sensed my mood and tenderly wrapped her arms around my waist.

"What's wrong, sweetheart?" she asked, nuzzling my neck.

"I can't stop thinking about Chow Li and how lonely he must be up there in those godforsaken mountains. I wish there was something we could do for him."

"There is! It's only seven o'clock and even though it's Christmas Eve, to most of the Chinese, it's just another Saturday night. I'll bet you anything Chow Li shows up like clockwork tomorrow to shop in the market place. Let's buy him something special tonight and surprise him when he arrives."

Jennifer and I strolled down to the market square and began stocking up on items that Chow Li wouldn't have purchased for himself if he lived for a million years. We bought a pair of leather mittens and a beaver fur cap. As practical as they were, I wondered if Chow Li would accept these gifts or if he would reject them in deference to his austere beliefs. Regardless, Jennifer and I were soon caught up in a frenzy of buying anything we thought would put a smile on his stoic cherubic face and soon found ourselves laughing at each other across a pile of assorted gifts. Besides the aforementioned mittens and cap, we would be presenting our two thousand-year-old friend with three woolen sweaters, an overcoat, an eel skin wallet, a fingernail clipper, a raincoat, four pairs of cotton socks and an over-stuffed pillow. I was handing the lighter items to Jennifer when I glanced over her shoulder and caught a glimpse of two robed figures, one short and one monstrous, quietly approaching through the darkness. My blood chilled as they stepped out of the shadows and the glowing street-lights revealed their identities.

On Christmas Eve of 1949, Chow Li presented me with Chang Sou.

"Jennifer," I whispered, as she was busily inspecting the eel skin wallet. "Don't turn around. Chang Sou is standing about thirty feet behind you. I don't want him to see your face."

The first thing that struck me about him was his size. He was enormous and had to be close to seven feet tall. He probably weighed well over three hundred pounds. Even through his loose fitting Buddhist robe, it was obvious that he was incredibly muscular with very broad shoulders and ramrod straight posture–almost militaristic. In those first few seconds only one thought came to mind: this was not a man from this time and place. I stood my ground as Chang Sou took a step in my direction and paused. His long blond hair, ice-water blue eyes and sunken, hollow cheekbones created an unmistakable Nordic appearance. He reminded me of a primitive, but much larger version of the SS officer who'd descended the guard tower the day we liberated Dachau. Was he the missing link that Himmler's German Ancestral Heritage Organization expeditions to Tibet in the 1930s were seeking? As I pondered the thought, Chang Sou spoke.

"Steven Ronson," he bellowed in a deep hollow voice. "Would you consider this historic moment to be an honor, coincidence or destiny?"

"None of the above," I said. "After touring that chamber of horrors you call a monastery, I can assure you that it is not an honor and this is no coincidence. Furthermore, I would hate to think that life could be so cruel as to deem you my destiny."

Taken aback by my reply, Chang Sou bent down to ask something of Chow Li.

"Please do not be so impolite," Chow Li admonished me in a nervous voice. "Chang Sou only wishes to be your friend."

My friend? The monster who murdered my mother in her sleep? I would choose the right time and place for my revenge. Forcing a smile, I walked towards Chang Sou, my hand outstretched. The giant quickly shifted his body sideways into a defensive stance.

"Why are you approaching me in this manner?" he shouted.

"Chow Li said you wanted to be my friend. In my culture, the proper form of peaceful introduction is to shake with empty hands free of weapons."

He mechanically reached out to me with a giant hand nearly the size of a catcher's mitt. It completely enveloped mine. I could sense an incredible amount of power surging through his body. It was like grabbing an open fire hydrant and feeling the vibration as the water blasted through. Chang Sou reached within his robe and produced a jade handled knife. I jerked my hand from his grip and stepped back.

"Why are you alarmed?" He smiled, revealing teeth that appeared to be sharpened. "If you are truly an immortal you should have nothing to fear."

"I haven't been an immortal for that long. Old reflexes are hard to break."

"All I want to do is cut your flesh and prove that you are an immortal. Are you afraid?"

That was the last thing I wanted him to believe.

"Sure, be my guest," I said, stretching out my arm to offer the upraised palm of my hand.

With lightning speed, Chang Sou lashed past my hand and sliced through the bridge of my nose, clean through the cartilage. I clutched my face as blood spurted between my fingers.

"You son-of-a-bitch!" I screamed, kicking him in the groin with all of my strength. My foot bounced off him as if he was made of stone. Chang Sou didn't flinch. Instead, he calmly tore a piece of cloth from the bottom of his robe and offered it to me.

"Clean your face."

I snatched the fabric and wiped the blood from my face as a familiar tingling sensation surged across the wound. Chang Sou watched the immortality formula perform its magic with clinical detachment. He would have made an excellent Nazi.

"I know that Chow Li has taken an oath forbidding him to reveal the immortality formula to anyone. How did you gain possession of it?"

Chang Sou stood expressionless while I explained how the pills had been taken from his monastery when the Japanese raided it in 1937 and their subsequent journey to Kobe and the SS laboratories at Dachau. I also told him they were originally destined for Adolf Hitler. His only reaction came when I told him that Germany had lost the war and Hitler was dead.

"Once again, my brothers came so close to their rightful destiny."

"What do you mean by 'my brothers'? Are you related to the people of Germany?"

Chang Sou's nostrils flared in pride.

"Interesting. You are the first person who has ever asked that question. My ancestors came from a great city, located far to the north of here. They prospered for thousands of years until a great flood. Most of our tribe headed north, while my ancestors traveled south through this region before building a city of magic in the great mountains of the underworld."

"What was the name of this city of magic?" I asked.

"It would mean nothing to you."

"Maybe not, but I thought you might have been referring to the ancient underground city in the Himalayas called Agartha."

The giant was confused. "How could you have possibly known this?" Chang Sou asked, casting a suspicious eye down at Chow Li.

"Albert told me," I said.

"That Christian dog spoke of Agartha?!" Chang Sou roared, the veins in his neck bulging as if about to burst. "He should consider the limitation of his injuries a sign of his good fortune. If I ever get my hands on Albert, I will personally make him endure each of the eighteen levels of death, then slowly roast him alive!"

"You bastard, you will do no such thing!"

I turned to see Jennifer standing beside me facing Chang Sou with her fists clenched by her sides. I'd completely forgotten about her. Chang Sou didn't reply as he silently studied her from head to toe with bestial anticipation.

"The flesh of a young woman has a sweetness and delicacy that can never be surpassed," he said, slowly licking his lips. Like a tiger fixating on its prey, Chang Sou never took his eyes off of Jennifer as he crouched down on his hands and knees, and rested his chin on the street.

"Chow Li," I asked, "what in the hell is happening here?"

Chow Li remained mute as Chang Sou began taking panting breaths that quickly hyperventilated his face into a mass of crimson rage. His pupils dilated and enlarged until his eye sockets completely filled with black. His lips retracted into a demonic scowl that revealed a jagged set of razor-sharp teeth dripping such copious amounts of saliva that a trickle dribbled down his chin, forming a small puddle on the ground before him. I had no idea what kind of creature Chang Sou was becoming, but I knew what was going to happen next.

I dove in front of Jennifer at the exact second Chang Sou leapt. We collided with a resounding thud as I furiously grappled with him and tried to get a grip. His body was a wall of rock-hard, sinewy muscle and he cast me off like a rag doll, slamming me to the street twenty feet away.

Jennifer hadn't time to react and had barely turned to take a step when Chang Sou was upon her. He flipped her over and clawed away her hair to expose the creamy white skin of her neck. I raised my head to see the streetlights reflecting off his sharpened wet teeth as he reared back to deliver a fatal bite to her jugular vein.

"No!" I screamed as his head snapped forward.

He jerked to a stop less than an inch from her skin, splattering Jennifer's eyes and hair with a shower of viscous spittle. Panting heavily, he appeared confused as he tilted his head from side to side and curiously sniffed her cheek.

Chang Sou rolled off Jennifer and sat down stupefied on the street beside her while he gazed mournfully down at her and clumsily stroked her hair. Chow Li approached and rested his hand on the giant's shoulder.

"What is the matter, my child?"

Chang Sou stared up at him, helplessly. "Could this woman be the reincarnation of Yang Kuei-fei?"

"This I do not know," Chow Li said as he bent down and tenderly kissed the giant's forehead. The relationship between them was clearly obvious and I knew then and there that Chow Li himself was completely incapable of ever killing Chang Sou.

Chang Sou leaned over and sniffed Jennifer's hair. She was trembling with wide-eyed terror, much too frightened to move.

"This woman reminds me of Yang Kuei-fei," he said in a low throaty whisper. "She has her brilliant green eyes of Imperial jade."

I seized the moment and snatched Jennifer away from him. He looked at me anxiously, but didn't lift a finger to reclaim her.

"Who in God's name is Yang Kuei-fei?" I shouted as Jennifer lay beside me in shock.

"Yang Kuei-fei was one of the most beautiful Chinese women who ever lived," Chow Li replied. "She was the favorite concubine of Emperor

Tang. Chang Sou saw her only once, when she came by my temple one morning to inquire about a flower she'd seen growing in the sacred forest. That chance encounter was the beginning of a powerful obsession that lives within him to this day. For the next year, Yang Kuei-fei and Chang Sou exchanged poetry by messenger. Soon afterwards she was forced to flee Chang'an during a military coup and was captured just a short distance from here. Emperor Tang's generals believed she was responsible for the coup and strangled her in the general's presence. Chang Sou was inconsolable for months. Before she fled the city, Yang Kuei-fei sent a message to Chang Sou promising that if anything happened to her, she would one day reincarnate and return to him."

Suddenly, Jennifer jumped to her feet and charged into Chang Sou, knocking him flat on his back.

"You fucking bastard!" she screamed, pummeling him with her fists. "I'll kill you!"

"I am deeply sorry if I have offended you," he said, making no attempt to shield himself from her blows.

I grabbed her around the waist and quickly pulled her away as she continued to flail with her arms and legs. Her adrenaline was pumping and it was like trying to contain a wildcat.

"I hope you burn in hell!" she screamed as I hurried to put distance between them. One swipe from his tree trunk arms could have easily broken her neck and I had no idea how much longer he was just going to sit there. All I knew was that he must have really loved this Yang Kuei-fei because a good five minutes had elapsed and the formula still hadn't managed to control his emotional upheaval.

As if he could read my thoughts, Chang Sou sat up straight as an arrow, folded his legs in a lotus position and closed his eyes for a minute. When he reopened them, I could see that the immortality formula had done its job. The broken-hearted beast had been completely replaced by an ice-cold Aryan superman, devoid of all emotion or weakness.

"I apologize for my outrageous behavior," he said, looking past us as he lifted his giant frame off the street. "Steven, you and I have important matters to discuss, but, this is neither the time nor the place for such negotiations."

Then he strode off into the darkness with Chow Li waddling after him. I slumped down on the street to catch my breath, but Jennifer was still wound up, pacing back and forth with her arms folded.

"Did you see that?" she fumed. "Chow Li never raised a finger to help either one of us."

"Yeah, I noticed, but at least we now know both of their weaknesses."

Jennifer stopped pacing. "Oh, really? And what do you think Chang Sou's weakness is?"

"You. Chang Sou believes you're the reincarnation of this Yang Kuei-fei person. Don't get me wrong, you look about as Chinese as I do, but if Chang Sou's convinced you're the reincarnated love of his life that gives us one hell of an advantage. As long as he believes that, he's practically defenseless around you."

"So, what if he is?" she shouted. "What do you expect me to do? Sleep with that creature to save humanity?"

"No, that's not what I had in mind," I said, cringing at the thought, "But we must consider all our options to stop him. Otherwise, millions, perhaps billions, will die."

Emotionally exhausted, Jennifer sat down on the street and buried her face in her hands.

"Chow Li and Chang Sou deserve each other," she muttered.

In early January of 1950, I was working one of those rare days at the Wu's noodle shop—a slow Sunday. Nevertheless, it was my turn for kitchen duty and there was always another dirty pan to wash or one more noodle sheet to dry. Jennifer was out front taking orders enjoying the day catching up on the local gossip with the few customers who wandered in. I was surprised when she popped her head into the kitchen.

"Trade places," she said, annoyed.

"Are you feeling all right?"

"I was until Chow Li walked in the door."

I quickly dried my hands and rushed out to see Chow Li standing at the counter. "What do you want?" I said, coldly.

"Please, Steven. Do not treat me like this."

"Why shouldn't I? You did absolutely nothing to protect Jennifer or me from that creature. If Chang Sou hadn't thought that Jennifer was the reincarnation of Yang Kuei-fei, he would've killed her. And you know what would have happened next?"

Chow Li warily shook his head.

"I would've spent the rest of eternity finding a way to destroy both of you."

Chow Li bowed his head. "You must really love this woman."

"More than you'll ever know."

"Then you must know how I feel," he cried, bursting into tears.

My anger dissipated. Chow Li wasn't a bad man, just a very weak one.

"Chow Li, why are you here?"

"Chang Sou has requested the honor of meeting with you, Albert and Jennifer in his monastery." He sniffled. "He knows you are a non-Buddhist immortal and have the will and power to stop him. He believes a truce could be negotiated that would be acceptable to you. Please. We are running out of time."

"You must be crazy. You seriously expect me to negotiate with a man who tortured my mother to death in her sleep? A man who tried to kill Albert and Jennifer?"

Chow Li dropped to his knees and clasped his hands. "I beg of you," he pleaded. "For the sake of all the innocents in this world you must put your personal feelings aside. I told him about your way of life in the Western world and he was fascinated. You must explain to him that there are many ways to enjoy the luxuries of the material world without resorting to death and force. Chang Sou and his monks are incredibly ignorant about even the most basic rules of business or commerce. For example, it is common knowledge in the West that money deposited in a bank will earn money over time. Therefore, an immortal could produce unlimited wealth by simply living long enough. I truly believe something good will come from this meeting. I swear on my oath he will not harm Albert or Jennifer."

"And what if it turns out that this is all a trap and Chang Sou still wants to be the master of the universe?"

"If he does not agree to change his ways, I will have no choice but to supply you with the means to destroy him."

I could scarcely believe my ears. "How?"

"The sleeping incense. It is derived from the dried stalk of a rare flower growing wild in the darkest part of the sacred forest. When burned, it produces a smoke that immediately renders an immortal unconscious, but unlike an overdose of the immortality formula, which provides nourishment to the body, the sleeping incense has no such beneficial powers. If unawakened, the immortal's body will begin to feed upon itself until death occurs."

"It certainly sounds like it has beneficial powers to me," I said, barely containing my excitement. "So, let me get this straight. If the three of us agree to meet with Chang Sou and are unsuccessful in convincing him to change his ways, you will supply me with this sleeping incense?"

"Yes. But I must have your word that you will do everything in your power to convince Chang Sou to pursue a peaceful path to enjoying a materialistic life."

"That won't be a problem. I just think you're going to be terribly disappointed."

"Don't be so sure. I believe Chang Sou will listen to you. He must, because we are running out of time."

"Why do you keep saying we are running out of time?"

"Because the fungus has returned."

"The fungus? The same fungus that nearly destroyed the forest a thousand years ago?"

"Yes. A thousand years ago the forest looked much the same as it does today. One morning, I noticed a beautiful red fungus growing at the base of a tree located near the monastery. I thought nothing of it until I returned a few days later and saw that it had grown quickly, smothering the base of the tree and stopping the production of pollen.

"When Chang Sou accompanied me a week later into Chang'an, he noticed the fungus as it had grown large enough to cover the base of twenty to thirty trees. The next morning I was horrified to find Chang Sou sitting peacefully upon a brilliant red carpet of fungi surrounded by neutralized trees. I knew it was only a matter of time before the organism destroyed the entire forest and allowed him to escape."

"What stopped it?"

"The power of light over the power of darkness. The fungus attacked the base of the trees where the pollen is emitted, but it didn't stop there. The fungus kept spreading up the bark of the tree and when it reached the treetops the leaves dropped off and sunlight flooded through instantly killing the organism. Overnight the tree's vitality was restored and its pollen production resumed. Chang Sou could not advance beyond the line of revitalized trees in front of the monastery without exposing himself to the pollen. The peasants of Chang'an could hear his scream of anguish echo through the mountains."

"Are you telling me that if Chang Sou had not stayed in the monastery he could've camped near the front line of the organism's progress and simply moved forward with it until he was freed?"

"Yes. But I assure you he will not make the same mistake twice. That is why you must convince him to change his ways before he is aware that the fungus has returned. Fortunately, the fungus has reappeared in a remote section of the forest, but it can spread quickly and eventually he'll see it."

"And even if I succeed in persuading him, but he reneges on his promise, you will deliver the sleeping incense to me?"

"That is correct. My word is my bond."

I instructed Chow Li to arrange a meeting with Chang Sou as soon as possible and sent him on his way. After dinner, I told Jennifer and Albert that Chang Sou had requested their presence at his monastery. Understandably skeptical, they listened while I explained how the ancient fungus had returned and, unless something was done quickly, Chang Sou would escape. It was a hard sell until I mentioned the sleeping incense. Albert nearly leapt out of his chair.

"The sleeping incense really exists?! That legend is as old as the immortality formula."

"Chow Li is desperate," I said. "If Chang Sou escapes, he knows what will happen. I've given Chow Li my word that I will do all I can to reason with him. Chow Li's gambling there's a chance I will say something that will convince Chang Sou to enjoy his materialistic desires without resorting to his historic pattern of violence and bloodshed."

Albert was still skeptical. "It sounds like a classic trap. On the other hand, Chow Li's promise to give us the sleeping incense is too good to pass up."

"Why do we have to go?" Jennifer asked.

"Good question. Chow Li didn't say. Yang Kuei-fei was the love of Chang Sou's life and maybe he just wants to get another look at your beautiful green eyes."

"Don't even joke about it," she snapped, emptying his ashtray into the sink. "When do you think we'll go?"

"If he remains true to form," I said, "Chang Sou will probably choose a Buddhist or Christian holiday."

Albert puffed on his cigar and chuckled to himself.

"Knowing how he feels about Jennifer, I'll wager the old chap picks St. Valentine's Day."

The old man barely had time to dodge the ashtray.

A few days later, I was awakened by the sound of Mr. Wu angrily berating the man he now referred to as "that crazy Buddhist monk." It was not yet sunrise, but Chow Li assured Mr. Wu that he had an urgent reason for waking us. Earlier that morning, Chang Sou had rousted Chow Li from his tiny temple and announced he was ready to embrace a pacifistic, though extremely materialistic, Western lifestyle in order to obtain his freedom. Chow Li was so excited that he ran all of the way to Sian.

"What is today's date?" I asked Chow Li.

"January 16th."

"Is there any religious significance to it?"

"None that are Buddhist," he said.

"And none that Christian, either," Albert interjected. "But believe me, Chang Sou didn't pick today's date at random. It must mean something." We were all drawing blanks when Jennifer stumbled out of her room to join us for some breakfast tea.

"I hope we don't have to walk there again," she grumbled.

"We won't have to," Albert said. "The Wu's have offered us the use of their bicycles."

"Bicycles?" I shook my head. "That's out of the question. You can't operate one because of your injuries and at least half of the trip will be uphill."

"And lastly," added Chow Li, "I've never been on one in my life."

"We can make it work," Jennifer said, suddenly bright eyed and bushy tailed after gulping down a cup of freshly brewed green tea. "Steven and I can pedal while Chow Li and Uncle Albert ride on the seats. I used to do it all the time with my friends in the Philippines."

"Let's go before I change my mind," I groaned. "We're going to look ridiculous."

It was impossible to retain a shred of dignity as Chow Li sat behind me and howled with delight as I pedaled as fast as I could to get sight unseen out of Sian while Albert clutched Jennifer's waist and struggled to hang on. It was very easy to tell if anyone spotted us during that early morning hour—all you had to do was listen for the sudden peal of laughter. Fortunately, the giant stone walls flashed by quickly and we sailed through the North Gate and into the fragrant poppy fields. We made good speed until we reached the hills and began to climb in elevation. Soon our leg muscles were burning with fatigue as we fought a losing battle with gravity. We went as far as we could before we pulled over and ditched our bikes behind some bushes.

"Now I know how it feels to be a rickshaw driver," Jennifer gasped.

We hiked the rest of the way up the trail to the stone Buddha and entered the sacred forest. A rancid musty odor hung heavily in the air.

"What is that awful smell?" Jennifer asked.

"The fungus," Chow Li said, "and it is spreading like wildfire."

We stepped onto a carpet of brilliant, furry blood-red patches popping up all over the forest floor. Their density multiplied with every step until it felt as if we were walking on a sheet of red velvet. It was absolutely beautiful, but horrifying because there was no way Chang Sou would miss it on his next trip to Sian. We had precious little time to make Chow Li's plan succeed, otherwise Chang Sou was a free man.

As we marched through the darkness, it began to feel like we were drowning in a rancid mushroom cellar. We covered our noses and breathed through our mouths, as we doubled our pace and raced towards the distant pinpoint of sunlight bouncing off the mountain wall of Chang Sou's fortress. Fortunately, the odor began to dissipate and we soon stepped out of the forest onto the emerald field.

I had only taken a couple of steps when I heard a sizzling sound. I looked down and saw my shoes were caked in a thick coating of mashed fungus, bubbling in the bright sunlight. Chow Li handed us pine branches to scrape off the crusty, reddish muck.

"I find it interesting that this organism reacts so violently to sunlight," Albert noted as Jennifer cleaned off his shoes.

"Interesting, yes. Surprising, no," Chow Li answered, picking the melted fungus from between his toes. "This organism is a gift to Chang Sou from the dark forces of the universe. I find it quite symbolic that it cannot live in the sunlight."

Chow Li faced the monastery and shouted something in Chang Sou's ancient tongue.

Within a few minutes we heard a creaking sound as the massive gates opened and Chang Sou appeared, easily pushing the center pine tree aside with one of his massive hands. He was dressed in an ancient Chinese military uniform handsomely constructed of rows of tiny metal plates with his long dirty blond hair swept up into a large knot on top of his head.

"That's exactly how he looked when his illusion assaulted me," Albert whispered.

"He is dressed as a warrior from the Han Dynasty," Chow Li said.

"My heart is filled with joy and I welcome you into my home," Chang Sou said, majestically sweeping his other hand toward the open gates of his monastery. "My disciples and I are eager to have you as our guests."

Chang Sou led us down the eighteen levels of the nine hundred foot staircase and we entered the giant cavern to see twelve hooded monks seated at a long wooden table in front of the giant honeycomb. Large clay bowls of steaming food lined the center, filling the air with an unfamiliar though not unpleasant smell that reminded me of corned beef and cabbage. Chang Sou directed us to sit at a small table placed at the far end, with Jennifer and I seated on one side and Albert and Chow Li across from us on the other.

All of Chang Sou's disciples shared the same similar facial characteristic: dull, lifeless eyes, completely devoid of emotion. All, except one and I would occasionally catch him stealing a glance at us from underneath his hood while the other monks dutifully stared down at the table. His eyes seemed to display a spark of personality the others did not possess.

Chang Sou stood and introduced us to his disciples in his ancient Chinese dialect. Then he called out their names to us in English. The curious monk was named Kusung and was now staring at us so frequently that I began to wonder if Chang Sou would take notice.

"Steven Ronson, I have invited you here today with all the respect due a fellow immortal so you may bear witness to this historic event. After exactly one thousand, nine hundred and eighty-four years of my imprisonment here, I am ready to depart this monastery. And from this day forward today, January 16th, shall be celebrated as the *Day of Enlightenment* as I begin my journey to learn the ways of the West."

The "Day of Enlightenment"? An interesting choice of words. Maybe Chow Li's crazy idea was actually going to succeed.

"In appreciation, are there any requests you wish me to grant you?" he asked.

Requests? I was expecting Chang Sou to chew my ear off about Western business, culture or whatever else crossed his megalomaniacal mind. This didn't make any sense. "No, um, none that I can think of. Are there any questions you'd like to ask me?"

"Only one—I understand you possess military experience."

"Military experience? I guess you could call it that."

"Excellent. Which English-speaking country would you wish to govern?"

I looked at Chow Li. This was certainly not the question I expected from a man who had any intention of renouncing violence or world domination.

Chow Li stood from his chair and nervously cleared his throat. "Chang Sou, it was my understanding that you wanted to ask Steven about the materialistic ways of the West."

Chang Sou arched his head back and roared with laughter.

"Chow Li, your unfailing hope to subjugate me with your tired pac-ifistic beliefs has been a constant source of amusement for almost two thousand years. And if I were to spend another ten thousand years in this deplorable monastery I would never consider such a thing. Regardless, there is no need for any of that now that the fungus has returned."

Checkmate.

The look of utter devastation on Chow Li's face convinced me that Chang Sou had completely deceived him. Regardless, none of it mat-tered now.

"I'm not interested in governing anyone," I said, flatly.

Chang Sou's blue eyes narrowed. "That is not an acceptable answer."

"It's the only answer you're going to get," I said, rising from my seat. "And Chow Li, you owe me some incense."

Chang Sou bolted from his chair with superhuman speed and rushed behind me. "You will join forces with me," he whispered, his hot fetid breath pulsing against the back of my neck.

"Go to hell," I said.

Jennifer screamed as Chang Sou reached around me and yanked her completely out of her seat by her hair, pressing the blade of his knife against her throat. "Perhaps we can see if she's taken the formula."

"For the love of God!" Albert shouted.

"Chang Sou, I beg of you," Chow Li pleaded as he knelt down in front of the giant. "Please do not harm this innocent child!"

"It is not my decision to make." Chang Sou shrugged. "Her fate rests in the hands of this Western immortal."

The bastard had me. At that moment my only regret was that Jennifer had not accepted my Christmas present in Yenan. One flick of his brawny wrist and she was dead. Still, I found it hard to believe that Chang Sou would actually harm the woman who resembled the love of his life. So, I gambled. "You would harm the woman who reminds you of Yang Kuei-fi?"

Bad move. At the sound of his beloved's name, Chang Sou gritted his teeth and pressed the knife against Jennifer's throat so hard a thin line of blood rose along the length of the razor sharp blade.

"Say her sacred name one more time and Jennifer will join her!"

Jennifer's eyelids fluttered as she slumped into unconsciousness. I had to buy time and buy it fast. Maybe there was a way out of this.

"May I have a little time to make my decision?"

"One hour, no more," he said, holding his knife firmly against Jennifer's throat.

Chang Sou commanded Kusung to escort me to the torture chamber on Level 2. As he led me away, Chow Li glared at him through steely brown eyes filled with an emotion completely foreign to his Buddhist beliefs.

For the first time in his life I believe he was experiencing hate.

When we reached Level 2, Kusung surprised me with an option: I could consume an incredibly high overdose of the immortality formula that would render me unconscious for hundreds of years—perhaps longer.

"How do you know Chang Sou will agree to this?" I asked. "He has no choice. Besides joining him, it is the only other way he can remove you as a threat. But you must make a decision soon. Otherwise, he will kill the girl."

"How do I know he won't kill Jennifer or Albert, anyway?"

"He will release them if you agree to join him or take the overdose," Kusung said. "If he kills them, he cannot control you." I understood the logic. Chang Sou did not have the power to kill me, but if he could incapacitate me for hundreds of years it would be just as good. And when I awakened the world would be his. I briefly considered falsely agreeing to join him, but what would my insurance be to protect Jennifer, Albert or anyone else once he realized my betrayal? Chow Li?

There was only one decision I could make.

CHAPTER

9

I tried to speak, but my tongue was glued to the roof of my mouth. I tried to move, but my arms and legs felt as if they were cast in solid lead. I saw only darkness because my eyelids were sealed with something akin to grainy leather. A greasy carpet of hair and beard blanketed my face and upper chest. The symptoms were similar to my overdose of the formula in 1945, except this was much more severe. This time I was completely paralyzed.

"Don't move," Kusung said as he gently pried my mouth open and inserted his index finger to loosen my tongue. Then he pinched an area of skin near the top of my cheekbone and peeled away a thick patch of encrusted mucus from my eyes. "You are in remarkably good condition," he said, touching the wooden spout of a goatskin pouch to my dehydrated lips. He squirted cool liquid into my mouth that gravity helped trickle down my esophagus. My taste buds awakened to the familiar tart sweetness of pomegranate juice. And this time it burned the hell out of my empty stomach.

"Kusung," I whispered. "How long have I been asleep?"

"A very long time."

"Six months?"

"Longer."

"A year?"

"Longer."

This was going nowhere. "Please Kusung, what is today's date?"

He paused. "It is the 16th of January 1959."

I had slept for exactly nine years.

My last memory was that of Chang Sou's hulking physique filling the doorway to the torture chamber on Level 2 where Kusung informed him that I agreed to take an overdose of the immortality formula if he released Jennifer and Albert.

"You are a very foolish man," he said. "The world will soon forget you."

"I'd like to say good-bye to Jennifer and Albert. I may never see them again."

Chang Sou was unmoved. "That will not be allowed. They must not know of your entombment here. I cannot chance Chow Li entering this monastery and attempting to free you once I have departed."

"What are you going to tell them?'

"That you have willingly joined forces with me."

"They'll never believe you."

"Not at first, but over time they will have no choice," Chang Sou replied as he unfurled two long white scarves and tied them around my eyes. "One thing I have learned about mortals is that their faith can be a very temporary thing."

Chang Sou spun me around until I became disoriented. He jerked me to a stop, grabbed my shoulders and pushed me backwards. Instead of a stone wall, my fingertips touched a smooth metal surface behind me. Chang Sou had placed me inside the Iron Maiden. Before I could react, he slammed the door shut, plunging a dozen metal spikes into my eyes, larynx and heart. No scream or cry could emit from my ruptured voice box. I squirmed in agony and listened to Jennifer sob as she, Albert and Chow Li passed by me on their way back to the surface.

Minutes later the door of the Iron Maiden was yanked open and I staggered from the renewed pain of a dozen metal spikes ripped out of my flesh. I tumbled to the floor, sliding across a pool of my own blood. Someone untied my wrists and lifted the scarf from my face. As my bloodied vision regenerated, I recognized Kusung kneeling over me.

"I hope you are nothing like Chang Sou," I said.

"None of us are like Chang Sou. There are only the blind and the guilty."

Kusung led me downstairs to the cavern where Chang Sou and the other monks were noisily feasting at the table. "You should eat," Chang Sou said, pulling a piece of gristle from his teeth. "It will probably be your last meal for quite some time!" Chang Sou tilted his clay bowl towards me to reveal what appeared to be a boiled head of cabbage– until I noticed the cabbage had human ears.

"What is that saying those Christian missionaries have? You should love your enemies? Well, I do love them. I love to eat them!" He roared with laughter while the other monks ignored him and silently tore away at their food.

I pushed my bowl away.

"You are foolish to deny yourself the experience of this ancient delicacy. These heads were taken from prisoners I captured myself during the Taiping Rebellion in 1864. They are extremely tasty after pickling in brine for eighty-six years!"

I could barely watch Chang Sou crack open a skull and scoop out the pickled brains with his fingers. Then he lifted the skull to his lips and drained the broth.

"As a final gesture of goodwill, I will answer any question you wish," he said, wiping his mouth across the sleeve of his robe. I could think of only one.

"How long will I sleep?"

"What does it matter? You will have no concept of time." He then realized the motive behind my question. "You are counting the days until you will be reunited with your beloved Jennifer! You must abandon such foolish thoughts. She will soon forget about you."

"I doubt it," I said.

"Enough of this triviality!" he thundered. "It is time for you to sleep." With a clap of his hands, Chang Sou summoned Kusung, who timidly shuffled over and presented me with a wooden plate neatly stacked with thirty small gray, gold-speckled squares.

"Would you like anything to drink?" he asked softly.

"Pomegranate juice."

"We have pomegranate juice," he replied timidly, producing a wooden bowl full of the crimson liquid. Holding my breath, I placed one of the soft doughy squares in my mouth and washed it down with a gulp of the juice. I downed the other twenty-nine pieces in quick succession.

"Impressive," Chang Sou remarked.

"I've had plenty of practice."

"Remember the world you see today. When you awaken it will be mine."

I was quickly beginning to feel groggy as Kusung led me across the footbridge to an open chamber prepared for me on the bottom level of the massive honeycomb. A fresh bed of straw lined the interior.

"Lie down and close your eyes," Kusung said. "The sleep will come quickly." I hoisted myself in and stretched out on the straw. The hexagonal interior was constructed of wax, hardened over the ages into a kind of petrified resin that resembled amber. Kusung replaced the opaque cover and welded it shut tracing a candle along the seal. I took a deep breath and slipped into a word of absolute darkness as an invisible hand dragged its long silken fingers down the length of my face.

And then I smelled smoke.

I panicked and tried to move but found I was paralyzed. I took another breath and realized it was incense. It smelled wonderful, and the scent reminded me of ripe cantaloupes.

"Very good," Kusung whispered into my ear. "Breathe deeply."

I was confused. Why did Kusung want me to inhale this incense? I'd fallen asleep easily and the sweet aroma was quickly returning me to consciousness. Had Chang Sou changed his mind?

Now I knew that nine years had passed in a flash.

After Kusung told me how long I'd been unconscious, he placed something doughy in my mouth. There was no mistaking the pungent odor of fermented fish.

"Why are you feeding me this?"

"The incense that awakened you stopped the effects of the overdose, but your body needs immediate nourishment or you will age quickly," he said.

"Pomegranate juice!" I pleaded, choking on the formula. I may have been asleep for nine years, but I could never forget that awful taste. Kusung raised his goatskin pouch again to my lips and squirted the juice down my throat.

"Where are Jennifer, Albert and Chow Li?"

"Tibet."

"When did they relocate to Tibet?"

"Soon after you went to sleep. They had to leave Sian right after China went to war with the United States."

"China is at war with the United States?"

"Indirectly. The United States and China found themselves supporting opposite sides during a Korean civil war."

"What do they believe happened to me?"

"They originally believed you unwillingly joined Chang Sou to save Jennifer's life, but they also believed you would have escaped at the first opportunity. Since they haven't heard from you in years, they have slowly resigned themselves to believing you had been seduced by his power as we all have."

It was exactly as Chang Sou had predicted.

"Is Chang Sou in Tibet?"

"Yes, but not in Lhasa. Chang Sou has built a mountain fortress in a remote area of southern Tibet, which he has named the New Agartha. He has been organizing his army there and preparing for world conquest since we left here in 1950."

"Since 1950? I've been here alone all that time?"

"Yes."

I could now feel the supernatural power of the formula rejuvenating my nutrition-starved body. I sat up and leaned against the inside wall of the chamber.

"You will not be able to walk like that," Kusung said, pointing to my toenails which now resembled the talons of an eagle. Pulling a knife from his bag, he pared away the excess nail from my toes and fingers. "I have arranged for us to spend the night at the home of Wu Tso-lin. But we must disguise you as a monk to get there safely. Since the Korean war, it has become extremely dangerous for an American to be in this country."

Kusung slipped one of his Buddhist robes over my head. It reeked of stale sweat and its rough fabric irritated my skin as if it were made of burlap. He reached under my armpits and pulled me out of the chamber.

The cavern was not as I remembered it. Except for the wooden bridge and the giant honeycomb, Chang Sou and his monks had stripped it bare. As we exited the tunnel and stepped into Level 18, I nearly tripped over a giant circular stone plug intricately carved with Chang Sou's familiar insignia of an inverted swastika surrounded by winged dragons.

"I don't remember that being over the entrance to the tunnel."

"It wasn't," Kusung said. "After we left the monastery, Chang Sou put it there to disguise the tunnel from thieves and soldiers."

"Weren't you worried about thieves and soldiers when you lived here?"

"Worried? They were our most reliable source of food!" Leaning against Kusung for support, I scaled the nine hundred foot staircase to the surface one unsteady step at a time. We'd just passed Level 2 when I stopped as an interesting thought occurred to me.

"Kusung, why are you here?"

"Chang Sou sent me here to retrieve you."

I released him and fell against the wall, "You came here to take me to Chang Sou?"

"I will do nothing of the sort. Chang Sou sent me here after he learned that the monastery had been discovered by the Chinese government and would be subjected to an archaeological excavation. I volunteered to transport you back to New Agartha, but he has no idea I have rebelled against him and awakened you. I can assure you my punishment will be most severe for I am the first of his disciples to ever do such a thing. Immortality no longer interests me and I will lovingly embrace a mortal death after I have committed enough earthly acts to counter the evil I have helped sustain. I believe liberating you is the first of these acts. If you desire, I will lead you to the location of Chang Sou's mountain fortress of New Agartha, but we must hurry if I am going to help you rejoin the others in Lhasa. Chang Sou has given me only enough of the formula to sustain us for a direct return to New Agartha and Chow Li must resupply us."

"How long will that take?"

"It took me thirty days to travel by foot from Tibet's Chonggye Valley to the Chinese border, and then five more days to reach Sian by truck. It is a shorter distance from here to Lhasa, and if we hurry we can make the journey in much less time. But, you must convince Chow Li to supply me with the formula or I will die before I can lead you to Chang Sou."

As we climbed out of the staircase, I could see sunlight flooding the entrance. The massive iron gates had been removed and debris and dried vegetation had accumulated inside into such a massive pile that Kusung had to lift me over it. Stepping into sunshine for the first time in nine years, I saw the reason why the Chinese had discovered the monastery.

The sacred forest had vanished.

In its place were acres of freshly plowed yellow earth. On the horizon stood one lonely tree, the ancient cypress, and beside it a symbol of the forest's destruction: a tractor.

"My God, what caused this to happen?"

"A Chinese government program called *The Great Leap Forward*," Kusung said. "It was supposed to advance China into the 20th century. Unfortunately, too much growth was attempted at once and it failed. It was such a disaster that it forced Mao Tse-tung to resign last year as chairman of the Communist Party." Kusung scanned the square mile of naked earth that had replaced the sacred forest. "I don't know how any of us would have ever survived this."

"You wouldn't have."

I adjusted the hood of my robe to cover my face and we began the trek to Sian. Without the forest the area looked much smaller and we traversed the entire distance to the ancient cypress tree in minutes. I peered over the edge of the cliff to view the valley below and saw rows of houses and other dwellings dotting the countryside. The dirt road leading into Sian had been widened and paved with asphalt. As an army truck roared past on its way to the city, a handful of soldiers sitting in the back turned and eyed us suspiciously.

"The most they will ever do is laugh at you," Kusung advised. "Nevertheless, remember two things: never look them in the face and never speak English in public until we are safely out of China."

I was astounded by Sian's growth. Most of the population now lived outside the massive stone walls. Many of the old shops and landmarks I remembered had been demolished or changed hands. The China Inland Mission now housed some sort of government facility and the Eight Route Army Headquarters was a museum with the 1939 Chevrolet we'd driven to Yenan proudly displayed outside. I was glad to see that the Wu's small brick home had remained relatively unchanged.

Ching-ling whooped with delight when she recognized me at the door and informed us that Tso-lin had gone to the market to buy vegetables for dinner. As Ching-ling spoke, I noticed her hair had become gray, deep lines circled her mouth and crow's feet crinkled her eyes. She had aged nine years, but in my mind I'd seen her only the day before.

"Look who's here!" Ching-ling announced as the front door creaked open and Tso-lin shuffled in from the cold, his arms wrapped around a large basket of produce.

"Steven," he cried upon seeing me. "You're alive! We couldn't believe it when Kusung told us you'd been hibernating in that monastery all of these years."

The years had taken their toll on him as well. His infectious smile revealed a paucity of teeth and his face was etched with an intricate pattern of thin lines, but the years had done nothing to temper the beauty of their souls. Their compassion and generosity warmed me and I was grateful they'd risked their freedom to welcome me.

"Do either of you have any idea what Albert, Jennifer and Chow Li are doing in Tibet?" Tso-lin and Ching-ling exchanged nervous glances.

Whatever they had to say, they were extremely hesitant about saying it.

"Chow Li is teaching ancient medicine at the Medical College atop Chakpori Hill," Ching-ling replied, pouring us a round of tea. "And Albert is operating a small missionary for the orphaned children of Khampas rebels."

Okay, that was two out of three. "And Jennifer?"

Tso-lin cleared his throat. I slowly sipped my tea and braced myself.

"Jennifer … has married another man."

If Tso-lin had reached across the table and plunged a knife into my heart it would have been less painful. This was the same Jennifer who'd poured her heart out to me that night in Little Italy. The same Jennifer who'd told me she loved me as we slow danced in Yenan. The same Jennifer who'd given me a Christmas gift inscribed with the one word that meant more than anything to me.

Forever.

Sensing my pain, Ching-ling leaned forward and cupped her weathered hands around mine. "I am so sorry, Steven. I know you loved her very much."

"Yes, I did. I mean, I still do," I said, struggling to maintain my composure. "Who did she marry?"

"A missionary she met in Tibet."

"Wonderful. Albert must have loved that," I said as Tso-lin and Ching-ling looked upon me with eyes moist with pity. "We have a long journey tomorrow and I'd like to retire for the evening," I said, my throat tightening. "I want to thank both of you for your warm hospitality in allowing us to spend the night. I will never forget it."

"Wait," Tso-lin said, handing me a leather folder stuffed with yellowed papers. "If you ever returned, Jennifer wanted you to have this."

It was my journal.

On the way to my room, I paused by what had once been Jennifer's bedroom. The door was open, but I couldn't bear to look inside. I entered my room and pulled back the sheet from the same bed I'd slept in nine years earlier. As I laid my head on the pillow, there was a faint tapping at the door.

"It's open," I said.

Kusung stepped inside.

"I know you are in terrible pain and I thought it might be helpful if we talked. I remember this girl. She was quite beautiful. You took the overdose of the formula to save her life."

"Please, don't remind me," I said, turning away.

"Steven, what did you expect? You must try to understand Jennifer's reality. Her reality is that you disappeared on January 16th, 1950 and for a young mortal woman, nine years is an impossible time to wait."

"And what about my reality, Kusung?" I sobbed, no longer able to control my emotions. "What about my reality? For me, January 16th, 1950 was this morning!"

For the next twenty-eight days, Kusung and I trekked over some of the most inhospitable terrain on this planet. We soon exhausted our supply of pomegranate juice and the taste of washing down Kusung's formula with water from melted snow triggered my gag reflex every time. Fortunately, I accidentally stumbled upon a discovery that made the process somewhat tolerable. One day I was too lazy to melt the snow and simply stuffed it in my mouth. The freezing cold numbed my taste buds just long enough to swallow the formula.

We began our journey hitching rides from Chinese truck drivers still sympathetic to the sight of two Buddhist monks trudging through the muddy snow. In five days we reached the Tibetan border town of Tachienlu. For the next thousand miles we hiked through Chinese occupied Tibet, making sure to stay far enough away from the main roads to avoid detection by the ever present P.L.A. patrols.

We arrived in Lhasa on the morning of February 14th,[th] accompanied by a flood of refugees pouring in from the Amdo and Kham provinces of eastern Tibet. Many of them were the families of Khampas warriors fighting to repel the Chinese Army. I was awestruck by the spectacular grandeur of the red-and-white Potala Palace, oddly out of place in the desolate landscape, and the castle-like appearance of the Medical College atop Chakpori Hill where Chow Li was teaching.

We walked past the palace, made a hard right, and headed north to the Sera Monastery. Along the way, I sighted massive flocks of vultures lazily circling to the east of us. When I asked Kusung why there were so many, he simply answered, "A sky burial."

The monks at the monastery's gate recognized Kusung and permitted us to enter. It had been five weeks since I'd last enjoyed the simple luxury of a bed, but no matter how badly my body hungered for sleep, there was something else I needed much more.

I needed to find Jennifer.

Using a mixture of sign language and broken Chinese, I managed to convey to the monks that I was leaving their monastery to do some sightseeing in Lhasa. They advised me to return before dark. The area outside the city was infested with packs of wild dogs, supposedly the reincarnations of criminals and they had killed more than one unsuspecting traveler.

I thanked them for the warning and set out with my sights on the Potala rising majestically in the distance. I wandered aimlessly through the city until I found myself drawn to the colorful commotion of the Barkhor Bazaar. Craving anything that would relieve my palate from the taste of fermented fish, I eagerly sampled the Tibetan native beer called, of all things, *Chang*. The milky, tangy brew was not my idea of a cold one, but it put a smile on my face and I ordered another.

The vendor eyed me warily not only because I paid him with Chinese yuan, but because I'd forgotten I was wearing a Buddhist robe. Embarrassed, I pulled the hood over my face and walked through a back street called Yak Alley. Aptly named, it was crowded with tables of vendors peddling freshly slaughtered Yak meat amid woolly carcasses strewn everywhere. My attention was soon diverted by a vendor hawking a rare luxury for Tibetans, imported Persian melons. The thought of a sweet, juicy melon sounded irresistible and I pushed my way through the melee until I could thrust my hand between the tightly compressed bodies blindly groping for a ripe one. Suddenly, the hungry mob surged forward and I crashed into the person in front of me.

"Excuse me," I said, regaining my balance and insatiable quest for the perfect melon.

"That's quite all right," a woman replied in perfect English, her back to me.

English? In Tibet?

The woman's blue padded Mao suit contrasted sharply with the other Tibetans' traditional chubas. The crowd shifted again and she fell backwards, tripping into me, dropping her melon to the ground and cracking it in half, revealing a fragrant orange interior.

"I'm so sorry," I said, kneeling down to retrieve the shattered fruit.

When I rose and handed her the pieces of melon our eyes met. She had the most beautiful emerald eyes I'd ever seen. They were feline, almost predatory in nature, with more than a hint of quiet desperation. I'd seen those eyes for the first time many years ago, on the other side of the world, in the back of a smoke-filled jazz club on 52nd Street. There was a whisper of gray around her hairline and her face had become more angular, but if anything, her maturity had made her even more stunning, even more beautiful.

"Do I know you?" she asked, curious about the American accent hidden inside a Buddhist robe, her eyes searching for my face in the darkened void beneath my cowl. I was lost for words and then I realized it was Valentine's Day. It was the ultimate irony to have the woman I loved look upon me that day as a total stranger. I reached up and pulled the hood away from my face.

Jennifer dropped the melon as her mind struggled to comprehend the impossible. Over the past nine years, she had slowly resigned herself to the fact that this moment would never happen. Could never happen. Confused, she slowly raised her hands to my face, her delicate fingers tracing my features. I slipped my arms around her waist and pulled her tightly against me.

"Jennifer," I whispered in her ear. "I love you so much."

At first, she numbly reciprocated and wrapped her arms around me. I could feel her heart beating against my chest. And then, with a sudden breath of determination, she shoved me away.

"You selfish bastard!" she shouted. "Did you think you could just walk back into my life whenever you wanted?"

I kept my cool and in a low voice calmly tried to explain that Chang Sou had lied when he said I had joined him. I calmly explained that I'd just journeyed thousands of miles through hostile territory to find her. And I tried to explain that what I did nine years ago, I did for only one reason. Because I loved her. None of my words mattered. Years of tear-filled, sleepless nights were unleashed in a torrent of vicious accusations of abandonment that could only be born of a broken heart. Hell hath no fury, indeed. I couldn't get a word in edgewise. Every time I tried to speak, she angrily cupped her hand over my mouth and screamed another accusation. Finally, I couldn't take it any longer. When she went to cover my mouth again, I pushed her hand away.

"Damn it, Jennifer!" I shouted. "Did you really believe I could ever leave you?"

That got her attention.

Unfortunately, it also got everyone else's attention and I now found myself surrounded by a menacing mob of Tibetans, curious to know why a Buddhist monk was yelling at a beautiful Western woman in English and reducing her to tears.

"Jennifer, get us out of here."

She snatched my hand and dragged me away as the confused crowd looked on.

"Listen," I said as she pulled me further down Yak Alley, "I know you're married, but I came to tell you the truth. I never joined Chang Sou. I was in deep hibernation all of this time."

She stopped. "Hibernation? Are you telling me you've been asleep for the last nine years?"

"Yes. That was my only real choice. I certainly wasn't going to join him."

She led me out of the dark alley into the high-altitude sunlight to get a better look at me.

"Congratulations, you look younger than I do."

"That's not funny," I said. "Chang Sou is out there somewhere building his New Agartha and I need to find him. How are Albert and Chow Li?"

"Albert's health is failing. He's become obsessed with the idea that Chang Sou is building an army of immortals somewhere south of Chonggye Valley, near the tombs of the ancient Tibetan kings. Chow Li is teaching student monks at the medical college on Chakpori Hill. Unfortunately, they rarely see each other. It's much too difficult for Albert to climb that hill and, for some reason, Chow Li won't visit us."

"Would it be possible for us to go up there now and visit Chow Li?"

"I don't see why not." She shrugged, glancing down at her wristwatch. "But we have to be extremely careful—foreigners can be deported simply for disturbing classes. The ancient secrets taught atop Chakpori are much sought after by non-Buddhists from all over the world. Even the Communists are frightened by some of their powers. Regardless, I know Chow Li will be delighted to see you."

Without thinking, I grabbed Jennifer's hand as I had a thousand times before. We had only taken a couple of steps when she stopped and released her grip. "Steven, I'm sorry, but I'm with someone else now. I've taken a vow and you can't hold my hand like that."

Reality was setting in quickly.

We continued in awkward silence and climbed the circular stairs to the summit of Chakpori Hill. The panoramic view of the Potala Palace, with Lhasa sprawled below us, was magnificent. Chakpori Medical College more closely resembled a medieval stone fortress than an institution of higher learning. Every year select monasteries throughout Tibet choose two of their most gifted monks to be sent there to learn the ancient healing secrets of the masters. The corridors echoed with the busy monotones of teachers instructing students. Jennifer and I stopped to peer through the keyhole in one classroom door and saw a Buddhist monk sitting on the floor lecturing an attentive group of about fifteen students. Using only his fingertips, he lifted himself completely off the ground and, with a gentle push, glided effortlessly across the room.

"Good God!" Jennifer exclaimed.

The entire class jerked their heads around at us as their teacher yanked on a rope, clanging a bell. Every classroom door burst open and within seconds we found ourselves jostled by a group of very irate Buddhist monks. They were pushing us towards the entrance when someone shouted something in Tibetan and the crowd stilled. There was no mistaking that high-pitched voice.

"Steven, I knew you would return!" Chow Li cried, pushing his way through the throng.

He didn't acknowledge Jennifer and quickly led us down a flight of stairs to a small room where I told him the incredible news that Kusung had rebelled against Chang Sou and freed me from the monastery.

"That is wonderful! Jennifer, would you kindly leave us alone? I have an important matter to discuss with Steven."

Jennifer said nothing and walked out.

"That was more than a little rude," I said after she closed the door.

Chow Li lowered his voice. "I'm sorry, but have you met her husband?"

"No, and to be honest with you, I'm not dying to meet the man who's sleeping with the woman I love."

"I understand, but it may interest you to know that I consider her husband to be one of Chang Sou's converts."

I was mortified. It was bad enough that Jennifer had married another man, but for him to be associated in any way with Chang Sou was unthinkable.

"What proof do you have?" I asked.

"When I first met this man I immediately sensed that his dedication to the teachings of Jesus Christ was a deception. He said he was from the German Lutheran Mission in Amdo. I have many friends throughout the Amdo province and they tell me no such mission has ever existed. I believe he is German, but certainly not a missionary."

"What do you want me to do?"

"I'm not sure. I was tempted to search through his possessions, but my beliefs prevent me from doing so."

"Mine don't."

He smiled. "I know."

Chow Li kept the promise he'd given me nine years earlier. His plan to kill Chang Sou and his converts was simple, but effective. We would flood the interior of New Agartha with smoke from the sleeping incense he'd stockpiled beneath Chakpori Hill. The only problem was that Chow Li didn't know exactly where New Agartha was located, except that it was somewhere south of Chonggye Valley.

"That won't be a problem," I said. "Kusung told me he would lead us there."

Chow Li was astonished. "He really said this?"

"Yes. Kusung told me that his greatest wish is to die a mortal death after he has performed acts that he believes will counter the evil he has helped to sustain. I'd say that leading us to Chang Sou would be pretty high on his list."

"It most certainly would be," Chow Li agreed.

Jennifer poked her head into the room. "Sorry to interrupt, but I have dinner to cook. Both of you are invited."

"Thank you, my child, but I have classes to attend," Chow Li said, showing us out. "But I'm sure Steven will be most delighted to join you."

"He still treats me like a little girl," Jennifer huffed as we descended the stone steps back to the street.

"C'mon, Jennifer. The man's two thousand years old. If you live to be a hundred, you'll still be a little girl to him."

Jennifer, her husband and Albert lived in a whitewashed bungalow on the north bank of the Ri Chu River, directly parallel to the Jokhang Temple. Except for the crucifix displayed in the front yard, there was no other indication that the structure was a Christian mission. The inside was sparsely decorated with a couch, a couple of unpainted wooden chairs and a few throw rugs. On the wall was a framed picture of Jennifer in her wedding dress, but no photo of her husband. Besides the traditional white dress, the only thing I noticed was that Jennifer wasn't smiling.

There was a loud bang as someone kicked the back door open. Jennifer put her finger to her lips. "You'll never guess who's here to see you!" she called out cheerfully.

"I don't care," a grumpy voice replied. "I'm in no mood for company."

Albert wheezed loudly as he dragged a lazy leg behind him. His jaundiced eyes widened when he entered the room and recognized me.

"My God, it's you! Where have you been all these years?"

"In deep hibernation in Chang Sou's mountain monastery. I was awakened and freed last month by one of his disciples."

"I find it incredible that one of Chang Sou's disciples has actually turned against him? Who was his Judas?"

"Kusung, the one who took me up to Level 2. He's with me here in Lhasa and will lead us to Chang Sou's New Agartha."

"He'll lead us to Chang Sou?" Albert asked, easing his tired body into a chair. "Good Lord, perhaps I've just witnessed my first miracle."

Again, the back door crashed against its frame. This time the footsteps were brisk and powerful.

The moment Jennifer's husband walked into the room it was as if a dark cloud had eclipsed our joyous mood. He appeared to be in his early forties, tall and muscular with closely cropped blond hair and blue eyes framed by round gold wire-rimmed glasses. My smile was returned with a petulant, sullen expression. I detested him on sight. Jennifer bounced over and kissed him on the cheek but he didn't kiss her back.

"Hi sweetie, how was your day?" she asked.

"My day was . . . pleasant," he replied in a heavy Bavarian accent. "Who is this man?"

"This is Steven Ronson," she replied. "Steven, this is my husband Franz."

"Ah, at long last I am honored to meet the legendary Steven Ronson," he said, his voice tinged with sarcasm. He didn't offer to shake my hand as Jennifer blushed with embarrassment.

Albert ignored him. "Steven, where did Kusung say we'd find Chang Sou?"

Franz stiffened at the mention of Chang Sou's name.

"Albert, there's something I really need to discuss with you in private," I said, motioning my head towards the front door. Albert wearily rose to his feet and followed me outside into the bitter cold.

"Have you gone mad?" he asked, shuffling his feet to stay warm.

"I saw Chow Li today at the Chakpori Medical College. He's making plans to dispose of Chang Sou by using the sleeping incense."

"That's lovely, but why did you have to pull me out into the bloody cold to tell me?"

"Because Chow Li has a very bad feeling about Franz. Where did you find this character?"

"Actually, he found us. When the Korean conflict began, Chow Li invited us to Lhasa. Unfortunately, he left us stranded the day we arrived to visit a monastery in the Chonggye Valley. The next morning at the Barkhor Bazaar, Franz introduced himself and told us he was the sole survivor of a German Lutheran Mission stationed in the Amdo province of eastern Tibet. He said all of the other missionaries had been slaughtered by the Chinese because they had been aiding the Khampas rebels."

"Chow Li told me his friends have never heard of any German Lutheran Mission in the Amdo province," I said. "And Chow Li believes that Franz is somehow connected to Chang Sou. You know the Germans had occult expeditions coming here before and during the war. What made you think Franz was telling you the truth?"

Albert shrugged his shoulders. "I've never had a reason not to believe him. He is a very Christian man who joins us daily in morning prayers, and he has been most generous in providing us with these living quarters. He's never expected anything in return."

"Never expected anything in return? What do you call Jennifer?"

Albert exploded. "How dare you judge my niece!? Jennifer waited years for you and I can't count how many nights I stayed awake listening to that poor child cry herself to sleep!"

The image of Jennifer crying herself to sleep made me feel foolish about my jealousy.

"Please forgive me, Albert. My heart was speaking instead of my mind."

"Steven, I understand how you feel. I probably shouldn't tell you this, but Jennifer and Franz argue constantly about you. I do believe the girl's never stopped loving you."

"I'd rather not think about that right now," I said, not exactly upset they were having marital difficulties. "I need to be sure about Franz. Can you get everybody out of the house so I can snoop around a bit?"

"Shouldn't be a problem." He trudged back inside. A minute later he reappeared with Franz and Jennifer in tow.

"We're going to the market to make you something special for dinner," Jennifer said as Franz wordlessly marched past me. "You're probably exhausted from your journey. Why don't you go back inside and relax until we return?"

I peered out the window to keep an eye on them until they disappeared. I was grateful for Albert's limp. The more he dragged his feet, the more time he bought me.

The door of the first bedroom reeked of stale cigar smoke. It wasn't hard to guess where Albert slept. The next one smelled seductively of jasmine perfume. I opened that door and zeroed in on a large pine dresser with a beveled mirror. I rummaged through its six drawers and found nothing but undergarments and socks.

Next, I searched the closet. It was crammed with dresses, Mao suits and shoes, and I found nothing more than that.

That left the bed. I flipped the mattress over and checked underneath. Nothing, but dust. I was running out of time and every sound made me jump. I studied the room for anything that seemed curious.

And then I saw it. The object was so unobtrusive that I hadn't noticed it. A dusty bronze statue on the floor, about eighteen inches tall, tucked neatly in the corner between the bed and the dresser. It was a bust of Bismarck the Great. Jennifer and Albert didn't know their German history, but I certainly did. Bismarck was the founder of the 2nd Reich, and an idol of Adolf Hitler. The bust was heavy and felt like it weighed about twenty to thirty pounds, but it didn't feel solid. Inspecting the underside, I discovered a deeply grooved plug in the center of the base about the diameter of a silver dollar. I retrieved a butter knife from the kitchen and twisted the plug back and forth. To my surprise, it loosened clockwise. It had been purposely threaded the wrong way. I turned the plug clockwise until it popped out. I shook the bust up and down and a small silver cylinder dropped into my lap. Inside was a tightly rolled piece of paper. It was a letter printed in German and emblazoned with the letterhead of the German Ancestral Heritage Organization. It translated as followed:

May 18th, 1942

Gartok, Tibet

Franz,

This letter hereby authorizes you to proceed at once to Lhasa. Gather as much information as possible about the following places: Potala Palace, Chakpori Medical College, Jokhang Temple, Sera Monastery, Norbulingka Palace, and Drepung Monastery. When completed, travel south, then southeast about 200 kilometers to the Chonggye Valley of the Tibetan Kings. The tombs are located at the furthest end of the valley, approximately twenty-five kilometers south of Tsetang. Be well armed at all times, particularly in the Chonggye Valley. That is the last place the 1941 expedition was sighted before we lost contact with them.

Wilhelm Teudt informed me that correspondence received from the 1941 expedition indicated that New Agartha was located somewhere due south of the Chonggye Valley.

In your travels across Tibet, you will undoubtedly come across many incredible discoveries. We have received reports that the Buddhist monks have developed many powers including the ability to fly and the secret to physical immortality. As fantastic as these powers may seem, you must discipline yourself and not become distracted. It is imperative that you keep focused on the sole purpose of your mission: to make contact and reunite Germany with our Aryan ancestors.

Colonel von Sievers sends his regards, and I have informed your family that you have been promoted to SS- Hauptsturmführer.

> *Reichsführer-SS*
> *Heinrich Himmler*
> *Berlin SW 11*
> *Prinz-Albrecht-Straße No.8*

At that moment everything had gone full circle. The ancient evil that had propelled Nazi Germany had never died and probably never would. As it had for eternity, it simply changed identities: Berlin– New Agartha, Hitler–Chang Sou. Only the times, names and places were different.

But I didn't have time to think about it.

Someone had just pressed the ice cold steel barrel of a gun firmly against the back of my neck.

"Roll the letter back into the tube," Franz commanded. "It is unfortunate you now know so much about me. I was going to do my innocent wife a favor and spare your life, but you have now left me no choice but to break her Christian heart."

"You obviously don't know much about me," I said. "If you did, you would know that if you fire that gun I'll survive. Then I'll have one more reason to kill you."

Franz spun me around to face him.

"During the war, so many men begged me to spare their lives," he said. "Of course, no matter how much they pleaded, I did my duty. I must admit, though, that their arguments were never quite as clever as yours. For a man to claim to be an immortal is a most creative bluff. Unfortunately for you, I've been in Tibet for almost eighteen years and know for a fact that no Buddhist monk would ever allow a Westerner access to the immortality formula."

"What makes you believe I found the formula in Asia?"

That caught him off guard. "Please proceed. You may have just bought yourself a little more time in this world."

I told the former SS Captain how I'd discovered the pills in Dachau and what I knew about the Thule Society. As I mentioned the names of Sigmund Rascher, Otto Krueger and Heinrich Himmler, his grip on the gun handle tightened and it was evident I was repeating information no one could know unless they were a very trusted member of the SS hierarchy.

"That's an ingenious story, but I don't believe a word of it. You could have just as easily learned that information from post-war Allied intelligence."

"Allied intelligence? Was the Thule Society even mentioned at the Nuremberg trials? C'mon, Franz, even for a Nazi you can't be that stupid."

"You dare call me stupid? You forget that it is I who is holding the gun. Well, I suppose there's only one way to settle this," he said, taking aim directly at my heart.

"Franz, I swear to God, if you pull that trigger, I'll kill you with my bare hands."

"God?" he sneered. "Not even God could help you now." Franz pulled the trigger and a bullet exploded deep in my chest. The pain was incredible. It felt as if a red hot poker had been jammed through my heart with the force of a jackhammer.

"Ah, for an immortal you bleed very much like a normal person!" He laughed as I rolled off the bed and sprawled onto the floor. "And now you have left me with a terrible mess to clean!" he said, casually stepping over me and proceeding down the hallway to rummage in the kitchen.

I waited thirty to forty of the most agonizing seconds of my life for the healing process to erase my pain. Hearing footsteps returning, I positioned myself flat against the inside of the door frame. Franz barely had time to register the sight of my missing body when I backhanded him across the throat. Like a boxer with his man on the ropes, I punched him repeatedly in the face and stomach until he slumped to the floor. I could have killed him right then and there, but I resisted. After all, he was still Jennifer's husband.

I dumped him onto the blood soaked bed and examined his pistol. It was a 9mm P-08 Luger. A classic example of German technology and very popular with SS officers. Franz opened his eyes to see me standing over him with the gun trained on his head.

"This is incredible," he gasped. "You are indeed an immortal."

"I've got to hand it to you Franz. You are a master of the obvious."

"Why don't you kill me?"

"Believe me, it would be my pleasure, but you just happen to be married to the woman I love."

"Isn't it strange? You and I are of such different ideologies and yet we both came to be with the same woman?"

"And which ideology is that? No Christian missionary would have tried to kill me simply because I discovered a letter describing his wartime activities from over fifteen years ago."

"But I am a missionary," he said proudly. "Not a Christian missionary, but like all missionaries I believe in spreading the word of my messiah."

"And who would that be?"

"Chang Sou. I am convinced he is the ancient Aryan messiah!" Franz raised himself off the bed. "I understand you have actually met this great man. Tell me, does he appear to be Asian?"

"No."

"Of course not, because he is a true descendent of the original Aryan race that survived the Great Flood!"

"Wonderful. Then why aren't you with him?"

"Because I have not been able to find him! Our SS occultists prophesied that the Aryan messiah would come to power soon after the German messiah and raise his army somewhere near the Chonggye Valley. In the summer of 1942, I led an expedition of fifty men into the Chonggye Valley, not far from the tombs of the ancient Tibetan kings. The area is fanatically guarded by monks from the Riudechen Monastery and the first night we camped we were attacked while we slept. Luckily for me, I'd walked away minutes earlier to relieve myself and returned to find every man lying in his sleeping bag with his throat slit. Himmler promised me a full SS regiment would be sent the following summer to exterminate these monks and continue our quest to locate Chang Sou. Unfortunately, by 1943 every available man was needed to fight on the Eastern front. But I will tell you this, on the day Chang Sou marches into Lhasa, I will be there to swear my loyalty to him!"

I could scarcely believe what I was hearing. If Franz had his way, the whole nightmare would start over again, except this time it would be far worse. Nothing could stop an army of immortals. Franz made his position clear. He'd do anything to help Chang Sou and his status as Jennifer's husband no longer made a difference. I made one last attempt to reason with him.

"Franz, after what I saw in Dachau, there's something I've always wanted to ask a dedicated SS man such as yourself. Don't you feel the least bit guilty over the atrocities the SS committed during the war?"

"Guilt? Who has time for guilt? In the SS, it was considered a weakness, a sign of human fragility that needed to be rooted out in order to strengthen the individual. I have never had a problem following any of the orders my superiors gave me, no matter how distasteful they may have been. Let me put it to you this way. Be they Jewish or Tibetan, I wouldn't think twice about tossing babies into an oven in order to build a better world. I've done it before and I would gladly do it again."

"And I pray that Jennifer will forgive me," I responded, pulling the trigger and blasting a hole in the center of Franz's forehead, splattering brain matter onto the whitewashed wall behind him. His eyes locked onto mine in horror before they rolled into his head and he slumped backwards onto the mattress. His death was instantaneous, quicker and more merciful than the innocents he slaughtered during the war. There was no doubt in my mind that his death saved countless lives. And perhaps I'd chosen to play God. Perhaps. But there was one thing I'd learned during the war—God could be extremely selective in preventing the death of innocents.

I shifted Franz's limp body to the center of the bed and covered it with the blood-stained linen sheet. Grabbing an empty wooden bucket from the kitchen, I dashed outside and dipped it into the freezing Ri Chu River. Slipping and sloshing, I feverishly mopped the bedroom floor before I was forced to rush back outside again, dump the bloody water into the river and refill the pail. Suddenly, I was startled by the sound of footsteps approaching in the darkness.

"Steven, is that you?"

It was Jennifer and I had no idea how I was going to tell her I'd just killed her husband.

"Yes, it's me," I said.

"What on earth are you doing outside here in the freezing cold?" she said, as Albert hobbled behind her. "And what's that in your hand?"

"It's a bucket. I'm mopping the floor."

"Mopping the floor?" She laughed, setting down a large sack of root vegetables by the front door. "Since when did you become so domesticated? By the way, did you see Franz? He said he wasn't feeling well and left us at the bazaar."

I leaned into Albert as he neared me. "Something terrible has happened," I whispered as Jennifer lit a mounted torch beside the door. "Don't let Jennifer go into her bedroom." Albert stared at me dumbfounded, but in the flickering light he saw something in my eyes that communicated finality.

"Jennifer, don't go inside!" he shouted.

"You must be crazy," she said, picking up her sack of vegetables. "I'm getting the hell out of this cold." Albert quickly staggered up the steps after her and told her to sit down on the couch. She refused and tried to push her way past him to the kitchen. I forced her onto the couch and held her down.

"Let go of me!" She squirmed.

"Jennifer, please calm down!" I said. "You can't go into your room."

"My room?" Jennifer glanced anxiously between me and Albert. "Why not?"

Neither of us answered.

"This has to do with Franz, doesn't it? What did you do to him, Steven?"

There was no other way to say it. "Jennifer, Franz tried to kill me."

"That's impossible!" she cried. "Franz is incapable of doing such a thing! He is the kindest, sweetest man I've ever known."

"Don't be ridiculous!" Albert admonished her. "You know how violent his temper can be! Do I need to remind you about the countless Tibetans he physically assaulted because they simply challenged his opinion about the war?"

Jennifer began to cry. "Please. Don't tell me you've hurt him."

"I'm sorry Jennifer, but I had no choice but to defend myself."

"Defend yourself against what, Steven? For Christ's sake, you're an immortal!"

"I told Franz, but he still tried to kill me," I said, pointing to the bullet hole on my bloodstained robe. I opened the top and showed her the circular welt over my heart.

"He did that to you?" she asked. Without answering I went into their bedroom and retrieved the silver cylinder containing Himmler's letter to Franz.

"Have you ever seen this before?" I asked, pulling the letter out of the cylinder.

"No." She sniffed, taking the paper from my hand. As I watched her lips silently move in translation down the page, her eyes began to well with tears. "How could I have been so stupid!" she sobbed, dropping the letter.

"I'm sorry, but his intention all along has been to join forces with Chang Sou. He told me he considered Chang Sou to be some kind of ancient Aryan messiah and would do anything he asked of him."

Jennifer rushed past us into the bedroom. After she locked the door, we heard a muffled wail of anguish.

"I hope the bastard burns in hell," Albert muttered.

"After what he did in the war, I have no doubt he will, but Jennifer's all alone in that room with his body. I wrapped it in the bed sheet as best I could, but there's blood everywhere."

"I'll take care of her and dispose of his corpse," Albert said. "Lhasa is in such chaos that no one will notice, but you'd better go. I have a feeling it's going to be a long night for me. Where are you staying?"

"The Sera Monastery."

"That's quite a walk. You may want to take something with you."

Albert went into the kitchen and emerged with a small clay bowl filled with hand-rolled balls of *pak*–roasted barley flour called *tsampa* mixed with yak-buttered tea. Besides the formula and some fruit, I hadn't much else to eat for the past five weeks and the pak tasted delicious. Before I reached the front door, I handed Albert back an empty bowl.

The temperature had plummeted and my robe provided little protection against the frigid Himalayan night. By the time I'd passed the Jokhang Temple, my teeth were chattering and the stench from the open sewers was nauseating. I doubled my pace and held my breath until I reached the lonely narrow dirt road leading out to the Sera Monastery. The city's lights faded with each step, and I soon found myself immersed in the night. It was the kind of darkness that could play tricks on a man's mind.

I pressed onward and kept my active imagination at bay by concentrating on the torches of Sera's gates flickering in the distance up ahead. As I trudged through the cold I found myself fighting an eerie feeling that a swarm of angry red eyes were tracking me in the darkness. I kept reminding myself that it was only my imagination, that there was nothing out there, but every time I glanced around I could swear that a multitude of tiny glowing embers were keeping pace with me. Before long, I could barely restrain myself from breaking into a blind panic and racing towards the monastery, but I calmed myself as an instinctive voice inside warned me not to run under any circumstances. I was jolted by a scampering sound as a pair of the glowing embers charged at me out of the darkness. I kicked out and they beat a hasty retreat with a menacing growl.

That was not my imagination.

I had walked straight into a pack of Lhasa's infamous wild dogs and they were closing in from all sides. And, except for the glow of moonlight reflecting off their eyes, I couldn't see them, but I could hear them snapping their teeth as they encircled me. While I no longer feared death, I did fear the unimaginable pain of being kept conscious by the formula as my body was eaten alive.

I desperately kicked at the ground in search of some type of weapon. There were rocks of various shapes and sizes and I groped around until I found one about the size of a baseball.

Hearing another rustle, I glanced up to see another pair of demonic eyes charging out of the void. I flung the stone with all my strength and was rewarded with a sickening thud as it crashed into the skull of the animal, knocking the beast unconscious.

It skidded along the rocky ground on its side and came to rest at my feet, heavily snorting for breath with its large canine teeth still bared like a wild boar. I cautiously backed away as the rest of the pack materialized out of the darkness and sniffed their prostrate leader.

Their attention temporarily diverted, I made a mad dash for the monastery yelling at the top of my lungs for someone to open the gates. I don't know if it was an adrenaline rush, the formula or a combination of both, but I never dreamed I could run so fast. Forget the damn dogs—Jesse Owens wouldn't have caught me.

As the monastery gates swung open I collapsed, gasping for air, into Kusung's arms. Far in the distance, I could hear the dogs mournfully howling the loss of their prospective meal.

CHAPTER

❖ 10 ❖

Three days later I was awakened by a gentle tug on my arm as one of Sera's monks politely informed me I had a visitor. I looked around the corner and saw Albert puffing on a cigar as he shuffled against the cold outside the front gates.

"I heard you had a run-in with some of Lhasa's best. Or should I say beast?" He chuckled.

"I don't think that's funny. It was absolutely terrifying."

"Oh please, those dogs haven't killed a healthy adult in memory," he said. "The only fatalities I know of have been children and the infirm. Besides, what are you worried about? It's not as if you have to fear death."

"True, I don't fear death, but I do fear pain. Regardless of my body's ability to heal itself, I've found that I experience pain the same as a mortal and let me assure you that being torn to pieces by wild dogs would not have been a pleasurable experience."

"I suppose it wouldn't be. Anyway, I'm not here to talk about dogs. There's something I want to show you." Albert said as three sun-weathered Tibetans walked up, accompanied by a yak with a tightly roped bundle strapped to its back.

"What's in the bundle?"

"Franz. I thought you might find it interesting to witness what the Tibetans call a Sky Burial."

We trekked across the rocky plain to the outskirts of Lhasa and climbed a series of stone steps until we stood on a cliff overlooking the valley floor hundreds of feet below. The Tibetans untied Franz's body, lowered it to the ground and respectfully unwrapped his corpse. According to Buddhist belief, it takes three days from the time the deceased is clinically dead until the spirit departs the body. This was the third day and Albert was wasting no time in disposing of the remains before the authorities got wind of anything. Prayers were offered over the naked corpse and then two men known as *body breakers* began their gruesome work. Using bone handled meat cleavers, they sliced the flesh off Franz's body until the blades scraped against the ivory white bones. As I watched them lift filets of flesh off the corpse, it was easy to understand why relatives of the deceased were forbidden from attending these rituals.

The bones were then hacked apart, pulverized and mixed into a paste with tsampa. Franz's skull was cracked open to reveal a shrunken lump of brain matter partially dried from three days of exposure to air. The cranial remains were scooped out by hand and mixed with another handful of tsampa and soon all that remained of Franz was a bloody stack of human flesh and a mound of yellowish paste.

A fire of dried cypress was ignited, sending a billowing plume of smoke high into the arid sky. It was like ringing the dinner bell. Within minutes, the sky filled with the enormous silhouettes of Tibetan vultures accepting their invitation to this morbid feast as they'd done for centuries.

Lower and lower they circled until a great mass of gray wings and feathers swooped down and enveloped Franz's remains. We couldn't see them feasting, but we could hear the chip-chip sound of their beaks ripping and tearing away flesh. Suddenly, the vultures stopped simultaneously and raised their bloody heads. The entire flock paused in deathly silence before erupting into an explosion of flapping gray wings.

"What happened?" I asked. "Why are they leaving?"

"I have no idea." Albert shrugged, walking over to consult with the Tibetans. A minute later he returned, chuckling to himself as he shook his head in disbelief.

"They tell me this sort of thing rarely occurs, but it seems that our friend Franz was such a despicable character in life that his flesh had become tainted with his evil deeds. The purpose of the sky burial is to return one's earthly remains to the universe so that other living creatures may benefit from it. In his case, it appears that even the cosmos has rejected him. The Tibetans are not happy about this because they must now collect his remains and cremate them."

While the disgruntled Tibetans began the arduous task of gathering the pieces of Franz's avian-scattered remains, Albert informed me that he wished for nothing more than to render assistance to Chow Li when the time came to attack Chang Sou's fortress. All he needed was a departure date.

"In order to determine that," I said, "I believe that an immediate visit to our favorite monk is necessary." We entered Lhasa and saw thousands of Chinese soldiers patrolling the streets of the ancient city.

"Something's brewing," I whispered.

"Indeed, something is," Albert said. "There have been Chinese soldiers garrisoned here since China invaded Lhasa in September of 1951, but I've never seen anything like this."

"Tell me Albert, is it my imagination or do these Chinese soldiers seem different from the ones I remember during the 1940s?"

"Something's changed and I don't believe it's for the better. These young men appear to be somewhat devoid of emotion and extremely indoctrinated. They're certainly not the same breed of friendly peasant soldiers I encountered in Yenan during the revolution."

Upon reaching the Chakpori Medical School, I assisted Albert up the steps to the summit where he was enthusiastically embraced by Chow Li.

"Franz is dead," I said.

Chow Li was appalled. "How did he die?"

"I killed him," I answered, ignoring Chow Li's expression of revulsion. "Your suspicions were correct. He's been trying to join forces with Chang Sou for almost twenty years."

Chow Li solemnly led us into his room where he requested a moment of silence to pray for Franz's departed soul. I knew the killing of another human being was practically beyond his comprehension. On the other hand, I knew that the bundle of sleeping incense stored underneath the Medical College wasn't going to be used to put Chang Sou and his converts to sleep.

"Albert is going to assist us, Chow Li. When do we leave for Chonggye Valley?"

"I have consulted a monk here at Chakpori who is greatly respected for his gift of prophecy and he has informed me that Chang Sou will begin his march on Lhasa soon after the Dalai Lama leaves the city."

Albert found this prophecy hard to swallow. "The Dalai Lama is planning to abandon the city? I can't believe he would ever do such a thing to his own people."

"Presently, he no such plans," Chow Li said. "But his relationship with the Chinese is rapidly deteriorating and he may not have a choice. From this date forward, we must be ready to depart Lhasa at any time.

Chang Sou has sent his disciples to monasteries throughout Tibet in search of converts for his army of immortals. When he learns that the Dalai Lama has fled, he will gather them together in his fortress in preparation for his march on Lhasa. That will be our only opportunity to eliminate all of them at once. Not one immortal can be allowed to survive."

"I will do everything in my power to ensure our success," I said. "In return, there is something I need from you. In Sian, you promised to supply me with enough of the formula until I could make it safely back to New York. I want the same assurance for Jennifer."

"Good God!" Albert exclaimed. "What makes you think my niece would participate in such a thing?"

"I know she will. I asked her once before and she turned me down, but that was before we lost nine years together. All I want is for Chow Li to supply us with enough of the formula to get us safely back to New York."

"I don't suppose there is anything wrong with affording her this protection," Chow Li said, handing me a jade box of the formula. "Albert, does this mean that you also want the formula?"

"Good heavens, no!" he scoffed. "I am looking forward to meeting my maker just as soon as he is desirous of my company."

Navigating the back alleys to avoid the Chinese soldiers, Albert and I safely made it back to the bungalow.

After fourteen years, our journey was finally coming to an end, but I still had one more bridge to cross. I had to convince Jennifer to take the formula. After she wouldn't answer my polite tapping, I opened the door of her bedroom to find her lying face up in bed with the shades closed and the sheets pulled up to her chin.

"I came by to make sure you were all right."

"I hope he burns in hell," she muttered, staring up at the ceiling.

"Don't waste your time with hate."

"I'm way beyond hate," she said, tilting her head to face me. "My uncle told me he was taking you to Franz's sky burial. How was it?"

"Well, let me put it this way, even the fucking vultures wouldn't eat him."

Jennifer stared at me in bewilderment, but as the meaning of my words sank in, a wry smile crept across her face. It lasted only a moment before she closed her eyes and began to sob.

"Jennifer, don't cry," I said, reaching across the bed to comfort her. "The nightmare's over. Everything's going to be all right. I promise you, we'll never be apart like that again."

"No," she sobbed. "I never want to lose you again."

"Thirteen years ago I asked you to take the immortality formula and you refused. I want you to reconsider. This afternoon Chow Li agreed to supply us with enough of the formula to get us back to New York where I have a forty-seven-year supply we can share. I'm not asking you to be an immortal forever. I just want to make up for some of the time we've lost together."

"And what happens to us after those twenty-three and a half years?"

"Who knows?" I shrugged. "Maybe we'll just sit around and grow old together."

"You really want that with me?"

"Do you remember what the inscription said on the Christmas present you gave me in Yenan?" I asked.

"Of course. It said: I will always love you forever."

"That's right. Forever."

Jennifer arched an eyebrow. "I suppose that by asking me to do something like this you're also asking me to be your wife?"

"Well, yes. As a matter of fact, it does."

"So, ask me."

"All right." I cleared my throat. "Jennifer Harrison, will you marry me?"

"No, you idiot." She laughed, pushing me off the bed. "Get down on one knee or something."

I held her hands as I knelt down beside the bed and looked into her eyes. "Miss Jennifer Harrison, will you marry me?"

"Yes, yes, yes!" she said, smothering my face with kisses.

"Good. Let's open this and get you started."

"What's in there?" she asked, curiously studying the ancient jade box.

"The immortality formula. And I guarantee you're going to hate the taste."

At ten o'clock in the evening of Tuesday, March 17, 1959, the three-hundred-and-seventeen-year reign of the Dalai Lamas passed into history. That evening, our dinner of yak stew was interrupted by an urgent knock on the door of Albert's bungalow. It was a teenage Tibetan student of Chow Li named Losang and he was terrified. Between ragged breaths, he informed us that the Chinese had fired two mortar rounds on to the grounds of the Dalai Lama's summer palace, the Norbulingka. Soon afterward, Chow Li received confirmation that the Dalai Lama had decided to flee Lhasa and he wanted us ready to leave at any time.

It had been steadily building up to that point. On the evening of the 16th, Albert and I ducked into an alley and watched a massive convoy of trucks filled with Chinese soldiers roll into Lhasa. Each truck towed a large object. Even though they were shrouded in tarp, they were quite familiar to me.

"What do you suppose they're pulling behind those trucks?" Albert whispered.

"Artillery. They're planning to blast the Tibetans into submission."

After Losang sprinted away to return to Chow Li, we began packing only those items we deemed essential for the arduous journey ahead.

Having arrived in Lhasa with only my journal and a burlap Buddhist robe, I had no sentimental decisions to make. But, for the last nine years Albert and Jennifer had made a life in Lhasa, and they were having a difficult time. Everything was abandoned in favor of warm clothing and toiletry items. My heart ached for Jennifer when she realized there wasn't another inch of room for a large jewelry box full of prized family heirlooms. She tearfully kissed each heirloom, including an antique shell cameo brooch that belonged to her late grandmother, and gently placed them back in the box.

Kusung tried to console her by telling her that rejection of material possessions would make her a stronger person. Regardless of the spiritual implications, when Jennifer wasn't looking I reached into the jewelry box, grabbed the cameo and slipped it into my robe.

We extinguished every candle and crouched on the floor in total darkness. My eyelids were growing heavy when we were startled by the sharp crack of a gunshot echoing in the distance followed by the roar of a crowd. I glanced at Jennifer's watch. It was 10:30 p.m. Suddenly, we were startled by the sound of brisk footsteps approaching the front of the house. There was a pause, followed by a single knock at the door. I hadn't been this nervous since the war. It was either Chow Li or the Chinese and none of us dared take a breath. Again, there was a single solid knock. I fully expected the door to be kicked open at any moment. Then I heard a familiar high-pitched voice.

"Steven, are you in there?"

I jumped up and unlocked the door. "Chow Li! What are you trying to do, scare us to death?"

"I apologize. The house was so dark I thought we had the wrong address." He was accompanied by Kusung and Losang, who were bent forward from the weight of large bundles of the sleeping incense strapped to their backs.

Chow Li informed us that the Dalai Lama had already slipped out of the Norbulingka dressed as a civilian. There was no telling how long it would be before the Chinese discovered his disappearance. It could be an hour, a day or a week. There was one thing I knew for sure—I didn't want to be within a hundred miles of Lhasa when they found out.

Shielded by the darkness of a moonless night, we followed the sandy banks of the Ri Chu River passing close enough to the Norbulingka to hear the cheering multitude of Tibetans camped outside who still had no idea their revered Dalai Lama had left the city.

We soon came to a narrow part of the Ri Chu that Chow Li insisted was shallow enough for us to wade across, which also meant it was shallow enough for a Chinese Army patrol jeep to drive across. And that's exactly what ran through my mind when I looked further down the river and recognized the glaring floodlights and pointed guard towers of a military camp.

"Chow Li, do those floodlights and guard towers happen to belong to the Chinese Army?"

"I'm afraid they do."

"You must be kidding me!" I said as the six of us made a muted dash to the river's edge and began wading across. I'd only taken a couple of steps into the freezing water when I realized that Chow Li had made a mistake. The Ri Chu was a lot deeper than he thought. By mid-stream, Kusung and I both had our hands full keeping Jennifer, Albert, Losang and Chow Li's heads above the swirling waters while the camp floodlights starkly illuminated our struggle for survival. Inch by inch Kusung and I fought against the current balancing on our toes until the water became shallow and we pulled the others onto the bank of the opposite shore.

I looked back to see the Chinese sentries facing the other way in their guard towers, too busy watching the thousands of Tibetans threatening to riot in front of the Norbulingka.

But now we faced another problem: hypothermia.

We were drenched with frigid water and the air temperature was well below freezing. Fortunately, we'd all brought a change of clothes. Without embarrassment, we stripped off our wet garments and pulled on our spare clothing. It was a battle to assist Albert who kept insisting he didn't need any help, but expediency took precedent over pride and we were soon on our way.

"What happened back there?" I asked Chow Li as we trudged deeper into the safety of the darkened countryside. "Albert, Jennifer and Losang could have drowned."

"I am terribly sorry. I was only trying to follow the escape route of the Dalai Lama."

The escape route of the Dalai Lama? Now we had to be doubly cautious. I had no doubt that the Tibetans had left men stationed behind for rearguard protection in case the P.L.A. picked up his trail. And that's exactly what happened when a dozen men on horseback charged out of the blackness and surrounded us. The red tassels braided into their hair and the daggers dangling from their belts identified them as Khampas rebels. Their Enfield .303 British rifles, each adorned with a pair of antelope horns, were pointed at us.

Their leader dismounted and addressed us in Tibetan. Chow Li smiled assuredly and answered him in his native tongue. Satisfied with what he heard, the Khampan commander motioned his men to lower their rifles and allowed us to continue. As I walked past him, he pulled a white scarf from around his neck and tied it around mine as a gesture of friendship.

"What did you say to him?" I asked Chow Li.

"I told him the truth. He was particularly impressed that you were an American soldier and is grateful you are supporting the Dalai Lama."

"Why did you tell him that?"

"The Dalai Lama passed through here less than an hour ago and he is under strict orders to shoot anyone who follows in his path. His brother was forced by the Chinese to fight in the Korean War and was killed by the Americans. I told him you were supporting the Dalai Lama, just in case."

"Just in case of what?"

"Just in case he wanted to avenge his brother's death."

We slogged through the snow and by daybreak reached the shores of the Tsang Po River. The Tsang Po was much wider than the Ri Chu, and the only way to get across was by ferry boat. Here we ran into our first real obstacle. The elderly Tibetan ferry tender would simply not less us pass. After trying to reason with him, a frustrated Chow Li returned shaking his head.

"We cannot continue. The ferry master will not let us cross under any circumstances. He has his orders and will shoot us if necessary."

"In that case," I said, "just tell him the truth."

"Which is?'

"Tell him we possess strange powers. The old man is probably superstitious. Tell him we are immortal."

Chow Li trudged back to the ferry master and began animatedly chatting with him, stopping only to point back at me and Kusung. The old man listened attentively for a minute before he reared his head back and howled with laughter.

Unfazed, Chow Li began walking towards the ferry boat. The ferry master unshouldered his rifle and shouted a warning. Chow Li ignored him and kept walking. The ferry master leaned into his rifle, took aim and shouted another warning. Upon reaching the ferry, Chow Li looked back with an air of indignation and calmly placed his foot on the rail of the boat.

Bang!

Jennifer screamed as Chow Li was blown completely out of his sandals and disappeared into the ferry.

Quivering with fright, the ferry master wheeled around and took hard aim at us. We instantly raised our hands in surrender. After a tense moment he lowered his weapon, dropped to his knees and buried his face in his weathered hands, sobbing.

His cries were soon interrupted by the sound of coughing coming from inside the boat. The ferry master peered between his fingers to see Chow Li dusting himself off and climbing out of the boat to retrieve his sandals.

Overcome with relief, the ferry master ran to him and threw himself on the frozen ground, hugging Chow Li's ankles as he begged for forgiveness.

Embarrassed, Chow Li pulled him to his feet and sternly chastised him for his violent reaction.

Minutes later the ferry master was happily singing an old Tibetan folk song as he poled us across the Tsang Po in his yak-hide boat. He cheerfully deposited us on the shore of the village of Kyeshong. Here, there was no need for Chow Li to explain our identities to these villagers as he had to the Khampas rebels. The old ferry master did all the talking, shielding us from the crowd and swatting away anyone who got too curious. The villagers informed us that the Dalai Lama had passed through the area only a scant three hours earlier.

And that's the way it was for the next five days. Every time we stopped at a village or monastery, we were told that the Dalai Lama had passed through before us, but the gap was widening. Riding on horseback, he was steadily gaining ground and because of Albert's condition, we had to rest frequently. We resolved that dilemma in the village of Dophu Chockhur by procuring two Tibetan horses that not only carried Albert, but also relieved Losang and Kusung of the backbreaking responsibility of carrying the sleeping incense. Henceforth, we picked up the pace.

It was apparent that the Dalai Lama was heading southeast, skirting along the border of Bhutan as he made his way towards India. The fastest and most obvious escape route would have been to journey west out of Lhasa and that's exactly where the Chinese were looking for him.

We stopped to feed our horses in the village of Chenye. Here we heard an eyewitness account of the fall of Lhasa from a Khampas warrior who'd left the city after us and was riding non-stop to catch up with the Dalai Lama. He told us that two nights after we'd left Lhasa, hand-to-hand fighting had broken out in front of the Norbulingka and the Chinese began shelling the city with artillery before dawn. Incredibly, the Potala Palace was only slightly hit, but, the Norbulingka was bombarded by hundreds of shells and the Drepung and Sera monasteries were blasted to rubble. The streets of Lhasa, particularly those surrounding the Norbulingka, were strewn with the corpses of thousands of Tibetan men, women and children. In the end, the Chinese had shown their true hand. When they thought the Dalai Lama had waited too long to come out, they decided to abandon their false diplomacy and murder him.

"Would you happen to know the status of the medical college atop Chakpori Hill?" Chow Li asked the Khampas warrior as he watered his horse.

"I'm sorry. The medical college was completely razed by artillery. It no longer exists."

At the news of his beloved ancient school's destruction, Chow Li released a wail of anguish. "Two thousand years of precious knowledge destroyed," he cried. "Why have the Han always been so cruel?"

We reached the Riudechen Monastery just as the setting sun was casting gigantic shadows over the Chonggye Valley. The tombs of the Tibetan kings were so large that I initially mistook them for the eroded bases of ancient hills. As we entered the monastic grounds, we encountered hundreds of horses being tended by their Khampan masters.

We'd finally caught up with the Dalai Lama.

We entered the monastery where Chow Li was warmly welcomed by four elder monks who represented the six hundred monks residing there. They seated us in a circular anteroom where we were served a steaming round of yak butter tea.

I was swallowing the last of the nutritious brew when a giant Tibetan swept aside a curtain to introduce the Dalai Lama, who slightly bowed his head and entered. He was dressed in a simple red Buddhist robe and appeared to be in his early twenties. I was immediately impressed with his peaceful and submissive demeanor. This was the man whom the Chinese feared so much? The giant Tibetan was the Dalai Lama's Senior Chamberlain who slowly guided the religious leader around the room, making introductions. Albert bowed and Jennifer curtsied as if they were being presented to the King of England. When I ribbed him about this later, Albert sniffed and corrected my ignorance. There was now a Queen of England.

The Dalai Lama's powerful stature among his people was plainly demonstrated when he greeted Losang. The young immortal swooned.

As I helped Losang steady himself, I found myself face to face with the Dalai Lama. Chow Li told him I'd served with the American Army during the war.

"In Korea?" the Dalai Lama asked in a singsong voice.

"No, I served in Germany during World War Two."

He was surprised. "You must have been very young. I have read about the atrocities the Germans committed against those of the Jewish faith and others they considered to be undesirable. It sounds almost too horrible to believe. Did you see any evidence of this?"

"Yes. I was among the first Americans who liberated the concentration camp at Dachau."

"Fascinating." He nodded. "I would relish the opportunity to speak with you at length about this dark chapter in mankind's history, but I am unable to do so at this time as there is another being written in my country."

The Dalai Lama chatted with us on a variety of subjects, politely deflecting any questions regarding his present dilemma. I got the impression it was simply too painful for him to discuss. When his Senior

Chamberlain quietly interrupted to remind him of his early departure in the morning, he blessed us and retired for the evening. After he withdrew, I found myself facing two somber-faced Riudechen elders who couldn't seem to take their eyes off Kusung.

"Chow Li," I said, beckoning him from across the room. "I think we have a problem."

The two elders approached Chow Li. They told him they recognized Kusung as one of Chang Sou's disciples who'd visited their monastery the year before seeking converts for his army of immortals. Chow Li invited Kusung over. He explained that, although their story was true, he was now aiding us in our quest to destroy Chang Sou. They appeared satisfied with his denouncement of evil and blessed him for his return to the path of spiritual enlightenment.

Their satisfaction turned to absolute rapture when I confessed to killing Franz, the sole survivor of the 1942 Nazi expedition to Chonggye Valley. They revealed how the 1941 Nazi expedition had deceived the Tibetans into helping them until they discovered the Germans' ultimate goal was to join forces with a lost civilization the Riudechen monks believed would unleash a great evil. Soon afterwards, the expedition vanished. The same scenario repeated itself in 1942, except this time one of the Germans—Franz—escaped, terrifying the monks as they rightfully assumed he would return with men and weapons. The cruel irony for the Germans was that, in 1942, Chang Sou and his disciples wouldn't arrive in Tibet for eight more years.

Afterward, we were shown to our quarters. The monks had set aside three small rooms for us. Kusung and Losang were assigned one, Albert and Jennifer another, and Chow Li and myself the third. The next few days would decide our collective destiny.

"Jennifer," I said, grasping her delicate hand before she entered her room. "I'd like you to stay with me tonight."

Albert was appalled. "That is an outrageous and disrespectful suggestion! Did you forget you are addressing my niece?"

"I was simply addressing my future wife."

"Is this true, Jennifer?" Albert asked, wounded. "Why didn't you tell me?"

"I'm sorry, Uncle Albert. I was going to tell you after we arrived home in Manhattan, but the truth is that I love Steven very much and have agreed to marry him."

Albert barely mumbled something congratulatory as he disappeared into his room with Chow Li.

Our sleeping quarters consisted of a small wooden bed illuminated by the flickering light of a single silver lamp filled with yak butter. It didn't matter. After fourteen years, Jennifer and I were finally alone. I sat down on the edge of the bed and watched in breathless anticipation as Jennifer stood before me and slowly undressed, staring deeply into my eyes. She allowed each piece of clothing to slip off her body and drop to the floor, revealing an athletic female physique more beautiful than my sex-starved mind had ever imagined.

At that moment, I felt as though I could've lived forever without air, food or water. I only desired her.

She bent down toward me. "We have a small problem," she whispered.

"We do?" I asked, nervously looking around the room. "What?"

"You're still wearing your robe."

I have never undressed so quickly in my life. Each thread and fiber covering my body was nothing more than a material obstacle to possessing her. After I disrobed, I pulled her onto the bed. Then she said something I'll never forget.

"You are the only man I have ever loved."

There is such a thing as hunger and there is such a thing as desire. And there is something that combines both in a way that is indescribable.

That would only begin to describe the magnitude of passion that consumed us. The immortality formula has a way of suppressing emotion in favor of logical behavior. Last night I learned that it didn't destroy emotion; it simply stored it up to be released at will. That night I released all of it.

I awakened to the first golden rays of sunlight creeping across the tombs of the ancient Tibetan kings. I had never felt such an exuberance and lust for life as I did that morning. My only regret was that I couldn't capture that exquisite moment and bottle it up to savor again fifty years later as one would a vintage wine. Curled up warmly against me, her beautiful head of auburn hair nestled against my heart, my precious Jennifer slept soundly, a woman finally at peace, perfectly content with the faintest of smiles upon her lips.

And for the first time in her life she would not be awakened by a nightmare.

We departed the Riudechen Monastery as Kusung directed us south to a remote village called E-Chhudhogyang. E-Chhudhogyang is infamous throughout Tibet as one of the most inhospitable places in the world. Chow Li told me of an old Tibetan proverb that states, "It is better to be born a beast than to live in E-Chhudhogyang."

Regardless, this wretched collection of hovels had a profound meaning for us, as it was located not far from the base of the mountain where Kusung claimed that Chang Sou had founded New Agartha. Only four of us departed from the Riudechen Monastery that chilly morning. Albert was stricken with fever and Jennifer volunteered to stay behind and nurse him. That meant we'd have to back track to the Chonggye Valley after we'd completed our mission. Even with the protection of the formula, I feared for her safety. After all, we were journeying into the unknown to commit the unthinkable– the murder of an immortal.

With the bundles of sleeping incense strapped to our two horses, we trekked for two days until we came face to face with a mountain called Yarto Tag-la. It was exceedingly difficult for all of us, particularly the horses, to climb this titan. Losang was the first to make it over the summit and he cheered at the unexpected vista that greeted him. We discovered that Yarto Tag-la led directly onto a picturesque plateau complete with grazing yaks and a small lake covered in ice. This was the idyllic beauty of Tibet that had haunted explorers for centuries. Sadly, I found it to be short lived, for within a couple of miles the green earth faded into a barren desert, and the howling winds engulfed us in choking clouds of dust. Barely visible in the swirling torrent, Chow Li raised his hand and signaled for us to stop.

"What is it?" I shouted above the wind. "What's out there?"

"Chang Sou. I am beginning to sense his heartbeat. We are getting close."

"Not quite!" Kusung yelled, shaking his head. "We have another five hours until we reach his fortress."

"If that is so," Chow Li said, "I am afraid his powers have strengthened considerably."

Meanwhile, his student Losang trudged quietly in the background keeping to himself. He hadn't said two words since we'd left the monastery. I dropped back and drew near him. "Is something troubling you, Losang?"

He nodded. "I am not afraid to die if my death aids in liberating the world from this evil man, but there is something that keeps troubling me. Is it painful when one is killed?"

He *would* have to ask *that* question.

"No, not really," I lied. What the hell. By the time he found out it wouldn't make much difference. "Kusung!" I shouted above the wind, scanning a wall of mountain peaks in the distance. "Do any of those contain Chang Sou's fortress?"

"Yes, you are looking directly at it."

"I am?" Each snow-capped mountain peak looked no different from the next. "Then how come I can't see it?"

"Because your eyes are deceiving you."

I closed my eyes and nearly jumped out of my skin. Embedded in the body of the tallest mountain was a massive, pulsating red triangle.

"Chang Sou has built a pyramid!"

"A what?" Kusung asked.

"A pyramid!" I shouted, pointing to the center tallest of three peaks in the distance. "Chang Sou has created a pyramid inside of that mountain." Chow Li, Kusung and Losang gathered around me while I knelt down and traced the outline of a pyramid in the sand.

"Where else do they build these pyramids?" Chow Li asked. "And for what reason?"

"No one builds them anymore," I said. "The most famous ones were constructed in Egypt thousands of years ago as tombs for their kings."

Chow Li erased the outline with his sandal. "That doesn't surprise me. Chang Sou has always held a deep fascination for the ancient Egyptian quest for immortality."

As we trekked across the sand, I periodically closed my eyes to study the pyramid's location within the mountain. The majority of the structure was buried beneath the valley floor while the upper point protruded about a hundred feet above the surface.

I was alternately opening and closing my eyes when I spotted something in the windswept sands ahead of us. I squinted hard and was amazed to see a pride of ten adult lions lounging comfortably in the sand.

Picking up our scent, they sat up, stretched, and began to amble lazily in our direction.

I tapped Chow Li on his shoulder. "Do there happen to be any lions in Tibet?"

"Lions in Tibet? Of course not!" Chow Li laughed. "They have been extinct in this country for centuries."

"Then I suggest you tell the ones heading this way."

Chow Li craned his neck forward and searched the horizon. His eyes went wide when he spotted the animals.

"Do not be afraid!" he shouted, with more than a touch of nervousness in his voice. "We are nearing Chang Sou's fortress. What you are seeing is an illusion he has conjured to frighten wayward travelers away. It is no more of a danger than a mirage."

As the distance between us and the animals shortened, all of us, with the exception of Chow Li, began to fall back behind the horses. The diminutive monk was now leading us single file and that was perfectly fine by me. If those lions turned out to be more than an illusion, Chow Li would be the first to know.

The wind reversed direction and we could smell their musky odor. The horses reared up in terror.

"I didn't know it was possible to smell a mirage," I shouted as Kusung and Losang fought to contain the horses.

The lions were about a hundred yards ahead when they broke into a charge. Chow Li chanted loudly as the rest of us crouched behind him and pulled the horses close to our sides for protection.

The pride was almost upon us when an enormous male shot into the lead and bolted straight for Chow Li. From over thirty feet away the animal sprang into the air with eyes ablaze, claws outstretched, and snarling mouth agape. I hunkered down, closed my eyes and braced for the impact.

It never came.

At the very instant the lion's claws would have ripped into Chow Li, its image froze in mid-flight and vanished. In quick succession, the other lions leapt into the air and disappeared in the same manner. Terrifying to be sure, but by the time the last lion attacked, I was confident enough to reach out and swat it away like an imaginary fly.

And that's when I received a shock. Though it disappeared in a flash, I could've sworn the palm of my hand had actually brushed against its leathery nose.

"That was fantastic!" I shouted above the wind, impressed by Chang Sou's display of magic and greatly relieved that I didn't have a six hundred pound lion sitting on my head.

"I'm glad you found it entertaining," Chow Li said, wiping his face.

"What's wrong? I thought you said we had nothing to fear because they were only illusions."

"Yes, they were illusions, but I've never encountered one of Chang Sou's illusions that was capable of doing this." Chow Li raised his chin to reveal three angry welts leading in a perfect line from his jugular vein across his throat. "I'm afraid his illusions are on the threshold of becoming reality. We must hurry for it appears that Chang Sou is reviving the ancient magic of the Bon religion."

"The Bon religion?"

"It is the religion indigenous to Tibet. Chang Sou and all of the early Tibetan kings buried in Chonggye Valley practiced it. Much of it has been absorbed into Tibetan Buddhism, but the pure Bon religion was governed by exorcists, shamans and high-priests, all yielding fantastic magical powers."

"That's interesting because when I slapped that lion it felt as though I actually touched something."

"You did touch something, but it wasn't a lion. It was energy disguised as a lion."

An hour later, we reached the base of Chang Sou's mountain. It rose like a steep hill before transforming into a nearly vertical face of solid rock that shot skyward for at least a thousand feet.

Perplexed, Kusung studied the mountain before informing us that something had changed. The main entrance to the fortress no longer existed. He pointed to a spot where the hill met the vertical face, but it was now sealed solid, probably in response to Kusung's defection.

We had to find another way inside.

"Look for anything that resembles an air hole," Chow Li advised. "If you find one, don't shout. Just raise your hand."

Leaving the horses behind, we fanned out and slowly walked up the hill. Almost immediately, Losang began flagging his arm. He'd discovered an air hole large enough for a man to slip inside, but judging by the blast of warm, humid air reeking of smoke and perspiration, Losang had stumbled upon an exhaust vent. We needed to find an opening where the incense could be sucked in, not blown out.

To me, the solution was obvious. The fresh air entrance would have to be located somewhere up the vertical face where it would catch the pre-vailing mountain winds—much like a ship's funnel at sea.

I tilted my head back and saw it immediately about eighty feet up the vertical face—a round entrance about six feet in diameter and more than sufficient to ventilate a large interior.

I picked up a piece of sandstone and flung it up at the opening. A small brown puff exploded off the mountain wall beside it and was imme-diately sucked inside.

Now all I wanted to do was scale that wall, light the incense, seal it up and race back to the Chonggye Valley as fast as the horses could carry me. When I pointed out to Chow Li that the sun was setting and we needed to hurry, he looked down at the ground and slowly shook his head.

"You must understand that we cannot leave unless we are certain that Chang Sou and every one of his immortals are dead."

"Chow Li, don't do this to me."

"I'm sorry Steven, but we must be absolutely certain; otherwise, all of our efforts will be in vain." Losang and Kusung stared mutely at us and offered no opinion.

"Fine," I snapped. "Let's get this over with as quickly as possible."

Climbing the wall was not as impossible as it first appeared. There were numerous pieces of jagged rose quartz crystal protruding out of the mountainside. Regardless, I didn't have an easy time of it. The setting sun was casting long shadows that severely distorted my depth perception and a couple of times I reached for a crystal that wasn't there.

Fortunately, Kusung was an experienced climber and patiently guided us up the mountainside one at a time. After he'd safely escorted all of us to the ledge of the entrance, he went back down to retrieve the bundles of incense while we huddled together and braced against the powerful suction of freezing wind.

Kusung led the way inside followed by me, Chow Li and Losang. The tunnel banked down sharply to the left and we were soon immersed in total darkness. We gingerly crawled into the icy bowels of the mountain, inching our way in a slowly descending circle as the freezing wind continuously pummeled our backs like an icy whip. The roar of the wind was deafening and I soon became numb with cold. Sensory deprivation was a problem and the only thing that kept me from losing my senses was Chow Li who kept ramming into my back.

My thighs were beginning to cramp when I glanced up and noticed the faint outline of Kusung ahead. There was light coming from around the bend.

I crawled out of the tunnel and joined Kusung on a narrow ledge just below the pyramid's ceiling. He was lying on his stomach peering over the edge. Whatever Kusung was watching below had him completely mesmerized.

I crept up alongside as I heard the booming echo of a man's voice reverberating throughout the pyramid's massive interior. I looked down to see at least a thousand men in black robes assembled on the pyramid floor approximately five hundred feet below us. They were fixating upon a man with long blonde hair, ranting and gesturing wildly from behind a stone altar. Mounted on the wall behind him were two giant silver winged dragons flanking a glittering symbol of gold. I don't know if I've ever seen dragons look so formidable, but I could never forget that twisted cross.

It was an inverted swastika.

Chang Sou was addressing his army of immortals and, by the look of things, they were primed and ready for action.

I pulled back from the edge as Chow Li and Losang emerged from the tunnel.

"What do you see down there?" Chow Li asked.

"Chang Sou and his army. We don't have much time."

I pulled him up to the precipice while Losang waited behind. After a moment of observation, Chow Li sat back on his haunches.

"What is Chang Sou saying?" I asked.

"He is aware that the Dalai Lama has departed Lhasa. They plan to march on the city tomorrow."

"Who are all those men down there?"

"He addressed them as his lost brothers, but I recognize many of them as monks from the Sera, Drepung and Nechung monasteries."

"I think we've seen enough," I said. "Let's fire up the incense and get out of here."

Suddenly, the lights below grew dim and a hush settled over the crowd. The silence was broken by the sound of music. I looked down to see three monks sitting at the foot of the altar, plucking strange stringed instruments cradled in their laps. It had been a long time, but the eerie melodies were unmistakably familiar.

I closed my eyes and understood why Hines, Jack Scoville and Charlie Parker had been so impressed. The discordant, yet extremely soothing and seductive sounds were not of this world.

My musical flashback was shattered by a high-pitched scream as a naked Tibetan woman was carried overhead by Chang Sou and forced down onto the stone altar. After he secured her wrists and ankles, Chang Sou raised a gold knife for all to see before plunging it deep into her heart and burying it to the hilt.

After she stilled, he untied her limp corpse and tossed it onto the frenzied crowd where it was passed hand over hand, showering those dancing underneath with blood.

The altar was wiped clean and another victim was selected by Chang Sou from a group of terrified Tibetan women lined up behind the altar. Those yet to be chosen waited with heads bowed in submission shaking uncontrollably with fright, some urinating, as they waited their turn to be sacrificed.

I looked over at Chow Li to see he'd closed his eyes. How many times had this scenario repeated itself over the centuries? How many times in the last two thousand years had Chow Li simply closed his eyes? I became overwhelmed by rage and grabbed Chow Li by the throat.

"Look!" I screamed, forcing his head over the edge to watch the slaughter below as another female corpse was thrown onto the delirious crowd. "You're not closing your eyes this time. Take a good look! You should have stopped this bastard centuries ago!"

Two large hands calmly grasped mine as Kusung wrenched open my grip.

"You may be right," Chow Li said, gasping for breath as he touched his neck with trembling fingers. "I may have made the mistake of putting too much faith in . . . "

He was cut short as another scream reverberated through the pyramid.

"Untie the incense!" Chow Li commanded. "When you see that I have begun to physically engage Chang Sou, ignite it and escape through the tunnel as fast as you can."

"What do you mean by physically engaging Chang Sou?" I asked. "Don't tell me you're going down there. You'll never make it out of here alive!"

"I am sorry, but Chang Sou must never kill again."

Before I could say another word, Chow Li jumped off the ledge, flipped over onto his back, and floating down to the pyramid floor as gently as a leaf. Shouting his teacher's name, Losang leaped after him and descended in the same fashion.

Chow Li landed undetected at the rear of the mob and was beginning to make his way forward when Losang landed beside him. Chow Li was shocked, but there was nothing he could do but allow his faithful student to follow him to his death. They were working their way through the crowd and had almost made it to the altar when Chang Sou spotted them.

He pointed at Chow Li and shrieked his name in a voice so hideous it silenced both the mob and the music. Monks tried to restrain Chow Li, but they were promptly pushed away by Losang who was then viciously beaten and dragged underneath a churning mob of black robes.

With no one standing between them, Chang Sou and Chow Li faced each other as the crowd of immortals stepped back and kept a respectful distance. They warily encircled each other for a minute, and then Chang Sou charged forward.

Chow Li deftly stepped sideways as Chang Sou roared past him and crashed into the stone altar. The surrounding immortals let out a collective gasp. Shaking his head to recover his senses, Chang Sou spun around and charged again. Again Chow Li stepped aside, but not before sticking out a tiny leg to send the giant tumbling across the stone floor eliciting a ripple of laughter from the throng.

At the sound of this disrespect, Chang Sou went berserk and attacked a handful of immortal monks standing nearest to him, knocking them to the ground with one roundhouse swing of his cinder block sized fist. He then turned his attention back to Chow Li and lowered his head as if he was going to charge again.

Instead, he paused. Chang Sou slowly raised himself until he stood completely erect and the raging blood drained from his face. I don't know if it was the formula getting a handle on his emotions, but he seemed to realize that Chow Li had caught him in a classic psychological trap: the angrier he became, the calmer Chow Li would react. And Chow Li would win.

Chang Sou passively approached Chow Li and rested his massive hands on the diminutive monk's shoulders. Caught off guard by his sudden change of demeanor, Chow Li could do nothing more than manage an uncomfortable smile. Chang Sou smiled back before slamming Chow Li backwards with such force that I could hear the crack of his skull hitting the stone floor. He scooped up the unconscious monk and tossed him hundreds of feet into the air.

"Light the incense!" I shouted to Kusung whose hands were shaking so hard he fumbled the lighter. "Give it to me!" I yelled, snatching it away. Flipping open the steel cap, I flicked the flint wheel and sparked the wick. As I touched the flame to a branch of the incense, I read the inscription engraved on the lighter:

"A man who has taught me how to live and die."

Fanned by the winds blasting through the tunnel, the incense quickly began to smolder, forcing Kusung and I to back away as thick white smoke billowed and spilled off the ledge. Meanwhile, Chang Sou and the crowd below were kicking Chow Li's body around the pyramid floor as if it were a soccer ball.

The smoke from sleeping incense silently cascaded over the ledge like a phantom waterfall and collected on the empty floor before rearing up like a white tidal wave in slow motion. As it proceeded to engulf those standing at the back, the immortals reached for their throats and collapsed in convulsions. Hearing their screams, those closest to the wave turned around and tried in vain to outrun the wall of death rolling inexorably toward them. It was the ultimate irony to watch these swastika worshipping men be annihilated in what had now become a giant gas chamber.

Alerted by the commotion, Chang Sou glanced up from kicking Chow Li's body to see the wave of smoke sweeping toward him. Raising his eyes to the source, he recognized Kusung perched high on the ledge.

"Kusung, you traitorous snake!" he screamed. "How dare you join forces with these servants of Buddha!"

At his command, the surviving immortals rushed behind the altar and disappeared into a passageway.

Kusung was terrified. "If they capture me I will be tortured for eternity. We must go!"

Suddenly, the prostrate Chow Li sprang to life. He grabbed the hem of Chang Sou's robe and pulled the giant off his feet.

"Not yet!" I shouted, straining my eyes through the lethal fog.

Chang Sou and Chow Li became a single blur as they furiously rolled around and wrestled under the thickening smoke. But they were tiring. Chow Li pushed Chang Sou away and stood up. Gasping for breath, he outstretched his tiny arms in what looked like a final reconciliatory gesture.

Chang Sou staggered toward him but faltered and fell to his knees. The smoke parted to reveal Chow Li standing over Chang Sou, tenderly stroking the dying giant's long blond hair as he whispered something into his ear. Then Chow Li looked straight up at me. His two-thousand-year odyssey had come to an end. As he locked his eyes upon mine, I was shocked to hear his voice resonate clearly in my head.

"Never forget the oath you have taken."

The phrase echoed over and over in my brain until a fresh blanket of thick white smoke rose up and spilled across the pyramid floor.

Then he was gone.

I didn't have a second to mourn for there was no time to waste. The immortals had reappeared directly below our ledge and were literally climbing the walls to get to us.

With the wind safely blowing the smoke behind us, Kusung and I dragged the burning incense into the tunnel as a myriad of faces, grotesquely twisted by convulsions, desperately tried to claw their way to reach us. One by one they fell back and disappeared into the white oblivion. Dropping the burning incense to shield our escape, we held our heads down against the blasting wind and crawled away quickly until the tunnel straightened to reveal a clear sky full of stars.

Now we had to seal the tunnel, not only to seal Chang Sou's fate, but to protect ours as well. From our vantage point I counted eleven of the fortress's exhaust vents billowing smoke, transforming the hillside below into a forest of deadly white geysers. Unless we found a way to block the tunnel and stop the flow of air into the mountain, we'd never make it back to our horses alive.

Kusung and I re-entered the tunnel and probed the walls for weaknesses until we discovered water dripping from the roof. Digging our way into the moist earth with our bare hands, we pulled back just as a torrent of rock cascaded down and completely filled the tunnel.

Returning to the entrance, I was relieved to see the exhaust holes were no longer spewing smoke and the wind was carrying the poisonous haze off into the distance. We recovered our horses and rode through the night, crossing into the Chonggye Valley around noon. The sight that greeted us made my heart race with anxiety. Black smoke billowed from the monastery and the ancient castle above it. As we kicked our heels and galloped across the valley, I recognized the wreckage of military jeeps and trucks littering the monastic grounds.

The Chinese army had arrived.

There had been a battle and, from the looks of things, the Tibetans had fought back hard. There were gaping sections in the five-foot-high surrounding wall, as if it had been hit by artillery at point-blank range.

As we came closer we heard voices and laughter coming from the courtyard. Kusung ducked down and sprinted along the shattered perimeter to the back of the monastery. At his signal I raced to him as he raised his head and peered over the top of the wall.

"Do you see anything?" I gasped.

He sat down and numbly stared at the wall. "Steven, you do not want to see this."

I poked my head over the wall to see the Chinese crucifying Albert. They had lashed his naked, withered body to a ten foot high cross, binding his wrists and ankles to the beams. Six soldiers milled around the base, taunting him and taking turns throwing his pants and shirt into the air and spearing the clothing with their bayonets. The ground shook with a powerful rumble that sounded like a wave of approaching thunder. I turned to see two silver aircraft, emblazoned with red stars on their tails, rocket out of the cloudless blue sky and roar past us at ground level as the helmeted pilots waved stiffly to the cheering soldiers on the ground.

I'd seen this all before.

It was the vision I'd experienced at the Black Onyx on New Year's Eve of 1946.

Incredibly, Albert was still alive and, judging by the way he squirmed against the ropes, suffering in great pain.

He stopped writhing and threw his head back against the wooden beam as he gazed up at the sky. "Deliver me from this evil!" he screamed at the top of his lungs, startling the soldiers below him. They stopped throwing his clothes in the air and stared up at him contemptuously.

One of them climbed a ladder and held an open canteen just out of reach of Albert's parched mouth. As he leaned forward to take a sip, another soldier viciously rammed the bayonet of his rifle into the ex-missionary's stomach.

The oppressed had become the oppressor.

"For the love of God, deliver me from this evil!" he screamed.

It was the most horrific sound I'd ever heard wrenched from the depths of a man's soul. My only thought was I would do anything in my power to never hear it again.

I turned to Kusung. "Are you ready to do business with these people?"

He nodded and we bolted over the wall.

They didn't have time to raise their rifles.

Kusung instantly snapped the first soldier's neck he grabbed while I yanked another's weapon away, a very effective submachine-gun called an AK-47, and shot the others. Albert was in dismal condition. His fingernails had been ripped out and cigarette burns dotted his torso. Kusung reached around the base of the cross and lifted it completely out of the earth, depositing it gently on the ground with Albert still attached.

"Why did they do this to you, Albert?" I asked, untying the bloody ropes that had burned their way down to his wrist bones. "Where's Jennifer?"

"The Chinese are hell bent on revenge," he muttered. "They arrived yesterday afternoon, only hours after the Dalai Lama left, and began executing the elder monks. I was awakened by the sound of gunshots and tried to negotiate with them, begging them to spare the others. I thought I was making progress until I made the mistake of mentioning Christianity. I don't know what I was thinking. These are not the same Chinese I taught twenty years ago. The very mention of religion seemed to infuriate them. They answered me by reciting Mao's infamous statement that 'Religion is poison' and insisted that people like me were enemies of the state. Their commander decided that if I believed in Jesus Christ so much then I should find it an honor to die like him. I've been tied to that cross since this morning. Thankfully, Jennifer never saw what happened to me."

"Where is she?"

"They took her and the surviving monks up the hill to the Chingwa Tagtse Castle. They're going to truck them off to China tomorrow morning."

"How many monks survived?"

"I'm not sure. When they realized they were going to be slaughtered the monks fought back with incredible bravery. At one point they almost overwhelmed the Chinese, until they broke out their flamethrowers. That settled things rather quickly. There are probably no more than twenty survivors."

Twenty survivors—out of six hundred.

"How many soldiers are up there?"

"I don't know. I'm amazed they didn't come running down here when you opened fire. Then again, they've been shooting off their guns all day in celebration of their so-called victory. Bastards. It takes a lot of guts to shoot an unarmed monk."

Albert was in desperate need of medical attention. He was bleeding profusely from the bayonet wound to his abdomen and suffering from exposure.

"Would you mind carrying me inside of the monastery, old boy?" he asked. "I'd much rather die in the shade."

I lifted him up and carried him inside the shattered building. The corpses of executed monks were everywhere and the stench of decomposing flesh was unbearable. Albert asked me to leave him a rifle.

"You're not going to do anything rash, are you?" I asked, prying a rifle from the hand of a dead Chinese soldier and laying it across Albert's lap.

"Of course not," he said. "I don't believe in suicide, but I have no intention of allowing some brainwashed Communist soldier to use this wretched old body for target practice."

I returned outside to collect rifles and ammunition while Kusung picked up each of the wounded Chinese and snapped their necks with his powerful hands. I handed Kusung one of the Chinese guns just as he finished applying the *coup de grâce* to the last wounded soldier.

"What do you know about that castle?" I asked him, pointing to the imposing battle-scarred structure high atop the hill.

"The Chingwa Tagtse Castle is very sacred. It is the birthplace of the Fifth Dalai. Both the Potala Palace and the Chakpori Medical College were built during his reign in the late seventeenth century."

"You don't say," I said, studying the steep hill for a way to reach the summit undetected. Then I saw it. A drainage ditch running along the hill that intersected at the top with the castle's outer wall.

We scampered across the courtyard and dove into the ditch. There were no signs of life coming from the castle above. My combat experience was telling me that this was much too easy. Keeping low, we made our way up the ditch to the summit and followed the outside of the wall around to the castle's mammoth wooden door.

Kusung put his ear to the wood and heard nothing. Grabbing onto a large iron ring, he planted his feet and pulled with all of his strength while I nervously aimed my gun.

The door opened to reveal at least a dozen Chinese soldiers sitting cross-legged on the floor, peacefully eating their lunches. The whole damn lot of them looked up at us in wide-eyed surprise, their mouths full of food and rice bowls resting in their laps. Curiously, their rifles were nowhere to be seen.

Kusung and I opened fire and blasted everything in sight. The air exploded with rice, chopsticks and human flesh. The unarmed soldiers sitting by the door never had a chance. But the ones at the rear were armed, took cover and immediately began returning fire.

We soon found ourselves standing unprotected in the middle of a ferocious fire-fight. Within seconds we were blasted off our feet.

"Oh my Lord Buddha," Kusung moaned, fingering the bleeding bullet holes in his chest, "I am in so much pain."

After almost four hundred years, this turned out to be Kusung's first experience with the wound healing powers of the immortality formula. The poor guy was in so much agony he probably thought he really was going to die.

"You're going to be all right," I whispered. "Close your eyes and play dead."

Lying on my back, I heard the soldiers shuffling around as they crawled out of their hiding places. Sliding my hand across the ground, I gently turned the barrel of my submachine gun in their direction and curled my finger around the trigger. When they stepped out of the doorway I snatched it up and fired. The smoke cleared and revealed seven dead Chinese soldiers still holding their rifles. Their bayonets had been fixed.

"How do you feel?" I asked Kusung as he curiously examined the small pink circles dotting his chest.

"Like I have been reborn within the same life." He grinned.

"Well, don't celebrate just yet. You might be reborn a couple of more times before the day is over."

Kusung went inside the castle to mercy kill the wounded. He reached down for the first man's neck and recoiled in horror. "This man is a monk from the monastery!"

"What?"

"This man is a monk from the monastery!" he shouted, pulling the soldier's cap off to reveal the monk's shaved head underneath. A quick check of the surrounding bodies uncovered the same thing. Now we knew why they weren't armed. Kusung held the dying monk in his arms and apologized profusely for shooting him. In a weak voice, the monk blessed

Kusung and forgave him. He told him the Chinese had disguised the surviving monks as decoys in case the Tibetans launched a counter attack before Chinese reinforcements arrived from Lhasa.

Before he permanently lost consciousness, the monk said something that chilled me.

"They also dressed the girl as a soldier."

I raced from body to body, ripping their caps off. Jennifer was not among them. My relief was interrupted by the sharp click of approaching footsteps coming from a hallway to our right. Kusung slid across the floor and peered around the corner. He counted five Chinese soldiers, but noticed that the center one was unarmed and appeared smaller and, more slender than the other men.

We decided that I would take out the two on the right and he would shoot the two on the left. When they turned the corner we carefully opened fire from less than ten feet away. The four men slumped to the ground as the center soldier screamed out in terror.

"Steven, don't shoot!"

Jennifer passed out in my arms and Kusung dribbled some water from his canteen across her face until she came to.

"What did they do to you, Jennifer?"

"They kept me up all night and threatened to kill me if I didn't tell them where the Dalai Lama was hiding. I told them I had no idea what they were talking about, that I was here on an archeological expedition with my uncle. They didn't believe me and kept insisting I was lying. This morning I asked if I could take care of my uncle because he still had a fever. A little while ago they came into my room and said they were taking me to join him."

Kusung and I looked at each other. We knew what that would have meant.

"Can I have something to eat? I'm starving."

Kusung searched around until he found a bowl of rice uncontaminated with blood and debris. As Jennifer wolfed the rice down with her fingers, she asked, "Where's my uncle?"

"Jennifer, the Chinese hurt him very badly."

She set down her rice bowl. "In the past twenty-four hours I've seen the Chinese execute hundreds of monks with a bullet to the back of their necks. Just give it to me straight and be specific. What did they do to my uncle?"

"Specifically, they tortured and crucified him."

Jennifer threw her bowl of rice away. "Is he still alive?"

"Yes, but he won't be for long unless he receives proper medical attention. I left him inside the rear of the monastery."

"Did you succeed in killing Chang Sou?"

"Yes. He and his entire thousand man army of immortals"

"I can't believe it," she said. "After all these years, it's finally over. Where's Chow Li?"

"He didn't make it."

It was the standard reply I'd made a hundred times during the war when a GI inquired about an ill-fated friend, but this wasn't a battle hardened veteran I was talking to.

"I'm sorry, Jennifer. I rode straight here from Chang Sou's fortress. I haven't had a chance to deal with the loss myself. The truth is Chow Li sacrificed his life to ensure we survived and Chang Sou did not."

Jennifer had never forgiven Chow Li for failing to defend her when Chang Sou attacked her that Christmas Eve in Sian in 1949 and the news of his heroic death surprised her. "He gave his life to save us? I guess I was wrong about him. What happened to Losang?"

"He joined him," I said, handing her a Chinese rifle. "Do you know how to use this?"

"Yes, I used to go hunting for ducks in Sian with Mr. Wu."

The three of us collected ammunition and quietly made our way back down the hill. When we got to the courtyard we split up. Kusung ran around to the entrance to ready the horses while Jennifer and I went inside to retrieve Albert. As we passed through the courtyard, Jennifer noticed the cross covered in bloodstained ropes on the ground.

"Is that what they did to my uncle?"

"Yes."

"Bastards," she said, cocking back the bolt of her rifle.

The quiet was broken by the sharp crack of gunfire erupting from the front of the monastery. Jennifer and I ducked into the rear entrance where I'd left Albert. We found no sign of him except for an ominous trail of smeared blood leading into an adjacent room. We cautiously turned a corner and froze. Jennifer gasped and dropped her rifle at the sight of her uncle. The former missionary had been propped naked on a Buddhist altar with his legs folded in the lotus position. His corpse stared back at us through empty, bloody eye sockets. A metal crucifix had been jammed into his heart and his genitals had been severed and stuffed into his mouth.

Before I could react, three Chinese soldiers popped up from behind the altar and opened fire. Stumbling backward from the impact, I squeezed the trigger of my AK-47, emptying the entire clip across them in one sweeping motion. They cried out and fell back behind the altar.

The entire firefight lasted no more than two or three seconds. Because I was aiming my weapon and not bracing myself, I slammed my head against the stone floor and was briefly knocked unconscious. When I awoke, I discovered that my wounds had healed, but Jennifer was still lying in the same position in which she had fallen, arms and legs spread akimbo, like a rag doll that had tumbled off a dresser.

"Jennifer," I whispered. "Are you all right?"

She didn't respond.

"Jennifer," I repeated, crawling over to her. "Are you–"

I was horrified to see fresh blood still dripping from her mouth. I touched her cheek and her eyes fluttered open. "Jennifer, I don't understand. Why aren't your wounds healing?"

"Steven, I'm so sorry," she said, gasping for breath. "Oh my God, I'm so sorry."

There have been times in my life when I have been terrified. There have been times in my life when I have been paralyzed by fear. It happened many times during the war, but it was always because I feared for my own life. Now I felt so utterly powerless and devoid of hope that it dwarfed any fear I had ever experienced.

"Jennifer," I said, fighting to remain calm. "Please tell me you've been taking the formula."

She could only stare up at me, terrified. Then she began to cry. She was afraid. And there was absolutely nothing I could do to help her. Nothing I could do to protect her. Her breath became shallow as a sickly ashen color began to spread across her face.

Then, as I cradled her head and watched in stunned disbelief, her eyelids began to slowly open and close. Each time opening and closing a little less wider than the moment before. Each time opening and closing a little slower than the moment before. Like a dying butterfly opening and closing its wings over the most beautiful green eyes I had ever seen in this world. And know I will never see again.

Until they finally closed one last time.

Forever.

I heard my voice scream in the distance as I sobbed and clutched Jennifer's head against my chest. No power in the universe could have relieved me of that pain. Jennifer's death pushed me far beyond the threshold of any anguish I could imagine.

For the first time in my life I craved death. I prayed for death. I wanted to embrace death and become its messenger, whether for myself or for those responsible for stealing my beloved from me.

I softly kissed Jennifer's lips, brushed her hair away from her face and gently laid her down upon the cold stone floor. Numb with grief, I systematically picked up every rifle and piece of ammunition I could carry and walked outside. I was now a man in hell, consumed by the fire of hate as I followed the crackle of gunfire around to the front of the monastery. There I found hundreds of fresh Chinese reinforcements blasting away at Kusung who was pinned down behind an overturned jeep. The Chinese were safely concealed along the outside of the monastery's main wall and appeared to be in no great hurry to scale it. I waited until Kusung opened fire, and the Chinese ducked, before I ran across the open field.

"I thank my Lord Buddha you are here," he said after I dove headfirst into the dirt beside him as bullets pinged off the jeep's chassis. "Dying is a terribly painful experience and I have felt its extremely unpleasant effect at least twice in the past fifteen minutes."

"Jennifer and Albert are dead," I said, carefully taking aim and killing a Chinese soldier with my first shot. "I want every one of these bastards shipped off to hell before the day is over."

Kusung look at me incredulously. "How is it possible that Jennifer is dead? I thought she was taking the formula?"

"Obviously she wasn't," I said matter-of-factly, as my gun recoiled and another Chinese soldier slumped backward.

The Chinese were well entrenched behind the wall and unless they lifted their heads to take aim, there was no way to get a clear shot at them. At any rate, we'd run out of ammunition long before we could get them all and I wasn't thrilled about the prospect of engaging them in hand-to-hand combat.

"This is going to take all day. Let's take turns rushing them."

"What?' Kusung said, looking at me as if I'd just lost my mind. "We'll be shot!"

"Correct. When I rush forward, you'll shoot the Chinese who raise their heads. When I fall, you'll run out and I'll shoot the ones who aim at you. In that way, we'll keep moving forward until we're practically sitting in their laps."

Kusung was not thrilled at the prospect of becoming a Chinese clay pigeon. "Getting shot that many times will be most painful."

"Yes. But not as painful as getting a steel bayonet in the belly a hundred times over and over again. And that's exactly what's going to happen in a few more minutes when we run out of bullets."

I slammed a fresh clip into my gun and charged the wall as a row of Chinese heads popped up, all smirking at the utter futility of watching a man rush headlong to his death.

Kusung's aim was excellent and he quickly picked off five Chinese in succession.

I had only advanced a couple of yards when I was blown completely off my feet by a fusillade of lead. As the formula healed my wounds, I waved Kusung onward.

He scampered out from behind the jeep and ran toward the wall. Steadying my weapon atop my kneecap, I took aim like I was at a penny arcade. At least a half a dozen Chinese fell backward before Kusung whizzed past me and was shot down.

And that's how we spent an otherwise typically sunny Tibetan summer afternoon, advancing a few yards at a time until we finally reached the wall. There, in a desperate last stand, the dozen surviving Chinese frantically turned their flame-throwers on us.

The oily smoke cleared to reveal us charred and naked, but still very much alive as our bodies regenerated before their disbelieving eyes. We casually picked them off one by one. Screaming hysterically, they lost their sanity long before they lost their lives fighting an enemy who would not die.

The next morning Kusung and I buried the bodies of Albert and Jennifer Harrison in the Riudechen Monastery courtyard. Before I wrapped Jennifer in a white sheet I stroked her face and spoke to her as if she were still alive. I told her how much I loved her, that I would *always* love her, and that I would see her again.

Yes. I would see her again.

And at that moment, I realized that of everything in this world that dies, hope dies last.

Pulling that sheet over her face was the hardest thing I've ever done and I found it impossible to place her body in that cold, hard earth. Kusung understood my grief and buried her while I tended to Albert's final resting place. We did this all while ignoring the swollen corpses of over two hundred Chinese soldiers rotting in the Tibetan sun. I'm sure the bellies of the Chonggye Valley vultures were quite full that week.

In Albert's room, I rummaged through the last of his worldly possessions, coming away with three thousand dollars in American currency, the keys to his Park Avenue apartment, and his missionary Bible I intended to deliver to his relatives.

Kusung went through Chow Li's belongings and discovered ninety days of the immortality formula as well as various ancient Buddhist artifacts he would present to the Dalai Lama.

All I had left of Jennifer was her grandmother's cameo. I had intended to surprise her with it on our wedding day. Now, I would carry it with me for the rest of my life.

CHAPTER

❖ 11 ❖

Towing two Tibetan horses loaded with supplies, we departed the Riudechen Monastery under the cover of darkness and began our final journey out of Tibet. Our only problem was that Kusung was unfamiliar with the area south of E-Chhudhogyang. I suggested we guarantee our safe passage by convincing the Tibetans along the way that the Buddhist religious artifacts in our possession were of great importance to the Dalai Lama.

It turned out that my suggestion was a monumental understatement. The resident lama at our first stop, the Thosam Thargayling Monastery, was thrilled that the small golden Buddha and other relics Kusung showed him had not fallen into Chinese hands. He confirmed that they all dated from the classic period in Tibetan history during the eleventh century when Buddhism overtook Bon as the nation's religion.

The inscription on the base of the Buddha revealed it had once belonged to Saint Milarepa himself and was in his possession when he defeated the evil Naro Bon-chung in a legendary battle of magical powers.

We departed Thosam Thargayling armed with a letter from the lama attesting to the authenticity of the artifacts and asking all those who came in contact with us to render assistance. We trekked south for nearly two weeks, skirting the eastern border of Bhutan until reached the last village in Tibet, Mangmang, and crossed the Indian border at the Khenzimana Pass. We applied for asylum when we met an Indian government official in the village of Chhuthangmo.

Unfortunately, things here got a little sticky as I was obviously not Tibetan. I told the Indian official a long-winded tale of being abandoned in China after the Christian missionaries were expelled in the late 1940s and fleeing to Tibet in 1949 to be sheltered by the monks of the Sera Monastery. The Indian official believed my story and promptly made arrangements for me to travel south by rail to Calcutta where he promised I would be quickly processed back to the United States.

We continued south through India for another week until we reached the Bengal and Assam Railroad Station at Tempura on the Brahmaputra River. Here, we boarded a steam powered passenger train built during the glory days of the British Empire. It was a welcome relief traveling by rail after nearly three weeks on foot and horseback.

At Parbatipur, I bid farewell to Kusung before he journeyed a thousand miles west to the new home of the Dalai Lama, a small village north of New Delhi called Mussoorie.

We divided the remainder of the formula. Kusung took just enough to last until he reached his goal: a private audience with the Dalai Lama, where he intended to reveal the historic truth about Chow Li and Chang Sou. Then he would experience something he'd never done in his three hundred and eighty-eight years on this planet. He would lie down, close his eyes, and die.

I stood on the train platform and cheerfully waved goodbye to Kusung as the steam locomotive belched puffs of black smoke and chugged its way out of the station. Kusung was the last of the Buddhist immortals. When he dies, an incredible two thousand-year-old legacy will die with him.

I waved my hand vigorously until the train rounded a bend and his smiling face disappeared from view. Overwhelmed with emotion, I slumped down on a wooden bench and broke down. My fourteen year adventure had finally caught up with me. Chow Li, Albert, Kusung, Losang and Jennifer–especially my beloved Jennifer–had all walked into my life, left their indelible mark upon my soul and left. Was this the kind of joy that immortality would ultimately bring me? The formula was originally created to force humans to stay on this plane of existence. Back then, people didn't want to stay here, they wanted to move on. Somewhere over the past two thousand years the priorities had been reversed. I now found it ironic that even with the promise of heaven most people would do anything to prolong their earthly existence. And this I understood. Even though I no longer feared death and was actually beginning to become curious about the experience, I was still much more curious about life. I wanted to stay a while. The only drawback was that those closest to me, those whom I loved, were all gone. I was completely alone.

Once again, I had embraced solitude.

I opened my eyes to find myself looking into the face of a very young, beautiful Indian girl with large brown eyes and long black hair that flowed down to her waist. No doubt drawn to the sight of a grown man crying, she stood before me wide-eyed and curious, and extended her hand. In that tiny hand was the lavender flower of an East Indian Lotus. It was a simple offering from one complete stranger to another, powerfully demonstrating that no matter how long I lived, and no matter how many people walked in and out of my life, I would never truly be alone.

True to the official's word in Chhuthangmo, I was met at the Calcutta train station by an Indian officer who had been briefed on my predicament. I was elated to learn that my papers were in order and I would be flying out of the country that evening on the westbound Quantas Airlines' weekly around-the-world flight. Accompanied by the official and a reporter from the *London Daily Mail*, I was driven outside of the city to the Calcutta Airfield. Much to the reporter's dismay, I was in no mood to discuss the flight of the Dalai Lama or to give him any eyewitness account of my exodus from Lhasa. It was the last thing in the world I wanted to discuss.

I was more interested in learning about the historic events that had transpired since my departure from America in 1946. I was surprised to learn that General Eisenhower was now completing his second term as America's president and that the Russians had not only developed their own atomic bomb, but also a very advanced rocket program capable of sending objects into outer space.

On a personal note, I wondered aloud if a New York jazz musician named Hines Winston had ever achieved any degree of fame or notoriety. The reporter had never heard of Hines, but informed me that I had a guest waiting for me in the Qantas reception room. There was a guest waiting for me? The thought was absurd. No one besides the reporter from the Daily Mail had been informed I was arriving. I opened the door to the Qantas office and was politely greeted by the receptionist. Before I could respond, a young female voice spoke from behind me.

"It's really good to see you, Steven."

I turned around to see Erika dressed in a stylish blue overcoat with her blonde hair cut to her shoulders. She was as beautiful as I remembered her from Munich in 1945. But, I noticed three things: she'd lost her German accent, there was a young teenage boy wearing some type of school uniform standing beside her, and . . . she hadn't aged a day.

I warmly embraced her with a kiss on the cheek.

"Steven," she said. "I'd like you to meet Charlie."

"I'm delighted to meet you, sir," the young boy said, extending his hand.

I clasped it warmly. "It's great to meet you, Charlie."

"My mother tells me you play the alto saxophone."

I smiled at Erika. "Why, yes. As a matter of fact I do play the alto saxophone, but it's been quite a while."

"Charlie, I need to speak with Mr. Ronson," Erika said. "Why don't you go watch the planes land and take off?"

The young boy nodded and pantomimed playing a saxophone as he headed for the door.

"He's a fine young man," I said. "And he plays the alto saxophone?"

"Yes, he plays the alto saxophone. Just like his father."

My intuition told me she was going to say that. The moment I laid eyes on Charlie, I felt the connection. And things were starting to add up. Erika knew I played the alto saxophone. She knew I'd be here. And she hadn't aged a day. There was no doubt in my mind. "Erika, we have a saying in America: *cut to the chase*. I could ask how you knew I played the alto saxophone. I could ask how you knew I'd be here in Calcutta. But considering you haven't aged a day, I think we both know the answer to that question. So tell me, is your mother's first name Maria?"

"Yes, my mother is Maria Orsic. However, I believe my biological father's name may surprise you."

"Go ahead. Surprise me."

"My biological father's name is Otto Krueger."

That surprised me. "Where is your father?"

"This I cannot tell you. He would be prosecuted as a Nazi and I would never allow such a thing. You may not believe this, but my father is innocent. The reason he left Dachau was because he became aware of the sadistic treatment of the prisoners and the human medical experiments. He is in hiding and has given me the last of his supply of the immortality formula. My father is a good man who was deceived."

"Your father is a good man? You can't be serious. I read his letter where he offered Hitler the formula."

"My father had no idea how evil Hitler and the Nazis were until he worked at Dachau. None of us knew. Do you remember how upset I became that night in Munich when you told me what you'd witnessed at the camp?"

"I remember. Where's your mother?"

"She escaped to Aldebaran."

"Aldebaran? The star that's sixty-five light years away?"

"Yes. She too was deceived by the Thule Society. She believed that Hitler was going to save Germany and do many wonderful things. They convinced her to help them."

"Then why did your mother meet with Nazi officials in Kolberg in December of 1943 to offer Hitler an escape to Aldebaran in that flying machine the Germans were building?"

"My mother only made that offer so the Nazis wouldn't defund the project. It wasn't until the seventh prototype was completed and tested in late 1944 that the machine was truly capable of making the journey. She waited until the Russians were closing in on Berlin and left for the Aldebaran solar system in March of 1945."

"I still don't understand why your mother went to Aldebaran. She wasn't considered a war criminal or wanted by anyone."

"My mother felt directly responsible for Hitler's rise to power," Erika said. "Because of her telepathic gifts, she was the one who initiated contact with the Aldebaranians and passed their knowledge of psycho-kinetic power on to the Thule Society. She went to Aldebaran to beg their forgiveness and attempt to convince them to give this planet another chance. In person, my mother can be quite persuasive."

"Are you in contact with her?"

"Yes, telepathically. And she's safe, but because they were deceived and millions of people died, the Aldebaranians will no longer permit any physical contact with Earth until we evolve to the point where we can regain their trust. My mother tells me that may take hundreds of years."

Then it hit me. "Erika, you're taking the immortality formula so there's a chance you could be alive if your mother returns. And if you're taking the formula, you've been having visions. That's how you know I played the alto saxophone. That's how you knew I'd be here."

"Yes, I have visions. I've seen you performing on stage in New York City. I named my son, Charlie, after your hero Charlie Parker. I saw you many times with Jennifer."

Just the mention of Jennifer's name made me pause. "If you saw me with Jennifer then you know that no other woman will ever replace her."

"I understand your love for Jennifer, but you have a son and he needs you, Steven. Will you at least try to be a part of his life?"

"Of course. He's not taking the formula, is he?"

"Don't be ridiculous. He's only thirteen," Erika scoffed as she reached into her briefcase for a tightly rolled sheet of parchment bound with a ribbon of gold silk. "This is from Chow Li. He smuggled it to me from Lhasa with strict instructions to hand it to you only if you'd safely made it out of Tibet. Otherwise, I was to burn it."

"How did you get in contact with Chow Li?"

"My mother and Chow Li had been communicating telepathically since the German expeditions to Tibet in the 1930s. They were determined that the Nazis not locate Chang Sou. The Thule Society believed they'd made a mistake in supporting Hitler after he outlawed their organization. They believed that Chang Sou was the real Aryan messiah and wanted to bring him to Germany, but Chow Li tricked them into believing he was somewhere in Tibet."

"How did your mother find Chow Li?"